They Think I Invented Pizza:
Dungeon Pixies

They Think I Invented Pizza: Dungeon Pixies

Printed in the U.S.A. and Great Britain

1st edition

Front Cover Art by Manuel Aguila
Instagram @manuaguila_tattoo

Back Cover Art and Interior Art by Kiit Watson
Instagram @kdrawsok

For more information, see www.joshwalker.fun

forgottenplacespublishing@gmail.com

ISBN: 978-1-944621-29-2

Library of Congress Control Number: 2023916013

Josh Walker

Dedicated to my sweet son Cloud, an old soul whose passion for life helps remind me that it is okay to get excited about the smallest blessings in the day-to-day.

Josh Walker

Acknowledgments

First, I have to thank my son Cloud. He is who he is, and I love it. My second thank you goes to my other two children Esperanza and Dastan. Without my three children, this book would not exist. They—along with my wife—have become the greatest inspiration in my life. Thank you to my wife for always supporting me, and thank you to my other family: my parents, siblings, nieces, and nephews. Thank you to Manu Aguila for his incredible front cover. Also, thank you to Kiit Watson for the back cover art and the interior art. I'm excited to work with you on this project and future ones. Thank to all the video game companies who have filled my brain with ideas for this book. Thank you to the people with whom I've played those games. Introvice receives special mention as one of those people. Please, look him up on youtube. He goes by the same name there as he does here and in the book as a character. I want to give a huge thank you to all the amazing BETA readers that helped me with reviewing this book: Trent Newbury-VanLove, Introvice, Kuroochii, Katie Erickson, Rich Winters, Makaela Fowles, the Howe family, Aaron Turpin, Stephanie Keesling, Kole Hyde, the Nelson family, Shandy Star Mager, the Chavez family, Landry Hyde, the Steelman family, Syd and Brian, and the Jasperson family. Also, a thank you to Trail Ridge Middle School. My annual visits to speak with you guys about folklore is always fun, and I have you all in mind as I write this series. Last but not least, I want to thank Brian Cotter for the incredible job he did with the first audiobook. For as long as he is willing, he will be the voice of the They Think I Invented Pizza series. Finally, thank you to the readers and supporters I've had over the years. Without you, I'd have given up on writing a long time ago.

Foreword

During a snowy day in April, I took my wife to the women's clinic for a routine prenatal check-up. She was well into the third trimester but still a week away from the due date. We were expecting to do an ultrasound, hear a heartbeat, so on and so forth. At the appointment, the doctor informed us that we needed to get to the hospital. Ready or not, we were going to have a baby that day. We left the clinic and headed toward the nearest hospital.

Outside, heavy wet snow had continued to fall. My small sedan was not adapted to snowy roads, so when I hit a drift, my car became stuck. Even so, I knew I had to take my wife to the hospital. For such a situation, I kept a snow shovel in the trunk. Using it, I began to dig us out. Once free, we resumed our course.

Before we reached the hospital, my car bottomed out three more times. Each time, I dug us out. In the end, we arrived at the hospital with plenty of time, and that day, my son was born. Due in part to being big Final Fantasy fans—and also to recognize the stormy circumstances in which he was born—we named our son Cloud.

It has been a joy to see him pursue each of his interests. When something earns his attention, he dedicates himself to it in full. I can see how happy those hobbies make him. His passion for learning and growing in those areas reminds me of how innocently cheerful life can be. And he spreads that cheerfulness to everyone that takes the time to know him.

My life is certainly better because he is in it. One thing I wanted to offer him in return was dedicating this book to him.

After the release of the first <u>They Think I Invented Pizza</u>, many people asked me if the triplets were based on my children. The answer is yes. Being a dad is my favorite thing. I love listening to my kids' conversations. I love watching them grow. I love seeing their interests and how different they are as people.

In the first book, the triplets were side characters. As the cover of this book indicates, the triplets are ready to take center stage. I hope part of the love I have for parenting translates to the page and I can share that love with readers. With that, I want to welcome readers back to the world of Round.

Josh Walker

August 18th, 2023

Josh Walker

1: Insomnia is not a Problem

Like he did every night, Pete the pizzaman sat on his bed, preparing to slap himself to sleep. Back on Earth, he had never been able to do something so silly. But he wasn't on Earth anymore; he was on Round, a world that followed video game rules. One of those rules was that he could slap himself to sleep. But he had to activate the skill Slap'm Silly beforehand.

Otherwise, he might end up lowering his HP to 0. And if he did that... Well, he wasn't sure what would happen. He might respawn somewhere. He might return to Earth. He might die. Either way, he didn't want to find out, so he'd remember to activate Slap'm Silly.

The bed on which he sat resembled any bed from Earth. Though, the condensed padding came in the form of feathers rather than dense foam and springs. During his first night in Round, Pete had considered the bed's construction. The only thing he could come up with was that the feathers held their shape through some type of barrier magic. On the side of the room nearest the door, his bed rested against the wall.

On a wall to his right hung a mirror. It was large, round, and bordered with black metal. Craftsmen had shaped the metal to resemble flowers. As far as mirrors went, it appeared to be a good one. Even so, it reminded him of his childhood fear—which remained an adult fear; though he'd never admit it—of Bloody Mary. When he was only five, his eleven-year-old cousin told him the story of Bloody Mary. Since then, he never liked mirrors.

To his left, a chest of drawers held place. At the time, Pete didn't use the piece of furniture. There was no need. He had an inventory. As he thought about his inventory, Pete wasn't sure what purpose the chest of drawers served. Like Pete, everyone on Round had an inventory space, so why would they need a chest of drawers? Could there be limits to an inventory's capacity? If so, having a chest of drawers to store the extra items would make sense. When Pete had a chance to ask Max, he'd learn more about how inventory worked.

Max was the talking anthropomorphic cat who'd sent Pete to Round. As such, Pete assumed Max would understand how the inventory on Round worked. Pete would have asked someone else, but he worried the question might be... Well, he feared it would make him look crazy. It reminded him of when he didn't know how to close his prompt windows.

A fine, polished wood formed the floor and walls of the room. It was a darker color like oak. The contrast of the lighter and darker shades in the grain comforted Pete. It was pretty and artistic.

As Zoey had appeared on Round, they'd moved a second bed into the room and pushed it against the opposite wall. On that bed, Zoey sat across from Pete, legs crossed, hands in her lap. Raising an eyebrow, she asked. "You aren't going to slap yourself to sleep, again...are you?"

"Ummm..." Pete turned his head in her direction but refused to make eye contact. "I'd rather not answer that question."

"You are going to give yourself a concussion, you know?"

Pete shook his head back and forth, disagreeing. "Concussions don't exist in Round. If they did, there'd be a debuff icon for them."

"Even though you haven't seen an icon like that, it doesn't mean the icon doesn't exist." Zoey let a coy smile slip across her lips. "Have you considered that you *have* seen it? But you don't remember...because you forgot...because concussions make you forget things? Have you thought of that?"

"If that were the case, I'd forget other things too." He argued.

"How do you know you haven't?" She asked.

"I'd remember if I forgot." He shrugged. Then he decided to change the subject. "What are your plans for the night?"

She wore the armored uniform that she used to deliver pizzas, so he assumed she wasn't planning to sleep. It consisted of a blue leather corset to protect her torso. Dark leather shoulder pads provided defense for her neck and shoulders. Steel plates formed her skirt. Her hat resembled a standard pizza driver's base-ball cap. Though metal lined the inside of the hat. Dark Leather wrapped around the metal. In that sense, it was as much a helmet as a hat.

"I'm not sure," She pursed her lips to the side. "We've been in Round three weeks. Other than my first night here, I haven't felt sleepy. It's possible that I don't need sleep anymore? Anyway, I was thinking about going to farm tomatoes tonight. We're running low. Also, Rumpke said the Trash Pandas are setting up for Harvestfest. They could need some help."

"Harvestfest?" Pete asked.

"It's like Halloween." She explained.

Pete chuckled.

"What's funny?" Zoey raised her eyebrow.

"Last Halloween," Pete explained. "You dressed up as a vampire." His laughter grew as he struggled to get out his last words. "This Halloween, you can be a human."

"I guess I can be." Zoey offered a sympathetic smile. "I don't understand why that is so funny, though. Why are you laughing so hard?"

Pete stopped laughing, confusion forming on his face. "Because it's ironic? That makes it funny?"

"If you say so." She stretched. "I'm going to go help Rumpke now."

"Be careful," he said, a worried tone replacing his jovial one. If she planned to farm tomatoes, it signified she'd be fighting the monsters that dropped tomatoes. Pete's interface referred to the monsters as nightshade terrors. One of his first quests as a pizzaman on Round involved hunting the monsters. As a level one pizzaman, they had almost dropped his HP to 0. If not for a fortunate level up which replenished said hp, Pete might have died.

Though, he knew he shouldn't worry about Zoey. She was level eleven, and the monsters that dropped tomatoes capped at level six. Still, he felt uneasy about her being in the forest at night. Then again, she was a vampire; she thrived in forests at night. Even so, he couldn't help but ask. "Do you need me to go with you?"

"I'll be fine." She assured him, winking, "no need to worry. Afterall, I am stronger than you... That is an objective fact...according to our character sheets."

She wasn't wrong. Each of them had a virtual character sheet. To make his character sheet appear, Pete only had to think about it and think it open. At that point, the window would appear as an opaque-intangible square. The square would hover in front of his vision. This was the same for other windows: the inventory, his skill tree, quest notifications, and his battle log. When he wanted to close a window, he'd have to focus on an X in the top right corner of the window. Then he needed to close his eyes with forceful intent. This caused the windows to shut.

"That hurts." Pete held his hand over his heart. He would have argued about who had the higher stats, but he would have lost. Being a vampire gave Zoey higher attributes than a human like Pete. On the character sheet, those stats were strength, dexterity, agility, vitality, and spirit.

When she first came to round as a level one noob, he'd already leveled more than once. Even so, her stats matched his in every parameter. As it stood, he no longer possessed a significant level advantage. As their levels evened out, her abilities had surpassed his.

That said, he had a plan to break the leveling system. If it worked—he hoped with all his heart it would work—he'd be able to strengthen his areas of deficiency. And part of his leveling plan involved slapping himself to sleep.

"It does hurt. Doesn't it?" She shrugged her shoulders as she stood. Then she strode to the door, walking with the same confident attitude as always. The difference this time was how her metal skirt made a quiet tinging with each step. He hadn't noticed it before, not with the ambient noise from working in the pizzeria or mountain forest. Yet, in the quiet of the night, he picked up on it for the first time. Zoey stopped by the door leading from their makeshift bedroom to Mod's bakery...also known as M&P's Pizzeria. "Do you need anything while I'm out?"

Pete shook his head no as Zoey spun and slipped out the door.

As Zoey closed the door behind her, she took in the empty bakery that doubled as a pizzeria. She wasn't sure which word to call it. Pizzeria or bakery? Before Pete's arrival on Round, it was a simple bakery. Yet, one of the first things Pete did on Round was help convert the bakery into something that sold pizzas. And Pete didn't waste any time in making that change. Max had sent Zoey to Round days after Pete. By the time she arrived, Mod's bakery was already serving as a pizzeria. It was during afternoons and evenings, anyway. It was still a bakery in the mornings, providing bread and baked goods for the town.

One of the main reasons Pete opened the bakery in the first place was because the world of Round had assigned him the job of being a pizzaman. One of the rules the gods of Round—the citizens referred to them as moderators—was that a person could only gain experience and level up doing their job. Anyone who broke this rule met harsh punishment from those moderators. Zoey and Pete weren't one hundred percent sure what said punishment entailed. Though, they did understand it was bad. They deduced this by watching the fear Round's citizens had for the moderators.

At night, the calm silence of the restaurant was a stark contrast to the lunch and dinner rushes. Those rushes became more and more common as word of pizza spread throughout the town of Greenlake. Sooner rather than later, she suspected word of pizza would spread to areas outside of town. If the popularity of the food grew enough, they might have to open new stores all over the region.

Zoey dropped her shoulders and inhaled a deep breath—not that she needed to breathe—and she relaxed, appreciating the stillness of night. To her right, a picture frame window revealed a perfect lake view. The lake's gentle waves reflected the moonlight, shimmering as the water rippled and shifted.

"Still awake?" A voice to her left caused Zoey to jump. She looked in that direction and saw Mod on the other side of a counter. He had a sheepish grin. "Sorry, didn't mean to scare you."

"No," she shook her head. "It's fine. I'm a vampire, after all. If anyone should be sorry, it's me...for letting someone sneak up on me at night." She made eye contact with him. "Why are you awake? Couldn't sleep?"

"I have to make sure the store is clean...make sure everything is ready to go tomorrow." He scratched his head. "I was about to turn in for the night."

WHACK! A sound from Zoey and Pete's room interrupted the conversation, forcing Mod to ask. "What was that?"

"Mmm…" Zoey considered before answering. "It was Pete slapping himself to sleep. He thinks it's going to make him stronger or something."

"Okay…" Mod waited for Zoey to elaborate, but she didn't.

A knock at the restaurant's front door sounded. Zoey and Mod looked at each other, then at the door, then back at each other before Zoey volunteered. "I'll get it." She guessed it to be one of the Trash Pandas, the gang of raccoon raiders turned garbage men. She didn't think anyone else would be awake so late.

Zoey hopped over to the door, pulled it open, and froze. Instead of someone whom she knew, three strangers stood there.

The first was a clean-cut man with dark hair; he wore a white tuxedo. The second was a bearded pirate. The third was wearing clown make-up and a black derby cap. His t-shirt had horizontal black and white stripes. Red suspenders held up his black slacks. *A mime?* Zoey wondered.

"Sorry to intrude." The man in the tuxedo spoke. "We saw through the window that you were awake and thought you might be able to help us."

Zoey composed herself. "Of course. What can I do for you?"

"We are adventurers." The tuxedoed man explained. "My name is Intro." He held his hand open, signaling to the pirate. "This is Flowerbeard." He used his other hand to signal toward the mime. "And this is Fredalic, but you can call him Fred."

Fred waved.

"Hi," Zoey waved back before turning her attention to the pirate. "Your name is Flowerbeard?"

"Yeah," the pirate explained. "Because pirates use eyepatches."

"But you don't have flowers in your beard, and you don't have an eyepatch." She said.

"Right." The pirate agreed.

"And you never have flowers in your beard?" She asked.

"No," he shook his head, annoyance creeping into his voice. "What's your point? Like whatever. Stop talking."

"Sorry about that," Intro interjected. "Flowerbeard gets cranky when he stays up too late, but he's a good person."

"Okay," Zoey squinted her eyes together. "What was it you needed help with?"

"As adventurers, we have a unique ability. It allows us to identify towns with dungeons." Intro explained. "Within the last few days, we realized that there is a new dungeon in Greenlake. We wondered if you have seen it."

"Dungeon?" Zoey scratched her chin. She possessed a deep familiarity with dungeons in the MMOs and RPGs she played back on Earth. Even so, she lacked any knowledge of how they worked on Round. Until Intro's question, she wasn't aware that dungeons existed on Round. "What does a dungeon look like?"

"Shiny," Flowerbeard answered.

Fred nodded his agreement with Flowerbeard. Then he stepped back and dropped to his hands and knees. All the while, he kept eye contact with Zoey.

"What is he doing?" She asked.

"Making a bench," Flowerbeard answered, sitting on Fred's back.

Again, Fred nodded his agreement.

"Okay…" Zoey vacillated in saying anything else.

In high school, she'd been witness to plenty of awkwardness. For example, she'd seen boys stammering as they asked her out. She recalled when George beatboxed in the middle of English class to impress everyone. And she remembered a group of students planking in the cafeteria. They planked as a form of protest to free George from ISS after he got in trouble for beatboxing.

In college dorms, that awkwardness became a nightly occurrence. For example, every Friday was karaoke night...and nobody knew how to sing.

Despite her practice with awkward events, all she could do was stare at the mime who pretended to be a bench and the pirate who sat on that human bench.

How was she supposed to respond to that? Should she encourage them and tell them they were doing a great job? Would that be patronizing? She didn't want to come off as rude.

"It's shiny," Intro said these words with assertive, practiced politeness. It pulled Zoey away from her thoughts about human furniture. "The dungeon...that is. It is shiny and shaped like a door. The frame isn't shiny. The portal inside of the frame glows an iridescent light. You step through it, and you're in the dungeon."

"I don't think I've seen anything like that," Zoey told him. "But I hope you find it."

"In any case, I want to offer you thanks." Intro offered a slight bow of the head and began to pivot away from the door. At the same time, the pirate stood, and the mime returned to his feet. "Have a great night."

As they walked away from the pizzeria, Zoey watched for a moment, unsure what to make of the interaction. Then with slow caution, she closed the door behind them.

Josh Walker

2: Harvestfest Preparations

Zoey waited a few minutes before leaving M&P's Pizzeria. She didn't want to run into the same trio of adventurers from before. It wasn't like they seemed evil, but something about them was weird, and she wasn't sure if it was good-weird or bad-weird. At that moment, she was not ready to spend more time with them to deduce which they were.

Once outside, Zoey closed the restaurant's door, and she scanned her eyes over Greenlake. At night, the town appeared calmer. The lake's lazy tide beat in a slow rhythm against the shore. Its ripples reflected the stars back at the cloudless sky. The water extended as far as the eye could see; even Zoey's enhanced vampire vision couldn't see the other side.

Along the lake, cabinlike businesses and homes extended up a sloped hill. Large dark windows held place in the buildings, reflecting the moonlight.

During the day, elves, pixies, humans, and dwarves filled the streets. At night, those same roads remained empty. Natural sound came in the form of a gentle breeze. It whistled through the plentiful trees and bushes. Her vampire ears picked up the feint timbre of wildlife.

Zoey made her way up the sloped hill, passing Wanda's Windmill and the school on the way to the city gate. As she prepared to break past the city limit, she heard a voice call out behind her. "Are you on the way to help Rumpke set up for Harvestfest?"

"Nick," Zoey smiled. Then she hopped, spinning to face the city guard. He wore his usual rusted armor, sword sheathed on his hip. His red hair matched the color of his thick mustache. "I'll try and help as much as I can." She wrinkled her forehead. "Isn't it a little late for you to be up? Don't you have to work early tomorrow morning?"

"I do." He nodded. "But I have to work nights, too."

"Do you ever sleep?" She asked.

"Yes."

"When?"

"That's confidential," He answered monotone.

"You don't trust me?" She squinted her eyes together.

Instead of answering with words, Nick growled. Zoey recognized the sound as Nick's annoyed sound, and she thought to herself, *He takes his job too serious. It's not like I'm planning to learn his sleep schedule to commit some crime...a prank...yes...but not a crime...*

"You asked about Rumpke. To answer your question from before, I am on my way to help him now. I'll keep an eye on him for you." Zoey grinned, considering how Rumpke might be able to help her with her future prank against Nick. Though, she didn't spend too much time thinking about it, knowing she'd have plenty of time to plan for it later.

"Thank you," Nick nodded, taking a few steps beyond her as he finished speaking. "Now, if you'll excuse me. I need to finish my patrol."

She watched him for a moment before she continued along the path which led her out of town. A few minutes later, the route took her through the stone archway which marked the town's edge. When she passed under it, she entered a grassy green field. As she crossed the area, she took in the vastness of the clear night sky. She'd always been a night person. That love for nighttime rooted in her childhood. During her formative years, she'd spent countless summers camping in empty country fields near her grandpa's house. Even so, there was an unfamiliarity to Round's sky.

The strangeness came in the size of the stars.

They seemed bigger and closer than the stars on Earth. And the constellations she knew so well were nowhere to be seen. Instead, unfamiliar patterns maintained their positions overhead. Between the yellow and white lights, she noticed streaks of green, blue, and purple.

Distracted by the sky, she didn't notice as the field inclined, and she began to walk up a slope. Though she did recognize when trees began to appear on each side of her. With each step, the incline steepened, and the trees became thicker and taller. Once in the Forest Mountain, she began toward the Trash Panda hideout. The night breeze whistled through the branches, rustling the leaves.

"BOOO!" Rumpke jumped out from his hiding spot behind one of the bushes.

Instead of jumping back in fear, Zoey caught the short, raccoon humanoid by his bronze harness, and she held him with his feet dangling above the ground. Keeping an even tone to her voice, she said, "boo."

Where most of the Trash Pandas stood two to four feet tall, Rumpke was the tallest. Zoey estimated his height at five feet, not much shorter than her. As such, his feet were only a few inches above the soft, grassy earth.

"You knew I was there?" He asked.

"Yup," she answered.

"And I didn't scare you?" He hung his head, scratching the back of it with his right hand.

"Nope.

"Well…" he forced an uneasy chuckle, "I'll get you next time."

"You can tell yourself that, but I am a vampire." She winked. "I have excellent night vision."

"Right," he smiled. After a few seconds of awkward silence, he asked. "You came to help with Harvestfest set up?"

She lowered him until his feet touched gently

against the ground and let him go. "I did."

"Great," he pointed deeper into the forest, "The rest of the Trash Pandas are that way. They've already begun set up."

"Lead the way." Zoey held her hand out in the direction which he had pointed. She felt like some fancy butler holding some invisible door.

Rumpke began in the direction, and Zoey lowered her arm, walking a quarter step behind him. They continued that way, pressing through the thickening foliage and forest detritus. The situation reminded her of when she'd gone hiking with her dad.

All the while, she remained aware of her surroundings, listening to the crickets, hanging on to every sound which carried in the light breeze as it whistled through the branches. She tried to filter out any abnormal resonance. As calm and safe as she felt with Rumpke by her side, nightshade terrors might still be in the area. She didn't want one to sneak up on them. Where she didn't hear any monsters, she did hear something else...voices up ahead.

They spoke in muffled tones, and she couldn't make out any words. Along with the voices, she heard excited laughter and scurrying footsteps. It rang busy, reminding her of students working to set up the school gym for prom.

With the vegetation blocking her from seeing the source of the voices, she focused her ears. When she did, the voices became less abstract. Most spoke about Harvestfest. Others gave instructions about where to set up games and decorations. Then she began to see lights through the thick vegetation. Seconds later, Zoey and Rumpke emerged from the forest and entered a clearing.

The space came in the shape of a perfect circle. The diameter of it spread sixty paces in each direction. A cave sat on the far edge of the clearing, covered with vines and bushes. She recognized the cave must be the entrance to the Trash Panda hideout. Countless raccoon humanoids rushed in and out of the cave. Some carried boxes. The Trash Pandas spread throughout the whole clearing. They set up games and positioned lights on bushes. Some held candles or cast spells. Those casting spells created multi-colored flames. The flames hovered fifteen feet in the air.

Zoey recognized some of the games: bobbing for apples, a ring toss that used witches' hats as the targets. They even had a pin the tail on the donkey. Though, this version of the game used a drawing of a chimera, a creature with a lion's head, a goat's body, and a snake for a tail.

There was also a temporary structure in the center of the clearing. They'd built it with metal rods and wrapping resembling tin foil. A square metal sheet rested a top, and a sign beside it read, 'Spirit Shrine.'

Most raccoons wore plate, harnesses, battle skirts, leather armor, and the like. Though some wore dresses and had a notable femininity to them. She wasn't sure if it had something to do with how they walked or how their eyelashes curled out. But she could tell they were female.

One of them wore a red bow in her hair. When she saw Rumpke and Zoey, she jogged over to them. "Rumpke," she shouted as she drew close, jumping to hug the warlord. "I wondered where you snuck off to." The woman raccoon drew back and smiled at Zoey. "And who is your friend?"

"R...r...right..." Rumpke stammered, and Zoey took note of the raccoon warlord's uncomfortableness. She guessed that if his face weren't covered in fur, she'd have been able to see him blush. When he stopped stammering and began to speak, his words came fast and nervous. They had spaces in weird places. "I was busy getting Zoey here...this is Zoey...that's

her name. She's a vampire, but she's a nice one. Harvestfest...she's here for Harvestfest...to help us set up for Harvestfest...that is." He inhaled and exhaled a deep breath before finishing with a normal voice. "Zoey, this is Rosie...don't worry though...she's not a flower...she's a raccoon... I mean, that is obvious, you can see."

Zoey reached out her hand. "Nice to meet you, Rosie."

"You as well, Ms. Zoey." Rosie took Zoey's hand and shook it. After releasing her grip on Zoey, Rosie turned to look at the field. "I better get back to work. We have so much to do still."

"Right," Rumpke agreed. "Back to work. Work is good."

Rosie ran back toward the center of the field. When she was out of earshot, Zoey whistled to tease Rumpke.

"What was that?" Rumpke wrinkled his brow and glared back at Zoey.

"Nothing," she said, casting her eyes off to the side and feigning innocence. After a few seconds of awkward silence, Zoey decided to change the subject. "So...you don't know anything about dungeons? Do you?"

"Do I know about dungeons?" Rumpke's scoffed, his demeanor returning to normal. "Of course, I know about dungeons."

"What can you tell me about them?"

He considered before answering. "They have monsters in them...and loot."

"Have you ever seen one?"

"I have. In fact, my men found the entrance to one the other day." He said. "It's a glowing door about halfway between here and town. It's about thirty feet off the walking path. Why do you ask?"

"I came across some adventurers tonight." Zoey explained. "They were asking about one."

Rumpke rolled his eyes once before saying. "Of course, they did. That's too bad."

"Why's that?" She asked.

"Because," he answered, "they'll loot it before we can."

"Why didn't you go in before them?"

He shrugged. "We couldn't. We don't have an adventurer's pass. Normal people can't go into a dungeon without one. You either need to be a monster, undead, or have an adventurer's pass. After Harvestfest, we were going to send Cedric to buy one. Future City sells them. Though, there is no point in sending him now."

"Oh," Zoey said. "I guess that makes sense." She turned her eyes back to the field where the busy Trash Pandas scurried. It didn't make sense, but a lot about Round didn't make sense. She had gotten used to pretending to understand things until she *did* understand them.

On the far end of the field—where the trees rose above the cave entrance—she noticed a pair of lights. One was orange, and one was purple. The purple began to move left along the tree line. Every five feet, another light appeared while the purple continued along. The lights formed a simple pattern of purple, orange, purple, orange, purple, orange. Moving to the right, the orange light mirrored the movement.

Are those lights moving by themselves? She wondered. *No,* she realized, *something was carrying them.* She squinted and looked closer. The image came into clarity. A respective Trash Panda held each light, hopping from branch to branch and jumping from tree to tree.

The lights were flames, hovering over the open palms of each respective raccoon. The fires were negligible, no more than three inches tall and one inch wide. At five-foot intervals, the raccoons would stop, clap, and a new flame would appear. It held place where it took form, staying behind while the raccoons moved along.

Zoey turned her head to look at Rumpke. "What is with all the lights?"

"They are harvesting lights." He answered, keeping his eyes on the other raccoons as they worked.

"They remind me of lights we use to celebrate something we call Christmas."

"I've never heard of Christmas." He said.

In awe at the Harvestfest preparations, Zoey decided to put off explaining Christmas. Instead, she wanted to learn more about Harvestfest. "These lights are different than Christmas lights, though. There are no green chords and no glass bulbs." She wrinkled her forehead as the scent of the burning flames reached her, and she sniffed at the air two times. "It smells like sage."

"I don't know what sage is." He said. "But the smell will keep the bad ghosts away from the Harvestfest activities."

"Bad ghosts?" She asked. "Does that mean there are good ghosts?"

The raccoon leader's right eyebrow raised, and he turned his head to look at her. "Of course, there will be good ghosts. Have you never celebrated Harvestfest before?"

She shook her head no.

"What do you do with the spirits that appear this time of year? How do you get rid of them?"

She considered the question. It wasn't that she didn't understand it. Rather, she pondered over its implications. For example, did ghosts appear everywhere in the whole world of Round? Did they only appear in the forest? She needed to know more. "We don't have ghosts where I'm from."

"You have vampires but no ghosts?" He questioned.

"No," she rubbed her temples with her right thumb and index finger, thinking about how best to explain. Then she lowered her hand to her side. "I know it's weird—seeing as how I'm a vampire and all that— but where I'm from doesn't have vampires. We don't have ghosts. We don't have evil witches that fly on brooms, werewolves, monsters, or any of that stuff. Sure, sometimes people tell stories about how they saw something supernatural. Yet, there is no real evidence for their claims... So ghosts might be real back home...but nobody knows for sure."

"Have you seen a ghost before?" He asked.

"Nope," she answered and then asked. "You said Harvestfest is something you do to get rid of the ghosts?"

"Yes," he nodded his head one time and continued. "When someone dies, their essence remains dormant until the harvest. At that time, their ghost returns. For three days, they wander, seeking their place in the afterlife.

"At Harvestfest, we use these lights." He pointed at the orange and purple flames before lowering his hand, "to draw the spirits."

"And then what?" She asked.

"What do you mean?"

"After you get them here," she clarified. "What do you do after?"

"We use these." He reached into a leather pouch on his belt, retrieving an orb and holding it up. It was a perfect, white sphere about two inches wide. Light reflected off the surface, creating rainbows inside the ball. "If you hold this up to a spirit, they will enter it."

"I see," Zoey said.

"It isn't quite as easy as it sounds," Rumpke added. "For example, the spirits recognize the living, and they run from us. As such, we must dress up for

Harvestfest. We try to make ourselves look like ghosts or forest animals. We use costumes so that the spirits trust us."

"Makes sense," Zoey said. "After you put the spirits in the orbs, what do you do with the orbs?"

"On the third day of Harvestfest, we take the orbs and place them in the spirit shrine." He pointed at the tinfoil construct in the center of the field. "From there, the spirits can find their way into the afterlife."

"What happens to the other spirits?" She asked, "the ones that don't get brought to the shrine?"

"They must wander for another year." He said. "With each year that they don't enter the afterlife, they become corrupted. They become bitter…jealous of the living."

"Can they hurt people?" She asked.

"Not at first," he replied. "After enough time, they become a soul eater…"

"Don't forget about monster spirits." One of the other raccoons said, passing between Zoey and Rumpke, box in hand, on the way to decorate somewhere.

"Right," Rumpke snapped his fingers once. "I'd almost forgotten. Monsters that have died also return. Those spirits *can* hurt you."

Zoey shuttered. She and Pete had faced countless nightshade terrors to farm the tomatoes for the pizza sauce. She'd hate to meet them all at once.

Rumpke noticed her concern. "Don't worry. Small things like nightshade terrors absorb into the orb like any other spirit. Plus, their attack power is less when they are ghosts. For someone your level, they won't be able to cause more than one hit point of damage."

"That's a relief." She relaxed. "So Harvestfest isn't only a celebration of the harvest, it is for helping spirits to the afterlife?"

He nodded once, adding. "And it is for remembering those we lost over the year. Before we send them off, we have a final meal with them. It's important to remember the dead and respect from where we come."

"I can appreciate that." She offered an approving smile.

"Aside from a celebration," he added. "It is also a competition."

"Competition?" She raised an eyebrow.

"We have games and prizes." He explained, pointing at the bobbing for apples and ring toss before lowering his hand. "The main competition involves the orbs and spirits. Whoever captures the most spirits wins the grand prize."

"What's the grand prize?"

He shrugged before returning the orb to the pouch on his belt. "We don't know. After we send the spirits to the afterlife, the shrine generates the prize. It creates the prize based on the number of spirits we send."

"That is..." she paused, trying to think of a word to describe Harvestfest... Cool... Crazy... She settled on saying. "That is like Halloween, Day of the Dead, and Samhain all put together.

"What's Halloween, Day of the Dead, and Samhain?" He asked.

"Holidays where I'm from," she said, walking toward the center of the field to help with decorations. Rumpke walked next to her, and she explained Halloween to him.

3: Slapping Awake

As the sun rose the following day, Zoey arrived back at the bakery. She creaked open the front door and snuck in to find Mod. He'd already begun preparing bread and pastries. Around noon, he'd shift gears and start prep work for the pizza rush.

"Is Pete awake?" She asked.

"Not yet," Mod answered, not taking his eyes from the countertop where he kneaded bread dough. "You know how he is, though."

"I do." She inhaled a deep breath and let it out in a sigh. "Too bad, though. I'm not letting him sleep in today." She strode past the dining area, opened the door to the bedroom, and passed through the doorway. She took care to close the door behind her without making a sound.

"Hey, Pete," she said. "Are you awake?"

No one answered, so she padded over to his bed. "Pete?"

His eyes remained shut tight.

She shook him.

He grumbled something but didn't wake up...so she shook him harder.

His grumbling grew louder.

Mmm... She contemplated. She could slap him awake. That way, he'd slap himself asleep. Then she'd slap him awake. There would be a certain irony to it. Even so, she did worry about him getting a concussion, so she decided against slapping.

Instead, she shook him thrice, yelling, "PETE, WAKE UP!"

When that failed, she sighed. Then she had an idea. Using both hands, she vaulted onto the bed and began to jump. "EARTHQUAKE!"

Pete remained asleep.

Nonetheless, Zoey enjoyed jumping on the bed.

It had a different feel than Earth beds. Round's beds felt springier. It reminded her of a trampoline. In turn, that reminded her of the trampoline park back in Cheyenne. The last time she'd gone there was with Pete. They went for a dodgeball tournament.

Even though they lost, it was a lot of fun. Pete struggled to climb up the wall to the zipline. It didn't surprise her that he had a minus ten on his tree-climbing skill.

"Zoey," she heard Pete's voice and continued to jump as she looked down. He stared up at her with a confused expression. "What are you doing?"

"Jumping on your bed." She said, still jumping. "Isn't that obvious?"

"Why?"

"Because."

He sat up and stretched his arms over his head. Then he rested his hands in his lap. "That makes sense." Using care to not bump her or make her lose balance, he lifted the blanket. Then he slid his legs out and rolled from the bed. He landed in a superhero pose on the ground, one arm up and stretched behind him. The hand of his other arm touched the floor.

Zoey ignored the cheesiness of the pose and kept bouncing, "Harvestfest is tonight. There will be real ghosts."

"What?" He stood from his pose.

"Ghosts are real, and we get to see them tonight." She said and then jumped from the bed, doing a flip before sticking the landing. She received notifications:

Flipping proficiency raises by 2 levels.

Flipping proficiency reaches level two.

She blinked away the prompts.

"Ghosts?" He went pale. It was a reaction she expected. He never liked scary movies.

"Yup," she said, "but you don't need to worry. They won't be able to hurt you...and we get to catch them. It will be like ghostbusters...kind of...we won't have ghost traps and particle beams. Instead, we get orbs."

"Orbs?" He blinked twice. "I'm lost."

"I'll explain it all later." She promised. Then she changed the subject. "What are your plans for the day?"

"Hmmm..." He considered before saying. "I'm going to climb trees."

"Climb trees?" Skepticism tinged her voice.

I'm tired of having a skill in the negative." He struggled to keep eye contact. "It's embarrassing."

"Fair enough," Zoey said.

"After I climb trees," Pete said. "I want to try something with you. Then you can tell me about Harvestfest."

"I'm scared." She answered without hesitation.

"Don't be. This should make us both stronger...or...break the peel shield." He shrugged. "Either way, it'll be fun."

She glared. "If you break my shield, I will hurt you."

Pete ignored the comment. "If it breaks, we make you a more durable one."

Mod cracked open the door. "Guys, I need you to try something."

*　　*　　*

"Is that scrambled eggs on a pizza?" Pete used his fork to prod at the slice on the plate before him. He wasn't a fan of pineapple on pizza, but he accepted those who enjoyed it. Eggs though? This was taking things too far.

Zoey used her fork to cut off the tip of her slice and ate it.

"It is," Mod said, "and sausage, gravy sauce, diced onion, and sliced peppers."

"Why do you hate pizza?" Pete spoke with a somber tone. "What did pizza do to you?"

"Try it, Pete." Zoey scolded. "It isn't bad." She lowered her fork to cut off another piece from the slice on the plate in front of her.

"You're not my mom." He answered.

"If you don't like it," Mod promised. "I won't ever make it again."

"Fine…" Pete conceded. With caution, he used the edge of his fork to cut the tip from the slice. Once cut, he pushed the tip of the fork into the piece and lifted it close to his face. With his eyes, he examined it. Then he lowered it to his mouth and ate it with a begrudging disdain. As he chewed and swallowed, he squinted his eyes together and admitted. "Okay, that is delicious. We can…"

The doors to the restaurant pushed in, and a woman whom Pete didn't recognize barged through the doorway. She was a human with smooth, long, white hair. Thick, circular glasses rested on her nose, magnifying the size of her glaring eyes. A beige and orange floral dress rested on her broad shoulders, hanging down to her ankles. The bulkiness of it made it difficult to deduce if she were muscular or heavier set.

She swung her arms back and forth as she walked toward the table where Mod, Pete, and Zoey sat. She huffed and puffed to a stop. "The pizza I ordered yesterday never came."

"Mmm…" Mod thought for a few seconds, stroking his chin. He rested his hands on the table as he seemed to remember something. "Wait…you had the Pepperoni and green pepper, right?"

"That's right." She replied. "Why didn't I get it?"

"When you called, you said you would pick it up. You said you didn't want to pay the ten extra len for delivery. When you didn't pick it up, I figured you didn't want it."

"I WANTED DELIVERY!" She yelled.

"I'm sorry for the misunderstanding." He remained calm. "How would you like me to resolve this issue for you?"

She crossed her arms over her chest. "I want a pizza for free."

"Sounds fair enough." He agreed. "Would you like us to make that now or deliver it later?"

"Lunchtime would be fine." She answered. "I want a free dessert, too."

"Would a tray of brownies suffice?" He asked.

She nodded her head once. "You better not forget this time. I have lots of friends. I'll tell everyone you don't care about your customers. I'll destroy your business." With that, she spun on her heel and stormed out of the restaurant.

"She's a pleasant person," Zoey said, sarcasm inherent in every word. "Does she actually have friends? Or did she make up that part?"

"Her name is Tammy Escaron. The Escaron family is the wealthiest one in Greenlake. One of her sons— a man named Roger—is the only person in town with an adventurer's pass."

"What's an adventurer's pass?" Pete asked.

"An adventurer's pass," Mod replied, "is an item that attaches to the person that receives it. The attachment is permanent. They can't get rid of it after. When someone has the pass, it allows them to enter dungeons."

"Is that how the family became rich?" Zoey asked.

"It is," Mod confirmed. "Roger used the pass to

traverse dungeons. Aside from the loot, a person can level up at will in a dungeon. There are no moderator restrictions. This earned him great individual power and his family wealth."

"I understand why Tammy is so entitled now." Zoey said. "She knows no one will tell her no."

"Right," Mod agreed.

After an awkward moment of silence, Pete stood and said, "I'm going to climb a tree."

4: Mermaids Mermaiding

Pete didn't know a lot about trees. He couldn't recognize the difference between an oak and a juniper. The one thing he did know...he would learn to climb them. He'd climbed trees before. He'd done so with no trouble.

Growing up, he lived four blocks away from his grandparent's house. He spent many hours playing in their yard. That same yard boasted two large crabapple trees. He'd climbed those two trees countless times; he'd never fallen before. If not for Max lunging at his face, he wouldn't have fallen from the other tree either.

It didn't seem fair that his tree-climbing skill had dropped into the negatives. It wasn't his fault he fell out of a tree. Even so, he knew if he climbed some trees, he could push his skill back into the positive.

He'd put a lot of thought into the best way to approach his tree-climbing skill. This included the evaluation of the trees in the region. Near the Trash Panda's hideout, the trees had thinner branches with pine needles. They'd be no good for climbing.

The trees around the lake had thick trunks and sturdy branches. Not to mention, the spacing of the branches made them ideal for climbing. It was even easier than the crabapple trees when he was five.

He inhaled a final deep breath, held the air in his lungs, and blew it out. Then at the same time, he lifted his right leg onto a lower branch and his right hand to a higher one. And he began to climb, going up one limb after the other, ascending five feet above the ground.

Tree Climbing proficiency raises by 1 level.

Tree Climbing proficiency raises to level -4

Climbing wasn't as easy as he'd remembered. He

suspected that had to do with his negative skill. His right hand reached for another branch. And the branch where he'd been standing snapped. And he fell. He fell hard. He fell on his backside. If not for the soft mud to land on, he was sure he'd have broken his tailbone.

Tree Climbing proficiency lowers by 2 levels.

Tree Climbing proficiency lowers to level -6.

A third notification popped up, related to the other two, but it was something Pete hadn't seen before:

Didn't your mother ever warn you about the dangers of climbing trees? Stay out of them. It is for your own good.

Pete blinked in confusion at the prompt. Was the world itself conspiring to keep his tree climbing down? Was his inability to climb trees a sick joke to whatever created his prompts? Was the prompt right? Would it be for his own good if he gave up on tree climbing?

"Are you okay?" Zoey's voice asked.

Pete blinked the prompts closed and spun to face her. He remained planted firm with his butt sinking into the mud. "I'll never recover from this...not on an emotional level."

"Don't be a baby." She held out her hand. He took it, and she helped him to his feet. "I bet we can find an item that gives you a passive tree-climbing ability. It'd make sense to try leveling the skill with something like that. Otherwise, you might continue to level in the wrong direction."

"You know." Pete inhaled and exhaled a single, long breath. "You might be right."

Zoey winked one time. "I am right..." Then she

raised an eyebrow. "...you had something you wanted to show me?"

"Oh, right!" Pete said. "Do you have your pizza peel? The shield one?"

Zoey nodded once as she held out her left hand, materializing her pizza peel into it. At the point where the handle met the carrying surface, Zoey pushed a button, creating a foldable hinge. Then the peel locked into its shield form.

"Hold it out," Pete instructed. "I'm going to slap it."

Zoey's initial reaction was to ask why, but she knew better than to try and understand Pete's antics. Plus, she trusted him, so in the end. She held it out in front of her, bending her front leg at ninety degrees, extending her back leg behind her. In martial arts, they referred to her stance as an extended forward stance. It allowed her to brace for whatever Pete had planned.

"Okay," he said. "I hope this works." Then he lifted his hand. And with all the strength he could manage, he slapped against the shield's flat surface.

The Claddagh ring on his hand rang in a high pitch against the cold metal of Zoey's steel. At the same time, the sound of Pete's open palm against a solid, flat surface created a hollowed thwack. The timber resonated in the air. Ding...ing...ing... It reminded her of hitting a hollow metal fencepost with a stick.

Zoey's arms buckled against the force, and her feet dug into the soft earth. But she remained upright, and the shield absorbed the damage from the slap.

As the sound died off, a prompt appeared before Pete:

Slapping proficiency raises by 2 levels.

Slapping proficiency raises to level 112.7

He blinked the prompt away and asked Zoey. "Did your proficiency go up?"

Her forehead wrinkled in confusion as her eyes read the prompt before her. Pete couldn't see her prompt, but he could see her eyes tracing over the words as she read. As she blinked the prompt closed, she answered. "It did. My Pizza Peel skill jumped three levels, and my light armor gained one."

Pete felt the excitement growing in him. If he continued to slap the peel-shield, he wondered how high he could raise his Slapping and her peel skills. There was only one way to find out. "Are you ready for me to slap again?"

"Ready when you are." She told him, bracing for another slap.

*　　*　　*

From the cover of water—only the top of her head and eyes above the surface—Aqua watched. She didn't know why the young man slapped the young woman's shield. The sight of it confused her. As the mermaid looked closer, she realized she had seen the boy before. The last time she'd seen him, she wanted to tell him hello, but shyness won out. Instead of speaking with him, she pulled on his leg, panicked, and swam away.

She could swim up to him and his friend. She wondered what kind of friends they were. Was the young woman with the shield his girlfriend? The mermaid didn't think that was the case. If it were, why would he be slapping her shield over and over? That's an awfully strange way to treat a girlfriend.

Though, the force of the slaps against the shield

seemed strong. She wondered if they would be strong enough to defeat Charybdis. The mermaids didn't have anyone strong enough to defeat the monster. *I should go talk to dad about* it, she thought. And with that thought, she spun away from the bank: plunging into the water, swaying her green tail up and down. It moved in slow, powerful strokes, allowing her to descend in an accelerated dive. As she dove, she passed by fish, freshwater shrimp, and a miniature saurian. The latter had the appearance of something that was a mix between a small crocodile and a human. It swam past her using it's powerful, webbed—and clawed—hands and feet to pull itself through the water, leaving ripples in its wake.

She was glad that Greenlake only held miniature saurians. Some other species grew to be four...even five times the size of a mermaid. They had long, triangular snouts filled with pointed teeth, and thick green scales. The scales formed a natural armor around their muscular bodies. She shuttered at the thought of coming across one of those.

The deeper she went, the cooler the water became, and the tops of the seaweed forest came into view. They reached up at her like long, green fingers. Fish near the forest grew bigger, feeding on the plankton that thrived near the plant.

Aside from plankton, crabs floated near the plants. They snacked on the nutrient-filled leaves. They were round and blue with fat claws. They'd pinched her before...when she was a little girl. But the experience helped her learn that if she left them alone, they'd leave her alone. So she made sure to keep her distance.

She continued above the forest for a few minutes, thinking about the young man as she swam. She'd never seen anyone slap so hard. *Could he use a sword, too, or was he only good for slapping?* She hoped the man could use a sword. If not, she doubted he could slap Charybdis to death.

A dim, emerald light appeared far ahead of her, and she knew she was almost home. This insight gave her cause to speed up, and she moved her arms more effortfully. Her tailfin pushed against the water with a powerful force.

With each stroke, the light ahead grew in intensity and size. It illuminated the far edge of the seaweed forest. One light became two, and two became three. Before long, the entire town was lit up. And she was swimming through it.

Structures of the town sprouted up from a singular limestone foundation. The town's first architects buried that foundation deep into the sandy earth. Each house rose as a circular pillar. Some had entrances near the top, others had entries near the bottom, and most had them in both locations.

The entrances themselves were circular doors reminiscent of portholes. They required touchpad codes to open. Though some of the wealthier families owned biometric scanners. The mermaid girl's family was the former. In fact, from a financial perspective, her family might have been the poorest in town. Between her, her parents, her two brothers, and her two sisters, they struggled to fit in their tiny home. Even so, the value her familial relationships added to her life... It made her feel like the wealthiest mermaid in the world.

Shops owners and politicians housed their businesses and public buildings within stout domes. That type of setup made navigating the merchandise easier for the mermaids. It gave them space so they wouldn't bump into each other. Plus, the owners could look down from the ceiling and see the whole store at once. It helped them eyeball their inventory. They could also see if any customers needed help and catch any would-be thieves. Not that they had to worry about any mermaid thieves; no one in Greenlake had that job.

Within the town, three buildings stood out over the others. The Siren's Call'isuem, Club Shake-a-Fin, and the King's mansion. Where most buildings in town were limestone, mermaid architects built these three from glass, jade, and marble. Rumor was that they imported the marble from First Sea and the jade from Volcano Island. Though, that was so long ago that no one knew for sure.

Club Shake-a-Fin was more glass than rock. Each of its walls was transparent, allowing people on the outside to see all the fun happening on the inside. The walls formed a cube shape, much like the structures in the land part of Greenlake. Though, the walls were not flat. Instead, they were a series of stacked, concave, and convex diamonds. The diamonds jigged inward and jagged outward. They rotated in a checkerboard pattern. This design allowed lasers and strobes to reflect and refract. It created an unpredictable light show every night. The light even passed through the exterior walls, creating streams of iridescence.

The Call'isuem was a half bowl, similar to the design of a coliseum on the surface. The difference came in a glass sphere. A sturdy metal base held the glass structure. It allowed the edges of the glass to spread within meters of the stands. It gave the audience a great view of the happenings within the sphere.

Most of those were sporting events like raiderball. Though the town used the venue for guard certifications and training. When they did certifications, they allowed the public to watch. The Call'isuem also hosted the largest underwater rodeo in the world. It happened once a year.

Two hatches rested at the bottom of the sphere, connecting it to the sphere's base on each side. Those hatches led to separate underground tunnels. On one side, the tunnel stretched to an indoor stable. The majority of the stable held rodeo and farm animals. There were rideable seahorses of every color, hippocampi, and bull sharks. The bull sharks were the kind with horns. The other tunnel linked to the guard station inside the castle.

The officers in the castle looked more like medieval mermaid knights. They could transport prisoners or other combatants to the Call'isuem. Though, a prisoner had to do something awful to earn punishment in the form of a Call'isuem battle.

The King's mansion proved the most extravagant of all. Whoever built the castle—Aqua wasn't sure who it might have been—lined up tall spires to create the castle walls. The spires were of jade and wrapped in clear quarts. The same quartz formed the windows, and jade marked the window frames. A tall archway of Jade formed the front entrance. There, a miniature army of knights guarded against any intruders.

Aqua swam past the club, the arena, and the King's mansion. She did so without slowing down. Then she reached her home, swam straight in, and approached her father. "Daddy," she told him. "I found someone that can defeat Charybdis."

5: No Good Crisis Goes to Waste

Mod tried not to let the busyness of the business over-whelm him. Though, sometimes that is more difficult than others realize. Afterall, his pizzeria was one of the only places young pixies could find an afterschool job. Those pixies—not to mention Pete and Zoey—depended on the restaurant remaining open.

To keep it open, he had to realize a plethora of tasks. For example, he had to balance how many pixies worked a shift versus the number of orders he expected to receive. On weekends, he'd schedule more to work. On weekdays, he'd schedule less. He also needed to ensure the quality of each pizza he sent out. Luckily, his pizza-related skills were rising fast. His slapping proficiency was almost as high as Pete's. And his skill with the peel and bubble fork neared Zoey's.

He was responsible for other tasks, too. For example, he had to decide how much to charge for each pizza. The cost needed to be more than the cost of making the food. The price also needed to be high enough to pay pixies for their work. At the end of the day, he needed to pay himself too.

Of course, Pete and Zoey minimized his expenses. They did this by managing all the ingredients for making the sauce, cheese, and toppings. All Mod had to do was make the dough.

Every shift, he and his employees shared a quest called *Successful Shift*. And new orders appeared as sub-quests. When the sub-quests came up, the pixies spoke with each other to coordinate who would make which pizza. As they finished making pizzas, those piz-zas dropped off the sub-quest menu. At that point, Mod would receive a prompt to take the finished products and put them into the oven.

When the pizzas finished baking, a new sub-quest item would appear. It let the delivery experts—

Pete and Zoey—know which items to take for different deliveries. They could group deliveries together in their inventory. This allowed them to take more than one delivery at a time.

Once Pete or Zoey finished a delivery, the whole restaurant received a notification for a completed sub-quest. If they delivered over one hundred pizzas in a shift, they'd complete *Successful Shift*. Completing the quest didn't give any experience. Though, it did provide them more ingredients for making pizzas. That saved them money. Plus, the pixies received a boost in pay for the day.

At the time, the pixies had to add sub-quest orders themselves. Even so, Mod planned to talk to a tech expert in Futuretown. He hoped to integrate online sub-quest aggregation for his customers. That way, customers could order via their communication boxes. With as busy as the pizzeria had been, he hadn't been able to take the required time off to make the trip to Futuretown. He could send Pete to do it on a weekday.

Mod found himself in the middle of one of a rush shift. Between making pizzas, the pixies took calls. Customers also came into the pizzeria to make in-person orders. At times, while out on delivery, Pete and Zoey came across people who wanted to make an order. In those circumstances, even Pete and Zoey could add it to the sub-quest list.

As such, the sub-quest list grew faster than it shrank. As it stood, Mod and his pixies needed to make another two-hundred pizzas…and that was if no other orders came in. Under such circumstances, it was easy to become overwhelmed.

Even so, Mod trusted his team, and he trusted himself. He knew all he needed to do was keep putting the pizzas in the oven, pulling them out, cutting them, and sending them out. Afterall, every rush had an end. Not to mention, it was the rush shifts that had come to earn his store its reputation…and a healthy boost to his income. *In another month or two,* he thought, *I'll have enough money to apply to the Foodmaker's Guild.* Before opening the pizzeria, he had never considered joining the guild. It was an ambition he felt above him.

One hour went by, and the sub-quest list remained the same. During the second hour, the triplets—Hope, Skye, and Tornado—came in. They ordered a pizza, staying in the restaurant to accompany their fellow pixies. By the third hour of the rush, things began to slow down. At that point, Mod only had to manage one or two orders at a time. During that calm, Angel took the chance to take the chalk from beside the front door and draw on the slate wall. Shy joined her. As Angel drew, the pixies whispered something back and forth with each other. Then they giggled.

Nolan, Rice, and Tice spoke about music. At some point during the conversation, Nolan pulled out his guitar and began strumming a song. The melody began slow and ominous with resonating notes. Then it shifted to a faster melody. The sound of it felt appropriate for the upcoming Harvestfest celebration.

Using the atmosphere created by the song, Mod asked to no one in particular. "Have any of you ever heard of the Moderator's Footstep?"

"Our parents took us there once," Hope replied. "They never told us the story about it, though."

"But you saw the imprint in the boulder?" Mod scanned his eyes over the triplets.

They all nodded, affirming that they had seen the footprint in the rock.

"Well, the story goes like this." Mod began. "One night, a citizen of Greenlake looked across the lake. At that moment, he noticed the lights of Futuretown. He thought to himself, *Futuretown doesn't look that far away. If I built a bridge, I could reach Futuretown in half a day. There would be no need to take the three-*

day journey around the lake.

"As the man thought about making the bridge, a moderator appeared behind him. The moderator explained how building a bridge would be impossible. The man insisted he could build the bridge.

"So the moderator challenged the man to a contest. 'If you can build a bridge, I'll double your current experience points,' the moderator explained. 'But if you fail, I get all your experience points and with it your life.

"The man agreed to the terms of the contest. To begin constructing his bridge, he worked with other townspeople to move a boulder along the coast. It provided a solid foundation for the bridge, and with that foundation, the man began to build.

"For years, he labored, never willing to give up. He wouldn't let the moderator claim his life. Some say it took a decade; others say it took two decades. It could have taken longer. Even so, the man did finish his bridge. When he did, he called out to the moderator, and the moderator appeared.

"Angered at losing the bet, the moderator stomped his foot on the boulder. It caused the bridge to collapse, leaving a footprint in the rock. Despite his anger, the moderator fulfilled his promise. He allocated the man the promised experience points. Then he disappeared, and no one ever heard from him again."

"I thought a tornado made the footprint," Tornado said. "Tornadoes can break rocks."

"Not everything has to be tornadoes." Skye lectured his brother. "Sometimes moderators break things too."

Hope rolled her eyes, using the most mature voice she could muster. "Guys, it's a made-up story. Why would a moderator come to Greenlake? That doesn't make sense. Also, Greenlake is too temperate for tornadoes. I bet the rock has a foot shape from weatherization."

"Weatherization?" Skye and Tornado asked in unison."

Hope sighed and began to explain. "It means normal weather...like rain and wind...that kind of stuff. That's what made the boulder have a footprint shape in it."

"Weather like tornadoes, too." Tornado offered a proud nod with his assertion.

"That's a scary story." Nolan joined the conversation. "It's not as scary as the haunted island, though."

"Haunted island?" The triplets asked, eyes wide.

"There are more than thirty islands in Greenlake," Nolan explained. "But one of them is a place where you should never go.

"It is a smaller island, hidden behind one of the four larger islands which are visible from the coast. When I went there, it seemed to be the smallest island of all the islands in Greenlake."

"The smallest in Greenlake?" Skye's eyes widened further.

"I've never seen any smaller," Nolan confirmed.

"And you went there?" Hope asked.

Nolan nodded.

"That's crazy!" Tornado blurted. "No, thanks. No way. Nu-uh. No haunted islands."

"And when I went there," Nolan added. "Mist covered it. I couldn't see from one side to the other."

"What were you doing there?" Hope questioned.

"I went with some high school friends," Mod noted how Nolan's quick reply added credibility to his story. "We were having a party to celebrate the start of summer."

"I bet the mist made it a scary party," Skye said.

"No thanks to scary islands! Yes, thanks to tornadoes."

"After I anchored our boat," Nolan continued. "I turned to look at the others, and I couldn't see them... So I called to them...but they didn't answer. Since it was a small island, I figured I needed to walk a little, and I'd find them. It didn't work. The island seemed to stretch on forever. There is no way such a small island can stretch for so long. The mist made it be that way."

"That's scary," Tornado said.

"And there were creepy sounds...moans, shrieks, and howls," Nolan explained.

"How did you get away?" Tornado asked.

"I decided to fly up." Nolan paused for dramatic effect. "I thought...it would help me get over the mist..." He paused again.

After a few seconds, Skye broke the silence, "Did it work?"

"It did." Nolan grinned. "My friends had the same idea. Once above the mist, we returned to the boat and left the island, but not before we noticed a creeping shadow beneath us. It was shaped like a snake, but way bigger. I can only imagine what would have happened to someone without wings. They might have been stuck on the island forever. They might have been prey to the shadow."

"It was scary." Rice chimed in. "I was there."

"For real?" Skye's eyes were gigantic. Mod didn't think they could widen any more than they had.

"Yeah," Rice assured, adding. "But it wasn't as scary as the story of *Bear's Fruit*."

"*Bear's Fruit*?" The triplets asked.

And with that, Rice began the story of *Bear's Fruit*. "Once, a long time ago...a bear found itself in a fierce rainstorm. Of course, this was long ago when bears still inhabited Greenlake. Unable to find a cave, the bear sought shelter in the trunk of a hollowed-out tree.

"Rains and winds beat at the tree, but the bear

was not scared. He was a brave bear. Even so, his bravery would not save him. For the rains had weakened a nearby hill. Its soil gave way, creating a mudslide which enveloped the tree, taking the bear's life."

"The years passed, and the tree grew, enveloping the bear, taking on his shape and spirit. The tree became part of the bear, and the bear part of the tree.

"Centuries stretched, and time forgot the tree...until one day. On that day, a man came across the tree. Its branches held something the man had never seen before. Every limb was full of the foreign objects. They were spherical with a red and yellow glow.

"As fruit tends to grow on trees, the man assumed it to be fruit. When he reached up and plucked one of the spheres, his suspicion proved correct. The fruit had a firmness to it and a stem that stuck up like an apple's stem. Even so, the glowing golden red told him it was special. The man had to know how it tasted, so he took a bite.

"That's when he heard a voice, 'who has my fruit.' The voice asked. Terrified, the man dropped the fruit and fled form the tree, returning to Greenlake."

"I'm glad he got away," Skye said.

"That's the thing," Rice explained. "He didn't get away. For the rest of the day, the voice echoed in his head. *Who has my fruit? Who has my fruit?* It wouldn't leave him alone. At night, the voice in his head spoke louder and with more frequency. In time, it became a shout in his head. *WHO HAS MY FRUIT? WHO HAS MY FRUIT? WHO HAS MY FRUIT?* It wouldn't let him sleep.

"He tried to ignore, but the voice moved closer until it was outside his house. *Who has my fruit?* A moment later, he heard it inside his living room. *Who has my fruit?* Then it was in the hallway outside his bedroom. *Who has my fruit?* He pulled the covers over his head, hoping that would protect him from whatever came.

"He heard the voice again. *Who has my fruit?* This time, it was in the bedroom. He waited a long time without hearing the voice. All he could hear were his own heavy heartbeats. Thump. Thump. Thump. When he thought he was safe. He lowered the blanket. *YOU'VE GOT IT!"* Rice lunged at the triplets as he shouted the final line. All three squealed and jumped back."

"A tornado would get rid of the voice." Tornado tried to be brave for his siblings. "Voices don't like tornadoes."

"They say the last thing the man saw," Rice said, "was the transparent spirit of the bear."

As Rice spoke the final line, Rumpke and some of the other Trash Pandas entered the pizzeria. "I came across that tree once," Rumpke said. "The fruit looked delicious, but we had one of our Trash Pandas fall victim to the ghost bear. Now, we all know the story. That's not the scariest tree near Greenlake, though. There is one that is way scarier."

Mod raised an eyebrow. He thought he'd heard all the urban legends around Greenlake. But he'd never heard anything about another haunted tree.

Sensing Mod's doubt, Rumpke insisted. "It's true. Trash Pandas call it the lonely tree."

"Trees aren't talking things. They can't have feelings." Tornado said. "They can't get lonely."

"They might have feelings but can't talk." Skye hypothesized.

Hope looked at Tornado. "How would you feel if a tree said you didn't have feelings?"

"That makes me sad," Tornado answered without any further explanation.

"Anyway," Rumpke began. "The lonely tree is deeper into the mountain forest. When you get close enough to it, your communication box will receive a message. It uses a name in your contacts, so you think they are talking to you. Then it tries to lure you to it. If you get next to it, its roots will wrap around you and pull you into the earth, leaving only your head above the ground.

"From there, the spirit of the tree talks to you. They say it traps you there because it wants a friend. The problem is, once it has you, it isn't easy to get away."

"How do you get away?" Skye asked.

"You have to promise to return with more friends. Then it will let you go, hoping you fulfill your promise."

"The scariest thing in Greenlake," Mod offered, "are soul eaters. These other stories are stories. Soul eaters are real...and they *can* kill you."

"Ay," Rumpke nodded. "That they can. We missed a spirit during last year's Harvestfest. It became a soul eater about four months back. It took every Trash Panda we could spare to finally end the fiend."

"Alien portals are real," Tornado said. "They are scary."

"They are not real." Hope protested.

"They are real." Tornado insisted. "Pete told me he came to Greenlake through a magic portal. He said a magic cat named Max made him come here."

"You're making that up," Skye said. "Like the one time when you said our bodies are acid."

"Nucleotides," Tornado said. "They are acid."

Everyone offered Tornado a blank stare.

"Why are you looking at me like that?" he asked.

6: Harvestfest Day One

That evening, Pete and Zoey arrived at the Trash Panda hideout. When they arrived, the rest of the town was there for the Harvestfest celebrations. Pete took in the lights and games...the matriculations of people and Trash Pandas. The unity of it reminded him of the biggest holiday party he'd ever been to. Christmas. Halloween. Thanksgiving... It didn't matter which...this was bigger than all the holidays.

"It's alive," Pete said.

"Alive is an offensive word to vampires," Zoey said.

"I'm..." He examined her face to see if she was teasing, but he couldn't tell if she was or not. "...Sorry?"

"I'm kidding," She winked. "This place is alive. It's amazing how much work the Trash Pandas put into it. It's crazy how the town and the Trash Pandas celebrated apart from each other last year."

"I'm glad we could bring them together." He said.

"Me, too," she agreed.

"I'm glad you could bring us together too," a deep, male voice spoke. Pete didn't recognize it, so he turned to face its source. A man walked toward them. His slicked black hair shone in the Harvestfest lights. His blue eyes contrasted with his dark hair, giving them extra vibrance. He wore plate armor like Nick Warman's. Though—where Nick's boasted rust—this man's shone. The name Roger Escaron appeared above the man's head. Next to his name was LVL 45. It was by far the highest level Pete had seen in Greenlake. "With the raccoons adding souls to the prize pool, it means the prize I win will be that much better."

"What makes you think you'll win?" Zoey asked the man before Pete could answer.

"I'm Roger Escaron." The man said as if that were an answer to the question.

"Ah," Zoey said. "You're that guy. I met your mom the other day."

"Oh," Roger smiled at her. "I hope she spoke well of me. You are enchanting. How have we not met before?"

"Gross." Zoey glared.

"I'm Pete." Pete stepped between them, offering his hand. "This is Zoey."

"Of course, you are," the man patted Pete's head before sliding past him to look at Zoey. "Now, let the adults talk."

"Please, go away." Zoey remained monotone.

"Alright," Roger agreed, taking a few steps back from Zoey. "I'll be back later, though." He turned and strode away, saying loud enough for Pete and Zoey to hear. "I love when they play hard to get."

"I'd love to punch you in your ugly face," Zoey whispered to Pete, and they both chuckled.

For Harvestfest, Pete had gone to Wanda's. For his costume, he bought a pair of plastic vampire fangs. He had died his hair black and wore a black cape. Zoey had bought a matching black cape. They'd decided to be vampires together...the Count Dracula kind...not the paladin kind.

Though, once they'd arrived for Harvestfest festivities, one of the Trash Pandas had explained to them that people were supposed to wear costumes on the second day of Harvestfest. The other two days, people wore regular clothes. Pete and Zoey decided they'd use costumes all three days, anyway.

An echoing voice began to speak from the center of the festivities. Pete recognized the voice as Rumpke's. "Thank you all for coming. Now, it is time for the spirit-capturing contest." Pete and Zoey positioned themselves to be able to see Rumpke.

The raccoon warlord held an approximation of a microphone. The difference came in the head of the microphone. Instead of wire mesh, it was a glowing neon sphere. Rumpke continued to speak into the device, and it vibrated in and out with his words. "In the past, there have been two separate spirit-capturing competitions. One which the citizens of Greenlake did in and around the town. The Trash Pandas held their own competition in Forest Mountain. This year, there are no restrictions about who can go where. We will do the whole contest as one united town.

"Of course, this means there will be fewer winners, but the cumulation of souls should mean greater prizes. To capture souls, you will need spirit orbs. We will station Trash Pandas near our hideout's entrance. Their only responsibility will be to ensure everyone has enough orbs. If you have questions about how orbs work, you can speak with those Trash Pandas. The archway at the town entrance will also have city guards with orbs. They can also help you." Rumpke finished as Nick stepped next to him, and Rumpke handed Nick the microphone.

Nick lifted it to his mouth. "The rules allow you to team up with others. For safety's sake, we recommend you do so. You can have up to five members on each team. Though, the number of souls captured will count on a per capita basis. If one person catches ten large souls, that counts as ten. If a team of two people catches ten large souls, it only counts as five."

"What is the difference between a large soul and a small one?" Pete—keeping his eyes directed at Nick—leaned over to ask Zoey.

"I'm not sure," Zoey shrugged. "I've never heard those terms before."

"Me neither," Pete said.

Nick continued. "This means that a bigger team

does not mean a better one. If you insist on hunting souls in the Forest Mountain, remember there are monsters here. For Harvestfest, the laws of the moderators permit you to defend yourself against such monsters. Assure your team is strong enough to do so. If not, remain in town or the grasslands outside of town. We don't want your soul to be one we must capture this year." He handed the microphone back to Rumpke.

Rumpke took it and added. "The contest will continue for three nights, beginning at sundown and continuing until dawn. On the third night, we will meet before daybreak and turn in all the souls at the shrine." Rumpke pointed to the shrine set up in the middle of the meadow. "The shrine will generate a prize commensurate to the quantity and quality of the souls captured. Nightfall is in fifteen minutes. Take the time to form teams, get your spirit orbs, and formulate a plan for how you will approach the contest. Good luck." The sphere on the end of the microphone dimmed as Rumpke turned his back to the crowd and entered the Trash Panda hideout.

Pete looked at Zoey. "We're a team, right?"

She wrinkled her forehead and teased. "I'm not sure. I'm still deciding."

"Decide faster," he urged. "We need to get some orbs."

"You've convinced me to join your team." She patted his back. "Afterall, you would be hopeless without me. Let's go get those orbs."

*   *   *

"Please," Hope asked her mom and dad. "I've never done a Harvestfest before. Tornado, Skye, and I will stay in town. We will stay away from monsters. It will help us learn to be responsible. Please, let us do Harvestfest."

64

Her father—Josue—was of average height for a pixie. He had dark blue wings and black-framed glasses. To hide his balding head, he wore a baseball cap.

He wasn't sure how the triplets' participation in Harvestfest would help them be more responsible. Though, he wasn't against the idea of them participating. If they remained in town like Hope suggested, he knew they'd be safe too. Nonetheless, he wanted to make sure his wife was okay with them doing Harvestfest before he gave the okay, so he looked at her.

His wife—her name was Flor—had jet-black hair which hung inches past her shoulders. She was thin with purple wings and a fair complexion.

When Josue looked at her, she looked over at him. They'd married fifteen years ago. In that time, they'd learned to understand each other. As such, when their eyes met, the unspoken communication went something like, *Are you okay with it?*

I am. Are you?

I am too.

Okay.

The triplets' father looked back at Hope and her brothers. "It is fine, but you must stay inside the town."

"We will." Skye and Hope said in unison.

"Tornado," Tornado offered a nod of agreement.

*   *   *

"Thank you for agreeing to help me with this," Rosie said to the two raccoons beside her.

"It's no problem," Cedric answered. "We can win this year." He was a master thief turned master garbageman. He was also Rumpke's brother and one of the highest-ranking members of the garbage patrol. He was so effective at collecting trash that the citizens of Greenlake never saw him coming. Their trash would be there one second and gone the next. Cedric's wiry frame provided him plenty of strength to go with his small size. That smallness made it difficult for anyone to believe he was Rumpke's brother.

"I hope we win," Rosie said. "If we do, Rumpke could take notice of me."

"From the rumors I've heard, he's already noticed you." The other raccoon answered. His name was Ragoon, and he was the second in command of the Trash Pandas. He specialized in spear fighting. As a garbage collector, he used that spear to pick up litter and place it in a garbage bag.

"I've heard the same," Cedric confirmed, looking at Rosie. "Not to mention, Rumpke gets nervous around you. One time, he saw you, and his nose blushed."

"No way." It was Rosie's turn to have her nose blush. "You guys are saying that to cheer me up."

"No, we're not." Ragoon insisted. "It is absolute. It is one-hundred percent true. It is no lie. No fib."

Rosie offered a heavy sigh before saying. "Either way, I need to win. It will give me the confidence to tell him about my feelings. I can't keep waiting for him."

"Right, let's win this." Cedric and Ragoon agreed in unison.

*　　*　　*

Nick squeezed his eyes together, scanning them up and down the figure before him. Then he grumbled.

"Is that a grumble of approval?" Mayor Yam Hopler asked. "Or is something wrong?"

"I've never seen you wear anything other than your gnome outfit," Nick told her. "I didn't know you owned other clothes. As such, it was a grumble of confusion."

"There is no such thing as grumbles of confusion." She put her hands on her hips. "You don't like it?"

"I didn't say that." He told her. "Is it chain mail?"

"It is." She smiled and held her arm out so he could see the metal links of her sleeve. "See."

"And it's..." he paused. "...it's...rainbow colored?"

"You have a problem with rainbows?" She asked.

"What metal looks like a rainbow?" He asked.

"Steel...the smith plated it in some type of titanium." She answered. "It makes it light and durable. I got it at Wanda's. She said something about the rainbow titanium providing magic defense, so I bought it. When I put it on, it gave a huge boost to both magic defense and normal defense."

"Umm... humm..." Nick grumbled again. This time it was a definite grumble of affirmation.

"Right," she smiled back. "This Harvestfest's soul-catching contest is as good as ours."

*　　*　　*

Back in town, the spirits of the bugs looked like small, blue stars dancing through the night air. The small, quickness of the insects made them difficult to track. They were even more challenging to capture. Though, that didn't deter the triplets.

"If Mom and Dad don't let us go into the Forest Mountain, we have no chance at winning the soul-capturing contest," Tornado said while summoning a miniature tornado. He used the small funnel it created to guide the translucent insect spirits toward the orb he held.

"Mom and Dad want us to be safe." Hope reiterated. "When we are older, they'll let us go into the forest for Harvestfest. Plus, Greenlake has neglected insect spirits for too long. They are important too. Someone needs to take care of them."

"Did you know you can catch more than one spirit in an orb at a time?" Skye asked. He had affixed an orb to the end of a small chuck of wood. Then he did the same to another chuck of wood. Then he tied the two pieces of wood together to create what he called orbchakus. To keep up with the speed of the insects, he used his makeshift weapon to capture them mid-flight. Though, he hadn't realized he'd be able to catch more than two spirits at a time that way.

"No way," Hope's eyes widened as she looked at her brother, watching him spin the orbchakus around, absorbing multiple spirits per orb. With each spirit an orb took in, the orb grew brighter and brighter. "That's…wait…why didn't Rumpke tell us you could more than one spirit at a time?"

"Tornado!" Tornado yelled as his small funnel finished pulling a group of spirits into the orb he held. Then he looked at his sister. "It could be that… Mmm…Rumpke didn't know? It could be that he limits himself to catching the big ones. If so, he doesn't know how orbs work with small ghosts. It's like knowing waves exist, but not knowing those turn into tsunamis sometimes."

"That was a disastrous comment," Hope said, looking back and forth between each brother. "Get it?"

"That was a joke Dad told you, huh?" Skye asked, continuing to catch insects with his orbchakus.

"Yeah…" She admitted while hanging her head in shame.

*   *   *

Zoey leaped from the tree, landing on the Nightshade Terror Spirit below, holding her orb beneath her, so it would hit the spirit first. As the sphere touched the ethereal glow of the ghost, the creature went from being there to not being there. It happened in an instant;

it had absorbed into the orb before Zoey landed in a crouch on the grassy earth.

From a tree, Pete observed the event. "I knew that your eyes turn red sometimes. For example, they turn red when your battle log opens and whenever you're angry about something. Tonight, I learned that they turned red when you jumped out of trees."

She stood and looked up at him. "That's good to know."

"It's kinda intimidating." Pete teased. "It's not paladin-like."

"I'm a vampire paladin." she reminded him. "We aren't as boring as those other paladins."

"Yeah, you are the best paladin for sure." Pete agreed as he descended the tree, falling about halfway down and landing in a sitting position. The slipup didn't cost him any hit points, only pride:

Tree Climbing proficiency lowers by 2 levels.

Tree Climbing proficiency lowers to level -8.

A third prompt appeared:

Someday you'll thank me for this. Keep trying. Keep failing. How low will your proficiency drop before you realize it's essential for your tree climbing to stop?

"That doesn't make any sense," Pete argued with the prompt.

The prompt argued back:

Of course, it makes sense. Think about it. There's a reason you needed Zoey's help to get into the tree in the first place.

"You think about it." He shot back.

"Are you arguing with the system prompts?" Zoey asked, unable to hear the prompt's side of the conversation.

"Yeah," Pete hung his head as he closed the prompts.

"That's kinda…" she paused to think of a word. "Cute and sad…both at the same time. Is there a word for that?"

"Sadute," he replied as he stood.

"That's not a word." She told him.

"Yeah…" He sighed. "I know." Once on his feet, he looked around. "Did you notice all these spirits around us?" he asked.

"I did." She affirmed. "Cool, huh?"

"Yeah…" He did a complete 360 degree turn. "We're in a dark forest…at night…surrounded by ghosts. It's cool." He turned to his friend. "Zoey, why are we surrounded by ghosts?"

"I noticed something when my red eyes activated." She explained. "It appears my vampire powers let me control things."

"You're a paladin-necromancer?" He raised his eyebrow.

"Yup," She smiled. "And I'm about to tell each of these spirits to walk straight into spirit orbs. With this ability, it won't be difficult to catch them at all. This contest is as good as ours."

*   *   *

Nick and Mayor Hopler pushed through thick foliage to escape the well-tread pathways. They didn't choose to do this. Instead, they felt they had to. They hadn't seen any spirits along the path for hours.

As the city guard—and de facto mayor's assistant—Nick took the lead, cutting through the vines and branches, clearing the path ahead. He was glad he had his titan's sword to do the cutting. He'd won it during a battle against the Turkey Titan. His old sword wouldn't have kept its edge against the vegetation.

"I don't understand where all the spirits went." The mayor said. "Has it ever been like this for you?"

"Every year," Nick grumbled. He already knew the source of why they struggled to find any spirits. He'd hoped this year would be different, but since it wasn't, he knew he'd have to explain it to the mayor. "It's always like this for me."

"Are ghosts afraid of you?" She guessed. "Do you have some type of ghost-repelling passive ability? Are they afraid of your mustache?"

"No," Nick answered, cutting a branch to reveal a clearing ahead. "My problem is him." Nick pointed to the clearing.

As the mayor looked, she saw Roger Escaron trapping a spirit within an orb.

"Each year," Nick explained, keeping an even voice. "Roger follows me to make sure I don't win. I am awesome, so I understand why he's threatened by me. Even so, it's not sportsmanlike of him."

"Have you asked him to not follow you?" the mayor asked.

"I can't," Nick said. "As sad as it is for me to admit that someone can bully a city guard, that is what Roger is doing. He's bullying me. If I let him know it bothers me, he'll see it as an even bigger win than it is. It will ensure he does this again next year. It's best to ignore and hope he goes away."

"You should talk to him." The mayor insisted. "If not him...talk to his mom."

"Won't change anything," Nick said. "She's as bad as he is. His following us might be a good thing, though." Nick explained. "If Roger follows us, it leaves

Pete and Zoey with plenty of spirits to catch. If we catch some of Roger's spirits here, he'll lose to Pete and Zoey. That would be the best payback we can get."

"I'd hoped to win." The mayor hung her head. Then she squeezed her eyes together and spoke with a rare passion. "Even so, payback against Roger sounds good. Let's steal as many spirits from him as we can."

7: Harvestfest Day Two

After the first night of Harvestfest, all the participants returned to their homes. And Pete and Zoey had retired to their room. The first night of Harvestfest had been a busy one. Zoey estimated they'd captured over one-hundred spirits. Though, Pete hadn't kept count well enough to verify one way or another.

The only thing he did know was exhaustion. His tiredness overwhelmed him. Even so, he'd expected as much. They even had the foresight to speak with Mod ahead of time. He let Pete, Zoey, and the triplets have the next two days off. Mod knew they'd need the rest to compete once darkness fell.

As evening drew near, Zoey emerged first from the room she shared with Pete. She scanned the impeccable cleanness of the restaurant. When she saw Mod behind the counter, he waved at her.

She smiled back, asking. "How'd it go yesterday? Did you get by without us?"

"With the holiday, it might have been busier than usual." He admitted. "Though, we managed. I sent Mike and Tike on deliveries in your absence. They did well with it. They might be able to help Pete and you with deliveries. That is...if you guys ever need extra help."

"Sounds like a plan," Zoey told him, padding over to one of the dining tables, sliding a chair out, and sitting. As she sat, she lifted her legs, resting them on the chair on the other side of the table.

Mod stepped around the counter and began in her direction. "How'd things go with you and Pete?"

"My best guess...it went well. I don't have any metric to go by...so..."

"Metric to go by?" Mod reached the table.

"I mean, I haven't done this before. I don't know what is good and what isn't." She explained.

"Ah, that makes sense." Mod sat next to her. "You figured out a strategy, though? Yeah?"

Before she could answer, the front door clicked open. Mod kept it locked during business hours, and he was the only one with a key. So it surprised him that someone had opened it. Who would have the ability to pick a lock? He guessed one of the Trash Pandas, ex-thieves that they were. Though, he guessed wrong. As the door opened, it didn't reveal one of the Trash Pandas.

Instead, Roger Escaron stepped through the open door. Mod locked eyes with Roger. He wasn't sure how to react. If anyone else broke into his business, he'd yell at them and chase them out. He did not want to do that to an Escaron. In particular, he didn't want to do that to Roger. Afterall, Roger was the one with the adventurer's pass.

Zoey didn't possess the same reservations. "There's a reason we keep that door locked. Come back during business hours."

Roger fixed his eyes on her. It wasn't a typical stare. It was intense...like he wanted to see through her soul. It reminded Zoey of movies. To be specific, it reminded her of the part in a film when the heart throb looks at the awkward girl. Then said girl melts under his gaze. In other words, he was trying to impress Zoey. She was sure of that.

The problem was that Roger was no heart throb. He was the opposite of a heart throb. *What is the opposite of a heart throb?* Zoey wondered. After considering the answer to her question, she decided. *Roger is a heart arrhythmia.* She wasn't sure if that made sense as an opposite. But the point was that she didn't like Roger. His presence bothered her.

To make things worse, he said. "I'm not here for pizza. I'm here for you."

"Gross," she told him.

He blinked a few times, unsure how to respond. Then he composed himself. "It's...last night...with the competition....we didn't get to talk. I'd like to get to know you better."

"I live here. You understand that?" She asked.

"Ye..."

"It was a rhetorical question." She told him. "You don't need to answer it. I know you know that I live here. That's what makes it creepy. Breaking into someone's home makes you creepy... I'm not impressed. Go away. If you want pizza, come back during business hours. Thank you. Have a nice day."

"Yes, well...I was hoping we could go for a walk along the beach." He explained. "Get to know each other better."

"I was hoping you'd go away." She told him. "It looks like we are both disappointed."

"Listen..." This word came out forceful. Zoey wondered if Roger was beginning to lose his temper. Even so, he calmed himself before continuing. "Any woman in Greenlake would feel thrilled to be on my arm. You should take this chance while you have it."

"I'll risk it going away." She answered. "Now, will *you* go away?"

As the conversation progressed, Zoey noticed how Mod became more and more stressed. She knew how he didn't want to offend the Escaron family. Even so, he needed to stand up for himself. Since he couldn't do that. She would. Mod could cede to Roger, allowing him to break into the pizzeria. Or Mod could side with Zoey and risk alienating himself from the Escaron family. At the time, she was making the choice for him. Though she'd talk to him later. If he wanted her to apologize for his sake, she would.

"Okay, it is obvious I caught you at a bad time," Roger said. "We can continue this conversation later. Farewell, my lady."

"Go away," She answered.

Roger glared, then recomposed himself...and lost that composure. He finished by mumbling something resembling words. Then he hurried from the restaurant. Once he left, Zoey turned back to Mod.

Before she could apologize, Mod told her. "That was awesome."

*   *   *

For the second night of Harvestfest, Pete and Zoey used the same vampire costumes from the previous night. As the pair searched for spirits, they noticed a blue glow in the distance. When they saw it, they hurried in its direction. As they speed-walked, it illuminated the branches, creating reaching shadows that stretched as if trying to grasp at the pair of pizza delivery workers. The surrealness of it created a strange dissonance.

"It's like being in a slasher movie," Pete observed.

"Are you scared?" Zoey asked.

After considering the question, he answered. "No, if some slasher villain attacks us, I'll slap him."

"Do you think you can slap your way out of everything?" She asked.

"I am a pizzaman." He replied. "It's what I do."

"Fair point," she said as they reached the branches. "Think we should push through these? Or do you think it'll be quicker to go around?"

"It doesn't look too thick." He said. "It'll be better to push through."

"Right," She opened her status menu, equipping her peel-shield hybrid. Once she equipped it, it materialized in her hand. "Let's push through then. Stay close behind me." With that, she positioned the shield in front of herself and began to push into the vegetation.

Pete remained close behind her, tucked down so none of the branches would whip back and smack him in the face. Even so, he wanted to respect her space, so he didn't get too close.

"You can get closer," she told him. "I don't want you to get whipped."

"Right," he agreed. Yet, he continued to maintain a respectful space.

After thirty seconds of pushing through the vegetation, they emerged on the other side. There they discovered the source of the glow, a well-used fishing hole. The spirits of fish and some worms filled the space beneath the surface. Though, some fish spirits swam through the air inches above the earth and water. Others swam through the grass and earth itself. Their glow illuminated the grass with a celestial opalescence.

Unlike the tomato plant and insect spirits they'd encountered, the fish spirits remained unimpressed by Pete and Zoey's presence. This made it easy for Pete and Zoey to capture the spirits in their orbs until they ran out of orbs.

"We'll need to return to the Trash Panda hideout for more orbs." Pete realized.

"I hate to admit it," Zoey said. "But you're right. Let's hurry back before someone else finds this spot, though."

"Right," Pete agreed.

*　　*　　*

A rectangular stone doorway stood on the east edge of the forest. Instead of a door, an opaque blanket of colors filled the frame. They shifted like food coloring in water, creating neon waves of gold, crimson, cerulean, jade, silver, and tangerine. None of the colors overwhelmed any of the others.

In front of the doorway stood Nick. For Harvest-fest, he'd dressed as a sailor, wearing a white sailor's hat. He wore the costume's white pants and button-up shirt tight over his armor. It was so tight it appeared the buttons might burst apart. Any passerby could see the form of the armor beneath the costume.

Next to Nick stood the mayor. For Harvestfest, she had added a winged helmet to her rainbow armor. The helmet wasn't metal, and it would do little to protect her. But she cared more about the appearance. She'd spray-painted the headgear with iridescent paint that changed color depending on how the light hit it. She'd hired Tay—the town's seamstress and leather-worker—to fashion a sparkling red cape. "Is that what I think it is?" The mayor asked, looking at the doorway.

"It is." Nick nodded, pushing his hand against what appeared to be liquid between the frame. Even so, it felt like solid brick under his touch. Without an adventurer pass, he knew he wasn't getting through the portal.

"How long do you think it's been here?" She asked.

An answer came, but not from Nick. Instead, it came from behind the pair. "About a week."

Nick removed his hand from the portal, and he and the mayor turned toward the source of the voice.

Rumpke walked toward them. "We noticed it about a week back."

"You knew about this?" the mayor asked.

"We did," Rumpke said.

"You didn't think it was important to share this information?" Nick growled.

"We wanted to buy a dungeon pass, so we could explore it first," Rumpke replied. "If we told the town about it, someone else might go in before us…but Zoey said a trio of adventurers asked her about the portal. It's only a matter of time before they find it."

"A dungeon in Greenlake." The mayor contemplated. "There's never been a dungeon in Greenlake before. Once word about this gets out…"

"…once word gets out, adventurers will overrun Greenlake." Nick finished her sentence.

"Is that good or bad?" Rumpke asked.

"Both," the mayor told him. "It's good because the influx of people will improve the local economy. Wanda is going to make a killing selling to adventurers."

"It's bad because we don't have the infrastructure to support all the adventurers. They won't have anywhere to sleep; we don't have enough food for them all." Nick said. "Also, the Moderators like to keep an eye on their dungeons. It's best to avoid any extra attention from them."

"Roger is an adventurer," Rumpke observed. "Can you send him to open the chests before other adventurers discover the dungeon? It would keep the riches from the dungeon within the town."

"In the end, the Escarons would hoard the money like they always do." Nick used his thumb and pointer finger to stroke his mustache, considering how to proceed. Then he lowered his hand and said. "The benefit of having adventurers here outweighs the risk of repercussions from the Moderators. Though, we'll need to make sure everyone is following the rules. This applies extra to a certain pizzaman."

"Rumpke," the mayor added. "I'll travel to Futuretown tomorrow and register the dungeon with the Adventurer's Guild. That way, they can assign guards. In the meantime, can you station some Trash Pandas here? Have them ensure no one tries to get in without an adventurer's pass?"

"I can do that." Rumpke agreed.

"Make sure they are strong," Nick advised. "Monsters and undead are free to wander in and out of the dungeons. We don't want anything coming out and causing trouble to the town. If your Trash Panda guards kill anything, they can loot it and say they're doing their jobs as bandits."

"I'll assign individuals capable of keeping us all safe," Rumpke said.

"Thank you," Nick said. "I appreciate your cooperation with this."

*   *   *

For Harvestfest, the triplets had told their parents they wanted to be raiderballers. And their parents agreed to the costumes. But like the caring parents they were, they made sure the costumes served a practical purpose. They did this by buying authentic raiderball shoulder pads. The triplets wore said pads on the outside of their t-shirts. Hope and Tornado used midfielder pads which covered only the shoulders. Skye used a defender's pad which covered his chest and upper back as well as the shoulders. Authentic pads provided authentic protection for Harvestfest soul capturing.

Tornado sped down the shoreline, his tiny wings beating with a frantic ferocity as he chased after one of the insect spirits. Ahead of him, it zigzagged, its trajectory carrying it over the lake and back over the land.

"Careful," Hope shouted, following behind. "Mom and Dad don't like us flying over the water. What if you fall in? Remember?"

"Oh, right," Tornado shouted back. From there, he adjusted his course to go straight, keeping over the land. This worked to his benefit. It allowed him to overtake the zigzagging insect, trapping it in one of the orbs.

"You have to remember to stay careful." Hope reminded her brother as she stopped to hover next to him. "You won't always have someone here to remind you to stay safe."

"I'm sorry." Tornado hung his head.

"Seven, eight, nine, ten," Skye shouted from the nearby beach, counting each insect he trapped with his orbchakus.

As Tornado and Hope returned to their brother, Hope continued to reprimand him. He continued to apologize. This cycle broke when Skye yelled, "watch out," and sped toward his siblings.

Upon seeing this, Hope and Tornado turned their attention to their surroundings. Tornado noticed a saurian as it shot out from the lake waters, snapping its jaws toward Hope. The small crocodilian humanoids called saurians were common in Greenlake. Though, the species native to Greenlake was of the miniature variety. The species that attacked Hope was something else. It was bigger and had stripes across its back.

As the creature leaped from the water, Skye zipped to his sister's defense. He swung his orbchaku into the underside of the animal's jaw. It didn't do much damage, but it was enough to knock the creature off course, causing it to miss Hope.

The thing reoriented, standing on its hind legs. At full height, it was taller than the pixies. But not by much. But in terms of body mass, it outweighed them by a large margin. All three wondered how the new species of saurian had gotten into the lake, but none of the three had time to ask the question aloud. Instead, they needed to focus on defending themselves.

"Tsunami!" Tornado lifted his hands, and the lake's tide responded. It rose, slamming into the saurian, knocking it off its feet.

Skye took the opportunity to swoop in and hit the saurian on the head with his orbchakus two more times. As it turned to counter him, he darted away. But not before one of the scales on the beast's head scratched his leg, causing him to cry out in pain.

"Hang on," Hope hurried over to him, pointing her palm toward the cut. A flow of green light slithered from her hand and into the wound. A few seconds later, the light faded, and the injury had healed in full.

"Thanks," Skye said. "Watch out!"

The saurian charged toward Skye and Hope, lunging and chomping.

"Tornado!" Tornado shouted, catching the thing in a spell that created a spiraling gust. The wind lifted the creature, throwing it back into the lake.

From the water, it considered the pixies. Ultimately, it decided they weren't worth the trouble before retreating into the depths.

"We should move toward the plaza." Hope suggested. "It has insects, too, and it will be safer for us."

*　　*　　*

Rosie, Cedric, and Ragoon used their small stature and agility to their advantage. They did so by climbing into the treetops and scouting for spirit-heavy areas. Once they'd located a spirit, they'd use the same treetops to move, hopping from branch to branch. Then they'd arrive posthaste at the spirit-heavy location. They'd clear out the spot, and they'd repeat the process.

To help them win the contest, they'd decided to forgo costumes. They didn't want anything to slow them down during the competition.

From the tall branches, Ragoon looked for a new location. "Spirits are beginning to thin out. By the end of tomorrow night, there won't be any left."

"We'll have to get creative," Cedric said. "We should begin searching caves."

Ragoon shook his head in disagreement. "If we wander around random caves, our spirits might be in orbs this time next year. Winning isn't worth our lives. Though, I agree. We *do* need to get creative if we want to win."

"We have to win," Rosie said. Her voice broke with uncertainty. "There's no other option."

"We could move deeper up the Forest Mountain," Cedric suggested.

"That might work." Ragoon agreed. "If we go too deep, we'll come across NMs, so we must be careful."

"Guys, what's that?" Rosie pointed below them.

Ragoon and Cedric cast their eyes downward.

Below them—no more than five feet beneath their feet—the spirit of the Turkey Titan's enormous head stared back. It gobbled once, cocking its head with a curious stare. After two seconds of silence, it shrieked a battle cry and hopped up, snapping at them with its beak.

The trio of trash pandas jumped up a few branches. "Let's get out of here," Ragoon shouted as the trio began to flee through the treetops.

8: Harvestfest Day Three

Half-way through the third night of catching spirits with orbchakus, Skye felt confident he could modify a pair of pizza cutters into cutterchakus. He wondered if he could impress customers with his chaku skills if he used those skills to cut a pizza. Though—in the end—it didn't matter if he impressed them. He was going to have fun cutting the pizza. And fun was the point. At the time, he was having fun chasing insects up and down the plaza's edge.

"Don't go too far off," Hope reminded her brother. "Mom and dad don't want us to leave the plaza."

During the day, their parents never had qualms about them going anywhere in town. Greenlake was a safe place with safe people. Even so, the event with the striped saurian and the sighting of the Turkey Titan had everyone on edge.

For safety, some citizens chose to remain home for the final night of Harvestfest. That said, the triplets lived on a street along the plaza. Their parents might as well have restricted them to the front yard.

If they couldn't expand further out into town, they'd never win the soul-capturing contest. Not that they had much of a chance in the first place. All they'd managed to capture over the last few days were insects, some mice, and a snake. And Tornado had captured spirits of worms by opening cracks in the earth with his magic. This would reveal the spirit worms which wiggled through the air as if the dirt were still around them.

In the end, all three triplets understood how the contest was about putting the spirits to rest. If they hadn't taken care of the smaller spirits, no one in Greenlake would have. In that respect, their work during Harvestfest proved more important than winning any competition. They took pride in that.

*　　　*　　　*

As the triplets had given up on any hope of winning the competition, so too had the mayor and Nick. Between the dungeon portal and the Turkey Titan sighting, their focus had shifted. They cared more about the safety of Greenlake and its citizens. Not to mention, Roger Escaron had followed them all three days. He'd captured anything within one hundred yards of them before they could.

Nick was a competitive person... And he was more emotional than he'd like to admit. Where winning would have felt great, he was okay with losing. What was more difficult for him to accept was how he hadn't captured a single spirit. As such, he couldn't hide his disappointment. He wore it in his sad eyes and his drooping mustache.

"It'll be better next year," the mayor assured him as they walked along the forest path. "Roger can't follow us every year."

"Yeah..." he agreed, his voice quiet. "Next year we'll win...or catch one spirit...I'd settle for catching anything at this point."

"On the bright side," the Mayor said. "If we find the Turkey Titan, Roger will capture it for us. It will save us some trouble."

"I suppose that's true." Nick agreed. Nick'd love to capture the spirit of the Turkey Titan for himself. Though, he recognized its capture was more important than him being the one to capture it. If they didn't trap it during the Harvestfest competition, it would wander the forest for an entire year. In that time—if it became a soul eater—the whole of Greenlake would be at risk of destruction.

"How was Futuretown?" She asked.

"Futuretown?" He repeated, confused by the

question.

"You went today to report the dungeon to the Adventurer's Guild." She reminded him.

"Ah, right." He remembered. "It was the same as always. The guild said they'd send someone, but it might be a week before they can allocate the resources."

"Help me." A voice carried on the night air, interrupting their conversation. It was a voice that neither Nick nor the mayor recognized. It was soft, high-pitched, and calm. This contrasted the words which it spoke. "Help me."

In fact, it was so soft that Nick had to confirm he wasn't hearing things. He looked at the mayor and asked. "Did you hear that?"

She nodded that she had. "It was close."

"Help me," the voice repeated, and they began in its direction. It was a direction that didn't make sense, away from the path and into some thick bushes.

Nick took the lead, using his sword like a machete to hack away vegetation. When he heard the voice call for help a fourth time, he answered. "Don't worry. We're coming."

"Help me." The voice called again. This time it was behind them, back toward the pathway.

Did we go past whoever needed our help? Nick wondered. *How did we miss them?* His eyes widened when he realized what had happened. "Hurry, get back to the path!" He shouted, trying to do the same himself.

Knowing not to question Nick, the mayor followed his advice. But the way back to the path wasn't much easier than the one they'd followed into the bushes. She had to give up some speed to ensure she wouldn't trip, poke herself in the eye, or anything like that. As she struggled to return to the safety of the path, she called back. "What is it?"

"A lonely tree," Nick shouted at her. "I've seen them before, but never this far south. They draw you into the woods, then use their roots to... Aaggh!"

His sentence cut short as one of those roots wrapped around his leg and pulled. The force from the root and the speed at which he hurried tripped him. It left him parallel with the ground, three feet above it. When he landed, branches broke beneath the force, leaving new dents and scratches in his rusty armor.

The root around his ankle began to drag him. He knew he didn't have a lot of time. The tree would use the root to pull him into a dirt-filled pit near its base. As soon as he was in it, the packed dirt would pin him in place like a carrot in a garden, preventing him from moving. Over the next few days, the root would drain his life energy. He needed to free his leg before that happened.

He lifted his sword and hacked at the tree root. It chipped but remained intact. And it didn't let go. If anything, it squeezed tighter. All the while, the root continued to drag him, snapping bushes and branches along the way. In such circumstances, it was difficult enough to hold on to the sword, let alone swing it. Though, swing it he did...again...and again...and again...

On that fourth stroke, he struck true, and the root broke. He returned to his feet in time to hear the mayor scream. "IT GOT ME!." Rather than run in her direction, he looked at the ground. He guessed that if the mayor needed help, it was because a second root had trapped her. He identified that second root. Then he felled his sword onto it like a man using an axe to cut firewood, and the root broke.

"Are you free now?" He shouted.

"Yes," she answered. "It let go. I'm free."

"Good," he shouted back. "Keep running. I'm going to take care of the tree."

In his mind, he knew he shouldn't take on the

tree by himself. There were lots of reasons to not attack it. For one, he wasn't an arborist. Attacking a tree went against his job. In turn, it went against the laws of the moderators.

Moderators allowed self-defense. But they didn't allow someone to protect other people...not unless they had a job like Zoey. By being a paladin, she was able to defend others. In the case of Nick, saving the mayor from the root might have been enough to break the law. He grumbled as he came to this realization and whispered to himself. "Pete the pizzaman is becoming a bad influence on me."

With that, Nick began his charge toward the lonely tree. The closer he got to where he guessed he'd find the trunk, the thinner the bushes became. Those that remained turned dead and dry. Then there were no bushes at all, only the lonely tree.

From one hundred paces away, Nick saw the tree for the first time. It had four roots swinging around it like wild tentacles. Two of them were the ones he'd damaged. The other two were in good condition. Though, they didn't try to grab him. Was it afraid of him?

Between the tentacles, Nick recognized two glowing, purple orbs. He guessed them to be eyes. The leaves on the branches and in the tree's canopy were bright orange. He wondered if they took their color from the blood of their victims. *Victims,* he wondered, *has the tree killed any of Greenlake's citizens? Had it killed Trash Pandas? How had it sustained itself?*

As he observed the tree and wondered about its victims, he continued his charge. "Help me." He heard it say. Though, he didn't see a mouth. Then it swung a root at him, and another root, and another. Using his level 11 City Guard agility, he dodged around the lashes, jumping that way and sliding this way. When the distance between him and the tree had closed to six paces, he jumped feet first. He landed with his feet against the trunk as he dug the point of his sword into the bark between the eyes.

"Help... me..." The tree said one last time before the purple glow of its eyes dimmed to black.

*   *   *

Near the end of the third night, Pete found it difficult to remain motivated. At that point, soul capturers had cleared most of the spirits from the forest. He and Zoey hadn't even seen a spirit during the last two hours.

"Do you think we should call it a night?" He asked her.

"That's a good idea," She agreed.

"Try using your vampire eyes again." He told her. "Try to call something toward us."

"That only works when I'm in battle mode, doing something athletic, or when I'm mad." She reminded.

"So...think of something that makes you mad." He said.

"Like what?"

"Like Kim." He answered, reminding Zoey of her high school rival. Upon mentioning Kim, Zoey's eyes flashed from green to red. "See, that turned them red."

"Yeah," she glowered at Pete. "Thanks for bringing her up." Then she looked around. "It didn't work. There's no spirits around here for me to connect with." After confirming the lack of spirits, Zoey took a calming breath, and her eyes returned to green. Those same eyes looked at Pete. "You know you shouldn't bring up people like Kim while you are on a date."

"Date?" Pete stammered. "This is a date?"

"You're too easy to tease, Pete." She snatched his hat off with her left hand and roughed up his hair with her right one. "That's one of the reasons I like you."

All he could do to answer was blush as she replaced the hat atop his head. Though, he went from embarrassment to curiosity as he noticed an ethereal blue glow in the trees behind Zoey. He hyper-focused on the light.

"What is it?" She asked, noticing the change in his demeanor and turning to follow his line of sight.

"Do you see that glowing light?" he asked. "You said there aren't any spirits nearby, right?"

"There aren't," She confirmed.

"So for one to be big enough to give off that kind of light, it'd have to be..."

"The Turkey Titan," she finished his sentence for him.

With that, both sped toward the direction of the light. They put every ounce of running ability and agility to use, hoping no one else captured the spirit of the Turkey Titan before they did.

As they neared the glow, they confirmed their suspicions. The light was in the shape of a giant turkey. When they drew even closer, Pete recognized the familiar turkey. It looked the same as it had in life. When they were within twenty feet of the thing, they slowed to a stop.

While Pete reached into his pocket and pulled out an orb, he told Zoey. "Watch this." Then he threw the orb at the spirit. Instead of capturing the ghost of the Turkey Titan, the orb bounced off, and a prompt appeared:

This spirit is too powerful to capture. Wear it down with combat, and then try again.

"Wow," Zoey said. "The way you bounced the orb off the turkey ghost thing...that was awesome. Good work."

"It says we have to wear the spirit down before we can capture it." He told her.

"Like catching a pokemon?" She asked.

"I guess so," he answered. "I wish we had a masterball... Wait...do you think they have a master spirit orb?"

"You're so dumb." She chuckled.

"Yeah," he agreed. "So how do we wear the spirit down?"

"I have a few ideas," She said. "I unlocked a few skills on my skill tree that might help."

"Nice," he said. "You use those. I'll try to use my fire spell on them. Fire tends to damage spirits in video games." He hesitated before continuing, "or it heals them. Boy, do I hope I don't heal him."

"If you do, he'll be your friend." Zoey smiled. "You can have a giant pet turkey ghost. Isn't that what you wanted for Christmas this year?"

* * *

As they continued to banter, the Turkey Titan watched them. It scanned its head back and forth from one to the other as they spoke, deciding which it should try to eat first. At the time, the Turkey Titan didn't realize it was a spirit. It didn't know it couldn't eat.

"I wanted a new gaming PC for Christmas." Pete answered.

"That's not the same thing?" She teased.

"How would that be the same thing?" He asked.

"They both...ummm..." She thought for a second. "...glow in the dark?"

The impatient turkey spirit decided it would eat Pete. He was the one that threw the strange orb at it, after all. "Gawk!" it let out its battle cry as it flapped its wings and charged.

* * *

Zoey activated her ability Draw Hate from her paladin skill tree. It was an ability that—when active—made nearby enemies hate her. The recast of the effect was a full minute, and the ability lasted thirty seconds.

As the turkey shifted its attention from Pete to Zoey, she transformed her peel into its shield form. She held it in her left hand. She held her pizza fork in her right. Seconds after she had equipped herself, the turkey slammed its beak toward her. She wasn't sure she had the strength to withstand a square blow against her shield. As such, she held it overhead at an angle, causing the turkey's attack to glance off and miss to the side.

The turkey pulled its beak back. And Zoey watched that beak with an intense focus, not wanting to mistime her defense of its next attack. That was her mistake. She'd become so hyper-focused on the beak that she overlooked as the turkey swung its wing in at her from the side. It caught her, sending her tumbling to her side and causing her HP to drop by a few points.

Before she could roll back onto her feet, the Turkey was on her, slamming its beak downward.

A fireball from Pete's Strong Fire spell interrupted the attack. It caught the Turkey Titan in the side of its head, knocking the creature off balance, forcing it to stumble to the side.

It gave Zoey enough time to return to her feet. "He hits harder than I thought." She said as Pete stepped next to her.

"Yeah," Pete agreed, lifting his hand to hurl two more fire spells toward the gigantic spirit. They struck, but the health bar above the turkey didn't deplete. "He wasn't that much fun when he was alive either."

* * *

At that moment, three things happened. First, Zoey's hate spell wore off. Second, the giant turkey spirit remembered it was dead. Third, the Turkey Titan remembered who had killed it. Its eyes flashed with anger, and it charged with a renewed vigor, focusing all its efforts on its foe – the pizza delivery man.

*   *   *

Pete slid back to avoid the first attack. Then he tried to time a slap across the turkey's head as its beak struck against the ground. Where his timing was right, the material nature of the turkey was not. His hand went straight through the spirit without causing any damage at all. It was like the head wasn't even there. Even though Pete couldn't hit the turkey, it *could* still hit him. And hit him it did, pulling its head away a few feet before batting it back into him.

He lost track of where he was as the world spun. When he came to a stop, the world continued to spin. Pete groaned as he returned to his feet, stumbling to keep his balance and not fall back to the ground.

The turkey sped toward him.

Zoey lifted her hand and initiated her attack in the form of two spells. The initial one was a spell that came from her paladin tree. It caused holy-based damage against its target. The other spell she used was a more robust version of the first one, also from her paladin tree.

Instead of shooting from her hands like Pete's fireball spells, the Light of the Living spells began as lights. One light was the size of a lightbulb. The other was a smidge larger. The pair of lights appeared in the center of the turkey. She could see them through the spirit's translucence. The smaller light radiated in waves that expanded outward. The more significant light spun. As it did, it flung out rotating waves of light.

The Turkey Titan froze in place, shrieking as the light disintegrated the creature from the inside out. When the spells finally dissipated, the spirit fell. Rather, it almost fell because it never hit the ground. Instead, it hovered, moaning in pain.

As Pete's head began to clear, he realized this was the moment he'd been awaiting. He materialized an orb from his inventory into his hand. Then he threw it. The small sphere hit the spirit and vacuumed it in with a satisfying whoosh. As the turkey dissolved into the sphere, the orb took on a brilliant, happy yellow glow.

9: Another Boss Fight

From the treetop, Ragoon, Cedric, and Rosie searched for any sign of spirits. By the third day, they found themselves without any luck. No strategies they tried to encounter spirits worked. They'd tried waiting in place; nothing wandered near them. Among the treetops, they'd tried moving fast and quiet; they didn't sneak up on anything. They'd tried making noise to draw things to themselves; nothing came.

"I suppose it's a good thing that we ran out of spirits," Rosie said, kneeling atop one of the branches.

"How do you figure?" Cedric asked, using his right hand to keep a tight grip on the branch above his head.

"Because," Ragoon answered for her. "It means the citizens of Greenlike and the Trash Pandas have captured all the spirits. No spirits got left behind or forgotten. There won't be any soul eaters this year."

"Yup," Rosie nodded.

"That makes sense," Cedric said.

"All that's left," Rosie said, "is to clean up some of the leftover insect spirits."

They spent the next fifteen minutes cleaning up those insects. At the same time, they turned the process of the cleanup into a game. They'd jump from one branch to the next, seeing how many insects they could catch in one jump. Ragoon held the record with six. Cedric also had done six, but he miscounted on his jump, so he thought he only had done five.

It was Rosie's turn, so she sought a branch that was ten feet above another. She figured if she added some fall to her jump, it would give her more time to capture insects before she landed. Also, she chose two branches with a natural gathering of insect spirits between them. After her jump, she was sure she'd have the record. She only needed to get seven, but if she could do more, she would.

She stood on the edge of the branch, ready to jump, counting in her head. "One," She took a deep calming breath. "Two," she inhaled. "Three," she exhaled and jumped in the same motion, but as she fell, she didn't capture a single insect.

The reason she didn't is because something distracted her from below, a dark cloud. Even though it was dark, it still offered a weird glow...a mix of purple, and black, and yellow. Also, she realized it shared an iridescence with the spirits...and a transparent luminescence.

As she landed on the second branch, she allowed her eyes to focus on the thing. It was like nothing she'd ever seen. Short, pointed tendrils danced over the thing. They wiggled like worms trapped in the earth, unable to escape. It made the outline of the cloudy, dark, wormlike, transparently opalescent, glowing, purply thing difficult to determine.

Even so, it moved like a grasshopper, jumping in fast bursts from one position to the next. Before she could ask what it was, Ragoon answered. "It's a soul eater. That might be why we've had so much trouble finding spirits. If that thing's been eating them, who knows how strong it is now. We need to let Rumpke and Nick know. Don't let it see you."

"Too late," Cedric said, and the trio looked down at the thing.

From a stationary position, it stared back. Where it retained a shifting form, its outline did seem to keep a generic shape. Two knees poked up near the back, six legs total. And it had two large eyes on the side of a triangular head. The eyes were devoid of any color, empty voids of nothing.

It jumped toward them in a blurring flash, and they began to run.

*   *   *

Pete heard them before he saw them. He was sure the whole forest heard them with as loud as they were screaming. Then there was the loud crack of branches as they broke. As he looked toward the sound, he saw the Trash Panda group—Rosie, Cedric, and Ragoon—hopping through the treetops in Pete's direction. Behind the trio, it looked like an avalanche chasing them. A glowing purple object knocked over full trees and crunched over everything in its path. Where they couldn't make out of form of the thing chasing them, it did have a distinct, ethereal purple glow.

"What is that?" Pete wondered aloud.

"It's moving like an insect that jumps...like a grasshopper or something."

"That," Nick Warman stepped next to the pair—neither realized he was standing behind to them—and he continued to speak, "is a soul eater."

"Are we allowed to fight it?" Pete asked. "Or would that be violating the laws of the moderators?" Pete was going to fight it regardless of how Nick answered. The real question was, *Nick, will you help us fight it?*

"The whole point of Harvestfest is to put to rest the spirits of the departed. It is not a violation to vanquish a soul eater during Harvestfest." He explained.

The Trash Panda trio reached the clearing where Pete, Zoey, and Nick stood. At that point, the raccoons jumped from the treetops. When they landed, they looked like synchronized free runners, distributing their weight and rolling to not take fall damage. From there, they returned to their feet at a full sprint, not losing any forward momentum. They disappeared in the tree line on the other side of the clearing.

Three heartbeats later, the soul eater broke

through the tree line behind them. It was larger than Pete had realized, taller than he was...and wider than it was tall. Tendrils wriggled around its body as if worms covered it. Between those tendrils and the glow, the proper form of the thing remained challenging to determine. Even the grasshopper outline came and went.

Zoey acted before Pete, casting Light of the Living and Strong Light of the Living on the thing. This made the thing turn toward her. After, she used Draw Hate and Strong Draw Hate to increase the enmity the monster had toward her. "Pete, I will hold hate as long as I can. Try to figure out a strategy to damage this thing."

"Right," Pete ran at a looped angle behind the monster. He hoped to proc critical damage for attacking it from behind. As he closed the distance between himself and the soul eater, he cast Fire and Strong Fire, rotating back and forth between them as fast as possible.

Zoey rotated between casting her Light of the Living spells as the thing continued toward her.

Once Pete attacked, his battle interface activated. It caused a battle log to appear on the left side of his periphery. His HP and MP bar appeared near the bottom of his vision. Zoey's HP was next to his. The soul eater's health bar appeared at the top of his vision.

The Fire and Light of the Living spells proved especially effective against the soul eater. The waves created by the enchantments caught the individual tendrils. It caused those tendrils to light like angry, wiggling matches. As those lit tendrils writhed back and forth, they'd caught adjacent tendrils ablaze. Spell after spell landed. More and more of the soul eater caught fire, and the monster's red HP bar began to drop at a rapid pace. It went from full, to three-quarters, to half, to a quarter. Then Pete ran out of MP.

Pete hadn't realized his spell would prove so effective. With all the damage he caused, he worried about taking hate from Zoey. It was an unwarranted preoccupation. Zoey—like the quality tank she'd always been in the MMOs they played together—held the monster's attention.

Still ablaze, it swung at her with six angry legs, rotating at random. On occasion, it would use a full-force attack, jumping into her with all its weight. She deflected and parried as best she could. But one of the full-force jump attacks caught her shield square. It knocked her off her feet, sending her fifteen feet into the air.

She landed with a thud and a groan. If vampires needed to breathe, Pete knew the landing would have knocked the wind from her. Along with her landing, her HP dipped by twenty percent. As soon as it went down, he noticed it begin to regenerate. *It must be a passive ability from her skill tree,* he realized.

The soul eater sped toward where a defenseless Zoey lied on the ground; the fire on its tendrils had begun to extinguish. Though—with the damage it had taken—the tendrils had become less active, and the glow had begun to diminish. As such, Pete could finally make out the figure of the thing. Sure enough, it was an enormous grasshopper. *If a soul eater from a grasshopper is like this, I'd hate to see what one from a dragon is like*, Pete thought to himself as he charged. He reached it before it reached Zoey, and he attempted to slap it.

His slap went through the creature like it had with the Turkey Titan spirit. Physical attacks weren't going to hurt it. To make things worse, his MP wasn't regenerating fast enough for him to cast more fire spells.

The monster jumped high in the air—positioning itself over where Zoey remained on the ground—and the beast stomped downward.

She rolled out of the way, using her shoulder midway through the roll to leverage herself onto her feet. Then she turned and cast Strong Light of the Living into the side of the monster's enormous head.

The soul eater's HP dipped, but a sliver remained.

"Cast it again," Pete told her.

"I can't," she told him. "I'm out of MP."

It turned and growled at Zoey, preparing to hit her with another ramming leap.

At that point, Nick threw a soul-catching orb into the soul eater. In its weakened state, the soul eater couldn't resist the effects of the orbs and sucked into it.

"You couldn't have helped sooner?" Pete asked.

"I don't have any magic...no abilities to harm soul eaters." He explained. "I wouldn't have been able to do anything to it. Though, you two handled it great, son. Great work."

The worst part of fighting the soul eater and the Turkey Titan was how the monsters had not given experience points. The lack of XP caused Pete to sigh.

"Here, son," Nick held the orb out to Pete. "You can have the soul eater."

Pete reached out his hand. "You are the one that captured the soul. Is it even allowed for us to keep it?"

"If I want to give you the soul," Nick explained. "I'm allowed to give it to you."

"Don't you want to win the contest?" Zoey asked.

"I have no chance at winning the contest," Nick explained.

"What do you mean you have no chance?" Zoey raised an eyebrow. "You've had that much trouble catching spirits?"

"I haven't caught a single one," Nick explained. "Wherever I go, Roger follows, catching the spirits before I can. The mayor even gave up and went back to the Trash Panda hideout. Since it's the last day of festivities, she wanted to try some of the games they've set up.

"Only when she gave up did Roger stop following us, so it's like I said. I haven't caught a single soul and have no chance of winning the contest. If you and Zoey take this soul eater soul, it does give you a better chance of winning. That means Roger has a better chance of losing. I want you to take the soul because I want Roger to lose."

"Okay," Pete agreed with a deep inhalation. "I understand. For what it's worth, I hope Roger loses too."

"I have one other question," Zoey said.

"What's that?" Pete and Nick asked in unison.

"Was that soul eater chasing Ragoon, Cedric, and Rosie?" Zoey looked in the direction to where the trio of raccoons had fled. "Should we try to catch them and tell them they can stop running?"

"No," Nick said. "They'll figure it out."

10: The Winner Is

Toward the end of the third night of Harvestfest—hours before daybreak—the citizens of Greenlake and the Trash Pandas gathered near the Trash Panda hideout. Not a single soul remained in the forest nor in the town. Outside the lair, everyone played games, enjoying the Harvestfest festivities.

Of these games, the most popular proved to be ring toss. Townspeople and Trash Pandas lined up to compete against each other in friendly matches. To play, they'd line up with rings of plastic. Event organizers had set cones shaped like witch hats ten paces away, twenty paces away, thirty, forty, and fifty paces away. The objective of the game was simple enough. They'd toss the ring and try to land it on one of the hats. The further away the hat, the more points they'd earn.

The mayor and Rosie were in the middle of a friendly ring toss match. As Rosie tossed, she spoke. "And the soul eater chased us. I don't know for how long. After about fifteen minutes, we looked back, and it was gone."

"When Nick shows up," The mayor took her turn to toss. "I'll have to send him to investigate. We can't leave any soul eaters in the forest. It wouldn't be safe for anyone."

A grumble sounded behind the pair, and they turned to see Nick.

"Oh, Nick, I'm glad to see you here." The mayor told him. "Are you growling about the soul eater? There is no need to get huffy about it. If you don't want to go by yourself, I'm sure Rumpke will send some of the Trash Pandas with you. Together, the soul eater shouldn't be a problem.

Nick grumbled, causing his mustache to vibrate like an angry caterpillar.

Next to Nick, Rosie, and the mayor, the triplets played their own game of ring toss. "Tornado," Tornado said, throwing a ring. While the ring was midflight, Tornado used magic to manipulate wind currents. It caused the ring to land on the furthest away hat every throw.

"That's cheating," Skye said, keeping an even voice. He was making an observation more than complaining.

"We can play again after," Hope suggested. "This round, we *can* cheat. Next match, we will play without cheating. It will be fair for us to do one of each."

"That does sound fair." Skye agreed.

"Tornado," Tornado added.

In one part of the field, Roger played pin the snake on the chimera with the rest of the Escaron family. They didn't let anyone else play with them; they said it was a family contest...no outsiders allowed. Some talked about what they'd do with Roger's soul-catching prize. They were sure he'd win again. Afterall, he won every year.

A wide—but short—round barrel rested on the ground, filled with water. Atop the water's surface, apples bobbed up and down. They drifted around each other...sometimes bumping into one another. Pete watched them and said, "it reminds me of when I went to a dance in elementary school."

"Apples remind you of an elementary school dance?" Zoey smiled. "How do apples remind you of a dance?"

"The apples are like the students," Pete explained. "The apples are awkward students trying to dance and interact...and be cool."

"Apples are students?" Zoey repeated.

"Yup," Pete nodded.

"You're weird." Zoey took his arm in hers. "But it's a good weird."

"Thanks," Pete smiled.

Rumpke's amplified voice began to speak, and everyone stopped playing their games to listen. It took Pete a second to identify the spot from where Rumpke spoke. It was at the entrance to the Trash Panda's cave. "Along with Nick, the Trash Pandas have swept the forest and town. We've done three passes over every inch of territory. After this, we are happy to re-port that not a single spirit has escaped capture. So far as I know, this is the first time that has happened in the history of Greenlake.

"I'm proud of everyone. You did a great job. I want you all to feel proud. Some of these spirits have been waiting for years for us to help them find final rest. As such, if you win...or if you lose...know that you helped these souls find peace.

"With that, it is time to announce the winner of the soul-capturing contest. Everyone who has captured souls, please bring them to the shrine." Rumpke point-ed at the makeshift shrine—the one with metal poles that looked like someone wrapped them in tinfoil—in the center of the field. As Rumpke pointed, the tinfoil of the shrine began to reshape itself, creating a basket. "Once everyone has placed their orbs into the basket, the shrine will determine a winner. After, it will assign prizes."

"Well," Zoey said, "let's go see how we did."

All the teams made their way toward the shrine. The first teams to the shrine began to form a line. They took turns submitting their orbs to the basket and then stepping away.

Pete was never one to race to a line. For the sake of the contest, if he got there first, he'd still end up waiting for the people behind him. Zoey knew Pete was like this. She was too. As such, they began walking—but not hurrying—toward the line.

As teams added orbs to the basket, the orbs began to stack. When the stack reached the brim of the basket, the basket expanded. So many teams had caught so many spirits that the basket grew over and over. When Pete and Zoey put their orbs in, the basket had extended to be taller and wider than they were.

Pete materialized his orbs one at a time; he had to reach up to drop them in. Zoey did the same, only she'd materialize two orbs at a time, one in each hand. When they finished, they moved out of the way.

After Pete and Zoey finished, two more teams added orbs to the basket, and Rumpke began to speak. "Has everyone added their orbs to the shrine?"

"No," Roger spoke from where his family continued to play pin the snake on the chimera. "I haven't added mine yet." With that phrase, Roger made a show of strutting by everyone as he moved toward the shrine. He winked at Zoey as he passed her.

"Yuck," she glared.

"Yuck," Pete agreed. No doubt, Roger was yuck.

When Roger reached the basket, he took his time: removing each orb from his inventory one at a time, explaining where he caught the soul held within the orb, and dropping it into the basket. Then he'd count. "This is the first orb...that's twenty spirits...I've put thirty-two spirits in, now."

When he reached orb number fifty, everyone stopped paying attention to him. When he realized he no longer had an audience, he stopped making a show and hurried to finish. Then he returned to his family.

"Okay," Rumpke spoke again. "Now, has everyone placed their orbs in the basket?" He waited, and when no one answered, he went on. "Great, we will now activate the shrine."

When he finished saying this, Trash Pandas

wearing little white robes stepped up to the basket with orbs and shouted at the basket. "Hey, we're done now."

In response to their voices, the metal poles and tinfoil basket began to buzz. The bars shook the ground, causing loose earth to bounce like jumping beans. The metal started to light up, flashing in a rainbow pattern. Then all at once, the orbs within the basket disappeared, releasing every spirit into the air.

Every soul the town had caught over the last three days danced above the field. They flowed with a reverent grace like the current of a river. When a departed neared a loved one, they smiled a goodbye. Only seconds went by—no longer than a minute—but to the people below and the spirits above, it seemed longer.

Even the Turkey Titan's spirit had humble respect for the townspeople. It smiled at Pete as it floated by him.

Then the spirits began to flow in a circular pattern toward the shrine. When they reached the metal, they absorbed into it, using its posts to move into the earth.

One by one, every soul found peace in the afterlife. One by one, every living person found peace in knowing they'd done a good thing.

After the last soul disappeared, the metal returned to its natural grey, and a voice began to speak. "I am a reaper. For this year's Harvestfest, my kin have assigned me this shrine. In the history of Greenlake, no group of citizens has ever brought peace to that many souls during one Harvestfest. Do not forget them; they will not forget you. Someday you will meet again, and they will thank you for your efforts on their behalf.

"Due to the extreme nature of your success, the prizes this year will be of an extreme nature. They are prizes greater than any granted before. We will begin by granting the Third-place prize. Ragoon, Rosie, and Cedric, this is your team. Please, accept these gifts with the same gratitude with which I give them."

Pete wondered what prizes they received. He'd ask them later.

The reaper of the shrine continued to speak. "Second place is Pete and Zoey. Please accept these gifts with the gratitude in which I give them."

A prompt appeared for Pete:

You received ghost-slapping glove inserts. Wear these inserts under any pair of gloves. They will grant the gloves the ability to damage incorporeal beings with physical attacks.

"What did you get?" Zoey asked.

"Ghost-slapping glove inserts," Pete answered. "What did you get?"

"I got a ghost-stabbing pizza fork wrap," Zoey answered. "When I put it on my pizza fork, I can hurt ghosts by attacking them with my fork."

"Cool," Pete said.

"Not as cool as my first-place prize will be," Roger forced himself between them. "I'll make sure to tell you what it is.

"And in first place," the voice continued. "We have the triplets. You saved more spirits than anyone else. Large and small, you saved them all."

A stunned silence came over the crowd as people realized the triplets had won the contest.

"For your prize," the voice explained. "I will grant you something I've never given before..." the voice paused as the crowd waited to hear the prize. "Each of you—Skye, Hope, and Tornado—will receive an adventurer's pass. Please, accept this gift with the gratitude with which we give it."

An excited trio of triplets began to celebrate as

the whole town began to cheer for them. Almost the entire town cheered for them, anyway.

The Escarons did not.

Next to Pete and Zoey, Roger's mouth hung open in shock.

11: Kidnapped

Back in their room at M&P's Pizzeria, Pete had changed into his pajamas—made by Tay at Timmy the Taylor's smithing and clothing shop—and sat on his bed. He rolled the glove inserts over in his hands. He wasn't sure why they called them inserts. They looked like thin gloves made of cotton. It reminded him of the stretchy, one-size-fits-all gloves his mom used to buy him and his siblings when they were kids. He shifted his eyes from the insert to Zoey. "How do these work?"

A top of her own bed, she answered. "According to the mayor, they'll attach to the first item you use them on. For example, if you put them under a normal pair of gloves, they'll become part of that normal pair of gloves. Those normal gloves will become able to damage ghosts."

"I will save them for later." He said. "I'd love ghost-slapping gloves, now. But what if I get better gloves later? Then I'll have given the ability to slap ghosts to weaker gloves; that doesn't make any sense.

"I'm saving my wrap for later." She agreed. "They could have legendary loot...or epic loot...or what-ever they might call it in this world loot. I want to use it on an epic loot item."

"I hope they have items like that." He told her. "I'd love to have legendary-epic whatever they might call it ghost slapping gloves."

"Yeah, I'd love all that, too." She said. "But in a fork...not for gloves."

"How do you think you blocked the soul eater and Turkey Titan attacks?" He asked. "Why didn't they go through your shield?"

"My guess is that they have to materialize to hit me, and they do that a microsecond before the attack lands. When they are material, it lets me block it?"

"Ah," he nodded. "That would make sense."

"I know we didn't get experience for fighting those things," Pete said. "But between slapping myself to sleep and fighting those things, I have gotten some skill-ups." He pulled up his character sheet:

NAME: Pete   **RACE:** Human   **JOB:** Pizzaman

LEVEL 12

HP: 276/276

MP: 21/21

STR: 37

DEX: 27

VIT: 29

INT: 21

SPR: 16

AGI: 26

ALIGNMENT: Lawful Good

RELIGION: Christian

LANGUAGES: English, Spanish, Common

GENDER: Male

HEIGHT: 5'8

WEIGHT: 145 lbs

AGE: 20

EYES: Blue

Hair: Blond

LEFT ARM: Unequipped

RIGHT ARM: Unequipped

HEAD: M&P Combat Hat

BODY: M&P Battle Top

LEGS: M&P Battle Pants

FEET: Combat Boots

HANDS: Fingerless Titan Gloves

NECKLACE: Unequipped

EARRINGS: Unequipped

Ring 1: Silver Claddagh

Ring 2: Unequipped

ATTACK: 788

DEFENSE: 569

MAGIC ATTACK: 10

MAGIC DEFENSE: 48

PROFICIENCIES: Slapping Skill 401.6, Slapping Defense 112, Tree Climbing -12.4, Running 27, Tackling 1, Slashing defense 19. Light Armor 49.2, Pizza Cutter 23.3, Pizza Peel 7.2, Jumping 7.9, Evasion 21.2

Experience: 1650/1800

"Have you gotten any concussions, too?" Zoey asked him. "Do you remember what that concussion icon looks like yet? Is it a face with its eyes crossed out and birds spinning around it? Does it have stars instead of birds?"

He ignored her question, sad to see his negative tree climbing skill. Even so, he was excited to see his slapping skill and slapping defense had gone so high. "If I'm correct about how leveling works in this game when I gain my next level, I'm going to get some serious stat increases."

"When your intelligence goes up, will you stop slapping yourself?" She paused, letting a smirk spread across her face. "Or will your intelligence go down because you *keep* slapping yourself?"

Instead of responding to her comment about slapping himself, he changed the subject. "It's crazy how the triplets won the soul-capturing contest." No one expected that outcome. Pete didn't. If it wasn't Zoey and him that won, he was glad it was the triplets.

"For sure," she agreed. "I'm glad it was them."

"It's even better how Roger didn't finish in the top three," Pete said. "Did you see his face when he saw he'd lost? It was priceless."

"It is because he spent too much time following around Nick and the mayor. If he had focused on himself—instead of tormenting others—things would have worked out better for him."

"How have the skills on your character sheet advanced? Did they go up any with the contest?" Pete asked her.

"Mmmm… I'm not sure. I wasn't paying attention." She admitted, pulling up her own character sheet to check:

Josh Walker

NAME: Zoey **RACE:** Vampire **JOB:** Paladin
(Subjob) Pizzawoman
LEVEL 11

HP: 310/310
MP: 46/46

ALIGNMENT: Chaotic Good
RELIGION: None
LANGUAGES: English,
Japanese
Common

STR: 42
DEX: 37
VIT: 43
INT: 46
SPR: 32
AGI: 67

GENDER: Female
HEIGHT: 5'5
WEIGHT: 110 lbs
AGE: 19
EYES: Black
Hair: Green

LEFT ARM: Combat Pizza Peel
RIGHT ARM: Combat Pizza Fork
HEAD: M&P Combat Hat
BODY: M&P Battle Top
LEGS: M&P Battle Skirt
FEET: Combat Boots
HANDS: Unequipped
NECKLACE: Gold Pendant
EARRINGS: Obsidian Earrings
Ring 1: Silver Claddagh
Ring 2: Ring of Day Walking

ATTACK: 3740
DEFENSE: 1145
MAGIC ATTACK: 23
MAGIC DEFENSE: 600

PROFICIENCIES: Slapping Skill 11.2, Air Hockey 121.9, Tree Climbing 12.2, Pizza Cutter 12.4, Pizza Peel 325.5, Evasion 74.1, Pizza Fork 100.9, Light Armor 221.2

Experience: 739/1600

"When you slapped my peel the other day, my peel skill went way up. When we fought the Turkey Titan, I noticed a difference. It was super easy to maneuver the shield. It felt more natural."

"When you level up," he said. "I'm guessing your vitality will see a significant boost."

"That'd be great." She stretched her arms over her head. As she rested her hands atop her battle skirt, she added. "These clothes are uncomfortable. I think we need pajamas."

"But you don't sleep." Pete said.

"No," she shrugged. "But I relax...and I can't imagine it is comfortable for you to sleep in your torn old delivery uniform from Earth. It would be nice if we each had a pair of pajamas."

"Yup, it would." He agreed. Then before she could say anything else, he activated Slap'm Silly and slapped himself to sleep. He fell into his bed with perfect precision. His head landed on the pillow. His blanket floated down on him like a happy parachute.

*   *   *

Pete awoke around noon, sat up in bed, and stretched. He looked toward Zoey's bed. When he saw she wasn't there, he remembered their plans to farm tomatoes that afternoon. Because she didn't have to sleep, he guessed she went early. If so, she was waiting for him. He wished he didn't need to sleep. If he didn't need to sleep, he'd be able to play so many video games...if he were still on Earth.

Harvestfest required Pete to wander through a forest for three days. As a result, his joints ached; his muscles felt sore. To recuperate, he wanted to take an extra day and sleep. Even so, he understood how M&P's Pizzeria had already gone three days without its delivery drivers...Zoey and himself. It was essential to get back into a routine at work. To get back into the routine, he knew he had to work that day. To work that day, he needed to hurry.

After stretching, he stood and walked toward his chest of drawers. Though, he didn't walk like an average person. Rather, he took long, exaggerated steps, stretching his legs as he walked. At the same time, he stretched an arm back over his shoulder. Then he did the same to the other arm. If Zoey had seen what he looked like doing the morning stretch walk, she would have teased him for it.

When he reached the chest of drawers, he opened the top drawer. Even though he didn't have to use the drawers, he liked to. It reminded him of being back home on Earth. He reached into the drawer, pulling out his delivery uniform. He also removed a swimsuit before shutting the drawer. Then he hurried to the closet. From there, he removed a towel. Then he pushed his way out from his room, out from the pizzeria, and toward the lake's shoreline. There he would bathe to clean the muck and dirt which he'd accumulated during three days of soul-catching.

Once he'd left the restaurant and saw the lake in the midday sun, it amazed him. In truth, the lake never ceased to amaze him. It didn't matter if he saw it at night or during the middle of the day. The size...the shifting currents...the way the deep blue water contrasted with the surrounding jade vegetation...it wasn't something to which he'd ever grow accustomed. The beauty of it would always amaze him.

He walked toward the lake, moving along the sidewalk, passing a pair of dwarves along the way. At that point in the day, Greenlake was full of movement. Aside from the dwarves, there were some gnomes, many humans, and elves. The elves were like those from fantasy stories and video games, not like those from Santa's workshop. Pixies moved through the air.

As Pete passed the dwarves, he heard one of them say. "And then the triplets became adventurers."

Pete wasn't sure what it meant when the triplets earned their adventurer passes. He knew their parents would never let them go into a dungeon, not at their age. As such, he suspected the adventurer passes would go unused until the triplets became adults. Even so, he was happy that they'd earned the passes. It would make their adult life easier because they'd be able to earn more money for themselves and for their families. It was like having a master's degree back on earth...or a doctorate. *If I ever get back to Earth,* Pete told himself, *I should focus more on college.*

As he reached the Lake, he turned east and began to walk parallel to the shore. In time, he'd reach the outskirts of town, and he'd have some privacy to change into his swimming suit and bathe.

During his walk, he passed by tall, gnarled trees. They had thick trunks and wide branches which sprouted out like elephant trunks. For the most part, the ground was soft, made from clay, slate, and volcanic sand. He could see a volcano further east. Its white snowcap stood out in a range of green mountains.

When he emerged on the other side of the gnarled trees, the ground became soft black sand, nothing else. Opposite the lake, a green field of tall grass wafted in a calm breeze. That was his bathing spot.

He laid out his towel on the sand, placing his clean clothes on top. Then he changed into his swimsuit—leaving his dirty clothes next to his towel on the sand—and moved to the lake.

It was clichéd, but Pete stuck his toe in to gauge the temperature of it...colder than the last time he'd bathed. *That makes sense,* he realized, *we are moving into Autumn.* During the winter, he guessed he'd have to find a new way to bathe. The lake would be too cold.

For the time being, though, it was a tolerable temperature. In fact, Pete preferred it cold. He took a few steps back, got a running start, and jumped into the lake. With his increased attributes, his jump carried him fifteen feet high and twenty feet out. He landed in the water with a mighty splash. When he resurfaced, he noticed a prompt had appeared. It was about an increase to his jumping proficiency. He blinked the prompt away and began to swim. He hadn't been swimming for long when he felt a pull on his leg. The pull came with enough force to drag his head below the water. Despite his efforts, he couldn't free himself from whatever grasped him. He couldn't get back to the surface. Instead, he continued to go deeper and deeper beneath the surface. Also, he realized whatever had him was pulling him further toward the lake's center.

As a child, he loved learning about sharks. One thing he remembered was how when sharks attack, their victims say the attack didn't feel painful. They say it felt like a pull. Was a shark attacking him? He worried that was the case.

In a panic, he tried to kick at whatever held him, but it avoided him easy enough. *Panicked attempts to defend yourself won't work,* he told himself. *You must calm down, observe the situation, and devise a plan.*

Calm down is what he did. In that calm, he looked at his leg, trying to find what held him. It was a mermaid...the same mermaid he'd encountered during one of his other trips to the lake. When she noticed him looking at her, she smiled, releasing his ankle with her right hand. She continued to grip it in her left hand, and she waved with her free hand.

12: A Cat and His Vampire

White is a unique color because it can symbolize a lot of things. It represents new opportunities, beginnings, clean slates, innocence, and purity. People trust the color white; it puts their minds at ease. When someone wears white, others think the person in white is on their side.

That's why Vitalia used her white dresses. They gave off an innocence...a helplessness...a beneficial façade that she could use to her advantage. Her current dress was of a style reminiscent of medieval Europe with long hanging sleeves and a fitted hug at the hips and waist.

In her right hand, she held a table hockey paddle. Her left hand rested on the corner of the hockey table. She'd tied her blond hair back into a ponytail. Across from her stood Max the cat, wearing his pink tank top. "I prefer your tuxedos." She told him, hitting the puck toward him.

After he hit it back, he answered. "We're in a Pizza and Games. Tuxedos don't make sense in places like this."

The puck continued to go back and forth as they blocked each other's shots. "And why are we still hanging out in Pete's dreamscape?" She asked.

"I went through a lot of effort to create this." His voice sounded hurt. "It would be a shame to only use it once."

She rolled her eyes. "You could have asked him to help, you know? You didn't have to knock him out of the tree, send him through this dreamscape, and then teleport him to Round."

"There's not enough theater in that." He said. "Plus, he might have said no. We couldn't have that."

"And you think threatening him with permanent death as an ultimatum for not helping is a good way to earn trust? Later—when he needs your help—how will he trust you?" She saw an opening in Max's table hockey defenses and ricocheted a shot off the side wall.

He yawned as he deflected the puck back in her direction. "I shouldn't be helping them. If things get better, I won't have to. That's why we chose Pete. Remember? He's the player that breaks the game. Plus—if the moderators catch me in Round—they'll patch the world to block me out. In that case, Pete and Zoey'll be on their own."

Vitalia and Max had been working together for a long time. During that time, higher powers had blocked them from entering certain worlds. People in those worlds found themselves the subjects of demon lords or the slaves of warmongers. They didn't get happy endings. But worrying about what might happen wouldn't help anyone. She needed to focus on the current situation. "There's a dungeon in Greenlake. It's a matter of time before Pete and Zoey end up in that dungeon. The mobs they face will be above their level. Without help, they'll die."

Max considered Vitalia's words. They cause him to hesitate. And his vacillation almost allowed Vitalia to score a table hockey goal. He deflected it last second. Where many people saw Vitalia as Max's subordinate, she was his equal...his partner. When she expressed a worry, her worry had merit. This case was no different. If he didn't help Pete and Zoey face the dungeon, Pete and Zoey would die. But that was a problem for another day. "Without adventurer's passes, they won't be able to enter the dungeon." He said, "so we don't need to worry about that for now."

"Zoey is a vampire." Vitalia shot back. "Undead don't require passes."

His eyes widened. For a cat who prided himself on seeing the big picture, how could he have missed something so simple? "You're right. That could be problematic."

"If you were wearing a tuxedo," She joked. "You wouldn't have missed this."

Max ignored the teasing. "We should put a contingency in place, something to help Zoey should she end up in a dungeon."

"I sent a group of adventurers to the dungeon," Vitalia explained. "Told them to help Zoey should they come across her."

"I noticed." Max grimaced. "I trust Introvice. Did you have to send Fred, though? He's as likely to kill them as he is to help them."

"They're a team." She shrugged. "Where Introvice goes, Fred goes. Introvice will keep him in line."

"Or Fred will keep Introvice out of line," Max mumbled. "Also, did you have to keep Flowerbeard with them? His name's a lie. I've never once seen flowers in that pirate's beard. I'm not even sure he's a pirate. He might be a dude with a beard cosplaying a pirate."

"He's a pirate," Vitalia replied. "I saw his ship once. Remember? It was that schooner with the two masts."

"The same schooner he was using to scam the prince in First Sea?" Max lifted his fuzzy eyebrow. "The prince who won the nicest prince in Round contest?"

"He's a pirate...I think..." She answered. "He has to do his job to level up."

Max saw an opening in Vitalia's defense; he shot straight at it. "Well, if Pete and Zoey die, we'll have to find someone else to save Round from the Moderators. It's more important the Moderators don't recognize our influence. Their survival is secondary."

"Agreed," she deflected the puck. "Are you sure Zoey beat you in this air hockey? You didn't let her win."

"She needed to go to Round with confidence." Max winked.

"Are you sure Earth was the best choice for a hero? There are people on other planets who are stronger

and faster than Earthlings."

"The saviors of Round need to be from Earth." He assured.

"Why?" She raised an eyebrow. "Do you know something you aren't telling me?"

"Because," he answered. "There *is* something I haven't told you yet…"

At that point, the puck snuck into Max's goal with a frustrating metal ting.

Vitalia knew that Max had let her score. The pause in the game allowed him to change the direction of the conversation. And she'd let him change it. In reality, she didn't need to press for more information. She had deduced why the saviors had to come from Earth. "In the end, the dungeon will work to our benefit. Did you have anything to do with it appearing in Greenlake?"

"No," He removed the puck. "Though…magic had begun to accumulate in Greenlake. It had to be a dungeon manifesting. That's what made it a good starting point for Pete and Zoey."

"Magic accumulation can mean other things." She answered. "It could signify the Moderators were about to destroy the town."

"Well," Max put the puck back on the table and shot toward Vitalia's goal. "It's like I said. We can find new saviors."

Vitalia blocked the shot. "We're still going to pay Introvice a visit, right? Let him know how Zoey might be showing up in the dungeon sooner rather than later?"

"We are," Max confirmed, taking another shot. This shot found its mark, slamming into Vitalia's goal with a satisfying metal ting.

Josh Walker

13: Meeting a Non-Girlfriend's Dad

Fish feel comfortable underwater; of course, they do. It's where they live. But they wouldn't be comfortable on land. They can't live on land…not unless they are magic, land-living fish. Likewise, Pete was a human—not a water-living human—and he wasn't sure how long he could hold his breath. He began to panic.

Though, the mermaid appeared friendly enough. If he could communicate that he couldn't breathe, he hoped she would let him return to the surface. So as she waved hello, he put his hands around his neck, making the universal sign for choking. He wasn't choking…not by definition…but choking and drowning end with the same oxygen-deprived death. It was a death he didn't want to experience.

While he looked at her, using his eyes to beg her not to kill him, he examined her. Her bottom half had the shape of a dolphin. Green fish scales covered it. As she maneuvered her tail back and forth, some of the scales reflected light. If the light hit at different angles, the color the scale reflected would change. This led to a rainbow effect within the green.

Over her tail, she wore a teal skirt. Over where her right hip would be, she had a pocket. On the left, there was a logo made from palm trees. Teal highlights dyed her blonde hair.

The upper half of her body was human in all aspects. She wore a formfitting, black shirt… He wasn't sure if to call it a shirt. It was more like a swimsuit top. Even while drowning, Pete's curious mind never stopped. He wondered what fabric formed the shirt. It wasn't spandex. In some ways, it resembled a wetsuit. Though—at times—it seemed to ripple like a t-shirt. The shirt had a blue chibi turtle at its center. The turtle smiled while holding one of its fins with a thumbs up. Pete wasn't sure how it was giving a thumbs up because turtles don't have thumbs, but somehow the chibi image managed.

As the mermaid smiled and waved, Pete noticed sparkling white teeth. Her lapis eyes had a unique cuteness to them...like the eyes of a family pet begging for treats...or like the adorable eyes on some stuffed animals. They had a surrealism. The mermaid's skin was fair. Mermaids didn't get as much sunlight underwater, so this made sense to Pete.

While Pete observed the smiling mermaid, he continued to make the sign that he was choking.

"Oh, right!" Though it had taken her a few seconds, the mermaid seemed to understand. "I forgot." Still holding his ankle in her left hand, she reached into the pocket of her skirt with her right hand and removed a small black box, handing it to him.

He reached out and took it. A prompt appeared:

You received a necklace of water breathing. While equipped, you will be able to breathe underwater.

Pete used his character page to equip the necklace. It caused the chain with a bright white shell to appear around his neck. However, he continued to hold his breath. It wasn't natural for humans to breathe water; it went against all Pete's instincts. Though, he'd already been holding his breath for near a minute. He wasn't sure he could do it much longer.

"Breathe," she giggled, letting go of his ankle. "You'll be fine. I promise."

With her no longer holding his ankle, he considered swimming to the surface and escaping. Then he realized a swimming race with a mermaid was an exercise in futility. He'd never win. While considering this, he could hold his breath no longer, and he exhaled.

Giant bubbles escaped his mouth as the air left his lungs. Then by reflex, he inhaled...and...it worked.

The water flowed into his lungs like air. Somehow, he absorbed the oxygen from it. He exhaled and inhaled a few more times, his body craving the oxygen he acquired from each breath. Once his respirations returned to normal, he turned to the girl. "Thanks for the necklace."

"You're welcome," she let the smile fade from her face, allowing her forehead to wrinkle. "It is working, right? I wasn't sure it was going to work."

"Wait..." Pete allowed a look of concern to form on his own face. "You dragged me underwater, not knowing if I'd be able to breathe?"

"Yup," she stated with a matter-of-fact tone. "Don't worry, though. If it didn't work, I would have dragged you back to the surface. It's not like I would have let you die or anything. I'm not a monster."

"I see..." He considered her words. "Why did you drag me down here in the first place?"

"The thing is," She backed away from him. "I need your help. Rather, we need your help. The mermaids...that is...need your help."

"Help with what?" Pete asked.

"It's a long story." She began. "Charybdis is a nearby dungeon boss. He keeps sending creatures from his dungeon to attack our town."

"That wasn't a long story," Pete began to repeat her sentence in his head, counting each word. After counting, he said. "It was only eighteen words long. That's not long. A long story is something like <u>The History of a Young Lady Volume I</u> by Samuel Richardson."

"What's that?" The mermaid blinked twice with confusion.

"I...actually don't know," Pete confessed. "But one of my elementary school teachers told me it is the longest book. It's almost one million words long. That is way more than eighteen."

"That book has a long title, too." The mermaid

observed. "Samuel Richardson seems like a complicated man."

"He does. Doesn't he?" Pete chuckled. Then he
realized that as the conversation had continued, he'd
begun to sink. He could see the tops of kelp plants below him. For a few seconds, he tried to swim like the
mermaid, maintaining a position at a fixed point in the
water. At that point, two things happened. One, Pete
realized he needed to work on his swimming skill. Two,
Pete gained a new respect for synchronized swimmers.

The mermaid noticed Pete's struggles, and she
held his hands. From there, all he had to do was move
his legs back and forth with little kicks, and he'd maintain his position. "Thanks," he said.

"You're welcome." She answered. "By the way,
my name is Aqua."

"My name is Pete," he told her. "Pete the pizzaman."

"What's a pizzaman?" She asked.

"Someone that makes pizza," He said.

"What's pizza?"

"You know..." He paused for dramatic effect. "I
don't think I'll ever get used to answering that question."

"What's pizza?" She repeated.

"Pizza is," he told her, "flatbread coated in a
sauce made from crushed tomatoes. You take the flatbread and cover that with grated cheese. Then you
bake the bread, melting the cheese in the process. You
can also put meat, vegetables, or other ingredients on
the pizza."

"Like fish?" She offered an enthusiastic grin.

"I suppose." He said.

"And shrimp?"

"I dunno about..."

"And clams and seaweed?" Her eyes widened,
causing them to gleam with a child's innocence. "And

rock moss?"

"I guess…" Pete answered, deciding he'd rather change the topic than think about a slimy rock moss pizza. "So why do you think a pizzaman can help you protect your town from dungeon monsters?"

Her enthusiastic expression became pensive as she wrinkled her brow, pursing her lips to the side. She pursed them to the left, "mmmm…" Then she pursed them to the right. "mmmm…" Then she sucked them in, causing her mouth to appear like a lipless slit. "mmm…" Then she answered. "Because I saw you slap that other girl's shield. You slap harder than a rock golem playing slapjack. You must be strong."

"They have slapjack on Round?" Pete mused, "interesting."

"Of course, we have slapjack on Round." Aqua sighed. "Why wouldn't we have slapjack? What do you mean 'on Round?' You are kind of weird."

"Did you know that the etymology of the word 'weird' teaches us that 'weird' used to mean someone that had the power to change their fate?" Pete asked. "In that case, I'm weird for days."

"Ety-what?" She cocked her head to the side, confused.

"Etymology," he repeated. "It means the study of word origins…or something like that. And entomology means the study of bugs. So the etymology of entomology means the study of the origin of the word that means the study of bugs."

"Yeah…" She hung her shoulders. "you are weird."

"That's a little hurtful." He said.

"So was your explanation about bug word history."

"That's fair." He agreed. "I do slap hard, but I'm afraid I can't help you with dungeon monsters. I don't have an adventurer's pass. Unless I can use those monsters as pizza toppings, I'd be violating a law of the moderators by fighting them."

"About that," she explained. "We had a dungeon appear at the bottom of the lake about three months back. Along with the dungeon, our king received a notification that the town gets a single dungeon pass. We will use it to send someone into the dungeon to face Charybdis. Though, the king wants to make sure they are strong enough to defeat Charybdis before he sends them in."

"That makes sense," he said. "If he sends someone in, and they die, it's a waste of the pass. After, they wouldn't be able to send someone else. They need to make sure."

"You are going to be that person." She squeezed his hands and spoke with confidence. "You will be the hero that saves Greenlake."

"Last time," Pete said. "A talking cat asked me to save the whole of Round. Greenlake is less than that...baby steps, you know."

"Steps? I'm a mermaid. We don't take steps. Our babies don't take steps. I don't understand what you are talking about."

Pete nodded his understanding. Of course, mermaids didn't take steps. He needed to pick a better metaphor. "What I mean to say is that I can help you." A prompt popped up:

You've accepted the quest Saving the Merfolk. You've always been great at looking out for others, but the most challenging part of this quest will be looking out for yourself. Good luck with not dying!

"Good," She puffed out her chest, a hint of proudness to her movement. "Let's go meet my dad then." With that, she released one of his hands, spun to face the opposite direction, and began to swim.

Pete held on to her other hand for dear life, using both of his hands to grip her as she sped through the water.

While they moved more toward the center of the lake, she also descended. Pete remembered something about nitrogen... Was it nitrogen? Or was it oxygen? Whichever gas it was, the gas caused bubbles in scuba divers' blood. This happened when someone went down too fast. *Or was it when they came up too fast?* Pete wished he could remember. If the mermaid dove too fast, would his heart explode? He hoped not.

The pair sped over a kelp forest. While they did, Pete made out plankton, fish, fat blue crabs, and small crocodile things. He tried to focus on one thing or the other, but he was a fish out of water. Rather...a human out of land... *Does that make sense?* he wondered, *a human out of land?* He decided it would have to make sense. The sensation of the water around him, the speed at which the mermaid traveled, the unfamiliar environment...it disoriented him. He began to feel nauseous.

Before he knew it, they had passed over the forest, and he noticed a dim light ahead, one with an emerald sheen. It illuminated the far end of the woods. "That's my home." He heard Aqua explain, but he couldn't think enough to respond. All he could do was try not to vomit.

With each flap of her tail, the intensity of the light increased. So did the size of it. The light became a building, a tall round cylindrical structure. One structure became two, two became three. When they entered the town, Aqua began to slow.

With the slow pace, Pete's dizziness waned. When he felt confident that he wouldn't throw up, he took in his surroundings. The buildings—he realized—were houses. Each pillar appeared to belong to a different family. The diameter of the pillars varied, but none seemed to have more than one room per floor. Some of the pillars were only three stories tall. Others rose over ten levels.

Mermaids swam around the pillars. They weren't dressed how Pete imagined mermaids would dress, no seashells for tops. Rather, the kids wore t-shirts made from a similar material to Aqua's... cotton that looked like the material from a wet suit. And the adults wore what adults wore. That is to say, some business-men...errr...business-mermen wore white shirts and ties. Though, even the dress shirts had a bit of a wet-suit look to them.

All the merpeople wore pants designed to fit over a merperson fin, skirts, or dresses to cover their bottom halves. They were the most modest mermaids Pete had ever come across.

Aqua pulled Pete through town, and people stared at them all the while. They passed something called The Siren's Call'isuem; it reminded Pete of the Roman Colosseum. Near its entrance, Pete saw some mermen wearing armor. The armor would have fit in with the Roman Legionnaires. It was a handsome bronze with red accents. It included crimson seaweed which poked up from the helmets.

Then they went past a glass building called Club Shake-a-Fin. Since it was the middle of the day, the club looked empty. Pete saw a dormant disco ball hovering at the center of the club. He hoped he'd see what the night club looked like at night.

Later, Pete saw more guards like those from the Colosseum. They stood outside a castle that looked like it was pure jade. Even the wall around it was jade. "That's the king's palace," Aqua said as they swam by it.

Opposite the castle, they came to another neighborhood with house pillars. Aqua pulled Pete toward the hatch at the top of one of the pillars. When they reached the hatch, she released Pete's hands and entered a code into the number pad by the hatch. As she punched it in, Pete held to the edge of the pillar like a child holding to the edge of a pool. When she finished inputting the last number, the hatch hissed, and she spun a doorknob. It resembled a steering wheel. Then she pulled the hatch open. "Go on in," she said.

Pete did his best to acquiesce, but being underwater, he proved more clumsy than usual. The mere chore of swinging his legs up lacked any amount of precision. It made him feel embarrassed. "I'm so sorry," he said.

"It's fine," she told him. "I'm sure you're doing better than I would on land."

When she said that, he felt better, and he finished swinging his legs into the hatch. Once he was in, he let himself drop. He should have looked before he dropped because Aqua's father was below him.

He landed atop her father, and they both tumbled to the floor of the family's living room.

14: Lost in Waiting

Nick was great at standing guard. Rumpke was great at annoying Nick. As they stood side by side, the question became, who was better at what? Was Nick better at standing guard? Or was Rumpke better at annoying Nick? As trees shaded them from the midday sun, it was a battle of wills. Nick remained determined to demonstrate his superior guarding. Rumpke wanted nothing more than to distract Nick...if even for a second.

So Nick stood to the right of the dungeon portal. He felt determined not to let anyone enter without an adventurer's pass. He'd also deny entry to the triplets...even with their passes. It wouldn't be safe to let them go in. They were still children. He wouldn't be able to live with himself if something happened to them.

Standing guard is a serious artform that requires focus and an understanding of technique. When Nick stood guard, he couldn't talk. He couldn't move. He couldn't smile. He couldn't even faint. It would be a violation of his guard protocols. Though, every ten minutes, rules allowed him to march. By marching, it helped him stretch his muscles and legs.

He also had an ability in his City Guard Skill Tree called Stand Guard. When activated, it prevented his muscles or feet from tiring. So long as he didn't move, the skill remained active. If it remained active, he didn't have to worry about sore feet.

While he stood, he used the periphery of his vision on each side to identify movement in the forest. As he watched, he activated the skill Search for Movement. It was an ability that would use neon lights to leave trails behind any movements. He could activate the skill once every five minutes, and it only lasted for thirty seconds. This left him four and a half minutes without the skill between thirty-second bursts with it.

In some cities, guard protocols stipulated that the guards be more reserved with their skill usage. In those areas, guards activated skills when they thought they saw something. Elsewise, they didn't use it. Nick disagreed with that standard. This was because using the ability sped up the leveling of his guarding skill. Also, as it leveled, he earned skill points. While using those skill points, he had unlocked Strong Searching for Movement.

Strong Searching for Movement allowed him to activate the skill every six minutes, and it lasted for forty-five seconds. When he stacked the abilities, he had almost double the time to scan with the ability. It made him twice as effective a guard. And being the most effective guard was the Nick Warman way. Someday he dreamed of writing his own guard protocols. He could travel the world and teach them to guards at castles. He could teach them to children who wanted to become guards.

All the while, Nick tried to ignore Rumpke.

Rumpke stood left of the dungeon portal. While Nick watched the forest like an angry statue, Rumpke watched Nick. "You might get stuck standing like that...if you stay that way for too long." When Nick didn't answer, Rumpke continued. "It's okay to relax, too. There's no immediate threat." Nick still didn't answer, and Rumpke sighed one time.

Then Rumpke turned his eyes to the forest. "When will those adventure society guards get here?" If on time, they would arrive any second. Then it would be up to Nick to find those adventurers housing in Greenlake. Rumpke had offered the adventurers a space in the cave, but Nick had rejected the idea outright.

Rumpke wasn't hurt or offended by the rejection.

He and Nick had a history of distrust, so it would take time to mend their relationship.

Rumpke turned his attention back to Nick. "Do you think that the Adventurer's Guild will send human guards? What if they send Raccoon guards?" When Nick didn't answer, Rumpke continued. "Then they could stay in our cave. I'd give them their own room." Nick remained motionless without making a sound. "While they were there, I could plan evil things with them. Finally, I could take over Greenlake."

Rumpke looked up at Nick and then back to the forest. Nick offered no reaction; he didn't even grumble. Though, his mustache looked angrier. Rumpke wondered if its corners had turned upward or if it was his imagination. *Angry mustache,* Rumpke thought. *I'll take that as a win.*

Nick could feel the corners of his mustache turning upward. This frustrated him. He didn't want to give Rumpke any reaction...not even an involuntary one like an angry mustache. Even so, he doubted Rumpke had noticed his angry mustache. He hoped... No... He prayed that Rumpke hadn't seen his angry mustache.

"Your mustache is angry," Rumpke said. "I know you didn't want me to notice, but I did. That means I win, you know. I got a reaction."

Nick took a deep breath. Rumpke guessed it was to keep calm. "Now you're taking deep breaths. That counts as a reaction, too." Rumpke knew Nick was about to lose it. All Rumpke had to do was push a little more. "For a city guard, you sure are tense. You should learn to relax, my friend."

"There's movement in the forest." Nick squinted his eyes together and leaned forward to get a closer look. It looks like someone is headed this way. Be on guard."

"You know," Rumpke stepped over to Nick and patted his shoulder once. "I saw your angry mustache. You don't have to pretend there's movement in the forest to hide that I was getting to you."

"Ggrrrr..."

"And there's no need to grumble at me," Rumpke said.

"Sir," one of Rumpke's Trash Pandas broke through the tree line. "We've spotted a soul eater in the forest. It's moving toward Greenlake. We tried to keep it distracted with guerilla tactics, but it's regenerating faster than we can damage it. We need your help."

"I told you there was movement," Nick said, keeping a neutral expression. Though, his mustache looked smug. It had an *I told you so air* to it.

What a pretentious mustache, Rumpke thought.

"We should go help them," Nick said. "The portal should be fine. It's not like someone can enter it without an Adventurer's Pass, anyway."

"Agreed," Rumpke said. Issues with the portal aside, Rumpke was the highest-level person in the area. As such, he felt a keen responsibility to protect his Trash Pandas from any damage the soul eater could cause. "Let's go deal with the soul eater."

*   *   *

"I don't think they saw a soul eater. I do think this is part of a plan you came up with to make me abandon my post." Nick complained.

After half an hour of searching, Rumpke, Nick, and the rest of the Trash Pandas couldn't find any trace of a soul eater. "We both know how soul eaters can phase in and out of existence. It isn't the Trash Panda's fault that this one phased out. Even so, we should keep searching. It's bound to show up again."

"You keep searching," Nick said. "I'll head back

to the portal. If the soul eater *is* real, and it turns back up, you can send someone for me."

"It is real, and it will turn back up," Rumpke assured. "Don't you worry about that. But you are correct. We've left the portal unguarded for long enough. You should make your way back there."

*   *   *

In video games, Zoey never enjoyed grinding for experience or drops. Grinding felt like a waste of time. To save time in single-player games, she'd use Game Genie, a Game Shark, Code Action Replay, or Save Pro Wizard. Those tools let her skip levels, cap her experience, and maximize her money. Though, she avoided doing that in multi-player games. It wouldn't be fair to the other players. She wondered if that was the purpose of the laws of the moderators. Did the moderators want to make leveling up fair for everyone? She hoped that was the case.

In Round, Zoey enjoyed farming for tomatoes. It let her wander through a beautiful, thick, green forest. She always enjoyed hiking. Also, whenever she found a nightshade terror, she got to practice with her fork and shield. Since Pete had begun grinding his slapping skill by slapping her shield, her peel skill had been a co-beneficiary. It had gone up by hundreds of points.

As soon as she found a nightshade terror, she'd be able to feel how those skill points carried over to reality. *Is Round reality?* She wondered. Sometimes it felt like a complicated 3-D video game. She assumed that the surreal nature of Round was what had allowed her to come to terms with being a vampire. Back on Earth, the transformation would have been a traumatic experience. On Round, it felt like a game.

Another thing that helped her come to terms with being a vampire was how she could travel in the sunlight. At the time, she found herself exposed to the sun. Beams of it worked their way through the canopy and found her skin, warming it where they touched. Of course, that was possible because she wore a ring called the Ring of the Daywalker. She'd found the ring at Wanda's Windmill of Wonderous Widgets and Wild Wafler. If not for the ring, the sun would have harmed her.

"AAAgggghhh!" A high-pitched shriek sounded to her left, accompanied by a night-shade terror. The creature leaped from the bushes at head height.

Using her shield, she intercepted it midflight. As it bounced and began to fall, she swung the point of her fork into the thing. In less than a second, its hit points had dropped to zero, and it disintegrated in a flash of light. She received prompt notifications. They indicated three tomatoes had dropped, and she'd earned a nominal amount of experience.

During the encounter, she hadn't noticed a considerable difference in her shield usage. She guessed that was due to the nightshade terrors being such a low level. With such a gap, she wouldn't see the difference. In a way, the easiness of it was boring. Though as simple and mindless a task as tomato farming had become, it was necessary.

Plus, it would be more entertaining once Pete arrived. He had planned to join her, but he hadn't yet. *He got distracted by something.* She convinced herself. *I'm sure he'll be here soon.*

On the other side of her, bushes rustled. She shifted to face the sound, raising her shield and bracing to block.

Sound rumbled in another bush...this time to her left. She spun to face it. Her left arm held her shield ready to block. Her right hand held her fork, prepared to counter. Though, it wasn't a nightshade terror which emerged from the bush. Instead, Hope's tiny, pixie head poked out. Her eyes squinted, and she wrinkled her forehead as she glanced left and right. Then she looked straight at Zoey. As she saw Zoey, her expression softened. Then she emerged from the bush in full. With a smile forming, she leaned back and said. "It's Zoey. You guys can come out."

Some of the bush's branches rustled as Skye and Tornado emerged. They fluttered next to their sister, one of them on each side. Too shy to make eye contact, Skye leaned his head down and waved at Zoey.

Tornado looked straight at Zoey and said. "We are looking for a dungeon portal. Rumpke said there was one. He said we couldn't go in, but we could see it. Mom and dad said we could come, but we had to be careful. Have you seen Rumpke? Have you seen the portal?"

Zoey stood upright, returning her weapon and shield to her inventory before relaxing her arms. "I haven't seen the portal yet." She put her finger on her chin. "Come to think of it, I haven't seen Rumpke today, either."

"He said he'd take us tomorrow..." Hope hung her head. Then she looked at Tornado. "But some of us are impatient and wanted to see it today."

Tornado looked back at his sister. "You were impatient too, Hope."

"We are all impatient." Skye smiled.

"Yeah, that's true." Hope and Tornado said in unison.

"Right," Zoey said. "I have to get back to the restaurant for the evening rush. But I can't leave the three of you alone in the forest. Let's get back to town. Rumpke said he'll take you tomorrow. It will be best to wait for him. Afterall, he knows where it is."

"Okay..." the siblings sighed in unison. Zoey could feel their disappointment.

"But," She added. "If we see Rumpke on the way

back to town, I'll ask him to take you today."

At those words, the triplets perked up, but none said anything.

"Alright," Zoey said. "Follow me."

The group began down the forest trail. During the day, the forest boasted a majestic beauty that only nature can provide. Red, funnel-shaped flowers hung from the trees. The deep shades of green demonstrated the health of each leaf. Each of the trees and all the bushes produced such leaves. The grass along the path was thick and full. In a pinch, it could be thick enough to become a comfortable mattress for a nap. Though napping where nightshade terrors wandered...it wasn't the safest idea. Still, the grass looked cozy.

An occasional vine hung, and as Zoey and the triplets descended, Zoey took the time to use the vines as swings.

"Why do you keep swinging like that on the vines?" Tornado asked.

"It's fun," Zoey said.

Skye wrinkled his face in confusion.

Zoey smiled. "Understand that I don't have wings. If I could fly like you three, swinging on vines wouldn't be as fun."

"That makes sense," Hope said.

When they were nearing the edge of the forest, and the trees had begun to grow thin, Skye pointed to the side and asked. "Guys, what is that?"

Zoey looked in the indicated direction. Through sparse trees and thinning foliage, she noticed something glowing. It was around three hundred meters away, but her vampire sight allowed her to see it with clarity. It was a doorway. "No way." Her eyes widened. "That's got to be the portal."

Cloud began to dance with his left hand on his hip, his right hand with one finger in the air.

"Yay!" Tornado said with a big smile. Though his

voice remained monotone.

Hope smiled but didn't say anything.

"Well," Zoey said. "Let's go take a closer look. But remember, you told your parents you wouldn't go in."

"Um, hum," Tornado agreed.

"Right," Hope said.

"Okay," Skye nodded.

The triplets and Zoey weaved through the trees toward the portal. Where the triplets hovered, Zoey had to through tall grass. As they went, Zoey made a mental note of the portal's location. If she saw the mime, tuxedo man, and pirate adventurers again, she could tell them where they could find the dungeon. As she walked, she kept her eyes on the portal. "That's strange."

"What is strange?" Hope asked.

"I don't see Nick, Rumpke, or Trash Pandas. There's no one guarding the portal." Zoey pursed her lips. "Someone should be."

If there was no one watching the portal, what happened? Was everyone okay? Did someone get hurt? Something had to have occurred.

Before Zoey could explain the potential of a dangerous situation, Hope looked at her brothers and said. "I'll race you there."

With that, the trio of pixies zipped away. Their wings flapped faster than a hummingbird's as they sped toward the door.

"No, wait!" Zoey shouted behind them. "I don't think..."

A low growl rumbled behind Zoey, cutting her sentence short. With a slow head turn, she looked back over her shoulder. Angry red eyes looked back. The eyes embedded themselves in the center of a purple cloud of smoke. "Soul eater!" Zoey shouted to the triplets as she materialized her shield and fork. "Fly as fast as you can."

She had not finished shouting her commands when the soul eater caught her shield center mass. Her arm buckled under the force, and the blow sent her flying. Off-balanced, she landed with a thud on her back and slid, tumbling. She could feel bushes and branches breaking around her before her momentum stopped as she slammed against a broad tree trunk.

"Uuufff…" she felt the air expelled from her lungs. As she didn't need to breathe, she recovered without delay and searched for the soul eater. It moved toward her in a flash. *Good,* she thought. *If it's after me, it's leaving the triplets alone.*

The thing leaped toward her, and she parried with her shield while sliding to the side. The creature's momentum carried it into the tree behind her, and the tree snapped like a twig under the force.

As it reoriented, she got a better look at it. The shadowy outline within the cloud of purple had the shape of a bipedal bird. It reminded Zoey of velociraptors in some of the dinosaur movies she had seen. Though, this soul eater was bigger than an ostrich or a velociraptor. Based on the shadow, she guessed it to be fifteen feet tall.

She shifted her eyes to the triplets. The three had followed her instructions to fly away as fast as they could. Though, she couldn't help but notice they flew straight toward the dungeon portal. Did they think they could hide in the dungeon? The soul eater was a monster; it could follow them in…assuming it could fit in the door. Not to mention they'd come across other monsters in the dungeon. To make things worse, Zoey couldn't follow them into the dungeon to protect them there… Or could she? Rumpke said the undead could enter dungeons. If she couldn't stop the triplets from fleeing into the portal, she'd have to try to follow them.

Her eyes returned to the soul eater. It was back

on its feet, preparing to attack again. As it leaped, she noticed its leg out, taloned foot aimed at her. She leaned back, bracing the back of her fork against the ground and aiming its point at the bottom of the soul eater's foot.

As the point of the fork met the bottom of the soul eater's foot, Zoey dematerialized her shield, dove, and rolled. She heard the dinosaur shriek in pain as she began toward the triplets. She tried to call out to them, advise them not to enter the portal. But they didn't hear, and she watched as their outlines disappeared into the iridescent doorway.

She dematerialized her fork, removing it from the soul eater's foot and returning it to her inventory. Then she sprinted in the direction of the portal. She could feel the soul eater behind her, drawing closer every second. At the same time, she could see the portal ahead, and she doubted the soul eater could fit through the doorway. All she had to do was make it. Would she make it? She wondered. She knew it would be close.

The portal was fifteen feet away. The soul eater was twenty feet away. The portal was ten feet away. The soul eater was thirteen. Five feet to go. Six feet until it had her. Then she disappeared into the portal, unsure if the soul eater had followed.

*   *   *

"You need new guards," Nick grumbled as he and Rumpke returned to the portal. "Or they need better training. I can train them if you want. I have the Nick Warman method. It will make men out of your... ... raccoons... That doesn't sound right, but it will make them tough."

"Keep your methods to yourself." Rumpke walked next to Nick. "If they say they saw a soul eater, they saw one."

When the pair reached the portal, they saw two men standing by the portal. One of the men called out, "Is one of you Nick Warman?"

Nick moved a few steps closer, so he wouldn't have to shout, "I'm Nick."

"We," the man by the portal pointed at himself and the other man, "are from the Adventurer's Guild. We are here to assume responsibility for the portal. You have no need to fear. Nothing will get in or out without further notice from us."

"Or out?" Nick asked. "Why would we worry about something getting out?"

"You see," the man explained. "The guild likes to lock portals. Then we register them. That allows adventurers to move into the area. When there are plenty of adventurers in an area, we unlock the portal. This protocol prevents monsters from escaping into nearby towns. As such, you have no need to worry."

"We should have asked them to put Roger in the portal before they locked it." Rumpke joked.

Nick offered Rumpke a reprimanding glare before returning to the Adventure Guild Guards. "Thank you for assuming guard duties. You may have noticed we left the portal unattended."

"We did notice that." The man answered. "We thought it strange to leave the portal like that."

"The thing is," Nick said. "There are reports of a soul eater in the area. We went to investigate. Though—as of now—those reports remain unsubstantiated."

"You're unsubstantiated," Rumpke said. "Those reports are legitimate."

Nick grumbled.

"We've noted your reports of a soul eater in the area." The Adventurer Guild Guard smiled. "We will be careful. You have no need to worry."

"Right," Nick said. "Thank you for coming. We will leave you to it then."

"What does leave you to it mean?" Rumpke asked. "Leave them to what? That phrase doesn't make sense."

Nick sighed before saying. "Let's go. It's been a long day. I'm ready to turn in."

Rumpke agreed.

15: Enter the Moderators

Geb wore his pet goose as a happy hat over his long navy-blue hair. Rather, the goose was part of a crown called a pschent. The bottom part of the crown was red with a golden snake curving out from its front. Where the crown would normally have a white egg, it had Geb's goose. The goose wore a blue wig, so his hair could match Geb's.

An ankh held place over Geb's bare chest, hanging from a golden chain. He wore a white linen kilt. A leather belt held it up. A pouch hung from the same belt, resting over his right hip. Sandals protected the soles of his feet. Aside from the goose and strange clothing, he looked like an ordinary man, lean and muscular with a slight tan. His normalcy contradicted the terrain over which he walked.

The landscape nearest him came dotted with lava pits which spit droplets of fire in his direction. He managed to avoid them. Where many would say he was lucky, his movements were purposeful. He understood the lava's natural activity; he knew the exact second it would spray. He walked at a pace to avoid that spray. Then a few steps later, he walked a half circle around a pit of quicksand. The pit looked the same as the rest of the ground, but Geb knew it was there.

Fifteen paces to his left, a harsh ocean tide beat against the coastline. In an hour, it would become a tsunami. To his right, volcanos threatened eruption. Though, he guessed it'd be another three days before they did erupt.

The stretch of land along which he walked shook and quaked. A violent wind pushed against him, and nearby tornadoes spun. Overhead, lightning flashed, and thunder boomed.

And Geb yawned, not impressed by any of it. He'd seen disasters before. He didn't recognize anything special to them. If he wanted, he could cause them...or prevent them. They were mundane, predictable, and boring.

Geb had lived in different worlds. As such, he knew how the curvature of a world determines how far away a person must be from something before they see it. Round was much the same. And in the case of Arbitration Tower—when its spire began to peak over the horizon—it told Geb he'd be there in thirty minutes. So when he saw the spire, his heart sank. Walking alone—him and his goose—was the only calm he knew. It was the only break in his otherwise chaotic existence. After some consideration, he slowed his pace, adding another fifteen minutes to his journey.

Despite his best efforts, forty-five minutes later, he came to the tower. From the outside, the structure boasted a smooth black surface, reflective like obsidian. A broad base supported the cylindrical design that stretched eighty floors up. Not even one of those floors had a window or balcony. Such things went against the purpose of the tower. That purpose was to protect the moderators and their secrets.

It wasn't that Geb—or any of the other moderators—felt threatened by anyone on Round. Though, it was better to be safe than sorry. And the tower's purpose was that of a stronghold. No moderator would be foolish to think otherwise. Higher-ranking moderators even used the structure to protect themselves from lower-ranking moderators...lower-ranking moderators like Geb.

When a building's purpose was to guard secrets, it wouldn't make sense to have multiple entrance points to a stronghold. It would make less sense to have one of those entrance points be a window. In the case of Arbitration Tower, it didn't even have doors.

A moat surrounded it. Aside from the lava which filled the trench, he knew the lava contained red dragons and the like. As he drew close to the tower, large stones at the base of the tower began to vibrate, creating a low rumble. The rumble shook the earth as the rocks started to hover, shooting one at a time to form a solid bridge over the moat.

As Geb stepped across the bridge, his feet made a hollow tip-tapping. Every time he crossed the bridge, it reminded him of the children's story about the goats. He loved that story.

When Geb reached the other side of the moat, he used his right hand to fish a whistle from his pouch.

The stones which had formed the bridge floated up from the lava, hovering in the air behind Geb. Then—like arrows—they shot back to their original position at the tower's base. Those which would have hit Geb curved around him.

As the boulders zipped around him, Geb moved the whistle to his lips and blew three times. In unison with the third note, a light formed around him, so bright he had to close his eyes to protect them. When the light dissipated, he opened his eyes again, and he was no longer outside the tower. The light teleported him to the tower's first floor.

Instead of a traditional walking surface—one made from marble, carpet, wood, or tile—sedimentary rock and sand created an uneven floor. Sandstone formed caves along the edge of the rooms, and it rose to form pillars at the room's center. Small sandworms, desert vipers, and antlions hid within the nooks and shadows of the area. Though, some larger sandworms left trails as they swam through the sand.

A narrow canyon divided the room at its center, only a tiny hop from one side to the other. The narrowness of the chasm contradicted its depth. Geb avoided an antlion pit as he plotted over to the chasm. Then he looked down. He didn't know what happened to people who fell into that endless dark; he wasn't sure if higher-ranking moderators knew. Whether they did or not, throwing dissenters into that dark was one of the leadership's favorite hobbies.

Geb disapproved of those hard-handed tactics. Even so, he understood the effectiveness of a powerful deterrent. He returned his whistle to his pouch, hopped over the chasm, and continued to a cave on the far side of the chamber. The cave hid a stairway. Geb used that stairway to go up to the next floor.

As the first twenty stories of the tower represented the element of earth, the second floor was much like the first. Though, it lacked the canyon. Geb continued to climb, beyond the twenty floors of earth, through another twenty that represented water, and past the next twenty which embodied fire.

When he reached the sixty-first story, marble formed the floors and walls. It was perfect and polished marble without a chip or blemish. Golden pillars stretched from ceiling to floor. A slight breeze blew through the room. Geb knew the draft could become a raging storm at the whim of leadership, but he'd never seen it happen. Someone would have to be crazy enough to invade the tower for that to occur. They'd also have to be powerful enough to fight their way to the sixty-first floor, defeating three high notorious monster—HNM—bosses along the way… It was an impossible feat.

As such, the sixty-first floor was the only floor in the tower without monsters. Instead, it served as the hub for the moderators. It was where higher-ranking moderators met with lower-ranking ones. Also, it was where lower-ranking moderators socialized with one another. Sometimes they even had parties. Those parties tended to get wild. If the moderators still had parents, their parents would not have approved.

At the time, plenty of those moderators moved about while a quiet melody played. He knew the music came from a spell rather than speakers, live performers, or other technology. Magic music always had a different sound to it. It was an internal permanence that resonated from the center of a person. Even at quiet volumes, it felt powerful and precise.

The melody was of a classical tradition, heavy on the strings. Its tonal vocals lacked any coherent lyrics. In effect, they functioned much like an instrument. Geb knew which moderators were there for recreation by how they swayed and tapped their feet to the music. Not to mention, they had smiles plastered across their faces. The moderators on business—those like Geb—retained a glower. If Geb's goose could have glowered, it would have, too. Moderator business was serious business... It merited respect.

Whether there for business or for play, most moderators in the tower weren't from Round. They came from adjoining worlds. They'd conquered some of those worlds... Some were in the process of conquest. Others were on a list for the moderators to conquer later. Geb himself wasn't from Round. After tens of thousands of years of life, he couldn't remember his home world, but he knew it wasn't Round. He scanned his eyes over the room until he found Enlil, Vulcan, Zonja, and Sidhe. They sat on a couch in the corner, and he began toward them.

Enlil noticed Geb first. Geb knew this because Enlil's skin went from a light gray—which blended with the marble of the wall—to a dark blue. As the skin shifted color, Enlil focused his pupilless eyes on Geb. The pure whiteness of those eyes matched his long beard and flowing white hair. He'd tied said hair into a ponytail. Enlil wore a golden crown atop his head which matched the accents of his jacket. Aside from those inlays, dark metal chainmail formed the rest of the jacket. Each ring was so small that it appeared like cloth. A matching material made Enlil's pants.

When Zonja saw Enlil turn blue, she shifted in her seat to look at Geb. Her red kapica headdress flowed behind her as she moved. She wore a white dress with a patched apron that matched the kapica's red. All in all, she appeared like an average girl, nothing intimidating, nothing threatening. She had normal dirty-blond hair and normal green eyes.

Vulcan lacked any of Zonja's subtlety. He was a towering mountain of man, covered in rippling muscles. His bronze battle skirt showed off powerful legs, each wider than the waist of a typical man. A single shoulder pad held up the skirt, connected by a strap that crossed the front and back of his body at an angle. Three protrusions rose from the shoulder pad. They had the shape of waves. The middle rise was tall enough to protect Vulcan's neck. A long brown beard covered his face. It concealed burnt scarring on his skin. Even so, he'd somehow managed to win the love of Venus...the moderator of love and beauty. A blacksmith's hammer rested on the ground next to him. The head was as wide as a coffee table and half the height of an average human. From that head, the hammer's handle rose ten feet into the air.

On the shoulder without a pad, sat Sidhe. At a glance, she looked like any other pixie on Round: small in stature, with tiny wings protruding from each shoulder blade. Green armor covered her thin figure. Engravings across the armor imitated the shape of leaves on a tree. Piercing emerald eyes matched the sheen of the armor. Those eyes contrasted against her messy green hair.

"About time you got here," Vulcan grumbled with his usual baritone. "We were beginning to think you fell in the moat."

"Now," Sidhe patted the shoulder on which she sat. "We have no need to be rude. Geb traveled a long way to be here. Plus, you know him. He does enjoy his walks. One should not rush the enjoyment of others." Each word she spoke came out melodic, gentle, and calm.

If windchimes could talk, Geb thought, they'd *sound like her.*

"One should not walk slow when he knows others wait for him." Vulcan shot back, his skin flashing the orangish-red of embers.

"Easy," Enlil admonished Vulcan with a glance. Then he looked back at Geb. "Though we were waiting a long time. Everything alright?"

"I got held up in the Volcano Islands," Geb explained. "A man was stealing when his job wasn't that of a thief."

"What was his job?" Zonja asked, unable to hide the curiosity in her voice.

"A steelworker," Geb replied.

"Do you think," Enlil said, "he might not have known the difference between the metal steel and the verb to steal?"

"That's what he claimed. He told me he was a steal worker, so he had to steal." Geb sighed. "Don't worry, though. I explained the difference before I destroyed his village. They won't make the same mistake again."

Zonja's eyes widened at Geb's explanation, but she said nothing.

"Why does Geb get to have all the fun?" Vulcan asked. "Can I be an enforcer again? I tire of this tower."

"No," Sidhe patted his shoulder again. "You're my favorite chair. I'd hate it if you left."

"Geb," Enlil said. "We have a mission for you."

"A mission?" Geb considered. Under normal circumstances, his job consisted of wandering from town to town. He'd talk with people, see if anyone was breaking any laws. If he found anyone violating the rules, he'd punish the town. Though, he didn't like to kill anyone. For the moderators to be scary, they had to leave people alive. When people lived, they could tell stories. That's how people learned about the moderators. If he killed everyone, no one would even know about the laws. "What kind of a mission?"

"Danu has recognized an influx of magic. It is in the town of Greenlake in the kingdom of Lakes." Enlil's skin returned to its grayish camouflage as he leaned back against the wall. "She wants you to investigate this influx. Likely, it is the formation of a dungeon. If not a dungeon, it might be something more sinister. Figure out what it is and return. This time...don't lose any time with your enforcement duties. The destruction of towns can wait."

16: Adventurers

After Zoey followed the triplets into the portal, she found herself with her knees bent, sitting atop her feet, a cold floor beneath her. She could hear the trickling and rippling of water, Though even her vampire eyes couldn't see through the darkness around her. It was suffocating, disparaging. It made her feel hopeless. As the weight of the dark bore down on her, she worried. Though, her preoccupation was more for the triplets than for herself. If she felt scared, how did they feel?

"Hello," She called out. "Hope, Skye, Tornado...are you here? Are you okay?"

If the triplets were nearby, they didn't answer her. She groaned as she stood. Still unable to see her surroundings, she moved with purposeful slowness. She was careful not to hit her head, arms, or legs against anything. The last thing she needed to do was to stand too fast and bump her head against something. If she gave herself a concussion, Pete would never let her hear the end of it.

She opened her mouth, preparing to call to the triplets a second time. Before she could make a sound, she heard Hope's voice call back to her. "Zoey, is that you?"

"It's me," Zoey answered. "Where are you?"

"One moment, please," Hope said. A few seconds later, a flash of greenish-white light filled the room. As the light dissipated, Zoey found herself in a circular tunnel. The diameter of the space was ten feet in any given direction. The walls, ceiling, and roof were gray stone. The edges were smooth but boasted uneven dips and mounds. Water trickled through cracks in the ceiling and walls, pooling into puddles in the dips on the floor.

Twenty paces ahead, Zoey saw the triplets. Tornado hovered, looking up and down the long passageway, eyes wide. Zoey wasn't sure if he felt scared, excited, curious, or all three.

Skye sat with his back against the right wall, head unmoving, scanning his eyes back and forth. He wore a neutral expression on his face.

Hope stood in the center of the tunnel facing Zoey. Hope had one hand on her hip, one in the air with greenish-white light flowing from her palm. As the light faded, the room remained lit.

Zoey's eyes met Hope's, and Zoey asked. "Did you do that?"

"Yes," Hope flashed a smile. "It's a spell called Light the Way. It's one of the spells I get as a healing pixie."

"That's a handy spell," Zoey said, "lifesaving. There's no way we'd find our way out of here in the dark. How long does the light last?"

"Two hours. Then I'll have to recast it."

Skye remained sitting as he said. "I want to get out of here. Which way should we go to get out?"

"I want to go both ways," Tornado said.

"We can't go both ways," Skye told him. "We need to pick one way."

"There can be treasures in both ways." Tornado looked at Zoey. "Right? We can get treasures both ways?"

Hope interrupted her brothers. "We should try to go one way. If it is a dead end, we go the other way."

"Ah, man," Tornado looked at his sister. "Wait...are you being serious? For real?"

"When you're older," Zoey told Tornado. "You can explore as many dungeons as you want. For now, we must get you three back to your parents before they worry about you."

"Ummm..." Tornado landed in front of Zoey, looking up at her. "If we find treasure on the way out, can we keep it?"

"I don't see the harm in that." Zoey agreed.

"Yay!" Tornado spun as he took flight. Zoey worried he would slam against the ceiling, but he stopped a few centimeters short.

"Well," Zoey said. "We should get going. Skye, which way do you think."

"That way." Skye pointed. "I hear running water in that direction. I read that if you get lost, you should follow running water."

"That makes sense." Zoey agreed, not sure if the fact he'd told her was true or not, but she chose to believe it was. "Let's get going."

As Zoey began down the tunnel, Skye stood and hovered, landing on her right shoulder and sitting. Tornado landed on her left shoulder and sat. Hope hovered overhead.

During the next five minutes, the walls, puddles, ceiling, cracks leaking water, drips of water, and floor began to blend. To Zoey, it all looked the same. Even so, the triplets seemed to notice differences. She listened to them play a game where they came up with different shapes for the puddles. One looked like a dog. One looked like a cat. One looked like a cordle. She didn't know what a cordle was, but one of the puddles looked like a cordle.

"What's that?" Zoey asked, noticing the tunnel widen up ahead.

"I'm not sure," Hope said.

"I'll go check." Tornado leaped from Zoey's shoulder and sped ahead before she could stop him.

Skye rolled his eyes. "He always does that. Dad says he should slow down and make safe choices."

"We should hurry and catch up," Zoey said as she began to jog.

When Tornado reached the wider portion of the passageway, he scanned the area, nodded once, and hurried back to Zoey.

"Don't move away from the..." Zoey began.

"It is a huge chamber full of water stuff." Tornado interrupted her.

"Don't interrupt, Tornado," Hope scolded.

"Oh, sorry," Tornado said, looking at Zoey. "I'm sorry for interrupting you. I'm very sorry. I'm so sorry."

"It's okay." Zoey smiled. "I wanted to remind you not to go too far away from the group. It isn't safe."

"I'm so sorry I interrupted." Tornado's voice broke like he was about to cry, tears forming in his eyes. "I didn't mean to interrupt you."

"It's okay," Zoey told him. "I'm not mad at you. Thank you for saying you're sorry."

"Okay," A tear began to fall; he used his sleeve to wipe it away. "You aren't mad that I interrupted you?"

"No," Zoey told him. "We aren't mad at you. Thank you for being brave. Can you tell us what you saw?"

"Yeah," Tornado smiled. "I saw a big room. It had water stuff. I saw some crabs. There were three guys there too."

"Let's go see it," Zoey said. "Tornado, can I ask a favor?"

"What you need?" Tornado asked.

"Next time we come to an opening or something like that, can you stay with the rest of us? It will help keep us all safe."

Tornado landed on Zoey's shoulder again. "I can do that."

"Thank you." Zoey turned her eyes to the passageway up ahead. "Let's go see this chamber you found."

When Zoey and the triplets reached where the tunnel opened to the chamber, they stopped. Zoey leaned her head toward where Tornado sat on her shoulder. "When you said it is full of water, you weren't kidding."

The ceiling rose hundreds of feet. The walls extended even further than that in each direction. The floor became a swampy field. Small rivulets crisscrossed through tall grass and around full trees and bushes. Quaint, wooden bridges stretched over the small waterways. A pond held place at the chamber's center. Waterspout spun at random intervals, stretching from floor to ceiling. The watery tornadoes died out in time for new ones to take their place.

Giant crabs crawled through the water, pinchers snapping at one another. The pinchers also snapped at anything into which they bumped. A few smaller bushes fell victim before the crab's ferocity.

To the right—about twenty paces into the chamber—stood three men. Zoey recognized them as the same three adventurers who had knocked on the pizzeria's door the other night: the man in the white tuxedo, the pirate, and the mime. The three men stared at Zoey and the triplets. Zoey waved at the men, and they whispered something among themselves. Then they approached Zoey.

As they walked, Zoey realized the water that filled the chamber was at least a foot deep. The men splashed as they tromped through it.

"Introvice," Zoey stopped waving as the men drew close. "Flowerbeard, Fred...I'm happy to see you three."

"You said you didn't know where the portal was." Flowerbeard glared.

"I didn't when I talked to you," Zoey answered.

"Likely story." Flowerbeard crossed his arms over his chest.

"I'm sorry about Flowerbeard." Introvice offered a respectful bow of the head for a second before he resumed. "Though, we didn't expect to see you. We didn't know you were an adventurer."

"I'm not," Zoey said. "I'm...a vampire..."

"A vampire?" Introvice squinted his eyes together. "And you live in a bakery?"

"That is accurate," Zoey said.

"I bet she's one of the dungeon monsters." Flowerbeard adjusted his pirate hat. "She didn't tell us about the dungeon because it's her home. The bakery was a cover. She didn't want us to find the dungeon."

"I don't care that you are in the dungeon," Zoey explained. "In fact, I'm happy to see you here. We wandered in by accident and don't know the way out."

Fred facepalmed and fell backward, splashing in the water and sinking until he submerged. Zoey saw bubbles coming up from Fred's mouth. "Is he going to be okay?"

"Why wouldn't he be?" Flowerbeard asked. "That was a rude question. Don't be rude. Like serious. Whatever. Stop talking."

"Why do you like to tell people to stop talking?" Tornado asked.

"I don't do that," Flowerbeard said. "I've never said for people to stop talking, so be quiet. Like...whatever."

"The pirate has a broken brain," Skye whispered to Zoey.

"You're lost?" Introvice repeated.

"We'd appreciate any help getting out," Zoey said.

"We can help, but I have a few questions." Introvice interlocked his hands and let them hang behind him.

"What questions?" Zoey sighed, trying not to feel frustrated.

"I get you are here because you are a vampire, and dungeons allow the undead to enter." Introvice looked at the triplets. "But how are they here?"

"They have adventurer's passes. We came into the portal to escape a soul eater attack." Zoey told him.

"I see," Introvice hung his head. "As you know, we are adventurers, and it seems your friends are too. Because you are adventurers, there is a problem."

"It's a big problem." Flowerbeard nodded his head once in agreement.

Fred remained underwater. Bubbles continued to float from his mouth to the surface where they popped.

"What problem?" Zoey tried to keep a calm voice. She knew it was essential to stay calm for the triplets, so they wouldn't panic.

Introvice let his hands drop to his side. "Once an adventurer enters a dungeon, they must defeat the dungeon boss before they can leave. No one has defeated the boss yet. The dungeon is too new for that. If you want, you can join our party, and we can try to find the boss together?"

Zoey considered the proposal. If they were stuck in the dungeon, it would make sense to team up with seasoned adventurers. That way, they could learn how dungeons work. Not to mention, they'd have extra help facing some of the monsters they'd come across.

"We should join them," Hope said. "We can get loot, kill a monster, and be home in time for dinner."

"I'm hungry," Tornado said. "Dinner sounds good. Zoey, do you have pepperoni?"

"I do." Zoey materialized a few slices of pepperoni from her inventory and handed them to Tornado."

"Thanks," Tornado said.

"I don't trust the pirate," Skye said.

"I heard that," Flowerbeard said.

"I don't care if you heard," Skye said. "I don't trust you."

"Stop talking." The pirate answered.

"See," Tornado put his hands on his hips. "I told

you that you tell people to stop talking."

"No, I don't." Flowerbeard argued.

Tornado looked at Zoey. "What's wrong with the pirate."

"Maybe he's hungry," Zoey said, turning back to Flowerbeard. "Do you want some pepperoni?" She materialized another handful and held it out to him.

"Yes," he grabbed it. "Thank you.

Zoey turned back to Introvice. "We'll take you up on the offer to join you. Thank you for your help."

As she finished speaking, a still-submerged Fred sat up. Where his upper body was above the water, his legs remained submerged. He spat out water in an arcing stream, and a prompt appeared in front of Zoey:

Fred invites you to join his party. Accept invitation? Yes or no?

17: A Dungeon Without Dragons

"When you navigate a dungeon," Introvice explained, Fred and Flowerbeard to each side of him. "The dungeon has three components. The first is puzzle-solving. Large chambers—like the one we are in—are puzzle rooms.

"Within the chamber, your party must discover clues. Once you discover clues, you use them to crack puzzles. Most puzzle rooms don't have a time limit. This is such a chamber. We have as much time as we need to solve the problem this chamber provides us. In some dungeons, there are puzzles with time limits."

"What happens if you fail a timed chamber?" Skye asked with timidity.

"That depends on the chamber," Flowerbeard answered. "It might kill you."

"That's not true..." Introvice said. "I don't think it is, anyway. Sure, there are rumors of dungeons that will punish you with death for failing a puzzle. I've never seen any for myself, and I've been through hundreds of dungeons. Upon failing a puzzle, most puzzle rooms will return you to the beginning of the dungeon or to the last puzzle room. You'll have to find your way back to said puzzle room for a second chance at solving the puzzle."

"It's like an escape room." Zoey realized.

"What's an escape room?" Introvice asked.

"It's a room where you solve a puzzle." She said. "Not a big chamber like this...a small room."

"Why would people put puzzles in small rooms?" Flowerbeard asked.

Zoey looked over to Flowerbeard. "For fun."

"Puzzles aren't children's games. They aren't for fun. That makes no sense." Flowerbeard glowered. "Who would try to make puzzles fun. The audacity."

Fred put his hands on his hips and nodded his

agreement with Flowerbeard.

"Children do puzzles as toys all the time," Hope said.

"I have a pile of puzzles in my room." Skye agreed.

"What's your point?" Flowerbeard asked.

"You said puzzles weren't children's games," Hope answered.

"I'd never say that." Flowerbeard wrinkled his forehead. "Of course, puzzles are children's games."

Fred nodded his agreement with Flowerbeard.

Tornado kept his eyes fixed on Flowerbeard. "You are crazy in the brain."

"Thank you," Flowerbeard said.

"Anyway," Introvice continued his explanation of how dungeons work. "The second part of the dungeon is clearing monsters from chambers and passageways. As you clear them out, solving puzzles will become easier. Even so, the monsters do respawn from time to time, so you'll never be able to clear a dungeon in full."

"We are lucky." Flowerbeard puffed out his chest. "No other adventuring teams have found the dungeon. Not yet. That means we have all the monster killing to ourselves. It's a great opportunity to level up. When more teams find the dungeon, you're lucky to ever see a monster."

"That makes sense," Zoey said. "So, if I understand well, the first two components of dungeon navigation are solving puzzles and fighting monsters." When she saw Fred nodding, she continued. "And you said there are three components. What's the third?"

"Boss fights," Introvice said. "The first adventurers in a dungeon must face the bosses."

"There's always a main boss," Flowerbeard interjected. "In most cases, there're mini-bosses, too. Most we've faced in a dungeon are five, but I don't know that there's a limit."

"What's the lowest number of mini-bosses you've faced?" Zoey asked.

"One time," Introvice explained. "We went through a dungeon without facing any mini-bosses."

"That dungeon was the worst." Flowerbeard spat. "Mini-bosses give some of the best loot drops. A dungeon without mini-bosses is a dungeon without good loot."

"Speaking of loot," Introvice added. "There will be loot chests spread throughout the dungeon. If one party member opens the chest, everyone gets one of its items. Most chests contain consumables... Those are things you consume to help you move through the dungeon...things like potions and stuff. Any that you don't use, you can save for later dungeons or sell."

"So if a chest has a potion in it," Zoey clarified, "and someone in our party opens that chest, we all get a potion?"

Fred did a double thumbs up to answer in the affirmative.

"You can sell the loot from mini-bosses, too, right?" Hope asked.

"You can." Introvice nodded. "Though, the loot from mini-bosses doesn't go to everyone. It will go to whoever's job can use it. For example, if it is a sword, it will go to someone that uses a sword. If more than one person can use a sword, it will drop to one of the sword users at random. If no one can use a sword, it could drop to anybody."

"That makes sense," Zoey said.

"Do you have any other questions?" Introvice raised an eyebrow as he waited for an answer. When Zoey shook her head no, he relaxed his expression. "Then let's go clear the room of some monsters. Stay close to us; be careful not to draw aggro."

"What does draw aggro mean?" Tornado asked.

"It means you don't go near the monsters, or

they will become aggressive and attack you." Zoey knew the term from all the MMOs she'd played. "It's better to find isolated monsters and kill them one at a time."

"Don't worry," Introvice said. "If you stay close, they won't attack. If you do see health bars and the battle menu activates, don't panic. Flowerbeard, Fred, and I have done this a lot. We can keep you safe."

"We can fight, too." Tornado offered.

"No, Tornado," Zoey said. "He's right. It is best to let them handle things. If something happened to one of you, your parents would never forgive me."

Tornado hung his head in disappointment, but he didn't say anything.

"Here comes the first monster." Introvice pointed at a level fifteen crab. It was about twenty paces ahead, far enough from the other crabs that it wouldn't aggro any of the others. Introvice took a few steps toward the monster as he activated an ability. For some reason, the ability dropped his health down to one hp. "Stay back, and we'll keep you safe." When he said this, the battle menu popped up. It displayed the hit points of the triplets, the three adventurers, and Zoey. It also showed the hit points of the crab.

"How are you going to fight with one HP?" Zoey asked. "If you get hit, you'll die."

"I better not get hit then." He continued toward the monster, materializing a dagger in each hand. He held the weapons with the point down, blades tucked against each forearm. To his right, Fred materialized a rapier. To his left, Flowerbeard materialized a cutlass.

What happened next was a flurry of movement that Zoey struggled to follow. Introvice flashed toward the crab only to backflip when he reached it. He spun many times before landing. All the while, his daggers pointed out, cutting into the crab's carapace like an angry bicycle wheel.

Flowerbeard shot left and right like a speed skater, bouncing and dancing around the monster. With each change in direction, he chopped at one of the crab's limbs. The way he circled and changed direction appeared to disorient the crab. He was behind it, to the side, behind it, and in front. His final attack lopped off the monster's clawed hand. It turned into light and evaporated before it hit the ground.

Fred's rapier stabbed in a rapid procession, targeting weak points between the joints in the shell. With each piercing blow, sparks flew. It reminded Zoey of fireworks...not any fireworks, though. It reminded her of the ones that people put on the ground. Once lit, they shoot out sparks in every direction. As with the fireworks, Fred's attack became a volcano of sparks.

While the three adventurers attacked, the crab's HP melted away to nothing. When it hit zero, the crab's body became small orbs of light that rose as they flickered out:

You defeated the crab. You gained 600 experience points.

Crab drops three crab shells. Fred receives one crab shell. You receive one crab shell. Hope receives one crab shell.

Crab drops four crab meat. You receive four crab meat.

The experience boost put Zoey within 200 of leveling up. She knew she'd have to go through her skill tree before they fought any dungeon bosses. From video games, she knew she'd want to ensure she had every possible advantage going into those battles.

"I got to level four." Skye smiled.

"Me too!" Hope and Tornado said in unison.

"Good job, guys." Zoey looked at Skye and then

at Tornado. "And two of you never even had to leave my shoulder."

"It's called power leveling." Skye smiled.

"They have power leveling here?" Zoey asked. On Earth, gamers used the term for two things. One is when a higher-level player helps lower-level players gain experience. Power leveling also describes when a player takes advantage of an exploit to level up faster than developers intended.

"Only in dungeons," Introvice explained as he returned.

At his side, Flowerbeard looked angry. "Why does she get all the crab meat. It isn't fair."

"I bet it's because I have a food-related subjob." She answered him. "It made the food items auto-drop to me."

"It's not fair," Flowerbeard repeated.

Zoey materialized the four pieces of meat and handed them to Flowerbeard, "here. You can have them."

"Thank you," he took them, allowing them to dematerialize as he added them to his inventory.

Zoey turned her attention to Introvice. "Isn't it risky fighting with one HP?"

"I have an ability that does double damage. But it only activates when I am at one hit point." He explained. "I supplement it with an ability that allows me to receive two physical hits before I begin to receive damage. It doesn't work against magic, but crabs only have one magic attack."

"What if they used the magic attack before you killed them?" Zoey asked.

"Their eyes glow blue before they cast it. It is an aura-based spell, so if they did use it, I could move away in time."

"It seems risky," Zoey said.

"It's not that bad." Introvice insisted. "You don't

get hit, you don't die. It's easy."

"Okay," Zoey said. "If you say so. Also...now that I know power leveling is a thing...it's important the pixies and I participate in the battles with you."

"Why's that?" Introvice asked.

"I have a friend. His name is Pete. Pete thinks that your attribute bonuses at level up tie to what skills you raise throughout the level." Zoey shrugged. "When it comes to stuff like this, I believe him. And if he's correct, it wouldn't benefit the triplets to level without skilling up at the same time. It would make them weak for their level."

"Your friend Pete is smart," Introvice said.

"Debatable," Zoey smiled.

The triplets giggled at her joke.

Introvice continued. "Not many people understand how skills relate to attributes at level up."

"You're telling me he's right?" Zoey's eyes widened. She thought he might be, but she didn't expect to confirm it with a seasoned adventurer.

"He is. In adventuring circles, some of us have noticed we get boosts that tie to skills. Though, we worry about what the moderators might think if they find out that we know about it. They might patch how leveling works, using standard attribute bonuses instead."

"I'll tell Pete to keep his discovery under wraps," Zoey said.

"Thank you," Introvice stretched his arms over his head before adding. "Now, you said you want to help the pixies fight some monsters?"

18: Underwater Palaces Belong in Cartoons

"Pete," Aqua looked through the hatch and into the living room below her. "That is my father...and you fell on him...great..."

"Hello, Aqua's Dad." Pete tried to act cool. Even so, he knew there was no acting cool toward someone after falling on them while wearing only a swimsuit. Even though it wasn't the worst first impression he left on someone – that other time was much worse. It was a struggle not to let the embarrassment show. "I'm Pete."

"He's the one that can defeat Charybdis." She explained.

With slow caution, her father returned to an upright position. He looked down at the footprint which Pete had left on his white dress shirt. Then he scanned his eyes to where Pete remained sprawled on the floor. "Hello, Pete." He paused, inhaling a deep breath. "I don't mean to be rude, but considering the circumstances, what I'm about to ask you is a fair question."

"Ask away," Pete stood up, using the living room floor like floor on land. Aside from the weightlessness, he almost felt like he *was* back on land.

"What makes you think you can conquer Charybdis when you can't even defeat the front door?"

"To be fair," he began. "Aqua is the one that thinks I can defeat Charybdis. I don't even know what a Charybdis is. But if she thinks I can help, I will try." He held his hand out again. "Like I said before, my name is Pete...Pete the pizzaman."

Her father offered Pete a hard stare, his eyes looking straight into Pete's. Then her father's expression softened, and he offered his hand to Pete. "My name is Kai."

As they shook hands, Pete said. "Nice to meet

you, Kai."

"I don't mean to be rude, Pete," Kai told him. "You seem like a nice enough person. Even so, I don't see you being able to defeat Charybdis. He's a water-based monster. Your swimming skill is…" he paused to consider how to phrase it. "Subpar."

"It is at even par," Pete told him.

"How do you figure?"

"It is at zero. Isn't that par?" Pete asked. "Wait…do merpeople have golf? How do you golf underwater?"

"Of course, we have golf." Kai's stern expression returned. "You do realize that every skill starts at zero. It isn't possible to be lower than that."

"Yes, it is." Pete hung his head. "I have a negative tree-climbing skill."

"A negative skill?" Kai asked.

"Yup," Pete confirmed.

"You realize that doesn't help your case as the potential slayer of Charybdis?" Kai raised an eyebrow.

"Yup," Pete repeated before asking. "How does underwater golf work?"

"Dad," Aqua returned to the conversation. "Worst case, we teach him how to swim. You need to see this guy slap stuff before you judge him."

"Right," Pete agreed, lifting his head and locking eyes with Kai. "Watch me slap stuff. I can slap with enough force to put Gallagher's sledgehammer to shame."

"What's a Gallagher's sledgehammer?" Aqua asked.

"He's the guy that splatters the watermelons," Pete explained, turning his head to look at Aqua.

"What's a watermelon?" Kai and Aqua asked in unison.

"It's a…" Pete let his head hang again. "…Nevermind…it's not important. The point is I can slap better than the best slappers... Wait, do they have slapping competitions here?"

Aqua ignored the question, speaking instead to her father. "Dad, if we teach him to swim. He can defeat Charybdis. He is super strong."

"How do you propose we get his swimming skill high enough to be useful?" Kai asked.

"I take him dancing." She replied.

"Dancing?" Pete said, remembering all the jr. high school dances he'd been to. During each, he held up the wall. Someone had to stand against it to make sure it didn't fall. By high school, he'd resigned himself to not finding dance partners. As such, he'd refrained from attending high school dances. In short, Pete didn't dance. "I don't dance."

"That's too bad," she told him. "Because you have to go to the club with me, and you have to dance...and party."

"Party? Mermaids have parties?" He asked.

"Of course they do." She swam closer to him, saying. "Everyone knows merpeople love to party."

Pete realized he wasn't included in the collective everyone because he did not know merpeople love to party. "How does partying teach me how to swim?"

"Before we waste time teaching a human how to swim," Kai said. "We should take Pete to the king. If the king tests Pete, and Pete passes, we can worry about teaching him how to swim."

"That makes sense," Aqua said, and without hesitation, she grabbed Pete's arm with both of hers and began up toward the hatch.

"Cool," Pete said as she dragged him through the water, her dad following behind. "We're doing this again."

"Don't be a baby," Aqua told him. "No whining allowed."

Pete tried to think of a witty retort, something

about how he wasn't whiney, but nothing came to mind. Instead, he remained silent for the rest of the way to the palace.

When they arrived, Aqua descended at the front gate of the palace. Pete had not realized it before, but a dome rested atop the palace wall, protecting the castle on all sides. The only entrances became small archways protected by guards.

Aqua released Pete's arm when he was about three paces above the seabed. He landed on his feet, and it pushed up silt.

A confused pair of guards stared at Pete, then at Aqua, then at Kai as he swam down to join them. Then the guards looked at each other and then back to Aqua. After an awkward silence, one looked at Aqua and spoke. "I'm sorry...I'm not sure I understand."

The other said. "Did you capture this human? You know you aren't allowed to take the humans as prisoners; those are the king's rules."

"This is Pete." She explained. "He's powerful. He slaps hard. He can use a sword." She looked at him. "You can use a sword, right?"

He shook his head no.

"He can't use a sword." She continued, picking up speed with each word. "But he can slap, and he's strong, and..." She paused, looking at him. "...can you do other things? Or do you only slap?"

"I can make small fireballs with my hands. Watch." He tried to cast a fire spell, but the water snuffed it out before it was even a spark. He looked back at Aqua. "Nope, I can only slap stuff."

"You must be an amazing slapper." One of the guards spoke with a dry tone.

"Can you slap something for us, now?" The other guard asked.

"Like what?" Pete asked.

"I don't know." The guard answered. "You're the

slapping expert. If you come here claiming you know how to slap things, you should bring things to slap."

"In fairness," Pete said. "I wasn't planning on being here today. If I knew, I would have prepared...brought a small boulder or something...wait...do you have any small boulders that you don't need? I could slap one of those."

"Sorry, we're fresh out of boulders." The guard said.

"Do you have any watermelons?" Pete asked.

"What's a watermelon?" The guard asked.

"You guys are missing out by not having watermelons," Pete said. "They are delicious."

"We're getting off track," Aqua said. "Is there any chance we can..."

"Merpeople have tracks?" Pete interrupted? "You have underwater trains that run on tracks? And you have underwater golf? But you don't have watermelon? You should consider a shift in priorities. More delicious fruit. Less non-sensical transportation."

The guard looked at Aqua. "Is he always like this?"

"I'm not sure," Aqua said. "I met him today. It appears he's using humor to deal with a stressful situation. It's a psychological defense mechanism."

Pete wasn't sure what a psychological defense mechanism was. He was okay with not knowing. At least he knew about watermelons.

Kai spoke next. "Do you think we could take him to the king? The king should have some type of test for him. Right?"

The guards nodded. It wasn't that they knew about a test. Nor was there a protocol in place for the situation. But letting the king decide made sense. After nodding, they moved to each side of the entrance, and a glass within the archway slid open. The guard on the right swam through the opening.

"This way, please." The guard on the left said, holding an open hand. Then he looked at Aqua and Kai. "Both of you will need to wait here."

Kai and Aqua agreed to wait at the gate, and Pete did his best to swim, following behind the first guard.

The guards, Kai, and Aqua did their best not to laugh at Pete.

Pete did his best not to feel embarrassed.

While he struggled to swim, Pete took in the strange beauty of the castle. "Are all the walls made of Jade?" He asked the guard.

"Or marble," The guard said. "For the most part, the floors are marble. There are some gold inlays, too."

"That is so cool," Pete said, looking at a few castle spires. They appeared to be like the pillar-houses that the other merpeople lived in. Like the other homes, these pillars ranged in height from three stories to ten stories. At the castle's center, a large pillar rose twenty feet. The difference between the castle pillars and the other pillars was how a wide base—more traditional of land buildings—connected the pillars.

When Pete followed the guard into that base structure, he recognized how the base created corridors and expansive rooms. Each gallery reflected light in a different direction. It was like swimming through a building made from a rainbow. "This place is like a cartoon," Pete said.

The guard nodded his agreement. "It is. Isn't it?"

A few corridors later, Pete followed the guard into a room the size of a football field. It was as tall as it was wide. Overhead, rays of colored light beamed through circular windows. A red carpet—no, it wasn't carpet; it was some type of moss—created a rectangular pathway to two golden thrones at the far end of the room. Mermaid guards lined the moss carpet-not-carpet on each side.

In one of the thrones sat a man with a dark beard and piercing green eyes. His muscles were larger than Pete realized muscles could be. Even his tail was ripped. He wore shiny golden armor with a sword on his hip. The sword's hilt was jade, shaped like an octopus, with its arms wrapping around to form a grip.

The other throne remained empty.

As Pete and the guards swam into the room, the man on the throne stood and asked. "Is that a human in my throne room?" His voice boomed and echoed. Pete wasn't sure if it was the king's voice that was so powerful or the acoustics of the room. Pete decided it was a combination of both.

The guards moved to each side of Pete and signaled Pete to stop swimming. Pete stopped, allowing himself to stand on the red carpet moss stuff. It felt soft under his bare feet. The fact that he wasn't wearing shoes reminded him how he wasn't wearing a shirt, either. *Great,* he thought to himself. *I met a cute mermaid's dad in my swimsuit. Now, I get to meet a king in my swimsuit. At this point, I should plan on going to my college graduation in a swimsuit, too.*

"This is a human." One of the guards said.

"And he is in your throne room." The other added.

"I thought my rules were clear." The king hung his head. "No kidnapping or imprisoning humans."

"This is no prisoner." One guard said.

"He's a champion." The other said.

"He's here to slap Charybdis." They both said in unison.

"Right," Pete agreed. "I am here to slap Charybdis."

"Slap?" The king raised an eyebrow. "Charybdis?"

"Problem is," one of the guards said. "We aren't sure if he knows how to slap. We need to test him."

"If you didn't kidnap him?" The king scanned his eyes back and forth between his guards. "How did he get here?"

"That's a good question." One guard said.

"Aqua didn't tell us." The other said.

"Aqua?" The king sighed, fixing his eyes on Pete. "Did Aqua kidnap you?"

"No," Pete fibbed, not wanting to get Aqua in trouble. She was the nicest mermaid he'd ever met. Then he realized she was the only mermaid he'd ever met. Still, he needed to protect her. "We're friends. I wanted to help."

"And she thinks you can help?" The king asked.

"She does."

"And you're good at slapping things?" The king asked.

"That's right," Pete confirmed.

"Okay," the king agreed, relaxing back into his throne. "Follow the guards to the Call'isuem. Let's test your slapping prowess."

Pete didn't know what prowess meant. He guessed it meant something like his ability or skill. At least he knew what a watermelon was.

19: I Don't Like This Kind of Test

The same two guards guided Pete to the castle's guard station. It was a small square room with traditional swords and spears in racks on the left wall. Rows of triple bunk beds lined the other wall. Merpeople beds—Pete noticed—had straps to hold the person in place as they slept...like a loose seatbelt. He imagined a bed without the straps, a mermaid floating away, and waking up in an unfamiliar place. It would be like that one time when he was five...when he sleepwalked from his bed and to the basement. He woke up on a giant beanbag. It was disorienting. A tunnel held place in the far wall. Some mermen soldiers moved about the space. Another merman floated near a desk.

The one at the desk stopped Pete and his escorts. "Is there a reason you aren't guarding the front of the castle?"

"You see," the first guard said. "This is Pete. He's a pizzaman. If you haven't heard of pizzamen, they are great warriors, powerful slappers."

"He might be strong enough to defeat Charybdis." The second guard explained. "The king wants us to test'm against Finnegan. It's hardly a fair fight if you ask me. But if he comes out against Finnegan, we'll know he's legitimate."

"I see," the desk attendant guard turned to two of the others. "Send messengers to inform the public. There will be a Call'isuem battle today...Finnegan versus Pete the pizzaman." The attendant returned his attention to Pete. "Make your way through the tunnel on the far wall. It will take you to the Call'isuem. Once there, remain on guard. Your test will begin shortly."

Within a thick glass sphere at the center of the Call'isuem, Pete stood. Around him, merpeople filled the stands. They all appeared anxious to see the supposed hero who could save them from Charybdis. He was still in a swimsuit; he was still barefoot. After the king's test, Pete would need to see about getting some clothes.

Though he could see the crowds of merpeople around him, he couldn't hear them through the glass of the sphere. He could see their mouths opening and closing. Some of them clapped. *The glass sphere must have some sound-blocking properties*, he realized. The sphere itself recessed into a broad metal base. The base provided the way into and out of the sphere, connecting the sphere to the guard station on Pete's side. On the opposite side of the sphere—within the base—was a second hatch. Pete guessed it went to another tunnel.

"Now," a voice began to speak. It reminded Pete of a Monday Night Football pre-game announcer. "We have the test you've all been waiting for. In the sphere, you have Pete the pizzaman, watermelon slayer."

People don't slay watermelons, Pete thought to himself. *Why do they think I can kill watermelons?* Then he remembered how many times he had brought up watermelons since he'd met Aqua. Then he thought about what type of watermelons would require slaying. Would they be like the nightshade terrors: vines for arms and legs, a melon for a head, pointed teeth, and beady eyes?

"Pete," the announcer continued, "is a master slapper with the strength of giants. If you had a boulder, he could slap it better than anyone."

Pete puffed out his chest, wishing he could hear the crowd cheering for him. Then he realized they might be booing him. What if they wanted him to lose?

"His opponent today will be a crowd favorite." Pete listened with great intent to the following line. "Finnigan the bull shark."

Pete chuckled at the name. Finnigan was a great

shark name because of the fin part. As the announcer announced the shark, the hatch on the other side of the sphere began to open. When it opened in full, a shark's head began to appear…inch by terrifying inch.

Though, Pete expected to see the shark's nose first. Instead, he saw two pointed horns. They curved like a bull's. Attached to the set of horns was a traditional bull shark. It was traditional for Pete anyway…what he expected a shark's head to be. It was broad with a wide, frowning mouth.

As the first dorsal fin appeared, it reminded Pete of boat's sail. He estimated it to be at least two feet tall and almost as wide. The second dorsal fin was a miniature clone of the first. Pectoral fins extended to each side like airplane wings. Powerful strokes of the shark's tail pushed it through the opening, and it did a small circle around the hatch before turning to face Pete. Above the shark's head, Pete saw words. They read Finnegan the Shark Level 14.

It's like he knows there's a crowd, Pete realized. *If he's a crowd favorite, I better not drop his HP to zero. I don't want to make the merpeople mad at me.*

"Let the king's test commence." As the voice finished speaking, the hatch in the sphere's base closed, and a chime sounded.

In response to the chime, the shark charged.

In elementary school, Pete had been a shark aficionado. He knew there were more than four-hundred species. By the teeth, he could identify about a quarter of those species. One thing he knew about bull sharks—the ones on Earth—was that they maxed out at around ten feet. At first glance, Pete thought this one was bigger.

Another fact that Pete knew about bull sharks was that they had more testosterone than any other animal. Under different circumstances, Pete might have wondered if an animal on Round had more testosterone than a bull shark. But he didn't have time to think about that. Instead, he needed to worry about not getting eaten.

As the shark charged, it lowered its horns to impale Pete, and he understood how bullfighters must feel...if they didn't have a cape...or shirts...or swords...and if they were underwater... After some consideration, Pete realized he didn't know what it was like to be a bullfighter. Bullfighters had it much easier.

Thirty feet separated Pete and the shark, and Pete considered his options. As he thought about how to defend himself, his battle menu activated. He tried not to let the battle log, HP bars, or anything else distract him. *Should I jump to the side?* On land, he would have felt more comfortable with this strategy. As it was, he wasn't sure how much the water resistance would restrict his movements. Plus, the shark had a super wide head. It would be tough to clear the mouth and the horns.

At Twenty feet, Pete noticed that mouth begin to...smile. It looked like a smile. Did the shark know what it was doing? Was it more than a mindless animal? The smile revealed sinister rows of daggerlike teeth. Pete considered trying to swim away from the shark. Though, he knew it would catch him.

When the shark was ten feet away, Pete considered activating Slap' M Silly and trying to slap his opponent. Though, the shark's horns were longer than Pete's arms. It would impale him before he did any damage.

Five feet separated them when Pete made his decision. With a precision that was driven by panic-induced adrenaline, Pete let his reflexes take over. Those reflexes caused him to raise his arms and grip the horns with his arms, one horn in each arm.

The force of the collision as his hands met the horns jarred his body. His elbows and shoulders took the worst of it, but he felt it down to his toes. Where Pete's body had taken damage—twelve HP of damage to be exact—the shark appeared unphased. It continued straight toward Pete, attempting to chomp at his core.

Using the grip he held on the horns, Pete swung his legs away from the teeth, and they missed by inches. The shark continued to swim in circles, turning its head back and forth and trying to bite Pete.

Pete continued to use his grip on the horns to evade by swinging his legs. Though, he realized he couldn't stay on the defensive forever. If he did, the shark would land a bite. It was a matter of time. And a bite is all it would take. Though Pete didn't have a stamina bar, he didn't need one to know he was tiring.

Plus, the initial collision with the shark had drained a quarter of his hp.

As Finnegan the shark thrashed up and down, left and right. All Pete could do was hold on for dear life...until his hands began to slip. Centimeter by centimeter, his hold weakened.

Finnegan the bull shark appeared to recognize this, so he chambered his head to one side before swinging it back with purposeful intent. Pete's grip gave way in full, and he zipped through the water, crashing headfirst into the arena's glass.

For a second, his vision blurred. Next to his HP bar, he saw an unfamiliar icon that looked like stars spinning above a person's head. *Huh,* he thought, *Zoey was right. There is a debuff icon for concussions.* The icon went away, his vision cleared, and he stood up. With his HP under half, he knew he'd have to be extra careful. With that thought in mind, he scanned the arena for Finnegan.

The bull shark headed toward him at full speed, horns gleaming with malice. Pete forced calm into himself, and he remained still, inhaling slow, deep breaths. *Five.* He began to count backward in his mind. *Four.* Inhale. *Three.* Exhale. *Two.* Focus. *One*. Finnegan stabbed toward him with a final lung, using all its momentum. Pete dodged the horns, using his hands to catch the shark's nose and flipping up and over.

Unable to slow itself, the shark's horns impaled the glass. And the horns remained stuck. It tried to free itself, whipping its tail back and forth, a tail which Pete was careful to avoid. Trying—and failing—not to look clumsy in front of the spectators, Peter swam-walked next to the shark's head. He was careful to avoid its tail. Then he lifted his hand, activated Slap' M Silly, and swung. His open palm connected with a hollow thwack,

The shark's body went limp, unconscious but not dead. A prompt appeared:

You defeated Finnegan the bull shark. Because you didn't kill him, you gained 0 experience points. Good on you for not killing him, though. Even though you can't swim, you are a good person.

A second prompt appeared:

Slapping proficiency raises by 4. Slapping proficiency increases to 405.6.

Evasion raises by 10. Evasion raises to 32.2.

"Thanks...I think..." Pete told the prompt as he blinked it away. As he did, he noticed the hatch which led to the guard station tunnel begin to open. Through it, swam the two guards. Without hesitation, they started toward Pete.

"Thanks for not killing him." One of the guards said.

"The merpeople would've never forgiven you for that." The second added.

"He seemed like a nice shark." Pete didn't believe himself when he said Finnegan was nice. In reality, he didn't think Finnegan was nice...not by any metric. Even so, he'd won the fight, and it was important to be a good sport.

The first guard wrinkled his forehead. "Bull sharks aren't nice. They try to eat you."

"Right," Pete agreed. "I meant that he seemed likable...by bull shark standards."

"Ah, yeah..." the first guard relaxed his expression. "By bull shark standards...that makes sense."

"You did great in that fight." The second guard joined the conversation. "I understand why those watermelons you slapped never had a chance."

Pete hoped someday he could clarify what he

meant when he brought up watermelons. For the time being, he chose to leave things as they were. "So I passed the test?"

"Sure did," the first told him. "Follow us back to the king's chamber. Aside from an adventurer's pass, he has a surprise for you."

The two guards began back toward the hatch, and Pete followed. As they entered, the hatch closed behind them, leaving them in a dim tunnel. As his adrenaline waned, Pete took a relaxing breath, and his nerves began to calm. Then a thought came to him, and his panic returned. *If Finnegan the bull shark was this difficult to defeat, how much worse is Charybdis?*

20: Triplets Trampling Trouble

"In adventuring, you have three main types of jobs." Introvice began. "You have your healers, your tanks, and your DPS."

"What's DPS mean?" Hope asked. She and her brothers had equipped the raiderball pads from their inventory over their usual t-shirts to protect themselves during the upcoming battles.

"It means damage per second," Skye answered. He was familiar with the term from some games he played on his communication box.

"Right," Introvice said. "DPS means damage per second. Party members in charge of DPS are responsible for lowering the HP of the monsters they fight."

Fred held up two fingers.

"Why does he have two fingers up?" Hope looked back and forth between Introvice and Fred.

"He means to say there are two types of DPS party members. There are those that do physical damage with a weapon, and there are spellcasters."

"I do spells," Tornado said. "Skye hits stuff. We're DPS."

"Skye hits stuff?" Flowerbeard asked.

In a shy effort to avoid eye contact, Skye looked down and nodded.

"He hits with orbchakus," Tornado said. "And pizza-cutter-chakus."

Fred offered an inquisitive cock of the head.

Skye held out his open hands and allowed a pair of pizza-cutter-chakus to form. In essence, it was a pair of straight-handled, wooden pizza cutters. A thick nylon chord connected the handles. Once the weapons had materialized, Skye went into a kata. It began by swinging the weapons in a figure-eight pattern. Then he zipped left and zagged to the right. All the while, he would switch from a figure eight to an inverted figure eight pattern. Then he'd flip the weapons behind his back and between his legs. At times, he'd let go of the weapon and let the rope roll around the back of his hand only to catch the weapon again. His weapon was a blur, and so was he.

Eyes wide, Flowerbeard spoke in a monotone voice. "That's impressive, but I bet I could do that too If I wanted, but I don't. It takes too much time. Like whatever."

"You say weird stuff," Tornado told Flowerbeard.

Before Flowerbeard could respond, Introvice interrupted. "We're getting off track. As I was saying, we have DPS like Tornado and Skye. In dungeon parties, aside from DPS jobs, there are healing jobs." He scanned his eyes between Zoey and Hope. "Are either of you a healer?"

"I have healing magic," Hope said.

"What spells?" Introvice asked.

"Fix an Owie," Hope answered.

"You have a spell called Fix an Owie?" Introvice asked. "I've never heard of that spell before."

"Yup," Hope nodded, then cast the spell on Introvice. "See...Fix an Owie."

"I also have Fix an Owie," Zoey said.

"But you are a vampire, right?" Introvice asked.

"Yes," Zoey nodded.

"And you have healing?"

She nodded again.

"A vampire healer?"

She shook her head no. "I'm a tank."

"A healing tank?" He scratched his head, trying to understand.

"I'm a paladin." She grinned.

"A vampire paladin?" He rubbed his eyes. "Is that allowed?"

"I guess so," She shrugged. "But we're getting off-topic. You were about to explain how we fight monsters as a team. You were going to say it's my job to get hit by the monster while Skye and Tornado damage it as fast as possible. Then you were going to explain how Hope's job is to stay back and restore HP to the party as we take damage from the monster."

"You've fought in a party before?" Introvice asked.

"You could say that," Zoey said. "I am still getting used to balancing enmity management abilities, but I have a few. I should be able to keep hate."

"That'll help," Introvice said. "So—in the end—all that remains is to practice with a few lower-level mobs. Set up as a party against that wall," Introvice pointed to a corner space. "Keep Hope in the corner for heals. That way, nothing can sneak behind her. I'll send Fred to go aggro a monster and bring it back to you. Zoey, as he runs by, pull hate."

"Got it." Zoey agreed, and she and the triplets moved to the corner, and Fred ran off to aggro a monster. While he did, Zoey materialized her fork and shield. Within thirty seconds, Fred was on his way back with a crab. When he ran past the group, the crab chased behind him. When it was near Zoey, she activated her skill Draw Hate.

The crab redirected from chasing Fred and scuttled toward Zoey. As it drew closer, Zoey noticed it moved sideways rather than forward. When it was close enough, it spun to face Zoey, and its claws snapped.

She raised her shield and deflected the first snapping claw to the left. Then she swung the shield down and to the right, blocking the second claw. Then she activated Strong Draw Hate as Skye maneuvered behind the crab and went to work. He whipped his cutter-chakus back and forth. With each swing, the blades dug into the carapace, and the creature's HP dropped.

Hope and Tornado remained in the back corner.

Tornado appeared to experiment with different spells. He fluctuated between lightning-based magic and fire-based attacks. Zoey admired the ingenuity of Tornado in choosing those spells. In traditional RPGs, water-based monsters are weak to fire or lightning magic. She wondered if Tornado had some knowledge about monster weaknesses from before. Or had he reasoned it out for himself? She'd have to ask him later.

Hope cast a spell on each party member called Don't Get Hurt. It raised their physical defense by ten percent. She followed up with a spell called Little by Little, which increased HP by a percentage based on the max HP. Since no one had taken damage, Zoey wasn't sure how much HP it regenerated.

The crab's attacks rotated in a predictable pattern. Left claw. Right claw. Left claw. Right claw. Between blocks, Zoey tried to stab with her fork but realized it didn't cause much damage against the hard shell. If the attacks didn't help keep the crab focused on her, she wouldn't have wasted the energy on them.

As Zoey lulled into a complacent sequence of left, right blocking with her shield, she almost missed the crab's flashing blue eyes. "It's going to use an AoE spell," She warned Skye, who hovered back and away from the monster. "Get some distance."

Foamy bubbles emerged from beneath the crab, forming a ring around it. The ring grew in height and diameter until the individual bubbles shot like bullets in every direction. From the time the crab's eyes flashed to the time the bubbles shot was a matter of seconds, but they were important seconds.

During them, Skye had given himself enough space to evade the projectile bubbles. And Zoey positioned herself between the spell caster pixies—Tornado and Hope—and the crab. Using her shield, Zoey intercepted the bubbles. They struck against the flat surface of her shield with a force she hadn't expected. It made her feel like she was trying to stop a car.

The unexpected blow sent her through the air. She landed with a thud that would have knocked the wind from her lungs. Fortunate for her, vampires didn't have to breathe. She slid across the ground, stopping beneath Hope and Tornado. Her HP had dipped to 160. She'd almost lost half her HP in one blow. Another bubble attack or two would drop her HP to zero.

She couldn't let that happen. She had to protect the triplets. As she went to stand, she realized she had a problem aside from her HP. Her body wasn't moving how she wanted. When she tried to move her left leg, her right arm moved. When she tried to move her left arm, her right leg moved. Her body control had reversed. She noticed an icon that looked like birds flying around someone's head. Was it an icon for confusion?

"The bubble attack," Introvice shouted to her. "It leaves a film over your body. Until it evaporates, you're body controls will be opposite."

As Zoey struggled to control her body, the crab scuttled toward her. Zoey was about to ask for Introvice's help when she heard Tornado shout, "firenado!"

In the periphery of her vision, Zoey saw a light flash from Tornado's body. A fiery tornado erupted around the crab. Wind cut into the hard blue shell. Heat rendered the carapace all but useless as the spinning fire burned away the remainder of the crab's HP. When the monster's HP reached zero, it fell in a slump.

You defeated the crab. You gained 600 experience.

Congratulations! You reached level 12!

With the level-up, Zoey's HP returned to full. And as the crab's body became light, the substance on her body did too. This allowed her to regain control of herself. While she pushed herself to her feet, she pulled up her character sheet. She wondered if Pete's slapping her shield had impacted her attributes like he thought it would.

NAME: Zoey **RACE:** Vampire **JOB:** Paladin
(Subjob) Pizzawoman

LEVEL 12

HP: 3270/3270
MP: 50/50

ALIGNMENT: Chaotic Good
RELIGION: None
LANGUAGES: English,
Japanese
Common

STR: 43
DEX: 43
VIT: 191
INT: 50
SPR: 36
AGI: 71

GENDER: Female
HEIGHT: 5'5
WEIGHT: 110 lbs
AGE: 19
EYES: Black
Hair: Green

LEFT ARM: Combat Pizza Peel
RIGHT ARM: Combat Pizza Fork
HEAD: M&P Combat Hat
BODY: M&P Battle Top
LEGS: M&P Battle Skirt
FEET: Combat Boots
HANDS: Unequipped
NECKLACE: Gold Pendant
EARRINGS: Obsidian Earrings
Ring 1: Silver Claddagh
Ring 2: Ring of Day Walking

ATTACK: 3794
DEFENSE: 4728
MAGIC ATTACK: 25
MAGIC DEFENSE: 606

PROFICIENCIES: Slapping Skill 11.2, Air Hockey 121.9, Tree Climbing 12.2, Pizza Cutter 12.4, Pizza Peel 325.5, Evasion 74.1, Pizza Fork 100.9, Light Armor 221.2

Experience: 339/1800

When she saw her vitality and hit points increase, she realized that Pete's training worked. Not only did it work, it raised her stats higher than she thought possible. At level twelve, her defense was four times higher than it had been at level eleven. Her maximum hit points had gone from 310 to over 3,000. *Pete was always good at breaking games.* She admitted to herself as she closed her character page.

Once Hope realized they had won the battle without casualties, she smiled. Her level had raised to five, and so had her brother's. As they hovered next to her, she told Tornado. "That was an awesome firenado. Good work."

"Firenados are disasters." Tornado beamed. "But they are not natural disasters. They are not natural. Like ghosts...but ghosts aren't disasters."

As Tornado finished his explanation about ghosts not being natural disasters, Skye joined his siblings. He said. "I got a new skill."

"What's it called?" Hope asked.

"Mmmm..." Skye squinted his eyes together. Hope knew he was examining the skill within his pixie skill tree. "It's called chucker. It lets me throw my cutter-chakus, and they come back like a boomerang."

"Cool." Hope smiled. She began to go through her own skill tree. She decided to put off learning any new spells, though she saw a few options. There was a spell that would increase the magic defense of its target. There was an AoE version of Fix an Owie. There was a spell that would increase the movement speed of its target. She didn't have the skill points to allocate into more than one or two skills, so she decided to wait. As they cleared the dungeon of other monsters, they might need a specific ability. If that situation came up, her options would be open.

"Is everyone okay?" Zoey asked.

"All good," Hope said.

Skye nodded and smiled.

"Tornado," Tornado said.

"Okay," Zoey said. Let's join Flowerbeard, Introvice, and Fred and clear this dungeon."

Tornado loved to think about disasters. As he helped to clear the chamber of crabs, this didn't change. During battles, he wondered what would happen to a crab if an earthquake and meteor shower occurred at the same time. He wouldn't know until he saw for himself. Too bad he didn't have a spell for summoning meteors. Though, he could use a spell to make small bits of fire fall like raindrops. Fire rain was kind of like a meteor shower. "Meteor quake!" He shouted as he combined his fire rain with an earthquake. The crab didn't stand a chance. Neither did the next crab. That trend continued until there were no crabs left in the chamber. At that point, the pixies were level ten, and Zoey had reached level fifteen. Tornado danced with joy. They were one tough party.

Skye listened with practiced intent as Introvice explained. "Now that we've cleared the chamber of crabs, we have some time before they respawn. We need to take this time to solve the puzzle."

"What is the puzzle?" Hope asked.

"Sometimes it's a hidden door. Sometimes it's a hidden switch to a door. In this case, we must figure out how to reach that opening." He pointed at a small opening against the far wall. "So far as I can tell, the dungeon continues through that door."

"That's easy." Tornado began to fly in the direction of the opening.

"Tornado, wait," Skye told him. "For us, it is easy because we can fly." Skye looked at Zoey, Introvice,

Flowerbeard, and Fred. "They can't fly. We have to figure out how to help them reach the opening."

"Oh," Tornado looped back, hovering beside his brother, "right. How do we help them."

"I'm working on it." Skye looked over the room. He studied the flow of the water, the shape of the wall and ceiling, and the patterns in the tornadoes which formed in sporadic formations. *No,* Skye realized. *There is nothing sporadic in their formations.* "Zoey, I know what we need to do to get you up there." Skye flew over to a spot in the water and pointed down at it. "Zoey, stand here." He stopped pointing, flying to a nearby spot. He pointed down again. "When a waterspout forms, jump here."

"What are you talking about?" Hope asked.

"Okay, I understand," Zoey said. "If the waterspouts are strong enough to lift us, we can use them to jump from one to another."

"Right," Skye said. "The force is strong enough, but it can only hold a person for a few seconds before they sink into it. That's why you must move from one to the next. I'll tell you where to jump."

"Okay," Zoey agreed. "Show me the way.

Skye watched as Zoey moved to the initial spot. No sooner had the spout lifted her when she jumped to the second spout. From there, Skye guided, saying, "jump here." Then he'd zip to the next spot. "Now, here."

Zoey made it through six jumps before she mistimed one and fell, splashing into the water. As she sat there, she looked up at Skye, "how many jumps is this?"

"Twelve total," Skye said, pointing at the different spout locations as he spoke. "Here, here, here, here..."

"Got it," Zoey said. "Let's try this again."

Six attempts later, Zoey found herself inside the

opening. It widened into a tunnel like the initial passageway where they'd entered the dungeon. She looked down at Fred, Introvice, and Flowerbeard. "I don't know how Skye saw that pattern in the waterspouts, but this looks like the right way." She moved her eyes to Skye. "Good work. You are one smart pixie."

Upon hearing Zoey's praise, Skye beamed with pride. He couldn't help but smile.

21: Moderator's Journey

Forests are more fun when they breathe, Geb thought to himself. It wasn't that they breathed for real; he understood that. Rather, certain conditions made the forest look like the ground was breathing. It occurred when tree roots remained trapped in loosened soil. Then—when the fluctuating wind caught the same trees—it lifted them in gusts. With each gust, the earth rose and lowered, making it look like the forest was breathing.

In the forest where Geb walked, there was no wind. Also, the trees looked thick. It indicated the soil was strong...healthy...and muddy. During his walk, Geb had experienced long moments in that rain. Where the canopy caught much of it, heavy droplets formed on the overhead leaves and branches. From those, the drops fell, pitter-pattering atop Geb's head.

Though, the water didn't bother him. Nor did the water bother his goose. They enjoyed the unpredictability of the weather. It kept their lives interesting; it made their long walks more enjoyable.

He did other things to keep his walks enjoyable. For example, Geb preferred to make his own rather than take a well-trodden path. In a forest, this meant pushing through the branches of trees and the foliage of bushes. It even meant finding his way over and around fallen trees.

Not to mention, whenever he strayed from trodden paths, he was more likely to come across a hungry predator: bears, tigers, and dragons. In the kingdom of Lake, the bears were small. They preferred eating berries to meat. And there were no tigers. Where he might have trouble was with dragons. The black-spotted forest hoppers frequented the area.

They—like their name indicated—boasted bright yellow scales with patches of dark black scales. Those scales created spots resembling those of a jaguar. Where all dragons were giant, the hopper-type dragons were on the smaller end of the dragon spectrum. In the case of the black spotted forest hoppers, they were quadrupeds. An average one stood five feet tall and nine feet long. Aside from their powerful hind legs, their bodies were narrow. What they lacked in mass, they made up for in nimbleness. They could hop from tree to tree in a flash with unmatched agility and precision.

Their faces were long and narrow, with recessed eyes. The bone above those eyes rose into short spikes. While jumping, a clear scale slides over the eye like a protective eyelid. It prevented the dragons from damaging their eyes on branches as they hopped. When threatened, they produced bursts of electrical energy. Due to this, some people referred to the black spotted forest hoppers as lesser storm dragons.

For his part, Geb had never seen one of these dragons. Of course, he hadn't. He'd never been to the Continental Bridge Forest. He had been in the area before. But the last time he'd visited was long ago. The forest didn't exist then. Much of the wildlife didn't exist either. In part, that's why he'd chosen to stray from the walking path. He wanted to experience new things: discover new fruit on the trees, see leaves with different shapes, and hunt unique wildlife. He hoped some of that wildlife would be dragons.

"Do you smell that, Cackler?" Geb asked his goose.

Cackler, the goose, honked in the affirmative before making a subsequent sequence of whistles.

"No, I don't think it's a dragon."

Cackler chirped a few more sounds.

"Yes, that's what I thought." Geb sighed. "Humans trying to hide."

Cackler murmured.

"They'd do that for two reasons," Geb answered. "First, they are afraid and want to hide from us. Second, they think we are defenseless, lost travelers, and they want to ambush us."

Cackler offered a few more murmurs.

"Yes, that's my opinion too. If it is the case, it should make for a fun encounter. See if you can get a view of them from the sky. Count how many there are and gauge how likely they are to attack."

Cackler honked once and then took off, ascending until he reached the canopy. From there, he weaved between branches until he disappeared behind them.

Geb continued through the forest, listening to every shifting sound. He used those sounds to determine the positions of the people around him. At first, the people moved away from him. Also, they had a stealthy quality to their movements. Whoever they were, they were good at hiding. It made it difficult for Geb to predict how many there were. He guessed between three and seven.

Once the people had met up, he heard their muffled voices. Though he couldn't make out what they said. *They are talking about what to do.* He knew. *They are deciding if they should attack me. If they choose to attack, they'll plan how to attack me.* He focused his hearing on the voices and picked out two words. "Easy target."

The people began to move away from each other. No longer grouped together, Geb began to count them. One. Two. Three. Four. Five. Six. Seven... There were seven.

Cackler honked as he made his way back down through the canopy, weaving in and out of branches at a wicked pace. As he drew nearer to Geb, he slowed before landing with a soft plop atop Geb's head. Cackler whistled a few things.

"There is an eighth further away?" Geb asked. "Interesting, I'd only counted six. They are clever. Where do you think they will ambush us?"

Cackler offered a sequence of whistles and murmurs.

"A meadow?" Geb smiled. "How do they plan to get me into the meadow?"

Cackler murmured once.

"So if I act scared of the sounds they make and move away from those sounds, in time, they'll attack?"

Cackler honked in the affirmative.

"Okay," sounds like a plan.

Geb and Cackler continued walking their path. A few seconds later, a haunting bellow came from their right. "OOOooooOOOOooooeww…"

"Oh, no! A ghost." Geb pretended to be afraid. Were he in an acting audition, he'd have never earned the part.

Though, his pretentions seemed enough to convince his soon-to-be attackers as the bellowing only increased in intensity. And it came from two bushes instead of one. "OOOooooOOOOooooeww…"

A guttural growl came from a third bush.

"Aaagghh!" Geb faked as he began to run away from the sounds. As Cackler had predicted, the path away from the sounds brought Geb to a meadow.

In the meadow stood four men.

The man in the center wore green brigandine. His left hand held a bow. He had a dagger in his belt, a quiver of arrows strapped to his back. He used the fingers of his right hand to stroke his red goatee. Sinister green eyes stared out from the shadow created by his chapeau.

To his left, a man stood with folded arms. He'd covered himself head to toe in dark ninja gear. The garb was baggy at the legs and arms. At the wrists and ankles, tight wraps held the attire over black leather gloves and boots. The boots had a fine polish with a split between the middle and ring toe. Geb had seen the design used before. It allowed people to use attachments on the boot. Most boot attachments were for climbing purposes. Though, he'd seen push dagger attachments to increase the damage of kicks. The man had a black leather vest over his body. He'd filled his toolbelt with shuriken, kunai, black eggs, and smoke bombs. A grappling hook hung over his left hip. Double ninjatos rested in scabbards angled across his back.

On the right, the man wore scale mail made from the scales of forest hopping dragons. He held a steel short sword in his right hand and a kite shield in his left. A shiny, silver pot helmet protected his head and face.

If the man wore the scales of lesser dragons, it told Geb that the men were strong enough to defeat lesser dragons in combat. Such a feat was beyond the capabilities of most humans. On Round, Geb doubted one out of every million people could accomplish it.

"Chances are we will kill you, anyway." The man in the brigandine spoke with a smooth charisma. "But if you want to get out of this unscathed, give us your valuables. Also, we want the goose. It will make a nice dinner for us."

Geb didn't offer a response. Instead, he stood still, evaluating the levels and classes of the men before him. In green, the man was a level sixty-two ranger. The one in ninja gear was a level sixty ninja. The armored one was a level sixty castle guard.

Cackler whistled four times. The sounds indicated the levels and jobs of the four men who attacked from behind. There was a level fifty-six Viking, a level forty-seven pirate, a level fifty-seven samurai, and a level sixty highwayman.

All Geb could do was hang his head in disgust. The men were not muggers, bandits, thieves, assassins, thugs. As such, they shouldn't be attacking travelers. To make things worse, one had the job of a highwayman. That meant it was his job to protect travelers. He was doing the opposite of his job.

There was also the question of where the men obtained the scale armor. If they killed a dragon, they'd need to have the job of poacher, hunter, or something like that. It was possible that the eighth attacker had such a job.

But since they were not nearby, neither Geb nor Cackler could see their job or level. In the end, it didn't matter. The other seven deserved punishment for doing things that weren't in their job descriptions. At a minimum, the eighth was guilty by proxy.

Geb shifted his gaze up. "You have broken the laws of the moderators."

"Yeah?" the man in green spoke as the other four men emerged from the bushes, surrounding Geb on all sides. "You hear that, boys? We broke the laws of the moderators. We're in trouble now."

All seven men began to laugh.

Through their laughter, Geb continued. "I'll grant you a punishment worthy of the crime. Of course, your lack of remorse requires further castigation."

The men laughed for a few more seconds, and then the man in green spoke, removing an arrow from his quiver and knocking it. "Forget what I said before...that you might survive this. You won't."

"You talk too much," Geb replied. "And I can predict what you'll say. It's boring."

"Oh," the man lifted his bow and took aim. "What am I about to say?"

Geb sighed. "You're about to say, 'what'd you do? What are you?' Then you'll figure out what I am."

The man smirked as he released the arrow, and it flew in Geb's direction.

Cackler reacted in a flash, leaping from Geb's

head, falling into a barrel roll, and catching the arrow. Then he opened his wings and took flight, climbing upward at a steep angle. As his wings flapped, he flung the arrow back at the man with the bow. The projectile flew with such speed that the man could not react. The arrow's tip cut his bowstring before embedding itself into the wet, grassy earth.

As Cackler zipped upward, the man with the bow growled and pulled out his dagger. In unison, the other men armed themselves with their respective weapons. These included swords, daggers, and spears. With angry disdain, they began in Geb's direction.

Geb looked at the samurai and said, "ha." He looked at the Viking and said, "ha." And he looked at the highwayman and then the pirate, "ha, ha." He said each word with a practiced emotionless tone. And each time he spoke the word, the ground shook and opened, pulling the men down to their necks into the mud. It was too fast for them to react.

The three remaining men charged Geb.

As they did, he removed his crown, and his head began to change form. His long blue hair became the scaly hood of a cobra; his face and mouth became that of an angry serpent.

Upon seeing the transformation, the three men slowed. Geb bared his fangs and spat venom into their eyes. One, two, three, they fell. Each screamed in pain, holding their hands over their faces.

"Cackler," Geb looked up. In his snake form, his voice came as a hiss. "Heal their woundsssss, remove their experienssssss."

Cackler cackled a cackle that would put any witch to shame, and blue dew began to form in the air. As the blue drops fell on the men, a sparkling aura surrounded them. It removed the venom from the eyes of the screaming men, and their pain subsided. Though, as it removed their ailments, it also took away their experience points. Their levels dropped to the thirties...the twenties...the tens...and stopped at level one. With the loss of levels, they lost their attribute bonuses, skill points, and abilities from allocating those skill points.

"Enough," Geb said as he saw their levels reach one. His head returned to its human form and returned his crown to his head.

Cackler stopped cackling, and the dew dissipated. Then he began to descend toward Geb.

As Cackler landed in Geb's crown, Geb looked at the men. "I will leave you now. Your loss of levels is sufficient punishment for your transgressions. Have a nice day."

The man in green pushed himself up to a kneeling position and looked up at Geb. "What'd you do? Who are you?" Understanding flashed in the man's eyes. "A moderator. You're a moderator."

"I told you that you'd say that." Geb yawned. "Dig up your friends before any predators find you. Your eighth friend, the one deeper in the forest. I only lowered his level to twenty. So long as you avoid dragons, he can protect you as you make your way to town. In the future, remember to stay within the bounds of your job. Don't think about stepping outside your responsibilities. Be good. Do as you're told. If you do, your faithfulness will be its own reward." With those words, Geb continued his journey through the forest.

At some point, it began to rain again. He enjoyed the coolness of the water as droplets pitter-pattered against his skin. It reminded him of fountains, waterfalls, and dolphins. He wasn't sure why it reminded him of dolphins, but it did.

22: I Can Swim

After his encounter with Finnegan the bull shark, Pete began to doubt himself. His HP hadn't recovered from that battle; it remained at under twenty-five percent. Did that mean if Charybdis was 25% stronger, Pete wouldn't be able to defeat it? He'd need a better strategy. He considered figuring out a way to level up before the fight. If he could do that, an attribute boost might help him. These were the thoughts running through Pete's head as he stood before the king.

Then the king began to speak. "Impressive how you handled Finnegan. That was some world-class slapping. Also, thank you for not killing him. I appreciate that."

"It's no problem," Pete answered. "It seemed like Finnegan was smiling; I wasn't sure if he was sentient."

"Sentient?" The king repeated the word. "What does that mean?"

Pete considered how to answer for a few seconds before he spoke. "It means that he can think, talk, has hobbies, and stuff. Also, I thought he might be a dad with baby Finnegan's swimming around his home; his wife takes care of them while he battles in the Call'isuem...something like that."

The king began to laugh. "A bull shark having a family? That's a good one. Your sense of humor is almost as good as your slapping."

Though it wasn't a joke, Pete pretended to act as if it were and offered a fake laugh to accompany the king's. When the laughing stopped, Pete decided to clarify, "but bull sharks can't talk, right?"

This time the entire room began to laugh with him. As they did, Pete realized it was unlikely he'd learn about bull sharks that day. As the laughter slowed a second time, the king began to speak. "As I was saying, you did an excellent job all around. I've never seen anyone defeat Finnegan. I doubt I'll see it again. That said, if you are to defeat Charybdis, you will need to raise your swimming proficiency. For the time being, where is your swimming proficiency?"

"It is at a solid zero." Pete hung his head.

"At zero," The king stroked his beard, considering. "I have some gear. It should be able to help you. Should you defeat Charybdis, you can keep it." The king turned to his guard. "Before I get it for you, I have one question."

"Yes?" *I hope it isn't a tricky question,* Pete thought. *I hope he asks me something like my favorite color.* After watching *Monty Python and the Search for the Holy Grail*, he'd practiced answering his favorite color. He wouldn't want to answer the wrong color by accident and have a higher power throw him into an abyss.

The king asked. "What is your favorite color.

Jackpot, Pete smiled. "Blue."

The king turned to his guard. "Get Pete the Pizzaman a set of natation armor. Get him one in blue."

The guard's eyes widened. "A full set? Boots and everything?"

"Boots and everything." The king confirmed. Then the king turned back to Pete. "As a secondary prize—of course—I will allow you Aqua's hand in marriage."

Speechless, all Pete could do was turn red. He wasn't ready for that. If he got married, Zoey would kill him. How could he turn down the king's offer and be polite about it?

"I'm kidding." The king and his guards laughed for a third time. "We haven't done arranged marriages for centuries. You can marry who you want. Aqua can marry anyone she wants. Wow, I didn't know someone could turn so red. You must think Aqua is pretty, huh?"

All Pete could do was turn redder. Lucky for him,

the guard returned with the blue natation armor. It gave him somewhere else to focus his attention…something else to think about other than the fatal consequences of marrying Aqua.

The guard rested the armor at the foot of the king's throne as if it were on display. He placed it down with unique care, putting down one piece of the armor after another.

First, he laid down the main piece. It looked like a wetsuit: one piece, form-fitting, covering from ankle to neck to wrist. Aside from dark blue protective plating on the arms and legs, the material was black. The plate mail interlocked at the knee and elbow joints, providing complete protection around the arms and legs. Pete guessed the plate material was a high-density plastic or a light metal. Until further inspection, he wouldn't know for sure.

Second, the guard set down a vest. The armor's vest was one-hundred percent plate. It looked thick and heavy. Pete hoped it was high-density plastic and not metal. If it were metal, he'd never be able to swim with it.

Next, the guard set down armored boots. They looked like medieval knight boots, except the water boots had long fins coming off the feet.

To the side of the boots, the guard set down a pair of gloves. The gloves appeared to be the same material as the wetsuit, with armor to protect the back of the hand. They were fingerless, aside from some stiff, black material that ran up and down the edge of each finger. Webbing connected the rigid material, making the gloves look like frog hands.

Last, the guard placed down a hat, one which looked much like Pete's armored M&P's Cap. Someone had even painted an M&P symbol on it. "We had the head gear special made. Aqua says it resembles what you use under normal circumstances?"

"It is," Pete shook his head. Despite his concerns about the weight of the armor, he had to hide his excitement at receiving new gear. Getting new gear in real life was way more exciting than getting some in a game. He couldn't wait to try it on.

*   *   *

After he'd left the palace, Pete had reunited with Aqua and Kai. Together, the trio returned to Aqua's house. Once there, Aqua showed Pete to a guest room. For privacy, the guest room had a tunnel that connected to the hatch above and the hatch below. The tunnel had a door that opened to its floor. The privacy design made sense to Pete. The tunnel served as a hallway would in a house on land. Once in the guest room, Pete finally had an opportunity to try on his new armor.

When he held it—it felt lighter than he had guessed—and he read its description. The description explained the plate was some type of plastic polymer that classified as light armor. It had a higher base defense and magic defense than his M&P Combat gear. Though, it was the passive traits that set the armor apart.

While wearing every piece of armor, Pete would lose seventy-five skill points in every category that involved land mobility: jumping, running, walking, climbing, so on and so forth. Though he would gain two-hundred-fifty swimming skill points. Once he saw these passive traits, he couldn't dress fast enough. He had tired of swimming around with less skill than the newborn merpeople.

Dressed in his new armor—hat atop his head—he swam into the tunnel and then the living room. Aqua waited for him there. "Wow," she said, looking him up and down. "You look great. How does it feel."

He swam right next to her, face to face. It felt easy and natural...like walking. With a two-hundred-fifty swimming skill, he could swim up and down without a thought. He could hover in place without any extra effort. He spoke with Aqua, maintaining the same height above the floor as her. "It feels amazing. Aren't I a great swimmer? Look at that. I can swim."

"That's..." she paused, trying to keep any awkwardness out of her voice. "...great."

Why doesn't she sound excited for me? He wondered. Then he realized that—to a merperson—bragging about swimming was like bragging about walking. On land, people didn't go around bragging about how well they walked. Her reaction made more sense. "Anyway," he said. "What happens now?"

"The king wants you to get used to swimming and moving around in your armor...so we're going to spend the day together." She smiled, inching closer toward Pete. "It'll be fun."

He tried not to blush. "Fun...sounds great...umm...uhh..." he struggled to think of something clever to say. "Fun is...uh...fun..."

"Right," she giggled, taking his left hand in her right one. "Fun is fun. Come with me." She swam up toward the front door hatch of her home.

Instead of dragging him, he swam alongside her as they exited the home and began toward the town. At a calmer pace, Pete could focus on the surroundings better than he had. He noticed how some tunnels ran between the buildings, like sidewalks. Though, he didn't notice anything resembling streets. This caused a question to come to his mind. "Aqua," he asked. "Do merpeople have vehicles?"

"Not in Greenlake," She said. "In the oceans, there are cities which are big enough to require vehicles, though."

"What do you call the vehicles?" Pete asked.

"Submarines."

"That makes sense." Pete lifted his eyes as a tall pillar came into view. "What's that? It's the tallest one I've seen."

"That's the mall." She explained. "I figured you're hungry. There're a few restaurants there. I figured we could get something to eat."

"That sounds great," Pete agreed.

As they swam into the mall's main entrance, Pete recognized how the mall was a broader, taller reproduction of the houses. A merperson's home was big enough to have one room per floor. The mall was big enough to have four or five stores on each floor. That, of course, depended on the size of each store. Instead of one hatch connecting the floors, there were four separate hatches. Plus, the hatches were wide enough to let many merpeople pass through them at once.

In the mall most of the stores were like the same ones Pete would find in the mall back in Cheyenne. There were plenty of shops with clothes, stores to meet every age and clique.

There were clothes with hand-crafted souvenirs for tourists. Pete wondered where tourists might come from. The ocean? A nearby sea? Some of the stores appeared to sell electronics. Although, Pete wondered how electricity worked underwater. He guessed that something else powered the electronics. If that were the case, he bet they'd have a name that was different than electronics. For example, if they were magic powered, he'd call them magic-onics.

There were shops that sold video games and anime figurines. When Pete asked why the figurines had legs instead of tails, Aqua explained how the merpeople and humans got the same television channels. They used the same streaming services. People above and below the surface enjoyed the same programming. He hoped some of that programming involved isekais where people from Round went to Earth.

There was an air tub store. Air tubs appeared to function like hot tubs, but the tub filled with heated air instead of water. He wondered how merpeople used the strange contraptions. Did they lower themselves down from above, keeping their upper bodies in the water until their tails were sitting in the air tub?

As Pete and Aqua made their way through the mall. They saw plenty of other merpeople. They filled the mall. There were so many merpeople it was difficult not to bump into anyone. The number of people and the speed of the movement disoriented Pete. Most teenagers and young adults dressed like Zoey, using bright colors and skirts. He noticed some kids using what looked like sports jerseys with numbers.

"What sport are those jerseys for?" He asked.

"Raiderball," Aqua said.

"Cool," he made a mental note to look up the rules of raiderball on his smartphone...whenever he got a chance.

Aqua and Pete came to a floor where every business was a restaurant. "Every five floors, there is a food circle." She explained. "They try to balance out the food on each floor. It doesn't make sense to have five kelp restaurants next to each other."

"Kelp...restaurants?" At that moment, he realized that merperson food differed from land-person food. They wouldn't have hamburgers because they didn't have cows. They wouldn't have French fries because they wouldn't have a way to fry anything underwater. Without fire, he wondered if they cooked anything.

"Yup," she said. "We have all sorts of restaurants with food from countries all around Round."

He began to look at the restaurants around them. It was a typical foot court with windows at the front of each restaurant where customers could order food. Above the restaurant windows were signs. He read the signs: Bubbles the Fish's Sharkburgers, The Kelp Deli and Sandwiches, Sarah's Sushi and Seaweed Rolls, and Tacos. Upon reading the signs, he asked, "How do you get the bread for the sandwiches and shells for the tacos?"

"We import it from the towns on land. They make the bread and shells with water-repelling flour. It keeps the bread and shells from getting too wet to eat." She explained. "Everyone here imports from a bakery in Futuretown. It's called Bob's Bakery."

"Do you have a favorite restaurant?" Pete asked.

"I do," she nodded, pulling him toward Bubbles the Fish's Sharkburgers. Bubbles is the best. You'll love this place."

At the service window of Bubble's restaurant, a giant goldfish with rainbow scales hovered upright. It reminded Pete of one of those characters from a children's cartoon. Behind the fish, Pete noticed a grill with some massive hamburger patties cooking. The grill appeared to be over some type of volcanic vent. A dome covered the grill, made from rock or coral. Air filled the dome, allowing the patties to cook. Pete wondered if the grill was a feat of engineering or of magic.

When the fish saw Aqua, he called to her. "Aqua, it's great to see you. I haven't seen you since Charybdis' last attack. I worried something had happened to you." His voice was like that of a grandfather speaking to their grandchild. But Pete didn't focus on the voice...not so much. Instead, Pete realized that if fish could talk, sharks could talk...probably... Pete would have to find Finnegan later and tell him it was a good match...do the good sportsmanship thing and stuff. Plus, he didn't want to be on Finnegan's bad side.

"Still alive and full of drive." She said, still holding Pete's hand as she pulled him so he hovered beside her.

At that moment—for the first time—Pete realized he'd been holding her hand the whole time. It wasn't like they were dating, though. At first, she was dragging him through the water; he couldn't swim on his own. After, it was a habit, and he did it without realizing it. He wondered about mermaid courtship rituals. Did holding hands mean the same thing as it did on land? He didn't want to give Aqua the wrong idea. She was a cool mermaid and all, but Pete liked...someone else...and he didn't want to hurt Aqua's feelings.

Taking the chance to release her hand, Pete lifted the recently free hand and waved. He tried to make it look natural, like he was freeing his hand to wave. "Hi, I'm Pete. Pete the pizzaman."

"I've heard of you, Pete." Bubbles said. "You're all anyone's talked about today."

"Talking about me?" Pete offered an embarrassed smile. He wasn't a fan of being the center of attention.

"No need to fret, my boy. They say good things." The fish offered a wide, toothy, goldfish smile. "Good things indeed. What can I make for each of you today?"

"From what are the sharkburgers made?" Pete asked.

"I'm afraid I don't understand the question." Bubbles answered.

"Merpeople make all underwater meat from tofu," Aqua explained. "They aren't made from shark or anything like that...in case you're worried about that."

"Ah...cool..." Pete proceeded to order a sharkburger with hot peppers. I do have one question, though."

"What's that?" Bubbles asked: removing a spatula from beneath the counter, turning, sticking the spatula into the dome of the grill, and pulling out a patty.

"If they aren't made from sharks, why do you call them sharkburgers?"

"Because they are big enough to feed a shark…most sharks, anyway… Finnegan will eat three in one sitting." Bubbles slapped the patty onto the bottom half of a bread bun. Then he began to add toppings: sliced kelp, lettuce, hot peppers, and the like. Then Bubble's handed Pete the massive burger. Pete thanked Bubbles for the sharkburger. As he sat down and began to eat it, he contemplated how to make an underwater pizza.

*   *   *

It took Pete over an hour to finish the massive burger. At the beginning of his meal, he was starving. By the end of it, he was more than full. Even so, he didn't want to offend Aqua or Bubbles, so he finished every bite…at the expense of his stomach.

Though, he wasn't too worried about it because, at that point, night had fallen over Greenlake. Pete could go back to Aqua's house and sleep. So long as he didn't have to go play a football game or compete in some soul-capturing contest, he'd be fine.

"We should go dancing," Aqua said.

"D…Dancing?" Pete stuttered. "After eating? I'm not sure that's a good…"

"Don't be a wimp," Aqua told him. "Dancing will be good for you. It will give you more swimming practice."

He had to admit that all the swimming around had helped him. Aside from his suit bonuses, he'd earned several swimming skill-ups. With each skill up, swimming felt that much easier. Those skill points were precious. They'd determine the outcome of his impending battle with Charybdis. "Fine," he agreed. "Let's go dancing, but on the way there, can we swim a little slower than normal?"

"Why's that?" She asked.

Pete didn't want to be like, *because I need to digest that massive burger I ate. At the moment, it feels heavy in my stomach, and if I move too fast, I will puke.* That would be a gross thing to say. "To save energy for dancing," Pete said.

"Oh," she said. "That makes sense."

Side by side—but no longer holding hands—the pair took their time and went to Club Shake-a-Fin. From the outside...at night...the club seemed like a different place than it had appeared to be during the day. Lights zipped like tangible lasers around the club. This applied inside the club and outside, where the glass provided no resistance to the light. By reflex, Pete dodged one of the zipping lights.

"They are harmless," Aqua giggled. You don't need to dodge them.

"Right," Pete agreed and followed Aqua to the line at the club's entrance. The closer they came to the club, the louder the music sounded. The current song had some EDM undertones. Although he could hear some harp and classical strings mixed in with the beat. It reminded him of Lindsey Stirling.

No sooner had the pair taken their place at the back of the line when one of the bouncers approached them. "The queen says you can come in, says it wouldn't be right to make the pizzaman wait."

"That's awesome," Pete said. "Back on Earth, everyone made pizzamen wait. Sometimes, I'd knock on a door, and it would be minus twenty out, and they'd make me wait three minutes in the cold. Then they'd come to the door and act surprised to see me there. Then they'd say, 'sorry, I was playing video games downstairs.' And they'd be in their boxers. Then I'd wonder if I've been playing video games wrong my whole life. Then I'd give them the pizza and return to the pizzeria..." Both the bouncer and Aqua stared at Pete with blank expressions. "So...the queen, huh?

Sounds great. What I meant to say with that story before was thank you."

"Right," The boxer spun and waved for Pete and Aqua to follow. "This way, please."

They followed the bouncer until they reached the entrance hatch. At that point, Pete realized there was a VIP entrance hatch next to the main one. The guard opened the VIP hatch and entered. Pete and Aqua followed.

Inside, merpeople danced a lot like land people do, shaking their hips back and forth, swinging their arms, and spinning. Within the crowded space, they'd move to different levels in the water—some higher and some lower—to not bump into one another. The special awareness seemed uncanny to a land person like Pete. He'd have to practice his swimming skill before he could dance like that. It would take a lot of practice. Not to mention...he'd need a dancing skill above that of a common house plant.

"Before you get to dancing," the bouncer pointed to a woman next to the disco ball at the center of the room. She had giant headphones over her ears. She floated in front of a turntable, seeming to control the music. "The queen would like to speak with you."

Upon hearing the woman was the queen, Pete took a closer look. She had a youthful face. Though Pete guessed her to be in her thirties. Her hair was long and red, her eyes a dark brown. Pete turned to Aqua and asked. "That's the queen?"

"That's her." Aqua nodded. "The king rules the day...and the queen rules the nighttime. It's kinda their thing."

"Cool," Pete said, and he and Aqua began toward the queen.

When she saw them, she waved a nearby guard over to her. When he arrived, she pointed at the turntable, removed her headphones, handed them to the guard, and left him to handle the music. With her DJ responsibilities accounted for, she moved toward Pete and Aqua.

With masterful grace, the queen maneuvered around the dancers at the club. With each movement, her long, green dress billowed behind her. When she reached Pete, she asked, "you are the pizzaman named Pete, yes?"

"I am," Pete nodded. "Am I supposed to bow or kneel or something?" He hoped he didn't have to kneel before the queen. If he did, he would sink, remaining in a kneeling position. It would be embarrassing. Aqua was still next to him. Would Aqua kneel? *Wait...can mermaids kneel without knees? Knee is a part of the word kneel. It's the first part of the word...four of the five letters.*

"No need for any of that," The queen said. "I wanted to thank you for not killing Finnegan. To be honest, none of us thought you had a chance against him. As such, we'd told him not to kill or maim you. Once he defeated you, we'd use it as justification to send you back to land.

"When you won, we had to reconsider your abilities. I've never seen anyone with an attack-based skill at your proficiency... To be certain, no one with so low a level. It is awe-inspiring."

"Thank you," Pete said.

"I wanted to ask you a question." Her eyes met his.

"What's that?" He struggled with keeping eye contact, so he chose to look at the spot between her eyebrows instead. It was a trick one of his high school teachers had taught him.

"Did the king make the joke about you marrying Aqua? It was my idea that he do that. I made him promise to do it. He said he did, but did he?"

Pete blushed and nodded in the affirmative.

"Oh, good," The queen smiled. "That was all I wanted to know. Please, enjoy your time dancing in the club."

"Thank you," Pete said, and he and Aqua found a space in the club and danced. Rather, Aqua danced, and Pete tried to dance, and Aqua laughed.

Josh Walker

23: Fred's Dungeon Scheme

Zoey's attributes shot up when she went from level eleven to level twelve. She noticed a significant drop in attribute boosts from levels twelve to fifteen. *Pete was right,* she had to admit. *Slapping himself to sleep will make him stronger.*

Between her level-ups, skill-ups, and victories over the higher-level crabs, she'd accrued thirteen skill points. As she looked over her skill tree, she saw four skills left to activate. To the bottom right was an ability called Weapon Boost. It seemed self-explanatory enough. She guessed it was either a passive skill that would boost her weapon skill on a permanent basis or a skill she could use for a temporary boost. In her case, that weapon was a pizza fork. Even so, she had a paladin skill tree. As such, she guessed the increase would apply to all weapons.

To the bottom left, she had an ability called Shield Slap. It connected to a third ability. Until she learned Shield Slap, she couldn't see what the third ability was. Then—at the top point of the skill tree—it read, *Apprentice Promotion.* It cost fifteen skill points, but for the time, it remained locked. *I'll need to learn the abilities from the novice tree before I can move to the apprentice one.* She told herself, and she began to allocate points to abilities.

She started with Weapon Boost and Shield Slap. They cost a respective four points a piece, leaving her with seven points. Upon doing this, she learned the Weapon Boost was a permanent increase to her pizza fork skill. Shield Slap was an attack skill with a timer.

She put five of those remaining points into the final skill. The skill tree called the ability Insult Your Ancestors. It functioned much like Draw Hate and Strong Draw Hate, helping her keep the monster focused on her. This prevented it from attacking her other party members.

The Apprentice Promotion unlocked. But with only two skill points left to allocate, she'd need thirteen more before she could activate it.

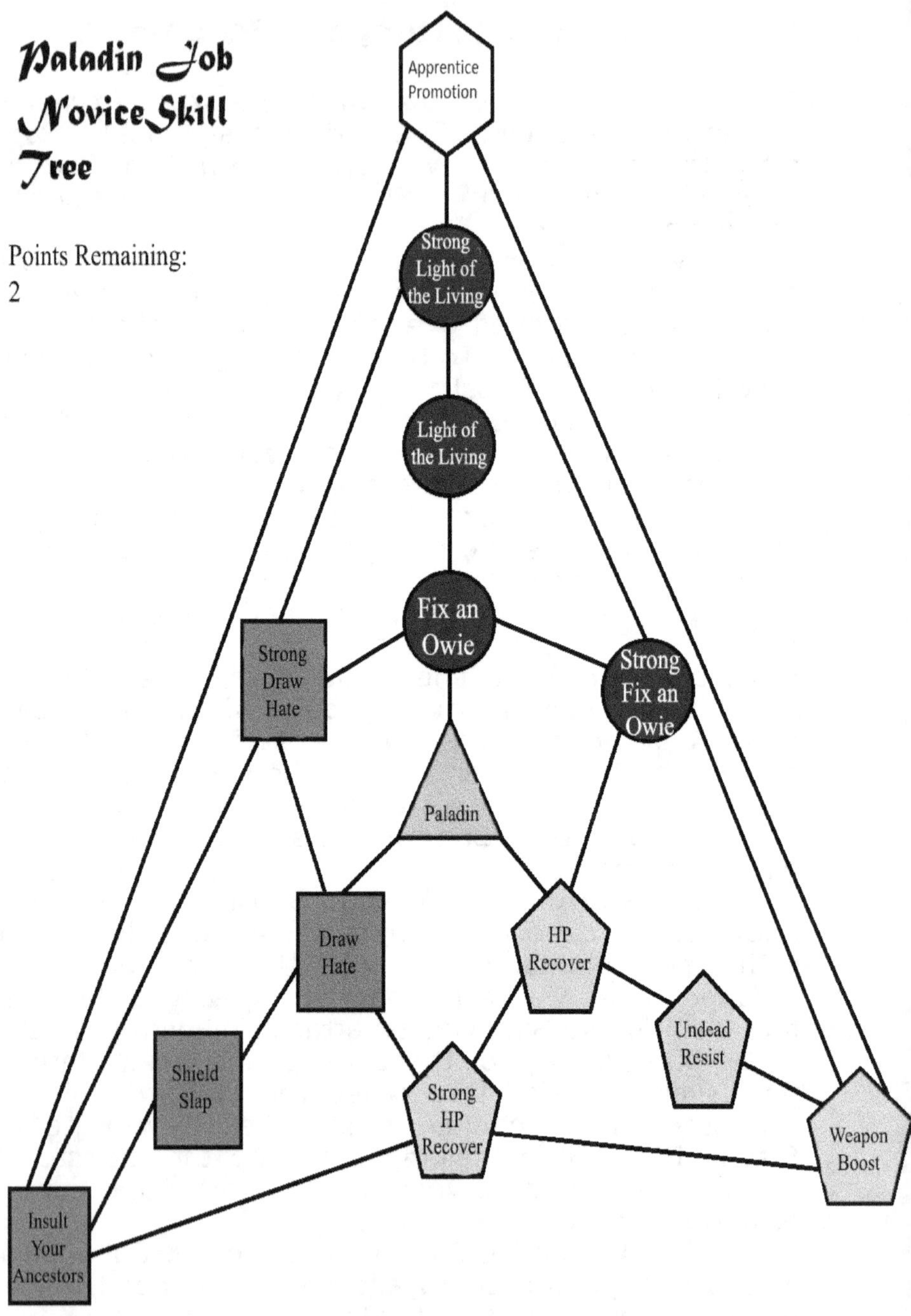

Paladin Job Novice Skill Tree
Points Remaining: 2
Apprentice Promotion
Strong Light of the Living
Light of the Living
Fix an Owie
Strong Draw Hate
Strong Fix an Owie
Paladin
Draw Hate
HP Recover
Shield Slap
Strong HP Recover
Undead Resist
Weapon Boost
Insult Your Ancestors

Zoey closed her window as Flowerbeard jumped from the waterspout to the tunnel's edge. It had taken him thirty-two attempts, but he'd made it. As he landed inside the new tunnel, he hit hard against the stone floor with an audible, "ooof." Gasping for air, he stood and said. "I...would...have...done...it faster, but...I...didn't...level...my...agility...stat...enough... I...could have...but what's...the point...like...whatever...stop talking."

Zoey patted his shoulder. "We know."

"Stop talking?" Skye wrinkled his forehead and whispered to Hope in confusion. "No one was talking."

Before Flowerbeard could answer, Zoey said. "Now that we are all here, we need to figure out what to do next." She looked at Introvice. "Is there any chance we clear this dungeon tonight? I'm sure the triplets' parents are worried sick, and it would be nice to get them home tonight."

"I don't see that happening," Introvice admitted.

"Then it would be best if we rest for the night." Zoey said, "recover our energy and try again tomorrow."

"I agree," Introvice pointed to a groove in the tunnel's wall. It looks dry there. We can make a fire. What do you guys have in the way of food?"

The group of adventurers began toward the space.

"If you don't have any food," Flowerbeard said as the group reached the space. "We'd be happy to share in exchange for some of your dungeon loot."

"We have food." Hope said as the non-pixie members of the party sat while the pixies remained hovering. "We work at a Pizzeria, so we always have pizza. That way, when you say, 'what's pizza,'..."

"What's pizza?" Flowerbeard asked.

"...see," Hope continued. "When you ask that question, I have a free sample to share. That way, you can try the pizza. Then when you like it, you go to the pizzeria and buy some. That's why I always have a free sample pizza to share."

Hope materialized a pepperoni pizza from her inventory, made with pepperonis from the Turkey Titan. One of Zoey's favorite things about having an inventory was how food stayed as fresh and hot as when it went into the inventory.

In her own inventory, Zoey kept an emergency cheese pizza. But she decided to ration it for later. There was no telling for sure how long they'd be in the dungeon. If they ran out of pizza, they'd only have crab meat, and Zoey wasn't a fan of sea food. Though, she wondered how a crab meat pizza might sell at M&P's. After the dungeon, they'd have plenty of crab meat.

As Hope set the pizza down in front of Fred, Introvice, and Flowerbeard, she explained. "We've cut the pizza into triangles like a pie. There are seven of us and eight slices. That means everyone gets one slice. Flowerbeard, you can have two, but you have to promise to stop being a grumpy pants."

"I'm not grumpy." Flowerbeard reached for a slice. "Your grumpy."

Hope slapped his hand away and stared him down. "Promise."

"Fine," he relented. "I promise."

"Good," Hope hovered back a few inches before landing and saying. "You may have a slice."

Flowerbeard tore the first slice from the pizza. As the cheese stretched, his eyes widened in excitement. Then he lifted the point of the slice to his mouth, bit down, and began to chew. At first, he chewed slow and cautious. Then—as the flavor hit his taste buds—he began to chew faster. Still with food in his mouth, he said. "This is delicious...the best food I've ever had."

Upon seeing their companion's reaction, Fred and Introvice each grabbed a slice. Fred had a similar reaction to Flowerbeard's. His eyes went wide. He ate with the excitement of a child trying a delicious food for the first time.

Introvice ate with practiced decorum. He gave no indication of how he felt about the food until after he had swallowed his first bite. Then he spoke, keeping an even tone. "This is delicious. Where does pizza come from?"

"Italy," Zoey answered.

"That sounds like a made-up place," Flowerbeard said while still chewing.

"Where is Italy?" Introvice asked.

"Europe," Zoey said.

"Now, I know you are making things up." Flowerbeard finished chewing and grabbed the second slice Hope had promised him.

Zoey shrugged.

"I've never heard of Europe," Introvice said. "Are you making it up?"

"No," Zoey considered how to answer the question for a few seconds before continuing. "But Italy and Europe aren't easy places to find. Most people haven't heard of them."

"Italy is in another world," Tornado added.

"Another world?" Introvice examined the pixie. "I can't tell if you're joking or not."

Tornado offered no clarification.

"What are the chances we get out of here tomorrow?" Zoey asked.

"To be honest," Introvice answered. "I don't think that great. We haven't even reached a mini-boss yet. If there is only one mini-boss, we could clear the dungeon tomorrow. Also, I should warn you about Fred."

Fred glared at Introvice, holding a finger up to his mouth as if saying to be quiet.

Introvice shook his head in disappointment as he

spoke to Fred. "What does it matter if I tell them? You promised us you'd moved on...haven't you? There's no need to feel embarrassed about the past."

Fred's glare intensified.

"What do you mean 'move on'...and 'embarrassed by the past.'" Zoey side-eyed Fred with new-found suspicion.

Fred's expression turned uncomfortable, and he hung his head.

"Fred grew up as an orphan." Introvice began. "On one of the Eastern Volcano Islands." At the mention of volcanos, Tornado went from daydreaming to hyper-focusing on the conversation. "To make matters worse, he received the job of mime. This meant he could never talk to anyone. It made for a lonely childhood."

"Why is that embarrassing?" Zoey asked.

"It isn't," Introvice said. "It's what he did after that earned him some embarrassment."

"This is the good part," Flowerbeard said as he shoved the remainder of his second slice into his mouth.

"As Fred entered adulthood," Introvice explained. "He won an adventurer's pass in a mime competition. Though, at the time, he had no combat experience. He was level one. He had no way to survive a dungeon crawl."

"So he exploited his party members," Flowerbeard explained. "He went into a dungeon, waited for other noobs to enter the dungeon, and if they died, he stole their stuff."

Introvice sighed. "Right, he grew as a solo adventurer by looting those whose hit points had dropped to 0. When he had enough gear to fight low-level monsters, he began to level. He began to join parties with lower-level members, encouraging them to fight stronger monsters. Once the battle started, he'd run away. If his party members survived, he'd earn experience. If they died, he'd loot them. It became a win-win situation for him."

"That's how he met you?" Zoey lifted an eyebrow.

"It is." Introvice stretched his right arm over his chest while pulling with his left against the elbow. "But once I realized he'd set me up, I decided there was one thing left to do." He switched to stretch his left arm. "I had to teach Fred how to survive. He was a fast learner, and we've been partners ever since."

"I joined them after," Flowerbeard said. "Introvice calls me his current work in progress...whatever that means."

"We warn everyone about Fred because sometimes he slips back into old habits. As such, I'd advise not taking on anything too powerful until you are one hundred percent sure you are ready...despite any encouragement that Fred might offer you."

Fred looked up at Zoey and shrugged his agreement with the assessment.

Zoey's eyes met Fred, and she considered what to say. After a few seconds of eye contact, she said. "We all make mistakes. It's how we respond to them that determines who we are. You seem to have responded well."

Fred smiled and quick-nodded a thank you.

With that, the adventurers—pixies included—turned in for the evening.

Tornado struggled to sleep. He missed his mom and dad. He missed his bed. He missed the painting of a tornado on the wall by his bed.

Skye struggled to sleep. He missed his mom and dad. He missed his bed. He missed the wifi for his communication box games.

Hope struggled to sleep. She missed her mom and dad. She missed her bed. She worried her brothers missed their mom and dad, too.

As a vampire, Zoey no longer needed to sleep. Instead, she remained awake. Watching the other adventurers, keeping an eye on the triplets. Her senses allowed her to feel the heartbeats of those around her. As such, she realized the triplets struggled to sleep. It hurt her heart to know they were more scared than they had shown.

After four hours, the triplets' nervousness outweighed their tiredness, and they didn't sleep. Around that same time, Zoey recognized that the adventurers had begun to stir. She decided to give them an extra push. "That's enough sleep. Let's wake up and get going. If we're going to get the pixies home today, we have a lot of work to do.

"Stop talking," Flowerbeard complained.

Zoey materialized an uncooked pizza dough and threw it over Flowerbeard's face. "I'll talk if I want to."

Fifteen minutes later, the group found themselves moving down a monster-filled tunnelway. Crabs—the same as those from the puzzle chamber—appeared at regular intervals. Other monsters joined them. One of the monster types was a cave snake. It was dark blue with gray stripes. There were also water bats.

Even though the cave snakes and water bats gave less experience than the crabs, they tended to attack in bunches. Zoey put her skill Insult Your Ancestors to good use. It had a short cool down which allowed her to cycle it with Keep Hate and Strong Keep Hate. Each time she used Insult Your Ancestors, a loud voice resonated in the air. It sounded like a loudspeaker at a concert. It would say, "YOUR MOM," "YOUR GRANDPA," or "YOUR UNCLE'S NEPHEW'S BEST FRIEND." Then it would follow-up by insulting the identified party.

The snakes must have loved their uncle's nephew's best friend because that insult made them extra mad. When one of the angry snakes managed to bite Zoey's ankle, she received an icon to show she had venom in her blood. Her HP began to dip at a rate of about five percent every ten seconds. Lucky for Zoey, only five seconds went by before Hope cast a spell to remove the venom, and the icon went away.

With the help of Introvice and his team, Zoey and the triplets made short work of anything they came across. Within half an hour, they'd worked their way through the passageway and were fast approaching a second chamber. Everyone unequipped their weapons to examine the chamber. From the outside, it looked much like the last chamber, minus the waterspouts. Also, a simple, waist-high wooden gate separated the tunnel from the chamber.

"That is a mini-boss room," Introvice said. "You can tell because of the gate. Once we open the door, we'll have to fight something big and scary. If you want to, you can stay here. Fred, Flowerbeard, and I can handle it."

"I'm going." Zoey looked at the triplets. "But I need you three to stay safe. Wait here."

The triplets didn't argue as Introvice, Fred, Flowerbeard, and Zoey padded over to the gate. The triplets waited nearby. "From our experience, boss fights come in three different forms. There are the damage sponges. They take a lot of damage and require a more passive strategy. In that case, tank like normal. If we come across one of those in a dungeon like this, it will likely be a giant turtle, a giant crab, or something like that.

"The second type of boss can hit you hard and fast. These are the equivalent of a glass cannon. If you encounter one of them, you must shatter it before it shatters you. Hit it with everything you've got. In a dungeon like this, my guess is it would be a killer whale or some large predator.

"The last type of boss is the one that uses terrain to its advantage. It will ambush, use special attacks, and wait for you to make a mistake. In the case of this dungeon, one of these might be an undead pirate."

Flowerbeard added. "If you recognize what type of monster we're fighting, call it out to the rest of us. That way, we can adapt our strategy."

"Right," Zoey agreed. By habit, she took a deep calming breath...then she remembered she didn't have to breathe. "Let's do this."

Fred nodded once: moving to the gate, pushing it open, and stepping into the boss room. With careful steps, he moved toward the center of the space. With each step, the water rose higher and higher, leveling out at his hips. As he walked, he materialized a rapier in his right hand and a dagger in his left. Flowerbeard took a position next to Fred, musket in his left hand and cutlass in his right. Intro materialized a dagger in his right hand. They stood back-to-back-to-back-to-back, forming a square in the center of the room. "Stay alert. It's in here somewhere."

"There," Zoey used her fork to point to the edge of the room where she noticed a large dorsal fin submerge beneath the water's surface.

"Uh, oh," Flowerbeard said as the fin dipped beneath the surface.

"What is it?" Introvice asked.

"It's a shark," Zoey said. "It's a big one."

"What kind of shark?" Introvice asked.

"Bull shark," Flowerbeard answered. "I saw horns."

Fred slumped his shoulders in disgust.

"Why is that worse than a different of shark?" Zoey asked.

"Bull sharks are smart." Introvice explained. "Some have high enough intelligence stats that they can learn to speak. This might be an ambush type boss and a glass cannon type boss at the same time. Keep your guard up."

"Great," Zoey said. Rather than wait for the monster to attack on its own terms, she forced its hand by activating Insult Your Ancestors.

"YOUR GREAT-GRANDFATHER WAS A VEGETAR-IAN." A disembodied voice shouted.

In response to the voice, a fin broke the surface and headed straight at Zoey. Her knees bent into an extended stance. She positioned the shield low, preparing for last-second adjustments. When that last second came, the shark dove under the shield, trying to grab her lower leg.

She activated Shield Slap, knocking the shark's head down and away. Rather than chomping into her calf, it bit down on the combat boot over her left foot. From there, it continued past her, pulling her off balance and dragging her along for the ride. All the while, it swung its head back and forth, whipping her against the floor and walls. She watched her HP dip by one hundred points. Then it went down by another two hundred, three hundred, four hundred. A few levels back, the attack would have dropped her to 0. As it was, she knew she needed to free herself. She couldn't continue to take the abuse that the shark was dishing out.

"Whirlpool," she heard Tornado's familiar voice. Though, her ears were underwater, so it muffled his shout.

She felt the shark release its grip on her boot as it began to spin in the maelstrom created by Tornado's spell. By the time Zoey had returned to her feet, Hope had cast a spell to restore Zoey's hit points.

"You guys shouldn't have come into the room." Zoey lectured. "I told you to stay outside."

Hope answered with a fast panic. "We saw it get you. Then we realized we can stay above the water. It can't get us if we fly high enough. We're perfect for this fight." Hope pointed at where the shark continued to spin in the water.

Above the whirlpool, Skye spun his cutterchakus at a speed that made it hard to see the rotations. Each time the shark spun in the whirlpool, the chakus slapped down into its face.

Hope repeated. "See. We are perfect for this fight."

All Zoey could do was watch in stunned silence as the boss's hit points melted away. When those hit points reached zero, a prompt popped up:

You defeated Finley the shark. You gained 1,000 experience points.

You received Finley's Fork

Skye received Finley's Chakus

Hope received Finley's Wand

Tornado received Finley's Staff

Introvice received Finley's Dagger

Fred received Finley's Rapier

Flowerbeard received Finley's Cutlass

"One mini-boss down," Zoey whispered to herself. "Who knows how many we have left to go."

24: Wandering and Wondering

Mod never had to worry about having employees, not before the pizzeria. Before that, it was him and his bakery. Of course, the pixies still hung out in the bakery. They were his friends. Plus, he gave them free food. Then he changed his business model, added pizza to his menu, and hired those friends as employees.

It was a lot of fun working with his friends. Even so, it created a lot of stress when they didn't show up to work. In the case of Pete and Zoey, he worried more than usual because they lived in the pizzeria. And neither had been there in the last twenty-four hours. They'd already missed one rush shift. He didn't know if they'd miss another. Of course, he worried more about their well-being than the store.

He'd heard about the scuffle they'd been in with Roger during Harvestfest. He wondered if Roger might have used his influence to chase them out of town.

Mod hoped that wasn't the case, but he couldn't think of many other scenarios. It was out of character for Pete and Zoey to leave for no reason. They wouldn't move to Futuretown and open a rival pizzeria, would they? No, he knew they wouldn't do that. But where were they? He hoped they were okay.

To top things off, the triplets hadn't shown. They were going to help Mod with the prep work before the rush shift. If they didn't show up, he'd follow up with their parents to ensure they were okay.

The bell at the bakery's front door rang, and Mod looked up to see Rumpke walking through. Rumpke froze in place. "Where is Zoey?"

"I haven't seen her today," Mod replied from the counter, where he kneaded a bowl of pizza dough. "I haven't seen her, Pete, or the triplets. They're all supposed to be here. Can you ask around town…find out if anyone has seen them? If they are missing, we need to get Nick and the city guard involved."

"I'll ask around." Rumpke agreed. "Nick might be busy, though. He's been dealing with a soul eater sighting...near table rock..." Rumpke's eyes widened. "You don't think the triplets, Pete, and Zoey came across the soul eater, do you?"

Mod's heart sank at the suggestion. His worry for his friends grew as he admitted. "In the past, they've spent time up there farming the nightshade terrors for tomatoes. If you find out anything, can you come back to me and let me know?"

"Will do." Rumpke spun and hurried out the door.

*   *   *

Rumpke wasn't sure where Nick might be. His best guess was he'd find Nick at the mayor's office. As such, Rumpke hurried in that direction, moving as a raccoon does. He weaved around people, hopping up and over things with boundless agility, and dipping through openings under fences. He had not grown used to walking around Greenlake in the plain light of day. It felt unnatural to him...wrong. At night, shadow and darkness cloaked all the houses. In the day, they were all so...bright...and cheery... He didn't like it. If he ever owned a house in town, he'd paint it gray. He'd frame the windows to look like sad faces.

Me? Own a house in town? He chuckled at the prospect. Then his laughter stopped as a thought struck him. If things with him and Rosie worked out. Would they have a family one day? If they did, they'd want to raise the little ones in town. *No,* he shook away the thought. Warlords don't live in happy towns. Then again...it wouldn't be so bad if they did.

He reached the large yellow municipal building and moved to the wooden front doors. He pushed them open and slid inside. His feet pattered over the tile as he turned left and headed toward the mayor's office. When he saw Nick and the mayor inside the office with the triplets' parents, he went from a fast walk to a run. When he reached the office, he hid outside the door, squishing himself against the wall and spying on the conversation.

"They didn't come home yesterday." The triplets' mother said. "We looked all over for them. We don't know where they went. Today, we told them they could go see the dungeon portal. They might have gone yesterday. We don't know."

"We'll do everything we can to find them," Nick assured.

"In the meantime," Mayor Yam Hopler spoke. She always spoke fast with few spaces between words. Even so, she seemed to talk faster than usual. No doubt it was because she was nervous about the triplets. "Why don't you go home. Get some rest. They might even be back home, waiting for you as we speak."

"You're right." The triplets' father agreed.

The triplets' parents fluttered toward the office's door, and Nick escorted them. He offered them words of encouragement. When the pixies left the office, they hovered past Rumpke without noticing him and continued down the hall.

Nick stopped next to Rumpke, looked down at him, and then back at the parents. Seconds after they'd left the hallway, Rumpke heard the building's front doors open. Once they'd gone, Nick asked. "How much did you hear."

"All of it," Rumpke said. "It's the same reason I'm hear. Mod had told me they didn't show up to work. Pete and Zoey are missing, too."

"Pete and Zoey?" Nick grumbled a few inaudible thoughts to himself before saying. "At least they're adults. They should be able to take care of themselves. For the time being, I must prioritize the triplets."

"Agreed," Rumpke said. "Where do we start?"

Nick turned his eyes down to the Raccoon. "You know there's a soul eater in the forest. All my guard force is out looking for it. If the triplets were in the forest, we would have found them."

"Have you found the soul eater?" Rumpke asked.

Nick grumbled an angry sound which Rumpke took to mean, 'no.'

"If they haven't found the soul eater, it means the triplets might still be out there," Rumpke said.

"I supposed," Nick agreed. "I'll let the search teams know to look for the triplets too. I have a different theory about what happened, though."

"What's that?" Rumpke asked.

"The triplets are a curious bunch." The mayor stepped between them, speaking as fast as ever. "And as you know, there was a brief period when the portal was unguarded." She scanned her eyes back and forth, side-eyeing both Rumpke and Nick. They hung their heads. "Nick believes the triplets might have entered the portal then."

"Of course, they didn't understand the rules about dungeons," Nick explained. "Like how they wouldn't be able to leave the dungeon until someone defeated the dungeon boss."

"You think they are alone in a dungeon?" Rumpke asked.

Nick nodded and grunted in the affirmative.

The mayor added. "We've asked the Adventurer's Guild to investigate, but they are processing the request. They say it can take days before they send someone."

"We asked Roger Escaron for help, too." Nick hung his head.

"What he say?" Rumpke asked.

Nick shook his head in disappointment before answering. "He said...and I quote...'I've never cleared a dungeon before. Are you crazy? Do you know how dangerous that is? There are bosses in there. Those pixies are as good as dead. There's no sense in getting myself killed too."

"So we have to wait?" Rumpke asked.

"I have a friend who is an adventurer," Nick explained. "Three days ago, he visited the Adventurer's Guild in Futuretown. He goes by the name of Introvice. If I can track him down, he'll help us."

Rumpke heard the doors to the municipal building open. Seconds later, an Adventurer Guild guard appeared. Rumpke recognized him as one of the guards who had shown up at the portal the day before. The guard marched up to Nick and the mayor, stopped, and saluted. Once Nick had saluted back, the guard relaxed and asked. "You requested adventurers to enter the dungeon, correct?"

"Yes," Nick said.

"This was to rescue children pixies with adventurer passes?"

"Yes," The mayor said.

The man took a deep breath. Rumpke didn't like it. It was the kind of breath someone takes before they give bad news. "As a preliminary step to process your request, we scanned the portal. When we did, we confirmed the entry of seven separate beings into the portal. Three of them are adventurers registered with the guild. They go by Introvice, Fredalic, and Flowerbeard." Rumpke noticed Nick perk up at the mention of Introvice. "Three were pixies who are not registered with the guild. I suspect those are the children." The man hung his head.

"What is it?" Nick asked. "Who was the seventh person to enter?"

The Adventurer's Guild representative forced his

eyes up to meet Nick's. They seemed apologetic. "About that...I'm afraid I have some bad news. The seventh entity to enter went in seconds after the pixies. It's like it was chasing them."

"The soul eater?" Rumpke guessed, anxiety building in his core.

"No," the representative said. "It was a vampire."

In unison, the mayor, Nick, and Rumpke exhaled with relief the air they'd been holding in their lungs.

"You aren't worried?" The representative asked.

"No," Nick said. "We have a resident vampire. She is a friend of the pixies. If they were with a vampire, it was likely her. She's tough enough to keep them safe... So long as they don't try to clear the dungeon, they'll be fine."

"She'll keep them safe or die trying..." Rumpke wrinkled his forehead in confusion. "...un-die trying? What's the correct term for when something undead dies?"

"Let's loop back to that question." The mayor removed the triangular hat from her head with her right hand and scratched her temple with the left. "As it stands, things are better than we could have hoped for. Zoey is a paladin..."

"Wait," the Adventurer's Guild representative interrupted. "She's a vampire and a paladin?"

"Yes," the mayor answered.

"How did that happen?" The representative asked.

"About that," Nick crossed his arms over his chest. "To put it in simple terms...we don't know. But she is a paladin and a vampire."

"Okay...understood..." the representative couldn't hide the surprise from his voice. "Please, continue."

"As I was about to say," the mayor returned her hat to her head. "Zoey is a capable paladin, and being a vampire makes her extra tough. If they meet up with Introvice inside the dungeon, I like their chances."

"I'm glad you feel that way." The representative said. "Even so, I will expedite your request for assistance. By the end of the day tomorrow, we should have adventurers inside the dungeon."

"Thank you." Nick saluted.

The guard saluted back before returning the way from where he'd come. They heard the municipal building doors open and shut as he left. "I'll go tell the triplets' parents what we've discovered. We still have two other problems to worry about." He scanned his eyes over to Rumpke. "The supposed soul eater that only your people have seen...I'm still not convinced it isn't a prank."

"It's not a prank," Rumpke assured. "It's a legitimate problem."

"Right," Nick stroked his mustache one time. "If there is a soul eater in the woods, the guards and Adventurers Guild will find it. It's a matter of time. That leaves us with one more problem."

"What is that?" Rumpke asked.

"Well, son." Nick put his hand on Rumpke's shoulder. "We know where the triplets are. We know where Zoey is. But there is one person who remains lost."

Rumpke nodded his understanding, saying. "Right, we still need to find Pete."

Josh Walker

25: Flowerbeard, Introvice, and Fred

"**T**he description on Finley's Chakus says that the blades on the cutters are coral." Skye offered a proud grin, hovering alongside Zoey and the others as they moved down the tunnel.

"It says my fork is coral, too." Zoey held the weapon up to examine it. "I'm not sure if they mean the tip or the whole thing."

"You're going to try it out, though, right?" Hope asked with a hopeful intonation. "My wand makes my magic better. I bet your fork will make your…" She paused to think. "…your stabbing things with a fork better."

"It has higher stats," Zoey affirmed. "Not by a lot, but it does add water damage to my attacks." She considered that implication. "Then again, water attacks might give hit points to the monsters in this dungeon. I should wait before I try this fork out."

"Mine says it does water damage, too," Skye observed. "I'll wait to use it, too."

"That happens a lot," Introvice explained. "Dungeon drops often don't work as well in the dungeon that drops them. But you might find yourself in a fire dungeon someday. Then those water attack bonuses will be huge."

Fred's head perked up, and he began to run, disappearing around a bend in the tunnel up ahead.

When Zoey saw no reaction from Flowerbeard or Introvice, it prompted her to ask. "Should we follow him?"

"No," Flowerbeard said. "That makes no sense. Why would we do that? I mean, I could if I wanted. But why would I? that's too much work."

"We don't need to follow him," Introvice assured. "Whatever he senses, he'll wait for us when he gets to it."

"He can sense things?" Hope asked.

"What kind of things?" Skye added.

"How can he sense things?" Tornado finished the string of questions.

"Yes, high-level enemies, and we don't know," Introvice answered the questions in the order the triplets had asked them. "When he senses something, it's either a notorious monster or a boss room. In the case of a boss room, the boss is higher level than what is normal for the dungeon. Depending on the boss's level, we could have some grinding ahead of us."

"Grinding?" Hope asked.

"It means you kill easier monsters over and over to raise your level," Zoey explained. "It's called grinding because sometimes it feels like a grind."

"You know a lot about adventuring for a non-adventurer." Flowerbeard squinted his eyes at Zoey. "Are you a spy?"

"A spy for who?" Zoey asked.

"Ummm..." Flowerbeard considered how to answer her question. "A spy for vampires?"

"I'm not a spy for vampires," Zoey assured. "I've played lots of JRPGs and MMOs."

"A likely story..." Flowerbeard pointed two fingers at his eyes, then at her. "I'm watching you, vampire spy." Then he pivoted to whisper at Introvice. "What's a JRPMO?"

"Fred's back." Hope pointed ahead.

Fred had rounded the bend on his way back to the group. His head hung; his shoulders slouched.

"That's not a good sign," Introvice said. "We should hurry ahead and see what's got him feeling down."

They began to jog in his direction. When the party reached him, he began to hand signal. First, he lifted his right arm over his head, hand parallel with the ground, palm facing down. Then he lowered his arm—

so both hands were in front of him—and held up eight fingers. Then he held his arms out to each side and made a wave with them, starting with his right finger tips and ending with his left. Then he made a scary face. Then he held up six fingers, followed by seven fingers. He finished with a shrug.

Where Zoey didn't understand the charades, Introvice translated them. "He found the final boss room up ahead. It's an octopus-type monster. It is three levels higher than us. He thinks we'll need to grind for six or seven days to get our levels high enough."

"Six days?" Skye's mouth began to quiver as he fought back tears. "That's...so many days."

"So many days." Tornado echoed.

"We have to be brave." Hope made her best effort to comfort her brothers. "We'll see mom and dad again. Don't worry."

Zoey's heart broke for the triplets, and she couldn't help them. She felt powerless. It wasn't fair for children to be away from their homes. There had to be something she could do to comfort them...no...not comfort...help.

As Zoey considered how to proceed, she watched the triplets land next to the wall. They sat there, dejected as emotional exhaustion overwhelmed them. Though...she had an idea that could help them.

She thought back to how Pete slapping her shield had raised her defense. When he leveled, she knew it would increase his strength, too. Attribute bonuses at leveling depended on skill-ups. She could let the pixies attack her shield like Pete had. If the triplets skilled up enough...they'd only have to level one time. In an hour, they could be ready to face a monster high above their level.

"If we are going to defeat the dungeon boss," Introvice said. "We should return to the room where we fought the bull shark. By now, normal dungeon mobs should have spawned there. Whenever you and the triplets are ready to join us. Meet us back there."

"I have an idea," she told Introvice as he spun and headed toward the room where they'd faced the bull shark. Fred and Flowerbeard had joined him.

While he walked away, Introvice's voice remained calm, comforting...in a weird way. "I don't know your idea, but I trust you have the triplets' best interest at heart. But for now, for their sake, they need a break. Let them rest and come to terms with the situation. When they feel up for it, join up with us, and we can talk about your idea."

Zoey was about to ask Introvice to stay, but she decided against it. Having Introvice and his team with her wouldn't help her power-level the pixies—or in the case of her plan—power-skill them.

"How are you guys doing?" She asked them as she stepped over to them, plopping down beside Hope.

"Okay, I guess." Hope spoke with forced maturity. Zoey felt terrible for her; it wasn't fair that Hope had to act like a grown-up when she was still a child. For that matter, it wasn't fair that any of the triplets found themselves in such a precarious situation.

Zoey couldn't help but feel guilty. Afterall, she was the one who suggested they flee into the portal. Then again, what was the other option? The soul eater at Harvestfest had formed from a grasshopper. By herself, it would have been more than Zoey could handle. And the soul eater which had attacked Zoey and the triplets was much worse than the one from Harvestfest. *It's not your fault*, Zoey tried to convince herself.

"I want to go home." Skye's voice cracked as he spoke. "

"Me too," Tornado sniffed, tears welling in his eyes and beginning to run down his cheeks on each side. He wiped them away with his sleeve.

"Guys," Zoey said. "I don't want to get your

hopes up, but it's like I said before. I have an idea. If it works. We still might make it out of here today."

"Thank you, Zoey," Hope said, forcing a smile. "I appreciate you trying to cheer us up. But we should take our time and be careful. It's better to make it home a week from now than not make it home at all."

"You know," Zoey set her hands in her lap. "You are very grown up for your age."

"Thank you," Hope said.

"The thing is," Zoey began. "I can make you strong enough that fighting the boss won't be risky. And I can do it today."

"That doesn't make sense." Tornado pointed down the tunnel where Introvice had gone with the other adventurers. "They said we need to level up for six days."

"That is what they said." Zoey nodded. "But let me ask you a few questions."

"Okay," Tornado agreed. "But no tests. I don't want a grade for my answers."

Zoey held up one finger. "First, what makes leveling so difficult?"

"The experience points you get from each monster go down as you get a higher level above them," Skye answered.

"And you have to wait for mobs to respawn," Tornado added.

"Good answers," Zoey said, lifting her second finger. "Second question is this. What level are the adventurers?"

"I checked." Hope explained. "When I talk to people for the first time, I change my settings to see their names and levels above their heads. Introvice is level twenty-eight. Fred is level twenty-six. Flowerbeard is level twenty-four."

"Right," Zoey said. "So if we were each as strong as a level thirty adventurer, we should be able to fight the dungeon boss...right?"

"No," Skye said this more as a question than a statement. He was asking, *what do you know that we don't?*

"What level am I?" Zoey asked them.

"Fifteen," Hope replied. "That means you'd need another fifteen to face the boss. My brothers and I would need twenty levels each."

"What should my defense be at level fifteen?" Zoey asked. "As a paladin who has high defense?"

"Hmmm..." Skye though for a second. "Based on books I've read, it should be around one-thousand-three hundred. That would be super high. For a level fifteen."

"And my hit points?" Zoey asked. "What should they be at level fifteen?"

"Around four hundred," Skye replied, his eyes searching her face as he tried to figure out what point she was making.

"Pete taught me a trick to get way higher attribute boosts at a level up." She explained. "My hit points are at 3,420. My defense is 4,731."

Tornado's jaw dropped open. He kept it open without saying a word.

"That can't be right," Hope said. "Are you sure you read your stat sheet right? You didn't make any mistakes."

"No mistakes." Zoey insisted. "And if my stats are right, would that make me strong enough to face this dungeon boss?"

"More than strong enough." Skye nodded.

"You think you can help us get strong like that?" Hope asked.

"I do," Zoey said. "And it's easier than you think. To put it simple, all you need to do is get a lot of skill points by hitting something way stronger than you." Zoey pointed at herself. "Or, in this case, someone way stronger than you."

"We can't hit you. That would be mean." Tornado said.

"It's called sparring," Zoey said. "Skye, I will practice fight you, but I won't punch back. It will get your skills up. When you do land hits, Hope heals me. We do this until you gain one or two hundred skill points to your primary skills.

"Then I can let Tornado cast spells on my shield. It will get my shield skill up, and his elemental-based magic skills will increase."

"It sounds like good training." Hope admitted.

"After we get your skills up, we need to fight monsters. Because you three are lower levels than the monsters in the dungeon, you won't need to kill many, and you'll gain a level. When you do, your attributes which relate to your skills will get a significant boost." Zoey finished her explanation.

"We have nothing to lose." Hope spoke with a renewed optimism.

"Nothing to lose," Tornado no longer had tears in his eyes.

"Nothing to lose," Skye shrugged.

"But before we get into any of that," Zoey said. "Introvice was right. You guys need a break. Let's have brunch.

*　　*　　*

"Do you think those kids will be okay?" Introvice asked his companions as they traversed the watery passageway.

Fred nodded that he thought they would be okay.

"Don't care." Flowerbeard stretched his arms over his head. "And if something happens to them, I call their loot."

251

Introvice ignored Flowerbeard's comment. "I mean, I get Zoey doesn't want to do anything to put them at risk, but they seemed desperate."

"Desperate people make mistakes." Flowerbeard lowered his arms. "That's why people should be more like me."

Fred offered Flowerbeard a confused expression, one which asked, *more like you?*

"Yes," Flowerbeard nodded. "More like me."

"How do you mean?" Introvice asked.

"I can't believe I have to explain this," Flowerbeard couldn't hide the annoyance in his voice. "I mean that people need to not care about stuff. If you don't care, you don't have to worry about losing it."

"Okay," Introvice smiled. He disagreed with the sentiment. Even so, he wasn't an argumentative person. If someone told him the sky's usual color was purple, he wouldn't argue with them. He'd let them remain happy in their ignorance. "But you do have to admit that Zoey would be a great addition to our team. She's a heck of a tank."

"Whatever...like stop talking about it...I don't care. Whatever." Under his beard, Flowerbeard began to blush. Introvice noticed because the pirate's nose had changed a bright shade of pink. *Does Flowerbeard have a crush on Zoey?* He wondered. *Why else would he be blushing?* Flowerbeard was fortunate because Introvice handled teasing others the same way he dealt with arguing. He didn't do it.

Fred increased his speed to outpace his companions. When he was ahead of them, he held up a hand, signaling them to stop. When they did, he pointed to the tunnel wall behind them.

As soon as he did this, an orb of brilliant light began to shine where he had pointed. It was small at first, no larger than a mason's jar. After a few seconds, it began to expand. Though, there was nothing threatening to its growth. It was the size of a watermelon. Then it was the size of a table. Once it was as tall and wide as a person, it began to fizzle out.

Once the light had dimmed to nothing, it left a cat in its place. Rather, it left an anthropomorphic cat in its place. He was a black cat with a white spot on his forehead. His vestment came in the form of a white tuxedo. It fit the cat with perfection that only the best craftsmen could produce and only with perfect measurements from the start.

"Hello, Max." Introvice nodded. "It is a pleasure to see you again."

"Pleasure is mine." Max pulled on the bottom of his jacket to straighten it. "How have Flowerbeard and Fred been behaving?"

Fred offered a wide, friendly, toothy smile and a hearty, exaggerated hand wave.

Flowerbeard glared. "I'm behaving better than that vampire sidekick of yours. You can tell her..."

Introvice held his hand up to silence Flowerbeard, stopping Flowerbeard midsentence. "They are behaving the same as usual."

"And the people we sent you to watch after?" Max spoke with a questioning tone. "How are they."

"We haven't met Pete yet. Though, we have met Zoey." Introvice straightened his own jacket. "She is strong like you say...didn't expect her to end up in the dungeon, though."

"She's here?" Confusion snuck into his voice. "I didn't expect her to end up in the dungeon either. She surprised us both."

"No one surprises me." Flowerbeard stuck out his chest. "I knew she'd come to the dungeon. Not surprised one bit."

"No one surprises you?" Max shifted his attention to Flowerbeard. "What about that crab sneaking up on you. As soon as Flowerbeard turned to look, Max said.

"Made you look."

"I expected you to make me look." Flowerbeard insisted. "I wanted to make you feel good about yourself."

Max stepped over to him and patted his shoulder twice while saying. "Sure, you did." Lowering his hand, Max looked back at Introvice. "As far as the dungeon goes, why is anyone in the dungeon?"

"Long story short," Flowerbeard said. "We wanted to scout the portal so we knew where the dungeon was. Then we were going to give Pete an adventurer pass and train him inside the dungeon. As soon as we found the portal, Zoey and some pixies sped into the portal before we could stop them. So we followed them in and acted like we were here the whole time."

"That makes sense." Max stroked his chin between his thumb and forefinger. "So you are here to keep her safe?"

Fred nodded yes.

"And where are Zoey and the pixies now?" Max asked.

"As it turns out...this dungeon will take us longer to clear than we would have liked. The pixies are children. The news of how long it would take was hard on them. As such, the children needed a break to come to terms with things. Zoey stayed with them for moral support." Introvice pointed down one of the tunnels and then lowered his hand to the side. "They aren't too far down that tunnel."

Without moving his head, Max scanned his eyes in the direction Introvice had indicated. Then he moved them back to Introvice. "Why are you stuck in the dungeon? The boss can't be much more powerful than you three."

Introvice shook his head in disagreement. "We can't face it in good conscience."

"You're worried about the children," Max observed.

"I am," Introvice confessed. "With mini-bosses, it's easy enough to make them wait outside the fight...protect them from risk."

Max held his hand in front of his face, rubbing his thumb and middle finger together as he spoke. Introvice interpreted the gesture as a sign of boredom. It was Max's way of saying he didn't care about the party's problems. "But main boss rooms require you enter with the full party."

"Also," Flowerbeard added. "We could need the lil buggers for additional DPS. For sure, we could use Zoey." He put one hand on Introvice's shoulder, his other hand on Fred's. "Between the three of us, we don't have a decent tank. And we don't have any spell-casters...no healer...no elemental dps."

"What are you saying?" Max cocked his head to the side, fixing his intimidating gaze on Flowerbeard. "Are you saying you're scared?"

"Listen, furball..." Flowerbeard's voice flared with anger at having his courage challenged.

Introvice held his hand up, preventing Flower-beard from continuing the rant which was sure to come. No doubt, that rant would lead to Flowerbeard picking a fight. If that fight ensued, it wouldn't end well for anyone...least of all Flowerbeard.

Though Flowerbeard's words had stopped, he continued to breathe with heavy anger. And his skin appeared red beneath his beard. Though with each breath, his skin returned to its normal color, and his temper calmed.

After a few seconds, Introvice spoke. "We're cautious. Better safe than sorry. Give us six weeks. If you do..."

"No," Max said. "You can't have six weeks. But I am not without a heart." Max materialized three vials, one between each finger. They were small, no longer than the fingers which held them, less than a centimeter in diameter. "These are enhancing potions." He tossed them one at a time to each respective adventurer."

"What do they do?" Flowerbeard asked, a tinge of resentment remaining in his voice.

"They'll provide a temporary boost to each of your levels. It will be like you are five levels higher for one to two minutes. I'll also provide each of you with a new weapon."

Fred wrinkled his forehead, cocked his head to the side, put an arm out to each side, palms up, and shrugged.

"I know you have weapons," Max smirked. "And they are magnificent weapons at that. The weapons I offer you are..." The tuxedoed cat fell back into a sitting position. It wasn't that there was a chair behind him. Instead, he was sitting on thin air as if it were a chair. "...specialized. They will be the best weapons for limited scenarios. Can you guess what one of those scenarios might be?"

"The boss room," Introvice answered with a humble voice, contemplating in his head what kind of boss would require specialized weapons. *If I know what makes the weapons unique*, Introvice realized, *it might give me some idea about a strategy to face the boss.* "You're giving us something to help us fight the boss. You want us to get it done now."

"And I won't take no for an answer." Max used his hand to cover a yawn. "You've wasted enough time in this dungeon. I need you outside with Pete and Zoey. To fulfill their purpose on Round, they must begin preparation. As we speak, an enemy journeys to Round."

"And who might that enemy be?" Introvice asked.

Max squinted his eyes, making him appear pensive. He remained that way for a few long seconds before answering. "Focus on one problem at a time, Mr. Introvice. You need to focus your energy on overcoming the dungeon boss."

"You are the one saying we need to worry about teaching Zoey and Pete." Flowerbeard pointed out. "You're the one that said an enemy was on their way to Round. Now you tell us not to think so far ahead. It seems contradictory."

"Yes...contradictory..." Max stood from his sitting position, walked over to Flowerbeard, and leaned so they were nose to nose, "contradictory like your face, good sir."

"That doesn't even make sense." Flowerbeard went to push Max out of his space, but the mischievous cat disappeared in a poof of smoke.

Though his physical body no longer remained present, Max's disembodied voice spoke. "I've placed your new weapons into your inventory. Use the vials, use the weapons, and defeat the dungeon boss. Do it now."

26: I Remember You, Fred!

Zoey held her shield in front of herself, using both arms to brace it. As she held it, the pixies attacked. Tornado cast spells against Zoey's shield until he ran out of MP. Then Skye swooped in, swinging his cutter chakus back and forth across the flat metal surface. Ting. Ting. Ting. Ting. While Skye attacked, a passive ability restored Tornado's MP.

None of the attacks caused more than a few HP of damage to Zoey. And as soon as she lost those HP points, they restored due to Zoey's HP Recover and Strong HP Recover from her paladin skill tree.

As a healer, this left Hope with little to do in the way of healing. Even so, she decided to spam her spells: Fix an Owie, Little by Little, and Don't Get Hurt. Much like Tornado, Hope cast until she ran out of MP. Then she'd have to wait for a passive ability to restore MP.

Zoey wondered if there was a way to speed Hope and Tornado's MP regeneration. In the RPGs Zoey played on earth, there were consumable items that restored MP like potions restore HP. "Hope, do they have ether on Round? For restoring MP?" Zoey asked her question while deflecting a flurry of Skye's attacks.

"They do," Hope said while casting Fix an Owie on Zoey. "But they cost more than potions. Middle-ranked adventurers use MP management and natural passive abilities over ethers. High-ranked adventurers will carry one or two ethers, but they won't use them. I mean, they'll use them to avoid death...in horrible situations. But they don't use them to restore MP in normal circumstances."

"I see," Zoey said. "That makes sense."

"Switch," Tornado said, waiting for Skye to move away from Zoey. Once Skye dropped back, Tornado shot a flurry of spiraling wind and ice into Zoey's shield.

As the spell slammed against her, Zoey heard Tornado's muffled shout. "Icenado!" As the icenado dissipated, he followed up with, "Firenado!" As the fire pushed against her shield, she saw the metal turn red hot. The color of the heated metal spread into the handle. Good thing she had an insulated grip, or it would have burned her palm. "Lightningnado!" Sparks danced around the shield as purple bolts of electricity struck it. "Fire," as the fireball hit her shield, she realized his MP was beginning to dip. She knew this because he stopped casting variants of his tornado spell. "Water!" The water spell felt like he was shooting her with a firehose. After the water spell finished, Tornado shouted. "Skye, it's your turn."

Skye swooped back in, whipping his chakus back and forth against the shield. Ting. Ting. Ting. Ting. Zoey had lost count of how many times they'd been through the rotation of magic and chaku attacks. She guessed it to be somewhere in the hundreds. Though, she couldn't be for sure. "How's everyone's skills? Are you getting skill-ups?"

"Lots of skill ups," Tornado said. "My elemental magic skill is at 372.4."

"What was it at before?" Zoey asked.

Tornado shrugged. "I can't remember."

"Last he told us, it was at twenty-seven," Hope said. "That is a lot of levels."

"345.4 levels," Skye said, still swinging his weapon against the shield. Zoey wondered how he'd done the math in his head so fast. "My chaku skill has increased by 632.7 points," Skye said before correcting. "Now, it has gone up by 633.1. Wait...633.6."

Hope finished casting a spell. "My healing magic skill is up by around two-hundred-fifty points. My buffing magic skill is up by around one-hundred-fifty."

"That makes sense," Zoey said. At first, her shield skill hadn't seen any gains because it was so much higher than the triplets' attack levels. As Skye's chaku skill had balanced with her shield skill, she'd begun to see increases. As it stood, her shield skill found itself in the same six-hundred-thirty range as Skye's chaku skill. Her light armor skill had raised ninety points.

"Switch," Tornado said. As soon as Skye had pulled back, Tornado shot his icenado spell.

*   *   *

Introvice walked with Fred on his right, Flowerbeard on his left. He wasn't sure how he would broach the conversation with Zoey that they were—in fact—going to fight the dungeon boss. Nor did Introvice understand how they'd keep the triplets safe. Sure, Zoey had mentioned having an idea about the dungeon boss. *Zoey is new to dungeons.* He worried. *Does she understand how dangerous final bosses can be?*

"You look nervous." Flowerbeard patted Introvice's shoulder one time. "But look at it this way. Max is forcing you to do the boss fight now. If it doesn't work out, it is Max's fault. You aren't responsible for what happens."

"You realize we could die in the boss room too." Introvice side-eyed his friend. "The triplets and Zoey aren't the only ones at risk from this fight."

"I don't believe that," Flowerbeard said. "With the vials, our levels are over that of the dungeon boss. We'll be fine."

"Have you looked at the weapons Max gave us?" Introvice asked.

"Yes, of course I have. What's your point? Like whatever. Stop talking."

Introvice smirked. "You realize you asked me a question, implying you'd want an answer. Then you told me to stop talking. Your instructions are unclear contradictions."

Fred nodded his agreement with Introvice's statement, offering a confused shrug.

"Okay," Flowerbeard sighed before he began to rephrase. "You can talk to tell me your point. Then stop talking."

Fred held up one finger, shook it, and pointed it at Introvice. Then he held his hand with his palm up, fingers inches apart. He finished by touching his thumb to the corner of his mouth.

"I don't care if I'm not his mom," Flowerbeard said. "I don't want him to talk."

Introvice ignored Flowerbeard's wants while keeping an even tone. "The point I'm making is I got a pair of daggers from Max. One has a fire imbuement. The other has an ice imbuement." Introvice looked at Fred. "Did yours have an element imbuement?"

Fred nodded and began to blow air before acting like he was a tree blowing in the wind. His legs became a firm trunk, his hands and fingers loose branches.

"Mine has a lightning imbuement," Flowerbeard admitted.

"What this tells me..." Introvice paused mid-sentence, lost in thought. "...what it tells me is that we will need to use many different elements to defeat this boss."

"That doesn't make sense." Flowerbeard considered such a scenario. "What kind of boss would have more than one weakness? That seems too easy."

"It would be too easy." Introvice agreed. "The more realistic scenario would be that the elemental affinity of the boss shifts."

"What does that mean?"

"It means," Introvice said. "The boss will be weak against one element one second and strong against it another. If you hit it with the wrong element at the wrong time, rather than harm it, you could heal it. The weapons that Max gave us indicate this fight will be more complicated than usual."

"We will have to be careful then. Once we're in, I'm sure I can figure it out." Flowerbeard puffed out his chest. "After all, slay'n bosses is kinda my thing." Then he stopped mid-step, turned to Introvice, and said. "But I know you're good at it too, so once we go into the boss room, you can be the one to make the plan. I mean, I could do it. Though, I don't want to take it away from you."

"Right..." Introvice said. "Thanks for that...I think..."

Fred pointed ahead, and when Introvice followed his finger, he saw the pixies and Zoey. They engaged in combat with one of the dungeon's blue crabs.

The enraged crustacean snapped at Zoey, but she blocked and avoided its attacks with artistic grace, using her shield to deflect each claw that came her way.

In the past, Introvice had fought in parties with tanks. Some of those were evasion tanks like ninjas. Others were samurais that relied on skill to deflect. And some were paladins like Zoey. They relied on heavy armor and large shields to protect themselves from damage. But she didn't fight like the traditional paladin. Rather, she leveraged a combination of evasion, skill, and armor to her advantage.

While she kept the monster's focus on her, the triplets made short work of it from behind. Introvice would never admit it, but the growth in their abilities surprised him.

Skye zipped between the legs of his enemy, striking at weak points between the joints in its carapace. His movements bordered on psychic, allowing him to move along with the weak points, lashing his weapon in an unceasing barrage.

Where Tornado had used powerful spells, he'd

gained a more precise control over them. He shot bursts of elemental magic like darts, aiming them at the same weak points over which his brother was taking advantage.

In unison, they struck a leg, and the crab crumbled to the ground. A short time after, its HP dropped to zero, and it disintegrated into tiny particles of light. At that point, Introvice's prompts notified that each of the triplets had gained a level. So had Zoey.

As the four cheered, Introvice, Fred, and Flowerbeard approached. When Zoey noticed them, Introvice called to her. "Congratulations."

"Thank you." She called back. Then she said something to the triplets who looked up and saw Introvice. With that, the pixies and Zoey began toward Introvice and his team.

When the two groups came together, Introvice said. "You all seem to be doing better."

"We're a lot stronger than when you left us." Zoey's smile widened.

"How many levels have you gotten?" Flowerbeard asked.

"Only one." The triplets answered at the same time.

"One level." Flowerbeard scoffed with an overabundance of sarcasm. "That'll be enough to beat a kraken."

Skye hovered toward Flowerbeard. "I gained one level..." He stopped near Flowerbeard's face. "And two hundred fifty strength points. My attack is in the thousands."

"Liar," Flowerbeard glowered.

"My intelligence went up by two hundred," Tornado added.

"Liar," Flowerbeard repeated.

"My healing skill and buffing skill both went up by two hundred points." Hope grinned.

"Liar," Flowerbeard said for a third time.

"Stop being jealous." Zoey lectured him. "Or I'll tell you what my vitality and hit points went up by."

"What did they go up by?" He glared.

"Are you sure you want to know?" Zoey asked. "I'd hate to answer and have you call me a liar."

"What did they go up by?"

"I'm not saying." Zoey winked one time. "But if you don't think Skye's strength went up, you should arm wrestle him. Test his strength."

"I could arm wrestle him," Flowerbeard replied. "But I don't want to. It's like...whatever. Anyone can arm wrestle. It isn't special."

"Right..." Zoey couldn't fight back her smile.

Introvice took a few steps nearer to Zoey before asking. "Did you all get as strong as you say? You aren't saying it to prank Flowerbeard?"

"We did," Zoey said. "That idea I wanted to tell you about before you left. You told me to bring it up later. This was it. Skill up to mega boost our stats by gaining one level. It seems to have worked."

"You didn't happen to boost the triplets' hit points by an abnormal amount." Introvice raised a optimistic eyebrow. "Did you?" He hoped Zoey understood the subtext of the question. If the boss could one-shot them, it wouldn't matter if the triplets were stronger.

"With my new level," Hope began. She spoke fast without pausing between words. "I gained some skill points. I allocated them to unlock a spell called More of Me. It creates three shadow clones around the target of the spell. Those clones absorb an attack each. They absorb magic and physical attacks. That should help keep us alive."

"Nice," Introvice offered the pixie a quick thumbs up. "That should help you stay alive. And if the three of you have made the gains you say you have, we have a shot at defeating this dungeon boss."

*   *   *

Outside the entrance to the boss room, Zoey, the triplets, and the other adventurers stood. The boss room entrance looked much like the portal to enter the dungeon. In essence, it was a doorframe with an opaque light where the door should be. The light shifted in color and intensity like food coloring in liquid. The triplets moved their eyes between each other and the door. "Should we go in?" Tornado asked.

"Not yet," Zoey answered. "Wait until everyone is ready. We don't need to Leroy Jenkins this battle." After she said it, Zoey realized no one in her group would understand the reference. Instead of understanding, the triplets offered her blank stares.

"I'm still worried about the triplets," Introvice admitted.

Zoey appreciated the concern. She worried about the triplets, too. She had worried about them since the soul eater attacked them. Though, things were much better than they had been two hours earlier. At least they had a plan and potential pathway to escape the dungeon.

"I'm not worried about them." Flowerbeard chuckled. "A pain in my neck they are."

On Earth, Zoey had played video games with many people like Flowerbeard. Their insecurities make them more competitive than they needed to be. She realized their angry and argumentative nature didn't mean they were mean. They wanted to feel special. And they hadn't learned that their uniqueness didn't depend on others. Often, their outbursts were cries for attention...supplications for recognition. She looked at Flowerbeard and said. "Even though they have made your life more difficult, you've made theirs easier. Thank you for your help."

Flowerbeard blushed, stammered a sound resembling, "you're welcome," and took cover behind Introvice.

Zoey looked to Introvice. "I'm worried about the triplets, too, but we have a good chance. Though, we should go over some potential strategies. Running into a boss fight without a plan…it never ends well."

"Right," Introvice said. "From what I can tell, elemental magic will have a big impact on this battle. The key to our victory will be identifying how that magic functions within the bounds of the fight."

"Within the bounds of the fight?" Tornado asked. "I don't think 'bounds' is a real word."

"It means we must figure out how to use your spells against the monster." Hope explained.

"Why did he not say that?" Tornado asked.

"He did," Hope answered. "He used different words to do it."

"That's too complicated," Tornado said.

"Yeah," Skye agreed. "If we use words like 'bounds,' we might as well say something like, 'it is essential to the attainment of conquest within the impending hostilities between the dungeon's potentate and ourselves that we grasp intelligence as it relates to utilization of rudimental enchantments against the aforementioned enemy.'"

Everyone stared at Skye for a few seconds, some of them blinking in confusion. Zoey broke the silence. "Well, that was a sentence."

"I'm not sure it was," Flowerbeard said.

Introvice chuckled. "Well, now we've said the same thing three different ways. Everyone understands that we need to keep our eyes open? When one of us understands how to use elemental magic against the boss, let the others know how it works. From there, we adapt our strategy to maximize damage."

"Aside from that," Zoey added. "We fight like a

standard party. Hope, you need to keep us buffed and healed. Most important, keep your shadow clone spell cast on your brothers and yourself. It's your only defense against attacks. Tornado, experiment with your spells. Watch for indicators from the boss of when to use what spells. Skye, if possible, I want you to stay out of this fight. All three of you," she looked at the triplets, "find a safe spot in the boss room and stay as far away from the boss as you can."

Introvice held up a small vial of glowing orange liquid. "The first two minutes will be critical. Fred, Flowerbeard, and I each have one of these vials. According to the item description, the liquid within the vial will raise our levels for two minutes. That does put us on a timer to defeat the boss. We'll need to make quick work of him."

"That's it," Zoey said. "Hope, buff us before we go in."

"Right," Hope began to cycle through her spells, casting More of Me, Little by Little, and Don't Get Hurt. She continued to cast until every spell was on each party member.

Once she'd finished buffing everyone, Introvice asked her, "how is your MP?"

"It's almost back to full. Buffs don't use as much as heals. Give it a few more seconds." Tornado began to count off seconds on his hand. When he reached three, he looked at her. "Back to full," she said.

"Once we're in, I'll pull hate," Zoey volunteered. "Everyone else, stay back. Once I have established aggro, everyone else, do your thing."

"Right," Introvice drank the liquid from his vial. Fred and Flowerbeard followed suit.

With that, Zoey stepped into the door. On the other side, she found herself in a dim room. The gray stone floor extended about twenty-five meters in each direction. From there, it angled up into walls made from that same stone. The walls curved into a dome high overhead. A single lantern hung from the center of the dome, providing the only lighting to the room. *No wonder it's so dim,* Zoey thought. Once the triplets and other adventurers had entered the room, the portal they'd used to enter the room disappeared. *One way or another,* she realized, *this is happening. There's no going back now.*

"The room is empty," Flowerbeard said.

"No, look at the floor," Introvice said. "The floor on the other half of the room is water…not stone. The reflection makes it hard to see."

Zoey looked at the floor. Sure enough, she noted the difference. Though slight, there was a noticeable shifting as the water's surface met the overhead light. She turned to the triplets. "Stay far away from the water. I'm going to use Insult Your Ancestors to draw the boss out."

However, before Zoey could use her ability, the boss erupted from the water. Its core was an obelisk with a rounded top and a beak for a mouth near the bottom. A beady eye rested on each side of its tapered face. The base of eight tentacles extended from the base of what Zoey could finally identify as a head. Yet only two of those tentacles had breached the water's surface. They writhed menacingly on each side of the angry face, boasting massive suction cups. Zoey knew that if one of those tentacles wrapped around her, there'd be no escaping it. As she prepared to fight the monster, the name Charybdis appeared above its head.

Its color shifted as it attempted to camouflage itself with the gray stone while its eyes took in Zoey and her party. One of the eyes froze when it saw Fred, and its skin flashed, becoming a violent red. Then the beak clicked as it spoke. "I remember you, Fred."

Fred shrugged his reply to the Octopus monster.

At that, it roared and swung at him with one of

the tentacles. He dodged as it began to swing with the other.

Zoey slid in and intercepted the attack with her shield. Then she cycled through her abilities to gain hate. She used Insult Your Ancestors, but the octopus remained focused on Fred. She used Draw Hate, but the octopus remained concentrated on Fred. She used Strong Draw Hate, but the octopus remained focused on Fred.

"I can't get the aggro." She called to the other party members as four more tentacles emerged from the water. All six swung in a flurry toward Fred. He dodged some, and Zoey blocked some, but some attacks found their mark. If not for Hope's spell which used shadow clones to absorb damage, the barrage would have made short work of Fred.

While the octopus attacked Fred, Tornado took the time to test his spells. First, he cycled through his weakest fire spell, shooting a small ball of fire at each tentacle. When the first ball hit a tentacle, it caused the octopus to receive a small amount of damage. When fireballs hit the next four tentacles, no damage happened. When fire hit the sixth tentacle, it healed the octopus to full HP. As the seventh fireball met the seventh tentacle, it exploded. The tentacle caught fire.

The octopus monster withdrew the tentacle into the water, dousing the flame. Then it changed strategies, continuing to slam three of his tentacles at Fred while redirecting two of them toward Tornado.

Hope recast More of Me on Fred to restore his shadow clones. At this, the—no longer on fire—sixth tentacle reemerged from the water and reached in Hope's direction.

Zoey stabbed the tentacle with her fork, but the point bounced off like rubber; the appendage continued to slither and writhe in Hope's direction.

"You have to hit that one with fire," Tornado

shouted as he zipped up and down to avoid the octopus's attacks. Amid his evasive maneuvers, he found time to shoot a fireball at the tentacle.

Again, the tentacle caught fire and retracted toward the water.

Introvice worked his way toward the retreating arm. He struck the tip of the tentacle with his fire-imbued dagger before it submerged back into the water. A different tentacle emerged, swiping at Introvice. It sent him flying into the wall. One shadow clone absorbed the initial damage from the blow. A second voided the injury he would have suffered as he crashed against the wall.

Flowerbeard used his lightning-imbued cutlass, testing it against the remaining tentacles. After three attempts, he found one weak to lightning damage. Then he began to hack away. It earned him the attention of another tentacle. Before, it had been attacking Tornado. A tentacle attacking Fred redirected toward Flowerbeard too.

With only two tentacles focused on him, Fred could test his wind-imbued rapier against tentacles. By accident, he healed the octopus when one of those tentacles absorbed lightning.

Skye had remained back, observing all of this. He called out to the others. "Each tentacle is weak to an element and strong to an element. When you find a tentacle you can damage, stay focused on it."

As soon as he had said this, all six tentacles retracted into the water. Zoey shouted to the others as she hopped away from the water, "It's preparing for a special attack. Get back and stay alert."

During the three seconds while the octopus was under the water, Hope restored everyone's shadow clones.

Then the attack came. According to Zoey's battle log, the attack was called Maelstrom. The octopus spun in the water, causing a whirlpool. As the spinning accelerated, so did the whirlpool until it shot out in blade-like waves. One. Two. Three. The waves tore away at the shadow clones. Lucky for the pixies, the Maelstrom attack stopped at three waves.

"Our level boost from the vials is almost gone," Introvice shouted at the others.

"We have seven seconds until we revert to normal levels," Flowerbeard added.

Before Hope could restore everyone's shadow clones, the octopus monster named Charybdis emerged from the water, six tentacles flailing.

27: King.com – Strategy Guide

After a full night's sleep, Pete's HP had refilled, and he had felt rested. Along with the rest of the merpeople—the king and Aqua included—he waited outside a glowing, door-shaped portal. It was about three hundred meters south of town, hidden in the kelp forest. He couldn't look in any direction without seeing people and seaweed. At one hundred feet away, that held true. At three hundred, it did too.

He could sense the excitement and tension of the merpeople waiting for him to enter the portal. Once inside, he would fight Charybdis. If he wasn't successful, they'd have no other way to defend themselves. It might mean the end of their town. It made him feel a pit in his stomach. "King, sir," Pete looked at the king beside him.

"Yes?" The king asked.

"How common are the attacks which Charybdis initiates from these portals?" Pete removed his hat and scratched his head. "I mean, does he attack once a day? Once a week? Once a month?"

"About twice a year," the king explained.

"Has he ever come himself?" Pete returned his hat to his head. "Or does he always send his minions?"

"To be honest," the king sighed. "We've never seen Charybdis for ourselves. The only reason we know he's the leader of the raiding parties is from the minions who we've captured."

Pete wanted to understand the battle into which he was about to enter. If he were back on Earth, preparing for an MMO raid, he would have found a website or two. Using the information on those websites, he'd learn how to counter every move. He'd memorize where to position himself to avoid super attacks. He'd understand every flaw the boss had and learn weaknesses to elements or weapon types. He'd exploit those weaknesses. As it was, his only source of information was the king. The king was king.com, video game strategy guide. "What are the minions?"

"He's sent lots of sea life to attack us. He appears to be able to control their minds. Though his mind control doesn't impact mammals. It only works on fish. After enough time away from him, his control wanes and then fades altogether."

"Only fish?" Pete asked. Then he remembered... "Does that include sharks?"

The king considered the question before answering. "Under normal circumstances, he sends devil crabs, giant lobsters, striped saurians, and sea snakes. Though, he has sent bull sharks and lemon sharks. Finnegan was one of the invaders that we captured. After he regained his senses, he felt terrible about what he'd done in attacking us. So he agreed to help us repair the damage he'd caused. He's become a great addition to our town.

"But it doesn't always work out that way. We've lost lives to these attacks. His minions have killed merpeople, destroyed our homes, wrecked our businesses, and stolen from us."

"Inside the portal, will I face other bull sharks?" Pete asked.

"No," the king said. "This is a boss room portal. It's a special type of portal that will leave you in the boss room. Bosses might have minions, but they won't be as powerful as bull sharks."

"And he doesn't keep any in there with him?"

"From the minions we've interviewed, Charybdis doesn't keep anyone in the boss room with him." The king said. "It will be you and him...no one else."

"Have the minions mentioned what Charybdis looks like?" Pete stroked his chin. "For example, is he a shark? Is he a merperson wizard? Is he something else?"

"He's a giant octopus." The king said.

Pete's eyes widened. "How giant is giant?"

"Not sure," the king said. "From our understanding, one of his arms is bigger than a person's. And giant suckers cover each arm. If he wraps one of those around you, the fight will be over. I'd target those and take them out as fast as possible."

"Good call," Pete agreed, formulating a plan for how he'd deal with the tentacles. In video games, octopi tended to have different elements associated with each tentacle. One might be weak against ice attacks, whereas another recovered HP when the player attacked it with ice. To win those battles, the player had to figure out which elements—thunder, wind, fire, ice, water, and earth—went with each element.

In the same battle, some arms would be strong against physical attacks. Others would be weak against physical attacks. Pete prayed this fight wouldn't follow that usual video game trend. If it did, he'd have to come to terms with a huge issue...the only element he could use was fire... And while underwater, he couldn't even do that. In the end, his attacks would have to be physical in nature.

"Did the minions mention anything about weaknesses?" Pete asked. "Like is there a weak point I can hit to hurt him?"

The king shook his head no. "To be honest, none of them ever saw him fight. We know little about his fighting style, attack patterns, or weak points. You'll have to figure those out for yourself."

"Understood," Pete wasn't sure he'd be able to figure those out for himself.

Even so, he had a backup plan. If the backup plan didn't work...he might find out what happens when his HP drops to zero.

The king materialized an adventurer's pass between his pointer finger and thumb and handed the pass to Pete. "With this, you'll be able to enter the portal. I wish you luck. Successful or not, you have my thanks for agreeing to this."

Pete took the pass from the king and materialized it into his own inventory. As he did this, he considered the king's phrasing when he said, *'you have my thanks for agreeing to this.'* Pete had nothing to agree to because there was never any choice in the matter. An outsider might see Pete as a prisoner forced to fight for his freedom. He didn't see things that way. He felt a genuine friendship with the merpeople. From the start, Aqua had been kind to him. He couldn't turn his back on her, not when she needed his help. Turning his back on people who needed help…it wasn't in his nature. When people needed help, Pete helped.

"You better come back," Aqua told him.

"I'll do what I can and can what I do." He said.

"Can what you do?" She furrowed her brow. "That doesn't make any sense."

"Sure, it does," Pete argued. "If what you do is canning vegetables for the winter."

"Canning vegetables? Is that a thing?"

"It is." He nodded. "Where I'm from, the winters get so cold that you can't grow vegetables. Instead, you have to put the vegetables in airtight cans. Those cans preserve the food."

"Do the vegetables taste the same after you can them?" She asked.

"No, they do not," Pete admitted. "But it is better than nothing. And if you use the vegetables in cooking, they retain the usual texture and flavor. Not much is better than a hot vegetable soup in the middle of December."

"What's a December?" She asked.

"Ah, right," he said. "I forget that you have different months here."

"Yeah," she said. "Also, merpeople can't eat

soup. I've seen it in anime and stuff, but we live underwater. Soup and water don't mix."

"Yeah...that makes sense." Pete imagined chunks of vegetable soup floating in the water as a merperson tried to eat them.

"What about pizza?" Aqua asked. "You said that is food?" A prompt appeared:

You've received the quest offer for 'Underwater Pizza.' Make a waterproof pizza for Aqua. Demonstrate you are the pizzaman you claim to be.

"After I defeat Charybdis, I'll make you one," he said. He'd have to talk to Mod about how to waterproof his ingredients. But if they could make a waterproof pizza, they could deliver to the merpeople, too. That would double the possible clients for the pizzeria.

You've accepted the quest Underwater Pizza. Sogginess has no power over you.

"Are you both talking about food at a time like this?" Kai asked.

"What do you mean time like this?" Pete asked.

"You're about to risk your life...and if you fail...the town faces its doom. We will have to move to new homes far away from here. This is—at best—a life-changing event. At worst, it's a life-ending event, and you're talking about food."

"Oh...that's what you mean by a time like this." Pete smiled. "When facing death...that is the best time to talk about food."

"Yup," Aqua agreed, looking at her father. "Food relaxes people. It helps them cope with stress, forget the scary things around them."

"That's why I'm a pizzaman," Pete said. "Food makes people's lives better."

"I'm still not sure I understand," Kai said.

"I'll make you an underwater pizza, too," Pete said. "Then you'll understand."

"I don't think I will." Kai chuckled, offering Pete his hand. "But I appreciate all you've done for us. Good luck inside that portal."

Pete shook Kai's hand. Then he shook the king's hand. Then he hugged Aqua, spun, and disappeared into the portal.

28: An Alliance

While still submerged, Pete scanned his surroundings. He found himself in what he could only describe as a swimming pool with a half-circle shape. By his estimate, that circle—if it were a full one—had a fifty-foot diameter. Pete had ten feet of space between him and the bottom of the pool. Above him, there were thirty feet between him and the surface. At the surface, the giant octopus named Charybdis flailed. Was it attacking something? Pete guessed that it was, but he couldn't see what. Its targets were on the other side of the surface. A prompt appeared:

Another party has priority in fighting the dungeon boss. Do you wish to form an alliance with this party? If you do not agree to an alliance, you cannot engage the dungeon boss.

"Yes," Pete said. "I want to form an alliance."

*　　*　　*

While Hope hurried to restore the shadow clones of everyone in the party, a prompt popped in front of Zoey's vision:

Pete's party wishes to form an alliance with your party. Allow? A majority of party members must answer yes to form an alliance. Between Zoey and the triplets, they had the majority. Within seconds, all four had voted yes, and a new prompt appeared:

Pete's party has formed an alliance with your party.

*　　*　　*

Once Pete received the notification that the other party accepted his alliance, he began to swim up. As he drew near Charybdis, he realized its head was above the water along with six of its eight tentacles. The two tentacles beneath the surface held firm against the rock. This helped Charybdis to remain in place.

Pete chose to put his energy into damaging the parts of the octopus that he could see. When he decided this, he swam next to the tentacle on the right side, lifted his hand, and slapped.

The tentacle went limp, and Charybdis flinched back in pain. Pete dove to avoid swinging tentacles as the octopus dropped beneath the surface. The tentacles continued to flail. Pete watched as the tentacle he had slapped withered into a dry husk of its former self. Then it fell off. An eighth of Charybdis's corresponding hit points dropped away.

The submerged octopus spun its head to look straight at Pete. "Who are you?" It clicked.

"Pete the pizzaman," he tipped his hat.

"I hate you, Pete the pizzaman." It went from violent red to a color resembling a burning fire, flashing oranges and yellow mixing with the red.

"Huh," Pete said as he raised his hand and slapped Charybdis across the face. It responded by slapping Pete with one of its tentacles. The blow caught him at an angle from below, lifting him like a baseball off the barrel of a bat. He shot through the water. And when he reached the water's surface, he shot out, rising ten feet above the surface before he fell back down. He landed on flat, hard rock.

Pain shot through his body as he tried to regain his senses. As his head began to clear, he noticed the icon for concussions. He reminded himself to never admit to Zoey that such an icon existed. Next, he saw his HP were half full...but they were going up somehow. Was someone healing him? The icon for concussions went away, and his head cleared.

He was on the ground, but he thought he was still seeing a hallucination...because Zoey stood over him. The triplets hovered behind her. Next to her, there was a mime, a pirate, and a man in a tuxedo.

"Hi, Pete," Zoey said, confusion inherent in her expression. "How'd you get here?"

"Mermaid," Pete answered, unsure if he should answer what he thought to be a hallucination.

Zoey squinted her eyes together. "Are you okay, Pete?"

"I'm not sure you're real." He replied.

"We don't have time for this." Flowerbeard pointed toward the water with his cutlass. "Here it comes."

Pete looked in time to notice a tentacle falling toward him. He rolled out of the way as Zoey hopped back. The tentacle shook the ground between them.

While his hit points finished healing back to full, Pete stumbled to his feet, spun, and prepared to slap. Charybdis drew back his arm, causing Pete to miss. He looked up at Zoey. "This is real life, right?"

Zoey sighed. "I told you that—if you keep slapping yourself—you'd give yourself a concussion."

Upon hearing this, he decided it was real life. Only the real Zoey could appear so disappointed in his choice to slap himself to sleep. He'd have to ask her about how she and the triplets were in Charybdis's boss room. But he'd have to do it after the battle.

The man in the tuxedo began to explain. "We've figured out that each arm is weak against a type of damage. "One is weak against fire for sure. How did you kill the other arm?"

"Ummm...slapping damage?" Pete's answer was more like a question than a solid response.

"Do you think it is weak against physical damage as a whole or a specific type of physical damage?" The man in the tuxedo ducked beneath a swinging tentacle.

With persistent determination, Zoey began to cycle through her enmity-boosting abilities. First, she used Draw Hate. Then she used Strong Draw Hate. She finished up with Insult Your Ancestors. Upon using her final ability, an echoing voice shouted at the octopus. "YOUR GREAT-GRANDMOTHER WAS BAD AT CROCHETING."

For the first time in the battle, Zoey earned the full attention of Charybdis. With one arm destroyed and one submerged, he used the remaining six to whip at her from every direction.

She used her shield to intercept attacks, her pizza fork to parry others away from her. She ducked, dodged, and danced, evading this way and that. When attacks snuck through her defenses, one of her shadow clones absorbed it. Pete wondered where the shadow clones came from.

When he scanned his eyes from Zoey to the triplets, he realized Hope was recasting a spell called More of Me. He guessed it to be the shadow clone spell. Then he realized each of the triplets was level eight. In the day since Aqua kidnapped him, how had the triplets gained so many levels? How had they ended up in the same battle with Charybdis as Pete?

"How did you get here, Pete?" Tornado asked. Pete realized the Triplets and Zoey must be as confused about him as he was about them. "Did you go through the dungeon too?" *Dungeon,* Pete wondered. *What dungeon?*

"No," Pete answered. "A mermaid kidnapped me and sent me here."

"Cool," Tornado said as he sent a massive wave of fire into one of Charybdis's tentacles. In an instant, the spell's strength overwhelmed the appendage, disintegrating it into nothing.

Charybdis roared backward before sliding down

into the water.

"Watch out." The man in the white tuxedo warned. "He's going to use his maelstrom attack."

"No, he's not." From the back wall where Skye had spent most of the fight, he swooped toward where Charybdis had sunk into the water. As Skye dove toward the surface, he spun his cutter chaku to his side. The sound the cutter chaku made reminded Pete of a jump rope on the playground when someone swung it to their side. Woosh. Woosh. Woosh.

An instant before Skye reached the surface, Pete noticed Charybdis peek his head up. *He's aiming the maelstrom attack,* Pete realized. The second the head appeared, Skye whipped his cutter into the center of the monster's forehead. It roared again, and a prompt appeared:

You interrupted maelstrom attack.

Pete blinked the prompt away as Zoey praised Skye. "Great job interrupting that attack."

As Skye retreated to his wall, a tentacle exploded from the water's surface, reaching for him. Like a skilled fighter pilot, he weaved this way and juked that way, avoiding the reaching appendage.

As the appendage pursued him. Pete watched as the pirate intercepted it, hacking into it with his electricity-charged cutlass. The tentacle stiffened, and the cutlass remained embedded into it. The appendage was stiff as a tree trunk as electricity coursed through it. Bolts of purple jumped from the pirate's weapon. They bounced around the suction cups, dipping beneath the flesh and sparking. A few seconds later, the tentacle withered and fell away.

"It's down to five tentacles." Zoey said, "Keep up the attack."

After saying this, she cycled through her abilities

to keep Charybdis's attention. When she got to the move Insult Your Ancestors, it yelled. "YOUR FATHER IS TERRIBLE AT SKYDIVING!"

One of the tentacles remained below the surface. Pete guessed it was still suctioned to the wall, holding Charybdis in place. The other four tentacles continued to whip at Zoey. She continued to tank them.

Tornado used a spell that sent a small ice needle into each tentacle. Then he pointed. "That one is weak to ice." Then he did another sequence of spells which sent gusts of wind into the tentacles. He pointed at one of the other tentacles. "That one is weak to wind."

The man in the tuxedo racked his ice dagger on the appendage weak against ice. In unison, the mime stabbed his rapier into the one weak against wind. The one weak to ice froze before it broke into millions of pieces of ice. The one weak to wind shrunk in on itself before falling off and disintegrating into nothing.

While the tuxedoed man and the mime eliminated their respective appendages, Pete had worked around the remaining tentacles, slapping each of them. Though, each seemed immune to his attack. "That's five tentacles down," Pete said. "Fire, wind, ice, lightning, and physical damage. Any idea what else we can try on the remaining three?"

Zoey kept those three focused on her. She did this by using Strong Draw Hate, Draw Hate, and Insult Your Ancestors. This time Insult Your Ancestors shouted. "YOUR ANCESTORS ARE SPACE ALIENS."

"That's actually true," Skye whispered to Tornado. "Octopus DNA is different than the DNA on Round. People that study it think it might come from space." Pete thought he had read the same thing about octopi back on Earth.

"What else is there to try?" the pirate asked.

"I have an idea," Zoey said. While still parrying, dodging, and blocking, she cast the spell Light of the

Living on one of the tentacles. The Holy damage healed Charybdis. Though, its maximum hit points seemed to cap at three-eighths of their usual maximum. Pete guessed it was because of the missing appendages. He was glad that healing the one tentacle had only healed Charybdis' core and hadn't regrown any of its arms.

Zoey used Strong Light of the Living on another arm. This time, the spell illuminated the tentacle from within. It reminded Pete of when a person holds a flashlight under their finger and looks at their fingernail on the other side. When the light from the spell dimmed, the tentacle evaporated away.

With only two appendages left, Charybdis fell back into the water, clicking out. "I surrender. Please, don't kill me."

Pete wasn't sure they could kill it. The tentacle which healed from holy damage would be weak against dark damage. He didn't think they had any dark damage. Then again, Tornado's cutter chaku attack to the head had caused damage. With only two arms left, they would have been able to make direct attacks on the head.

"We shouldn't show it mercy." The pirate said.

Zoey looked at the mime. "Fred, it seemed to know you. What do you think we should do."

Pete had seen the names of the three adventurers next to their health bars in his alliance menu. When he heard Zoey use the name Fred, he learned to associate it with the mime. He made a mental note to learn which of the remaining people was Flowerbeard and which was Introvice.

Fred shrugged at her before he began to walk in place. Then he made a cradle with his hands, opened his hands, put a hand on each side of his head, pretended to cry, and acted like he was swimming. He finished by pretending to cry some more, and then shrugged again.

The tuxedoed man translated. "He says when he was a boy, he had a pet octopus. One day he was walking along the beach when he accidentally dropped it. He was sad and swam in the water, looking for it. When he couldn't find it, he cried. In time, he had to accept he had lost his pet octopus."

"If that is the case," Pete said. "We should see if we can reunite a pet with its owner, shouldn't we?" Pete added. "I'm Pete, by the way."

"Introvice," the man in the tuxedo said, then he nodded toward the pirate. "That is Flowerbeard."

"He doesn't have flowers in his beard," Pete observed.

Flowerbeard glared. "What's your point? Like whatever. Stop talking."

"Guys," Zoey said. "How do you plan on talking to the octopus to let it know we accept its surrender? It doesn't seem like it plans on coming back up any time soon."

"I'll go talk to it," Pete volunteered.

"Talk to it?" Zoey raised an eyebrow.

"Yup," Pete grinned.

"Underwater?" Zoey placed her hands on her hips.

"Yup," Pete's grin grew. "I can't climb trees, but I can breathe underwater now. Cool, isn't it?"

"Yeah," Zoey smirked, flicking Pete's hat. "That's cool. "Go talk to the octopus. But be safe. If it attacks, we need to put an end to it."

"Right," Pete agreed, fixing his hat before turning and diving into the water.

He saw Charybdis curled into a ball at the bottom of the pool. When it saw Pete splash into the water overhead, it curled back like a scared puppy. Its skin was no longer red. Rather, it camouflaged against the gray stone. Pete's heart broke for it. Where it had once appeared nothing more than a heartless fiend, he recognized it as something more. At that moment, its driving force was human. It had fears and desires. It didn't want to die.

"Don't worry," Pete spoke to it with a gentle voice. "I'm not here to hurt you. I wanted to talk." He saw the monster relax, but it remained curled at the bottom of the pool. He neared within ten feet of Charybdis and stopped, hovering in place. "My name is Pete the pizzaman."

"I'm…" the monster struggled to get the words out between clicked sniffles. "I'm Charybdis."

"Charybdis," Pete said. "The mermaids sent me here because they are afraid of you. They don't like how you keep sending things to destroy their town."

"If I can't be happy," Charybdis said. "I don't think anyone should be. What good are towns or families if all they do is abandon you?"

"Fred didn't abandon you," Pete said. "He told us how you used to be his pet. When he dropped you in the ocean, he didn't do it on purpose. He looked for you. He cried when he couldn't find you."

"He…" Charybdis used one of his remaining arms to wipe away ink tears. "Didn't leave me on purpose?"

"He didn't." Pete shook his head. "He sent me to talk to you. We want you to know that we accept your surrender. We don't want to hurt you. We could even learn to be friends. You can be a family with Fred again."

"I'd like that," Charybdis said.

Prompts appeared:

You defeated the dungeon boss Charybdis. You gained 2,000 experience points.

You received Charybdis' Ring.

You completed the quest Saving the Merfolk.

Look at you being helpful. That one teacher from middle school would be very impressed. Your parents must be proud. The king might give you a medal. You gained 2,000 experience points.

You received one thousand len.

"Dungeon boss is a big title," Pete said. "How did you become a dungeon boss?"

"After Fred lost me to the ocean, I wanted to find my way back home to him," Charybdis explained. "For years, I thought he couldn't have lost me on purpose. Then I began to doubt. Then I became bitter with rage. All the while, I wandered the oceans, rivers, and lakes."

"And you found your way to Greenlake?"

"I did," Charybdis wiped away more ink tears. "Then I made a terrible mistake." He sniffled before continuing. "I...I grew too big to leave Greenlake. I no longer fit in the river. Then I received a notification that a dungeon had appeared in Greenlake. A single door led to the boss room of that dungeon." He scanned his eyes between Pete and the space where the door had been that Pete had used to enter the room. The door was no longer there. "I'd imagine that was the same door."

"It is," Pete confirmed.

Charybdis sighed before continuing his explanation. "I thought I could use the door to enter the dungeon. I thought another dungeon portal might help me escape to the ocean. But...but...when I entered the dungeon, the dungeon boosted my level and attributes. Then it made me the dungeon boss. It trapped me here."

"And that made you angrier," Pete observed.

Charybdis's gray skin began to turn blue. "It did. I know it was wrong, but that is another reason I attacked the mermaids. If I couldn't have happiness, I didn't want them to live in peace."

"I understand," Pete said, asking. "Do you want to go see Fred? I'm sure he misses you."

Using his remaining arms, Charybdis moved his head up and down in something resembling a nod. "I'd like that."

"Let's go." Pete held out his hand.

Charybdis reached out, allowing the tip of his tentacle to gently wrap around Pete's hand. Hand in tentacle, the pair swam back to the surface. Ink tears of joy and anticipation swelled in Charybdis' eyes.

As they breached the surface, Fred—the boy who had lost his trusty pet—stood as a man at the water's edge, tears in his own eyes.

Charybdis waved, releasing his grip on Pete's hand, retracting its legs in, and then pushing them out to propel itself in the direction of Fred, the boy who was once his master and friend. Though no longer that boy, Fred cried like a child as Charybdis slid onto the land, and the pair embraced.

"Hope," Zoey said. "Can you heal Charybdis?"

"On it," Hope cast every healing spell in her repertoire. As the spells took effect, Charybdis' lost limbs began to grow back. As they did, they wrapped around Fred in a soft embrace.

"I'm happy to see you," Charybdis said, releasing his grip and allowing himself to slide back into the water. "Pete told me you looked for me. I'm sorry I got lost."

Fred went through a sequence of signals ranging from spinning in a circle to making devil horns to pretending to jump rope. Pete couldn't follow any of it. After he finished, he smiled.

"Thank you for explaining," Charybdis said. "I always wondered what had happened. I missed you too."

A prompt appeared:

With the dungeon boss defeated, you will return to the underwater portal entrance. Teleportation will occur in thirty seconds.

"Did anyone else get a notification?" Pete asked.

Zoey answered first. "It says we'll return to the land portal entrance in thirty seconds."

"Did everyone's say that?" Pete scanned his eyes over the triplets, Introvice, Fred, and Flowerbeard. They all nodded yes that their prompt said they'd go to the land entrance. Pete looked at Charybdis.

"No," Charybdis answered with a panic in his voice. "It says I'll go to the underwater entrance."

Pete kept a calm tone. "I'm going to the underwater entrance too." He looked back at Zoey. "We can meet up on the shore. Bring Fred, so Charybdis and Fred can have a proper reunion."

"Right," Zoey agreed with Pete. Then she spoke to Charybdis. "I'll bring Fred to you on the lakeshore. Don't worry."

"Thank you," Charybdis said.

As Pete and the others teleported out of the dungeon, it left Pete with one more problem. *How am I going to explain Charybdis to the mermaids?*

29: Geese Have No Masters

Zoey, the triplets, Introvice, Fred, and Flowerbeard found themselves outside the dungeon. An early afternoon sun sent beams of light through the forest canopy. Zoey's natural vampire instinct was to draw back and hide in the shadows. But she reminded herself there was no need. She had the ring of the daywalker. It would keep her safe.

The entrance portal glowed nearby. It looked the same as always. Although, Zoey noticed a guard on each side of the portal. Those guards stared back at Zoey, surprised expressions on their faces.

After a stunned pause, one of those guards spoke, "Is one of you Zoey or Introvice?"

"I'm Zoey." She answered. Then she looked at Introvice. "He is Introvice. She shifted her attention back to the guard. "How can we help you?"

"You cleared the dungeon?" The other guard asked.

"We did," She replied.

The first guard spoke again. "We will need one of you to stay here and make a full report. That way, we can document dungeon expectations for other adventurers." The guard looked at Introvice. "I recommend that you stay." The guard looked back to Zoey. "And I recommend you return the triplets back home. Their parents have been sick with worry."

Flowerbeard interrupted the conversation. "I'm afraid I have to go. When we were in the dungeon, one of my pirate friends sent me a message on my communication box. Due to bad signal in dungeons, I received it now. My friend says a crazy man with a goose on his head attacked him and his party."

"A man with a goose hat?" Skye giggled. "I want a goose hat."

"Don't interrupt with questions." Flowerbeard

glared. "As I was saying, the goose-hat man lowered my friend's level to one and left him in a forest. I need to go make sure my friend is safe." Flowerbeard looked back at Introvice. "I promise to return and help with Pete and Zoey's training. Let Max know I'll be back...if you see that con artist again."

"Go take care of your friend," Introvice told him.

"Okay, bye." As Flowerbeard spoke, a prompt notified he had left the party. From there, he walked into thick forest vegetation, disappearing behind it.

The suddenness of the goodbye surprised Zoey. It wasn't that she imagined a goodbye hug or anything. But at a minimum, she expected a handshake. She didn't even get an individual goodbye, no see you later, no wave, nothing.

Introvice spoke to the guards. "I'll stay for your inquiry." While walking toward the guards, he asked Zoey. "After you get the triplets back home, can you take Fred to Charybdis?"

"Sure thing. We'll see you back in town?" She asked.

"You will." He answered without looking back.

"Cool, thank you for handling the inquiry." Zoey looked at the triplets. "It's been quite the adventure, but it's time to get you three back home. Let's go."

With that, Zoey, Fred, and the triplets descended the Forest Mountain.

"See you later, Introvice." Hope called out as she followed Zoey.

"Thanks for the help," Skye waved goodbye.

"Tornadoes and tsunamis." Tornado waved.

The group pushed through foilage in the direction which would take them to the trail. Once they reached the trail, they could follow the pathway back to town.

By her estimates, Zoey guessed there'd be hours of daylight left when they arrived. She felt she could even return to Greenlake in time to help Mod with the rush shift. She wondered how he'd held up being down employees. At that point, she wondered about Pete.

He said a mermaid had kidnapped him. Did that happen the same time Zoey went into the dungeon with the triplets? Had Pete missed shifts at M&P's? If so, she hoped Mod had figured out how to manage without any of his food delivery employees. *I'm sure he figured something out,* she tried to convince herself.

To keep her mind occupied, she pulled up her status page. She was still level 15 but needed less than 50 experience to level up. Next, she brought up her inventory page. With it open, she examined information on the Charybdis' Ring drop. She thought, *it's specialized against water damage. Other than that, the rings I have now are better.*

After closing the inventory page, she moved to her skill tree page. Before, she had needed fifteen skill points to move from the novice skill tree to the apprentice one. At that time, she'd only had two. That was no longer an issue. She had the fifteen necessary points to activate the next skill tree, so she did.

The center node of the new skill tree was active from the start. It was a square, indicating it was a usable skill. The words on the square read Dome Shield. When she held the shield overhead, the skill allowed the shield to extend an invisible barrier in a dome around the user and nearby allies.

As Zoey closed the skill tree menu, she saw Greenlake coming into view up ahead. With only one hundred paces between her party and the town, Zoey heard a familiar growl behind her. *Not again...* she worried. *Not now.* When she turned, she confirmed her fear. It was the soul eater.

*   *   *

Cackler rested atop Geb's head. Most would say Geb was the goose's master. But that wasn't how Cackler saw it. On the best days, he saw Geb as a partner. On most other days, Cackler saw Geb as the servant. After all, they'd been partners for years. During that time—excluding battles—Cackler hadn't moved.

On the other hand, Geb had moved. For example, Geb did all the walking. He was like a horse or a camel. If Geb were the master, he'd be riding on Cackler's back...he'd be making Cackler do all the menial travel tasks.

From atop Geb's head, the great and mighty goose took in the Forest Mountain. It wasn't his first time in the area...nor the second...nor the fifteenth. Atop Geb's head, he'd seen the whole world. And he'd seen it more than once. Though, it had been over one thousand years since the last time he'd visited Greenlake and the Forest Mountain. In places, trees—which had once stood tall—lied dead on their sides. New trees had taken their place.

"Do you see them?" Geb pointed through intersecting branches.

Cackler shifted his neck to change his line of sight to match Gebs, and he saw them. It was a group of five individuals. One was a young woman wearing blue armor with a shiny, silver battle skirt. The goose guessed the skirt was steel or polished iron. The man next to her dressed like a mime. Also, there were three pixies. Cackler honked to indicate he did see the group.

"What do you think they are doing in the forest?" Geb asked.

Cackler considered the question. They weren't too far from the town. As such, it was possible that the blue-armored woman and her friends were out for a walk in the forest. Then again, the dungeon portal was nearby. The blue-armored woman and her friends could be troublemakers. What if they tried to go into the dungeon without adventurer passes?

"Right," Geb agreed. "We should keep our eye on them."

In the early afternoon, the bright blue armor made it easy to track the woman and her friends. They didn't take long to leave the forest. From there, she and her friends followed the worn path toward town.

"They might have been on a walk," Geb said. "I can appreciate that. I love walks."

Cackler still wasn't sure about their innocence. His gut told him not to trust the woman. Her aura reminded him of vampires. If she weren't outside during the daytime, he would have thought she was a vampire.

"What's that?" Geb pointed to a spot in the field.

The grass was darker there. When the darkness began to shift, Cackler realized it wasn't the grass that was dark. It was a liquid resonance. The liquid began to fountain at its center; the fountain was small at first. Then it expanded until it reached a height of fifteen feet. Once it had, it became a sphere.

Cackler honked.

"You're right," Geb said. "That is a soul eater."

*   *   *

"It's the same soul eater from before." Zoey recognized the ostrich-velociraptor shape of it. She could never forget its intimidating size, towering over her. And this time, there was no dungeon portal where she could flee. Though, she hadn't realized how fast it moved. As it sprinted toward her, she called out to the triplets. "Get behind me. We'll have to fight."

Zoey activated Insult Your Ancestors. It called out, "YOUR FAMILY IS BAD AT DYING!"

As the soul eater closed to within seconds of striking, Zoey considered the insult. It was true. If the soul eater were good at dying, it wouldn't be a soul eater.

The angry creature leaped at her, lifting its right leg in front of it, and extending its foot, reaching with the taloned heal. It used the speed from its run along with its weight to drive the attack into Zoey.

She braced for it, keeping her shield between the talon and herself. Worry struck her mind. Was she strong enough to stand against the attack? Would the force of it run her to the ground? If she failed, what would happen to the triplets? She didn't want to find out... More than that, she couldn't find out. She had to stand tall.

When the soul eater struck her shield, something unexpected happened. Zoey didn't move an inch. It was like defending against the fury of a tantrum-throwing three-year-old. She felt the attack, but it had no strength behind it, not enough force to overpower her guard anyway.

And the soul eater's leg buckled, causing its body to fold over, glance against the shield, and deflect to the side. The creature rolled as it bounced over and over against the soft grass. When it stopped rolling, it struggled to its feet, stumbling. Zoey noticed the concussion icon over its head. Its hit points had dropped by one-fifth. It wasn't a lot of damage, but Zoey took the small victory, happy it was the soul eater that had suffered damage and not her.

As the concussion icon disappeared, Zoey stepped between the monster and the triplets. She kept her shield up and looked for Fred but didn't see where he'd gone. Had he run away? Knowing she couldn't worry about Fred, she used Draw Hate and Strong Draw Hate.

The soul eater came for Zoey with more care. When it was close enough to strike, it feinted with its head, trying to get around the shield and nip at her. To avoid getting bitten, she had to shift her stance. With practiced footwork and seventy-four agility points, she could protect herself. Even so, she saw no openings in the creature's defenses. If she couldn't attack back, she'd never win.

As she thought this, Fred flashed in the periphery of her vision. She wasn't sure from where he came, but she was glad he'd joined the battle. He dug the point of his wind rapier into the soul eater's hindquarter. It roared back, screeching three times before it spun to face him.

"Nope," Zoey told it. "You face me."

Then she activated Insult Your Ancestor. "RAPTORS ARE THE WORST OF THE CARNIVOROUS DINOSAURS, AND YOUR GRANDPA IS THE WORST OF THE RAPTORS. HE SHOULD HAVE STUCK TO CARROTS."

It spun toward her, whipping its tail into her ankles and causing her to trip. Her shield fell from her hand as she fell to the ground, leaving her defenseless.

While Zoey and Fred had kept the creature occupied, Skye had instructed Tornado. "Cast your wind imbuement spell on my chakus."

"Windstorm," Tornado had shouted, allowing a green light to flow from his hand. The light extended as a little tendril, reaching and enveloping Skye's weapon. It created a green aura around the cutter chaku.

As the brothers finished the imbuement spell, the raptor lunged at Zoey. It prepared to stab down with its talon.

"Nope," Skye said one time, zipping forward. He reached the soul eater while it was still in the air, spinning his chaku from down to up. The weapon caught the dinosaur under its chin, raising it into the air. The wind imbuement created a small funnel cloud, lifting the dinosaur further.

Instead of falling back down, the soul eater became trapped in the wild windstorm. The storm spun the dinosaur-like it was on some unforgiving carnival ride. And icons began to appear over its head. One looked like a vomiting emoji. The other was the confusion icon. One showed a sleepy face. The other was an emoji with Xs for eyeballs. Sky turned to Hope, "Cast your healing spells on it. It's an undead creature, so healing spells should cause it damage."

"Right," Hope cycled through each of her spells. The regeneration spells functioned like poison, damaging the soul eater over time. The instant heal spells burned into the monster.

In a short time, the soul eater had evaporated into nothing before it fell back to the ground. A prompt appeared.

You Defeated the Soul Eater. You gained 3,000 experience points.

Now the soul eater is at peace. You gained pride and self-respect. You weren't expecting a drop for this, were you?

30: Victory Loot

Pete and Charybdis appeared outside the dungeon portal. To their right, the townspeople froze at the sight of the giant octopus appearing in their midst. To their left, the king stood with all his guards. Those guards readied their weapons, preparing to attack.

"Wait," Pete called to them, holding up a hand. "He's nice. It's a long story."

The guards looked at the king, awaiting his instruction. The king smiled, signaling the guards to lower their weapons and saying. "Let's hear his explanation. It seems a better option than fighting a giant octopus."

"Thank you, your highness," Pete said. "Some might have guessed this is the dungeon boss Charybdis."

"Explain faster." An angry guard glared.

"Okay," Pete agreed, speaking faster. "I defeated him but didn't kill him. After, I learned he's good. He was attacking you because of a misunderstanding, and he's good. Also, he was trapped in the dungeon and didn't want to be there. Now that he is out, he can be good. He could even help guard the town."

"A monster integrate himself into town?" The same angry guard scoffed. "That is preposterous."

"You already did it with Finnigan the Bull Shark," Pete argued.

The guard blushed, unable to come up with a response.

The king put himself into the conversation, looking at Pete. "Are you sure he'll be willing to help us?"

"True blue, through and through," Pete told him.

"I don't know what that means." The king raised a questioning eyebrow.

"It means yes," Pete said.

"I'm not sure I trust him." The king scanned his

eyes to the octopus monster." Then he shifted them back to Pete and waited a few seconds. The pause made Pete nervous. "But I do trust you. If you say we should give him a second chance, we will do it for your sake."

Charybdis joined the conversation. "Thank you, King sir. I'm sorry I sent my minions to attack you. I promise I'll make it up to you. So long as I am alive, I won't let harm come to your town again."

The king returned his eyes to Charybdis, putting a fisted hand on each hip. "You assaulted us with some of the worst monsters we've ever faced. Day after day, we worried about the next attack. Even when one didn't come, we suffered."

Charybdis shied back, breaking eye contact with the king and looking at the ground.

"Even so," the king smiled, speaking softer. "We all make mistakes. The moderators know I've made my fair share. Not one of us is perfect."

"Highness," the angry guard said. "You can't be thinking about forgiving this..."

The king held up his hand, ordering the guard to silence. Then the king continued. "Every one of us requires forgiveness in our lives. I am no exception. As such, I extend forgiveness to you, Charybdis." The king glared at the guard who had interrupted him. "If any among my people desire to condemn you, they must prove their own perfection. They need to show they've never required forgiveness in their lives. They need to demonstrate they've led a perfect life. Are there anyone here who can prove as much?"

The guard shook his head no and hung his head in shame.

The king smiled at Charybdis. "Then I welcome you to Greenlake. Please, take time to acclimate. When you're comfortable, let us know where you'd like to work. We'll help you get started."

"Thank...you...King," Charybdis spoke with choked words. "I won't let you down."

"I know you won't." The king turned his consideration back to Pete. "And now let us turn our attention to the hero who saved our town. It seems Pizzamen—the slayers of watermelons—are every bit the brave warriors their reputations make them out to be. Let's have a round of applause for Pete the pizzaman."

Guards and townspeople alike shouted and clapped. The loudness of it caught Pete off guard. He was an introvert, not used to having people clap for him. In fact, the most anyone had clapped for him before that was when his mom had come to the melodrama he'd done in fifth grade... Pete played one of the trees.

As the cheering died down, the king said. "I promised a reward. That will transfer to your inventory now."

You received a Greenlake Vest.

Pete looked at the stats on the vest. It had a higher base defense and magic defense than his M&P Combat vest. Also, the Greenlake vest provided a twenty-five percent magic absorption of wind and water elements.

"Pete," the king said. "You and your friends will always be welcome in our town. Please, don't hesitate to visit." The king went from speaking to Pete to speaking to everyone. "Let us all return to our homes now, knowing we are safer today than yesterday. Never forget Pete the pizzaman and what he's done for us." The king spun—his guards falling in line behind him—and he began back toward the town.

Many of the town's citizens followed his example. Though, a familiar blond mermaid with teil highlights swam up to Pete and hugged him. "Thank you for saving us. I knew you could do it."

He hugged her back. "You're welcome, Aqua. I'm glad I could help."

She released her hug, and so did he, allowing her to hover back a few feet. "Now that you've saved us, you will come to visit me, right? You won't forget about me and stay on land?"

"I wouldn't dream of it," Pete promised. "By the way," he looked at Charybdis. "Aqua, this is Charybdis," he looked back at Aqua. "And Charybdis, this is Aqua."

"Nice to meet you," Charybdis clicked, holding out one of his tentacles for her to shake it.

She took it, and they shook hands...or whatever people call shaking hands when one hand is a tentacle. Would it be shaking tentacles? That didn't make sense because Aqua didn't have a tentacle. Pete decided to invent a word for when a hand shakes a tentacle. But he'd have to think of it later. "Nice to meet you," Aqua told Charybdis. "Thank you for deciding not to destroy our town."

"Thank Pete," Charybdis said. "For showing me that I didn't have to." Charybdis shifted his beak into the equivalent of a smile. To Pete, it seemed unnatural and a bit creepy, but he tried not to judge. "Of course, if I knew Greenlake had nice merpeople like you, I wouldn't have attacked it in the first place. I'm sorry for any distress I caused."

"Bridges over the water." She said.

"Thank you."

"Anytime," she smiled, looking back at Pete. "What are your plans now?"

"Well," Pete explained. "Charybdis has a friend waiting to reunite with him back on land."

"Ah," She looked down, disappointed that he didn't have more time to spend with her for the day.

"You are welcome to accompany us back to

land," Pete told her.

"That sounds great." She perked up. "Let's go."

When Aqua kidnapped Pete, the swim to the city was disorienting. While they swam back to the surface, he appreciated his surroundings. He looked back at regular intervals, watching as the town shrank behind them. It went from having detailed buildings to a small light to hidden behind the kelp forest.

When he couldn't see the town, he watched the wildlife. To that point, he hadn't noticed the miniature saurians. They were strange creatures that reminded him of crocodiles. But the animals had human-length hind legs.

While they swam, Pete told Aqua. "I'd like to start delivering pizza in your town. Do you think you'd be able to help with that?"

"What do you mean?" Aqua asked.

"I mean, I want to make a pizza recipe that won't get wet underwater. It will be like how Bubbles has his underwater burgers and stuff. If I can make a waterproof pizza, the merpeople can order pizza from M&P's. Then we can deliver it." Pete looked at Aqua. "Of course, we'd need your help to deliver it. If we could get a few of your friends to join you, everyone in your town can have pizza."

"If you can make an underwater pizza, and it tastes good, I'll see if I can help." She smiled.

"What is pizza?" Charybdis clicked.

Aqua jumped in to answer. "According to Pete, pizza is flatbread coated in a sauce made from crushed tomatoes. You take the flatbread and cover that with grated cheese. Then you bake the bread, melting the cheese in the process. You can put fish on pizza."

"Well," Charybdis said. "I like the fish part. Could you make it without cheese? ...and without bread? ...and without sauce? But you can keep the fish?"

Pete considered the question, realizing. "That

would be fish."

"I like fish." Charybdis's beak turned up at the sides into something resembling a grin. "I want to eat fish. I don't want pizza."

"I suppose that is fair." Pete sighed. "I would never *force* anyone to eat pizza." He decided to change the subject. "Hey, Aqua."

"Hey, Pete." She answered.

"I have a question." He said.

"What is your question?" She raised an eyebrow.

"Your town is Greenlake, right?"

She nodded. "It is."

"And the town up on land is Greenlake."

She nodded. "It is."

"How do you not confuse them?" He asked.

She tapped her finger on her chin, considering. Then she answered. "I suppose if you had to differentiate them, you'd say if you meant the water one or the land one."

"That sounds confusing." He said.

"Your face is confusing." She quipped.

Charybdis chuckled. His laughter came out as gurgled clicks and hums.

"That doesn't even make sense," Pete said.

The trio reached the lake's surface, breaching about fifteen feet from shore. As Pete took in the area, he realized it was his usual swimming spot. He could see the land version of Greenlake to the west.

On the beach, Zoey waited with the mime named Fred. The mime stood with an impatient awkwardness, knees bent. He swayed back and forth. His eyes gleamed with an expectant hopefulness. It reminded Pete of a child waiting for Christmas morning. When Fred saw Charybdis, Pete, and Aqua, those hopeful eyes lit up.

When Charybdis saw Fred, ink tears returned to his eyes. He curled up all eight of his arms and then pushed them out all at once, jetting himself forward. When he reached the shore, he slid onto the beach, wrapping one of his tentacles around Fred. As he pulled Fred into a gentle hug, Fred's feet dragged, leaving a trail in the sand.

Pete swam until the water was shallow enough for him to stand, and he stood. Then he looked at Aqua. She floated nearby. "Thank you for the fun adventure he told her."

With a powerful burst of her tail, she shot from the water in Pete's direction. When she reached him, she wrapped her arms around him in a tight hug. "Thank you for helping us. You saved our town."

"Anytime," Pete said, looking at Zoey.

Zoey had a curious expression. "Pete, you are friends with a mermaid?"

"I am," Pete said as Aqua released her hug, sliding back into the water. Only her arms and chest remained above the surface. "Zoey, this is my friend Aqua. Aqua, this is my friend Zoey."

"Nice to meet you, Aqua," Zoey waved.

"Nice to meet you too, Zoey." Aqua waved back.

Pete walked the rest of the way to the beach, unequipping the swimming armor that the king had given him to fight Charybdis. He switched over to his usual swimsuit. Though, he did keep his water-breathing necklace. The happy shell necklace felt appropriate to him. Pete looked left and right. When he didn't see Skye, Hope, or Tornado, he asked. "You took the triplets home?"

"We did," Zoey said, pointing at Fred and Charybdis. Neither Fred nor Charybdis had said anything to each other yet...not that Fred ever said anything. He was a mime after all. Instead, the pair continued to hug and cry. "It's only Fred and I here."

"And us," Rumpke's voice shouted from the direction of town.

When Pete turned to look, he saw Rumpke and Nick walking side by side. Nick shouted. "It's good to see everyone. I'm glad you are all safe."

"It's good to see you too, Nick." Pete smiled. "I'm sorry we worried you."

"Super sorry," Zoey agreed. "We didn't mean to disappear. The triplets and I got attacked by a soul eater. The only way we could stay safe was to run into the dungeon. I didn't realize we'd get stuck there."

While still walking, Rumpke nudged Nick with his elbow. "I told you there was a soul eater."

Nick growled at Rumpke as the pair reached the beach where Pete and Zoey stood. Once there, Nick asked. "Do you know where the soul eater went? Did it follow you into the portal after? We've been looking for it."

"Funny you should mention that," Zoey said. "After we left the dungeon, we were on our way back to town. The soul eater attacked us. With the experience we'd earned from the dungeon, we defeated it. It won't bother anyone anymore."

"Won't bother anyone anymore?" An unfamiliar voice began to laugh from overhead. When Pete looked up, he saw a man. "I'll ensure you don't bother anyone ever again."

The man wore a white skirt like what ancient Egyptians used to wear. The man had indigo hair under a red crown with a golden snake on its front. He wore a golden ankh on a necklace. At first glance, it looked like the man was flying. Then Pete realized a goose held the man by the shoulders. The goose wore a blue wig. It was the goose lowering the man to the ground. *This is one of the strangest things I've ever seen,* Pete told himself. As the man's feet touched down, he was less than five paces away from Pete and his friends.

Pete stepped toward the strange man as the goose released its grip. The goose began to hover over the man's right shoulder. Pete held out his hand to shake hands. "I'm Pete the pizzaman."

The man glared. "I'm Geb, the moderator." He pointed at Zoey. "Pete the pizzaman, I'm sorry to inform you, but your friend broke one of our laws. Now, your whole town will pay."

31: An Aggressive Appeal with a Peel

"**Z**oey, did you break one of the laws of the moderators?" Nick asked.

"Nope," Zoey replied. "So far as I am aware, I have not broken any laws of the moderators."

Geb smirked. "You are a convincing liar, Ms. Zoey."

"Go suck on a mango." Pete lowered his arm. "I don't want to shake your hand anymore. You, Geb, are a liar."

Geb kept a threatening tone, a sinister gleam in his eyes. "Ms. Zoey, not more than thirty seconds ago, you admitted to destroying a soul eater. Also, I saw you and the three pixie children destroy the soul eater. Might I ask by what authority you did so? What gives you permission to carry out such a thing?"

"The triplets?" Nick asked Zoey.

She nodded.

Geb stretched his neck to the left, causing it to pop. "After I take care of you," he stretched his neck to the right, and it popped again. "I'll go take care of the disobedient children. They'll learn their place."

"Your face will learn its place." Pete furrowed his brow and glared.

Geb cocked his head to the side, looking at Pete. "That doesn't make any sense."

"Yeah?" Pete answered, using his menu screen to equip most of his M&P gear. The one-piece he didn't equip was his M&P Battle Top. Instead, he equipped his Greenlake vest because it had higher stats. In a flash, Pete went from being in his swimsuit to being in full gear. His Greenlake vest looked much like his M&P Battle top. Though, the bandolier was thinner, and the vest's color was teal instead of blue. "Well...neither does your face."

"Do you have a problem with my face?" Geb

asked. "You keep bringing it up."

"Your face keeps bringing it up," Pete said. "Your big ugly…"

"Pete," Zoey held her hand up. "I've got this." She stepped toward the moderator. Pete trusted Zoey. So despite his impulse to pick a fight with Geb, he stepped back, letting Zoey take the lead. "Geb, there's been a misunderstanding."

"Oh?" Geb said. "Do you think so?"

"I didn't break any laws of the moderators." She told him.

"Are you asking me not to believe what my eyes witnessed, Ms. Zoey? I saw what I saw."

Zoey put a hand on each hip and frowned. "I know you saw us fight the soul eater. I'm not arguing you didn't see that. I'm asking you to consider why we fought it."

"You think you had a reason to fight it?" Geb laughed. "A menial peon breaks the rules and offers an excuse. You think this is my first rodeo?"

Wait, Pete wondered. *Do they have rodeos in Round?* His hometown of Cheyenne had the largest outdoor rodeo on Earth. Each year, it happened during the last full week of July. *Are Round rodeos different than Earth rodeos?*

Pete said. "No, we don't think it is your first rodeo. I didn't even think this was a rodeo. Are there animals? Where are the animals? I mean, I see your goose, but it doesn't look like a rodeo animal."

"I grow tired of your babble." Anger and impatience grew with each of Geb's words.

"Pete," Zoey looked at her friend and lectured. "Don't antagonize."

"Sorry," Pete hung his head.

Zoey looked back at Geb. "The thing is that I'm a paladin. It is my job to protect people. The soul eater was attacking us. I protected."

"A paladin?" Geb squinted his eyes together. Pete guessed he was activating the feature where you could see a person's job. "You are a vampire...and a paladin?"

"Yes," Zoey nodded.

"Interesting," Geb sighed. "That does explain why you engaged with the soul eater. Though, it does little to explain why the children attacked."

"They have adventurer's passes." Nick's voice shook as he spoke. His mustache quivered in fear. "The Adventurer's Guild in Futuretown issued a reward for hunting the soul eater. As adventurers, they have permission to participate in the hunt."

Geb considered Nick's explanation. Then he asked. "Have they registered with the Adventurer's Guild to take on the hunt? Does their Adventurer's Guild rank qualify them for a soul eater hunt?"

"No," Nick admitted.

In a flash, Fred appeared next to Nick. Fred pointed at himself, made a letter S in the air with his finger, and then puffed out his chest.

"Fred says," Charybdis spoke from the water. "He is an S-ranked adventurer, qualifying him to undergo the hunt. Lesser rank adventurers thereby qualify to participate in hunts with him."

"And are you registered for the hunt?" Geb asked.

Fred hung his head, shaking it no.

Rumpke explained. "Laws of the moderators don't apply to Adventurer Guild Regulations. They could participate in the hunt regardless of their registration status."

"I'm tired of your justifications and fancy words." Thunder sounded overhead as Geb spoke, and gray clouds began to form. "At best, you have skirted the laws." He pointed at Zoey. "Cackler, remove her level."

The goose flew high up, cackling as it made rain

fall on Zoey.

"Hey," Zoey materialized her shield and held it overhead like an umbrella. "Stop that."

After a few seconds, the rain stopped. As Zoey lowered her shield, she saw the goose swoop back to its position next to Geb. After it had found its place at his side, it murmured a few things to him.

Geb's eyes widened with surprise. "What do you mean it didn't lower her level? Why didn't it work?"

While maintaining flight, the goose shrugged, honking one more time for good measure.

Geb looked at Zoey. "Who are you?"

"I'm Zoey."

"Right," Geb growled. "I understand that. Why can't I lower your level?"

"Because we're not from Round?" Pete guessed.

"What does he mean they aren't from Round," Nick asked.

Fred patted Nick's shoulder. As he did, Fred held up a finger to his mouth, telling Nick to be quiet.

"Yeah, Nick." Rumpke agreed with Fred. "We can ask about this later. Now, it's not the time."

"That would make sense." Zoey agreed with Pete's assessment. "Because we're from Earth, we exist outside the moderator's jurisdiction? That means they can't punish us?"

"Earth?" Geb's eyes squinted with confusion. "What do you know of Earth?"

"It's our homeworld," Pete said.

"You know about Earth?" Zoey asked.

"You are liars," Geb shouted as he removed his crown, and his head became that of a cobra, and he spat venom at Pete and Zoey's faces.

Zoey jumped in front of Pete, raising her shield and blocking the venom. The substance was thicker than she'd realized...and sticky. It clung to her shield for a moment before it fell off. As it fell to the ground, it went from green to brown, hissing a hole into the beach while melting sand. Seconds after, it lost its acidity and appeared to be muddy water.

Zoey materialized her pizza fork in her other hand. "Get ready to fight, Pete. It looks like we haven't got a choice."

"Ha, ha!" Geb made the sound of mock laughter. With each ha, a hole opened in the earth. One opened under Zoey and one under Pete.

"Watch out!" Aqua shouted from the water as she saw the holes appear.

As Pete and Zoey fell into the holes, the earth sealed around them. It left their heads poking above the ground. Trapped like that, they scowled at Geb like angry cabbages.

The next thing Pete knew, a tunnel opened beneath him. It sucked him in like a vacuum as water filled the space around him. The next thing he knew, he was in the shallow water along the shoreline, Zoey next to him. They swam to the surface and looked toward the beach.

A confused Geb stared at the spaces on the beach where Pete and Zoey had been. "It was Charybdis," Aqua explained as she swam near Pete and Zoey. "He used two tentacles to burrow escape tunnels for you."

Another tentacle appeared beneath their feet. It lifted them, moving them toward the beach. "We won't fall for that again." Zoey hissed.

"That was a cheap trick," Pete said.

The surprise on Geb's scaley, snake face grew when he saw Pete and Zoey riding an octopus tentacle. "You cannot win," Geb said, regaining his composure. "But I thank you for making this interesting. It's been a long time since a rule breaker has caused me this much trouble."

"You're..." Pete jumped from the tentacle, doing

a flip and landing on the beach in a squat. From the kneeling position, he extended his legs and shot toward Geb. "WELCOME!"

Flying toward Geb, Pete bent his elbow and lifted his hand, preparing to slap. But before he reached Geb, the goose slammed into his back. It knocked Pete down. He landed face-first in the sand and slid to a stop. He spat out sand as he returned to his feet. As he did, he saw Zoey cast Insult Your Ancestors. When she did, a voice said, "EGYPTIAN GODS ARE THE MOST BORING GODS."

"That isn't true. We were the best." Geb snarled as he spat three spurts of venom at Zoey.

She deflected the first one with her shield while spinning her fork to knock away the second and third globs. Then she used Draw Hate and Strong Draw Hate on the goose.

The goose dove toward her, flapping its wings at sporadic intervals. Each flap sent a blade of wind in her direction. When it was closer, it extended its feet, boasting talons that seemed more appropriate on a bird of prey.

She placed her shield between herself and the goose, and the goose slammed into her. The blow knocked her off balance, and she stumbled back. Geb noticed the opening in her defenses. To take advantage, he de-materialized his crown. A sickle-shaped sword took the crown's place in his hand. Then in a flash, he swung it at her.

"Nope," Rumpke knocked the sword off course with his nunchakus. "You don't get to do that today, mate."

"Gah," Geb howled. "You will face judgment."

Rumpke and Geb began to trade blows.

Zoey fell backward, rolling to her feet. She looked up at the goose, watching as it ascended into the gray clouds which had formed overhead. Thunder began to rumble. Then a lightning bolt shot down. Zoey dove away. The beach where she had stood had turned to glass.

"Zoey," Pete shouted. "Remember Valhalla's Ascent in Viking's Journey Two?"

"I'm not sure this is the best time to talk about video games, Pete." She said.

Pete answered. "That's not what I mean. Do you remember how we used to exploit the game?"

Zoey's eyes lit up. "I think that will work."

"Let me know when," Pete said.

Zoey dropped to her knee, holding her shield over her head. "Now, go!"

Pete jumped on it, kneeling.

A lightning bolt landed next to them.

When Zoey felt him land on her shield, she stood as fast as she could and pushed.

At the same time, Pete looked up into the clouds, aimed, and jumped.

The combination of Pete and Zoey's strength shot Pete into the air. Lightning bolts continued to flash around him.

He ignored the bolts, knowing he couldn't change direction or dodge them. It was up to luck if he found his target...the goose.

When the goose looked down at him, he could see the surprise on its face; he heard the confused gaggle. And he knew it was too late for the goose. It wouldn't have enough time to react.

Then—as he lifted his hand to slap the creature— he saw something in its eyes that he hadn't expected. He saw fear. This caused him to activate Slap'M Silly before he slapped his hand across the goose. Its hit points dropped to one, and it fell unconscious. As it had lost consciousness, the clouds began to clear.

"Cackler!" Geb shouted, disengaging from combat with Rumpke and running to catch his companion.

As Pete went from rising into the air to falling to the ground, he realized he had left out a key detail in his plan. He didn't know how he was going to land. He guessed that his strength stat was high enough that he might be able to land like normal. If he did, he would try to land like a superhero in a movie with one hand punching into the ground and the other arm out to the side. If everything went to plan, there would be a cool shockwave sent out when he landed. Did physics work like that in real life? Did physics in Round work like physics on Earth?

Pete had so many questions about physics and his superhero landing that he hadn't realized how close the ground was. And that ground was fast approaching. Pete swung his legs under him in time to brace his fall. When his feet struck the beach, his knees buckled under him. They bent so far that his right knee slammed down. When it did, pain shot up into his leg. He punched, smashing his fist into the ground to help mitigate fall damage. His other arm went out to help keep balance. As he came to a complete stop, a shockwave went out. As he watched the wave send sand in every direction, Pete realized he'd done the superhero landing without trying to. He hoped it had looked cool.

"That was a nice landing," Zoey told him. "Did you do it on purpose?"

"If I said yes," he asked. "Would you believe me?"

"No," she said. "I would not."

"Cackler," Geb held the goose in his hands, looking down at it. Each time its chest rose and fell, the animal wheezed and groaned. "You aren't dead." Geb fought back tears. "Thank goodness you aren't dead." With the gentleness of a new parent laying their child to sleep, Geb kneeled and set Cackler on the ground. He looked back up at Pete, Zoey, and their companions. "You'll all pay for this transgression."

In response, Zoey activated Insult Your Ancestors. "KHOPESH'S ARE SILLY SWORDS."

"They are not." Anger flashed in Geb's eyes as the ground opened beneath him, swallowing him. Two seconds later, he shot up from the spot right below Zoey. It caught her off guard, and he was able to uppercut her with the pommel of his sword.

As the hard metal connected with her chin, her head whipped back, and she stumbled. Though, she knew a follow up attack might come, so she kept her eyes on Geb.

Like she had expected, a follow up attack came. Geb slashed his sword, aiming at Zoey's midsection. She struggled to see the attack. If not for already having her peel in position to block, it would have caught her across the stomach. Instead, she deflected, and the sword cut across her leg, causing her ten hit points of damage. "Agghh..." She groaned as she shunted away pain, and her eyes flashed a darker red than Pete had ever seen them. "That hurt."

Zoey countered with her pizza fork. But Geb deflected it with ease before punching straight into Zoey's shield. Her arm folded beneath the force of the blow. The peel bent, and her hit points dropped another thirty points. Even though she had plenty of hit points to spare, Pete knew she couldn't keep trading blows with Geb. Pete needed to join the fray. How could he help? If he could get close enough for one slap, he knew it would be enough, but how could he get closer?

An idea came to him, and he sprinted to Charybdis. While Pete ran, Rumpke hurried to help Zoey. When he reached Zoey and Geb, Rumpke worked a pincer, keeping himself on the opposite side of Geb. This way, Zoey and Rumpke could attack Geb at the same time. It kept Geb on the defensive, kept him from attacking with his debilitating speed.

"Hey, Geb," Charybdis clicked, slamming down

the tip of his coiled tentacle on top of Geb. The way it had wrapped, it resembled a heavy club.

Geb lifted his sword to block the tentacle, but an instant before it reached him, it stopped and uncoiled. Pete rolled out, landing next to Geb. Before Geb could react, Pete activated Slap'M Silly, lifted his hand, and slapped.

The battle log indicated that Pete had done twenty thousand hit points of damage. Yet, Geb still had around half his hit points. *Does he have forty-thousand hit points*? Pete wondered. *How strong is this guy?*

With Slap'M Silly still active, Pete slapped again. Geb lifted his arm to block the slap. Pete pushed through the guard, dropping Geb's hit points into a critical zone.

Pete lifted his hand to slap again, and Geb shouted, "I surrender."

"What?" Pete asked, not sure he'd heard right.

"If you kill me," Geb said. "It means my goose might not make it. Cackler is my responsibility. If you can ensure his safety. I surrender."

"I accept," Pete said.

A prompt appeared:

You defeated Geb and Cackler. You earned no experience. The system can't give out experience for defeating a moderator. The only thing you have earned is disdain.

You earned disdain for not giving experience. Pete thought. The prompt responded to his thought:

No, you get disdain.

"Whatever," Pete sighed aloud, blinking the prompts shut. Then he looked at Geb. "Let's check on your goose...make sure he's okay."

Geb nodded, dematerializing his sword while re-equipping his crown. Then he hurried over to Cackler, Zoey and Pete sped-walked behind him. Geb bent, picking up Cackler and lifting him, Zoey said. "I can help him." Zoey offered, pointing at where Geb had laid his pet goose on the ground. "I have a healing spell."

"Why would you help me?" Geb asked. "I tried to lower your levels and punish you."

"Because," Zoey said. "We don't like to see people suffer. And we don't like to see animals suffer. If we wanted to kill him, Pete wouldn't have used Slap'm Silly to prevent the attack from killing your goose."

"You said his name is Cackler?" Pete asked.

"It is," Geb nodded. "Please, heal him."

"Deal," Zoey said, casting Strong Fix an Owie on Cackler.

Cackler's breathing relaxed as the spell restored an eighth of the goose's hit points. "That was my strongest healing spell," Zoey said. "How many hit points does Cackler have?" Then she cast her base Fix an Owie spell.

"A lot," Geb answered. "Thank you for healing him even though I attacked you."

"No problem," Zoey said, looking at Nick. "Hope is with her parents. Can you go get her? She has stronger healing than me."

"I'll go get her." Nick agreed.

"Thank you," Zoey said, looking back at the goose. Her cooldown was back for Strong Fix an Owie, so she recast it.

"How did you hurt us?" Geb asked, looking at Pete. "At your level, you shouldn't be able to one-shot Cackler. You shouldn't be able to harm either of us. We each have a defense over thirty thousand. It should nullify an attack by any level fifteen. If you did any damage, it shouldn't be over one hit point. Was it an ability?"

"To be honest," Pete scratched his head. "I bet it's my 42,000 attack."

"42,000?" Geb, Zoey, Aqua, Charybdis, and Rumpke asked in disbelieving unison.

"That's not possible." Geb insisted. "A handful of moderators have an attack stat that high. There is no way a mortal could reach that."

Pete shrugged. "It is what it is. I don't know what to tell you."

Zoey cast the base Fix an Owie spell.

Cackler's hit points were a hair above a quarter full.

"And you got that strong without breaking any laws of the moderators?" Geb asked.

Pete said. "Do these questions mean you aren't going to punish us? Because I promise we haven't broken any laws."

Geb inhaled and exhaled one time, slow and deliberate. Then he answered. "You are skirting our laws. Your attack stat does not help your case. You are up to something. As a moderator, I know you deserve punishment. It will curtail whatever behavior you're carrying out to become so powerful."

"I'm lawful good," Pete argued. "It says it on my character sheet. If I broke laws, I wouldn't be lawful good."

"Show me." Geb insisted.

"Sure thing," Pete said. "But before that, can we go to M&P's? I'm hungry and could go for a slice of pizza."

32: We Insist on Moderation

Cackler the goose lied motionless on the table in M&P's pizzeria. Around the table sat Fred, Zoey, Pete, Nick, Rumpke, and Geb. Above him, Hope prepared to cast a sequence of her most potent healing spells. After a few of them, Cackler's hit points restored to full, and Cackler began to wake up.

"I better get back home now," Hope said. "My mom and dad miss me, and I miss them. That two days in a dungeon was a lot."

"Get back home." Zoey smiled at the pixie.

Hope offered a toothy grin and a wave goodbye before she sped through the window that took her outside. From there, she began in the direction of her house. Pete noted that the suddenness of the goodbye had an awkwardness to it. He also understood that children can be awkward. Adults too…Pete included himself among those awkward adults.

"You're thinking about how Hope's goodbye was sudden and strange," Zoey observed. "Aren't you?"

"Do you have mind-reading powers?" Pete asked. "Is that something you got as a vampire."

"No," she flicked his hat. "I know you."

"Oh," he grinned. "Got it."

Cackler woke up, realized where he was, and prepared to resume battle with Pete, offering an angry honk.

"No," Geb stopped his pet. "We have a temporary truce." Cackler calmed, turned to Geb, hopped on his shoulder, climbed atop his head, and sat. "About that truce. You say you have a lawful good personality?"

"I do." Pete pulled up his character sheet. He changed its settings so those around him could observe it. "You should be able to see it now."

Pete felt a tingle run through his body as Geb inspected the sheet. Geb stroked his chin twice before saying. "Your stats are broken. This shouldn't be possible. How did you do this?"

"I'd prefer to keep the secret," Pete said.

At that moment, Introvice pushed open the doors of the pizzeria, joining the others. Everyone stared at him. He stared back, asking. "What did I miss?"

"Everything," Zoey shrugged. "You missed everything. You missed a fight where Charybdis was on our side. You missed meeting Pete's mermaid friend. You missed an angry, overpowered goose sidekick."

"Cool," Introvice smiled, pulling up a chair and joining the others at the table. As he sat, he looked at the goose. "Is that the overpowered goose sidekick?"

Geb looked at Introvice. "His name is Cackler."

"Nice to meet you, Cackler." Introvice smiled. "My name is Introvice."

Cackler murmured a sound at Introvice.

Geb turned his attention back to Pete as he closed Pete's status page, and the tingle went away. "I see you are lawful good like you say. This does beget some confidence in you. Even so, I believe everyone at this table has skirted the rules."

"The question," Zoey said, "is what happens next?"

"You spared me and my companion," Geb admitted. "So I'll give you the benefit of the doubt. I'll assume that you've never broken any rules. That said...you must stop testing limits. I cannot continue to turn a blind eye."

At some point, Mod had stepped around the counter that separated the seating of his restaurant from the kitchen where he prepared the food. He had carried two pepperoni pizzas over to the table where everyone sat. As Geb finished saying the word eye, Mod set the pizzas before them.

"What's this?" Geb asked.

"It's pizza," Pete answered. "Zoey and I are pizza people. For me, it's my main job. For her, it's a subjob. In short, it is our job to make and sell pizza. It's like how it is a baker's job to bake and sell bread."

"Pizza isn't from Round." Geb squinted his eyes shut. "And when I was on Earth, it didn't exist there either."

"When did you live on Earth?" Pete asked.

"At the height of the Egyptian empire," Geb said.

"That was thousands of years ago." Zoey's eyes widened. "How are you still alive?"

"That's a funny question coming from a vampire." Geb rested his hands on the table. "But the simple answer is that moderators are immortal. Many of us have spent time on different worlds. We look to expand. If we do find a world worthy of moderation, we establish a system like that on Round, and we moderate. At one point, we looked at Earth. It was too primitive."

"What is Earth?" Nick asked.

"Does that mean you live underground?" Rumpke added.

"I haven't told you this before." Pete looked at Nick and Rumpke. "Because I didn't think you'd believe me. Zoey and I come from a different world. It isn't underground. Like how you call your world Round...we call our world Earth.

"Wait..." Nick stroked his mustache. "When Tornado keeps saying that you came through a portal from another world...he isn't making that up?"

"That's why when I met you, I didn't know how to close the prompt windows," Pete explained. "We don't have prompts where I live. When you met me in that field, it was my literal first minute on Round. I knew nothing about this place."

"That makes a lot of sense," Nick admitted.

"Wait," Rumpke held up a hand like a student at school trying to earn their teacher's attention. "Does Earth have raccoons? If I visit, will I fit in?"

"The short answer is yes," Pete said.

"But they don't talk or wear clothes," Zoey said.

"So if I go to Earth, I can't wear clothes?" Rumpke asked.

"I mean, you can." Zoey clarified. "But you'll have to pretend to be our pet wearing clothes we put on you."

"I'll have to think about it." Rumpke folded his arms over his chest.

"If we ever find a way back home," Pete said. "We can work out the details then."

"Right," Rumpke agreed. "That gives me time to think about things."

"Does this mean you are aliens?" Nick asked.

"We're getting off track," Zoey said. "We were talking about pizza."

"Right," Pete looked at Geb. "Pizza is from a place on Earth called Italy. Depending on when you were in Egypt, people called Italy by a different name. Though, people invented pizza way after you were on Earth. As such, you haven't had pizza. You should try it. It's delicious."

"Thank you." Geb reached for a slice, lifted it to eat, and Cackler snatched it, scarfing it down before Geb could react. Geb sighed, grabbed another slice, and—keeping that slice away from Cackler—took a bite. "This is very good. And it is your job to make this?"

"It is," Pete said. "Anything edible can go on pizza too. That's one of the reasons our levels and skills are high. We farm different edible items to put on the food."

"That explains the soul eater, too. You were hoping for a rare food drop." Geb said.

"If you want to believe that," Zoey said. "I won't

argue.

"Also," Pete explained. "The pixies, Zoey, and I have adventurer's passes."

"That also justifies your levels," Geb said. "I understand. Like I said, I'll let you off this time. But the other moderators might not be so forgiving. Please, tread with care."

"Thank you," Pete said.

*　　*　　*

Geb walked through the Forest Mountain, wearing Cackler as his happy hat. He found himself unsure how to proceed. To clarify, he pulled out his communication box, sent out a call, and held the box to his ear.

"This is Danu." A soft voice answered.

"I've investigated the influx of magic in Greenlake. The main source appears to be the dungeon portal." Geb said.

Danu waited a few seconds, giving Geb more time to add information. When he didn't, she asked. "Why did you call me to tell me this? You could have waited until you returned to the tower. Tell the nearest Adventurer's Guild about its existence and follow normal protocols."

"The Adventurer's Guild has control of the portal," Geb answered. "That's not why I'm calling."

"Why did you bring it up then?" Danu asked.

"You sent me on a mission to discover the source of a magic influx in Greenlake. That was the source." Geb explained. "I wanted to report on the mission before I brought up the reason for calling."

"And what is your reason for calling?" Danu kept a patient tone.

"There are two people in Greenlake. They say they are from Earth."

"From Earth?" Danu's voice sounded contemplative. "Do you believe them?"

"I do. Cackler couldn't lower their level. Their stats and levels existed outside of our moderation." Geb told her. "If they are from Earth, you can make one guess how they got here."

"You think it was Max and Vitalia?" Danu asked.

"That was my first impression," Geb said. "I'm not sure how else they could have come to Round."

She sighed. "Max must know about our invasion plans. Why else would he have chosen someone from Earth?"

"That does make sense." Geb agreed.

"In the end, did you punish the Earthlings?"

Geb sighed. "I couldn't justify punishment. At first, I thought they were skirting the laws of the moderators. After combat with them, I learned they'd been following our laws. One has a lawful good personality, too. If he had broken any laws, his character sheet would indicate as much."

Danu's voice took on a hard edge. "They survived combat against you?"

"If I'd seen them as capable opponents, I could have defeated them," Geb said, unsure if he was telling the truth. "I underestimated them, and they survived long enough to show they hadn't broken any laws." He omitted the part about how they'd one-shotted Cackler's hit points to zero.

"Remain in Greenlake," Danu ordered. "Befriend them. Learn their secrets. If they consider breaking one of our laws—even for a second—put an end to them."

"I will do it." Geb agreed.

"One more thing, Geb." Danu's voice softened. "Find out if Max caused all this. I'd love to reunite with my old friend."

"I'll see what I can find out." Geb cut the call, pivoting on his heel and returning toward Greenlake.

Cackler murmured.

"I suppose this does mean we will get to have more pizza," Geb answered.

Cackler murmured some more. This time, the sounds were higher pitched and faster.

"I like Pete and Zoey too, but I don't think I can help them with this."

Cackler honked.

"Listen, even if I put all my strength into helping them, the other moderators will overpower me. I can't disobey."

Cackler murmured.

"Yes, it will be okay for us to befriend them. For the time being, we *should* be friends with them."

Cackler made a high-pitched beep.

"The other moderators are going to send another enforcer. It's a matter of time. It will be up to us to keep Pete and Zoey on the straight and narrow, so the other enforcer can't hurt them."

Cackler murmured, lower this time.

"Well, if that is the case...if Max had something to do with Pete and Zoey being here...then there's nothing we can do to protect them. Let's hope that isn't the case...or let's hope we can't prove that's the case."

Cackler made a questioning honk.

"I'm not sure how we keep from finding out." Geb considered. "I guess we could walk up to them and say. 'Pete and Zoey, if a cat named Max sent you here, don't tell us. If we find out he sent you here, it makes us instant enemies. We'll have to destroy you... And if we can't destroy you, other moderators will. So if you know him, don't tell us.' That would be a weird way to start a conversation."

Cackler murmured.

"Yes, we can ask them if they like nature walks."

Cackler honked.

"If they say they like nature walks, we can ask them about picnics. You want to go on a walk and have a pizza picnic at the end of it, don't you?"

Cackler lifted his head and nodded. That was his plan. He wanted to have a pizza picnic.

Geb was okay with the idea of a pizza picnic. He wanted to have a pizza picnic too.

33: Slapping Himself to Sleep

After the rush shift, Pete, Zoey, and Mod sat at a table in the restaurant. Business had slowed to the point where they could send the inside-the-store workers home. Even so, orders could come in. Pete and Zoey waited to help in case orders did come.

Outside, the sun had set. Though, a clear sky allowed the moon and stars to beam light down to the lake. The lake's tide created ripples that reflected the light. As Pete watched the surface, he thought about what was beneath the water; he wondered about Aqua and the other merpeople. He hoped they were getting along with Charybdis.

"I'm glad you are both back," Mod said, supporting his chin on his hands with his elbows firm against the table.

"Sorry to abandon you like that." Zoey held her thumb out to point at Pete with it. "We didn't mean to abandon you. It happened by accident."

"Well," Mod smiled. "Next time one of you is the victim of a kidnapping, make sure the other one doesn't have plans."

Pete lifted his hand like a boy scout about to repeat the boy scout motto. "I promise the next time someone kidnaps me will be at a more convenient time for others."

"That works for me." Mod leaned back in his chair and stretched his arms over his head. Then he rested his hands in his lap. "In the end, I'm glad everyone is safe. It appears each of you was on quite the adventure."

"True statement." Pete smiled.

"And how are the triplets?" Mod asked.

"You'll be able to ask them yourself." Zoey nodded toward the open window. "Here they come."

As Zoey said this, the triplets sped through the

window. A few seconds later, the door pushed open. As it opened, the service bell rang, and the triplets' parents fluttered in.

Pete was not good with names, so he was happy when Mod said, "Josue and Flor, it's nice to see you."

They smiled and said hello to Mod. Then Josue looked at Zoey, and he and Flor hovered nearer to Zoey. After a few seconds of tears welling in his eyes, he began to speak. "Hope told us what you did for our children. You kept them safe. Thank you."

While he spoke, the triplets hovered toward the table. They landed on it, sitting with their legs crossed.

Zoey began to blush. "It was nothing… If anything, they kept me safe. They are capable children."

Flor added. "We'll never be able to repay you. But that doesn't mean we won't try."

While their parents spoke, the triplets hovered toward the table, landing on it and sitting with their legs crossed. From her sitting position, Hope looked up at Zoey and said. "It was scary. You helped us be brave."

"Thank you," Skye added.

"You're as cool as the ultimate EF5 tornado," Tornado smiled.

At that moment, Pete saw Zoey do something he'd never seen her do before. He saw her cry. She didn't ugly cry like the girl whose prom date didn't show up to the dance. She didn't sad cry like someone who'd lost a loved one. Instead, Zoey cried a single tear.

Pete knew it wasn't a tear of sadness. It was one of gratitude. She was grateful she could keep the triplets safe. Also, it was a tear of joy. She was happy things had ended how they ended. All she could do was say. "You're welcome, Mr. Josue and Mrs. Flor. You have amazing kids."

The front door of the restaurant swung open. Whoever had pushed it did so with enough force to detach the service bell from the doorframe. When the bell fell against the floor, it bounced once before settling. The collision cracked the bell and left a chip in the wood.

Tammy Escaron stormed through the doorway, holding an open pizza box. "You messed up my order again." She stomped over to where Mod sat at the table.

When Pete realized she was about to dump a pizza on Mod, it was too late. As luck had it, Tornado *did* react in time. The tiny pixie summoned a gust of wind. It caught Tammy square and pushed her back; she tripped and fell into a sitting position. Instead of tilting the pizza over Mod like she had intended, she had covered herself in gooey cheese and red sauce.

A stunned Tammy stayed that way, sitting, covered in pizza, and blinking. For the first time in her life, someone had stood up to her, and she didn't know how to react. In the end, she responded by screaming at Tornado. "DO YOU KNOW WHO I AM?"

"I don't care," Tornado spoke with a child's honesty. "You were mean to my friends. I don't like that. You need to be nice."

Tammy's eyes widened, but before she could speak, Roger stormed through the front door. Pete realized Roger had been outside listening to everything. He stomped over to the table and glared at Tornado. "How dare you speak to my mother that way."

"How dare she speak to anyone the way she was speaking," Skye said.

Roger stepped back and puffed out his chest. "I don't care if you three have adventurer's passes. That doesn't make you special. You three need to grow up and do something for the good of Greenlake. Until you do, know your place."

"Yeah," Tammy stood while pulling globs of melted cheese from her clothes. "Learn your place."

"You haven't heard?" Hope asked.

"Heard?" Confusion came to Roger's expression. "Heard what?"

"Remember how the triplets were stuck in a dungeon, and Nick asked you to help?" Mod smiled.

"What's your point?" Roger glared.

"You haven't stopped to ask yourself how the triplets got out of the dungeon?" Mod asked.

"The Adventurer's Guild rescued them," Roger smirked. "I saw the posting where they sought adventurers to enter the portal and save them."

"Wrong," Zoey said. "The triplets cleared the dungeon. Also, they were the first adventurers to loot the dungeon. You know what that means, right?"

Roger scoffed. "You're bluffing. There's no way they did what you say. I've been in dungeons. Small pixie children like these could not clear one. That's impossible."

"Skye," Zoey asked. "How much len did you three get while in the dungeon?"

"Three hundred forty-two thousand, six hundred and five," Skye answered. "Wanda is looking for buyers for items that we want to sell. After that, she estimates we will have around two million len."

Zoey scanned her eyes between Tammy and Roger. The pair looked horrified. "It seems you aren't the most influential family in Greenlake anymore. But don't worry. I have a suggestion. If you want people to continue respecting you, start by showing respect to others."

"Ridiculous," Tammy said. "People here know what we've done for..."

"What have you done?" Zoey interrupted. "Intimidate and bully? Having more money than others doesn't make you better than them. Being kind to others is what makes a person a good person."

"I don't need a lecture from…"

"From what?" Zoey smiled, showing off her vampire fangs as her eyes flashed red. "I dare you to say it."

"Tammy," Mod decided it was time to de-escalate the situation. "It has come to my attention that my restaurant might not be able to meet your high standards. I'll refund you for your pizza this time, but I ask you not to give us your business anymore. Please, leave."

"You can't do this." Roger snarled.

"They *can* do this." Geb stepped through the front door. "You both should leave."

"And who do you think you are?" Tammy snapped.

"I'm moderator Geb." He materialized a moderator badge in his hand, holding it up so Tammy could read it. "If you both continue to harass these people, I will revoke Roger's adventurer pass. Adventurers exist to serve the citizens of Greenlake. From now on, that is what I expect to see from him."

Tammy went pale. "Of course," she took her son's arm in hers. "We are so sorry." She pulled on Roger's arm. "Let's go." And the pair fled the restaurant.

Geb turned back to Mod. "Is it too late for Cackler and me to order a pizza?"

"Not too late at all," Mod answered. "What can I make for you?"

*　　*　　*

Pete sat atop his bed. Across the room, Zoey sat atop hers. Both felt exhausted. Between Harvestfest, mermaid kidnappings, and dungeon adventurers, it had been a long week. Where he couldn't speak for Zoey,

335

Pete was glad to get back into his daily routine: skilling up, bathing in the lake, farming tomatoes from nightshade terrors, and working a delivery shift.

"Did you have fun with the mermaids?" She asked.

He smiled. "I did. I want to take you to merperson Greenlake someday. They have a nightclub where you can swim and dance."

"Swim dance?" Zoey raised an eyebrow. "Is that a thing?"

"Yup," he smiled. "It's a lot of fun."

"Did you go swimming with Aqua?" Zoey let a coy smile slip across her lips.

Pete knew the smile. She was setting him up to tease him. He'd need to throw Zoey off her game. As he considered how to proceed, it caused him to hesitate before answering. "Yes…"

"Cool," she said. "She seems to like you."

"We're friends." He said.

"She is pretty, though." Zoey said.

At that moment, Pete knew the exact thing to say. After he said it, Zoey wouldn't know how to continue the conversation. Also, it was something he had wanted to say to Zoey for a long time. It was something he should have said a long time ago. "Yes, she is pretty, but not as pretty as you." Pete regretted it as soon as he had said it. Though, he couldn't go back on it. Plus, it wasn't a lie. To him, Zoey was always the prettiest.

Zoey's teasing smile became an embarrassed one. She blushed before stammering, "thanks… I mean…thank you."

"You're welcome." He smiled, changing the topic. "You showed Roger and Tammy tonight."

"You don't think I was too mean to them?" She asked. "I felt like I was being too mean."

Pete shook his head no. "You weren't bullying

them; you were putting them in their place. With the triplets creating new wealth for Greenlake, the Escarons won't have the control they used to have. It was a matter of time before someone told them off. If we are lucky, the experience will humble them. Imagine how awesome Greenlake will be with two adventuring families."

"Three," she reminded him. "Don't forget yourself. You have a pass now."

"Oh...right..." he materialized the pass from his inventory into his hand. "I'd forgotten."

"Are you going to continue skilling up a lot between levels?" She asked. "It seems to work."

"It does appear to work." He agreed. "But Geb was so strong. And he says other moderators are way stronger than him. I'm not sure it will be enough."

"It'll be enough." She said. "I have faith in you. You've never let me down before...especially not regarding power leveling in video games."

"Thanks," he said. "That means a lot."

"And with the dungeon nearby, you will have a place to level up between skill-ups. That should help." She spoke with a hopeful intonation.

"It will help get skill points, too." He said. "I finished up my novice skill tree. Some of the abilities in the apprentice tree are cool. They will help against stronger moderators...assuming we can't talk things out with them."

"Right, talking would be easier for sure." She agreed. "I unlocked my next skill tree too. Can you imagine what later skill trees will be like? I bet the master skill tree will be amazing." When Pete didn't answer, she sighed. "You miss Earth? Don't you?"

"A little," He admitted. "I'm sorry I got quiet. I didn't mean to. I'm getting tired."

"Tired?" She asked. "That reminds me. I had Tay make us something." A pair of pajamas materialized in

her arms. They came with a button up shirt and pants. "This is for you. It will make nighttime more comfortable."

"Thank you." Pete stood up to take them.

As he walked back to his bed, he used his menu screen to equip them. By using the menu, he went from wearing his M&P uniform to wearing pajamas in a flash.

Zoey used her menu to equip her own pair of pajamas. Then as Pete returned to his bed and sat, she asked him. "You aren't going to do what I think you are...are you?

"I'd rather not answer that question," Pete said as he activated Slap'm Silly. And like he did every night, Pete the pizzaman sat on his bed, preparing to slap himself to sleep.

To learn more about LitRPG, talk to authors including myself, and just have an awesome time, please join the LitRPG Group by Alernon Kong on Facebook.